LOVE
OF THE
GAME

LOVE OF THE GAME

A STARDUST, TEXAS NOVEL

LORI WILDE

WITHDRAWN

AVONBOOKS

An Imprint of HarperCollinsPublishers

AVON BOOKS
An Imprint of HarperCollins*Publishers*
195 Broadway
New York, New York 10007

Copyright © 2016 by Laurie Vanzura
Excerpt from *A Wedding for Christmas* copyright © 2016 by Laurie Vanzura
ISBN 978-0-06246583-2
www.avonromance.com

First Avon Books mass market printing: May 2016
First Avon Books hardcover printing: April 2016

Printed in the U.S.A.

10 9 8 7 6 5 4 3 2 1

To my brother-of-the-heart, David Vanzura. You're a shining example of what a good man should be. Thank you for your support and encouragement and for always being in my corner.

CHAPTER 1

It starts like this: an unexpected spark, instant attraction, the jolting jab of oh-so-you-feel-this-too? Flash fire in the belly. A corkscrew twist in the center of the chest. A physical ache that punches low and heavy and spreads out hard and fast through muscles and tendons, blood and bone.

Heady.

Erotic.

Thrilling.

Physical therapist Kasha Carlyle had felt it before, this hot flare, runaway-mine-train-express that stirred fear in the dark recesses of her mind. She'd resisted it then. Resisted it now.

But *this*? This here? This was something more.

Stronger.

Bolder.

Scarier.

Coal black eyes melted her resistance, seared it to ash. In that stopwatch moment when her gaze struck, and stuck to the steely stare of the Dallas Gunslingers' most valuable pitcher, Axel Richmond.

He'd just completed a physical therapy session with his trainer, Paul Hernandez, and he was sitting on a bench wearing nothing but red workout pants, his bare chest on display. Every glistening muscle

was finely etched. Not a drop of fat on him. He was a splendid specimen of adult male in top physical shape, life and passion oozing from
his pores.

The only thing that seemed out of place was the black tattoo over
his heart that spelled out *Dylan*.

One look and everything and everyone blended and blurred as
white-hot need transported them into their own little world far from
the sports medicine facility in North Dallas, where baseball coaches,
managers, administrators, and sports medicine specialists surrounded
them.

For a split second.

Then pure panic set in.

It was Tuesday, May seventeenth, and the second week of Kasha's
three-month probationary period at her new job working with injured major league baseball players.

And she was already falling in lust.

No. No. This simply would not do. Keeping her job was essential.

Now that she had Emma to consider, she urgently needed the
bump in salary to pay off the student loans that had gotten her
through her PhD. Not to mention the excellent health insurance
coverage. Finding out about Emma had changed everything.

Quickly, Kasha peeled her gaze from Axel's and she studied the
insignia on the wall above his head—the blue and green Gunslingers
crossed dueling pistols logo—but she didn't see a darn thing. Purposefully, she slowed her breathing, and forced herself to listen to the
conversation.

"I wish we had better news," Dr. Tad Harrison, the lead physician on the team, said to Axel.

Dr. Harrison had been the one to hire Kasha, and the one to
caution her that only thirty percent of probationary employees made
it past the first three months. "It takes a special breed to work with
these ballplayers. They're long on arrogance and stubbornness and
always think they know best."

"I have a lot of patience," she'd said because it was true.

"I heard they call you the Exorcist in your current job," Dr. Harrison had said. "Why is that?"

She couldn't keep from smiling. "My colleagues say I have a talent for taming difficult clients."

"And do you?"

"I consider physical therapy a calling." She folded her hands in her lap, and said without a hint of ego, "I was born for this work."

Dr. Harrison stroked his chin. "That's what Rowdy said too."

Rowdy Blanton was the field manager for the Gunslingers. He was also Kasha's brother-in-law, married to her younger adoptive sister, Breeanne, and he'd recommended her for the job.

"If I hire you," Dr. Harrison had continued, "it will be on your own merits, not your relationship to Rowdy. He got you this interview, but that's as far as nepotism goes."

"As it should." Kasha bobbed her head.

The uncertainty of the job was why she hadn't yet rented an apartment in Dallas. Every day, she made the one hundred and thirty-five mile, one-way trek to the stadium from her hometown of Stardust.

While she was optimistic, she was also practical. She'd learned that fate could derail even the best intentions and you had to be ready to flow whichever way the current took you. For the next three months, until she solidified the job, she would keep making that drive.

For Emma.

Her thoughts took off in a hundred different directions at once. Stalled. Spun. Gathered momentum like an encroaching hurricane. Realizing her mind had wandered, she forcefully shut down the unproductive thoughts and directed her attention back to the patient.

Axel Richmond.

One more look and Kasha was on fire and she hated it. The last thing she wanted right now was to meet a guy, especially this guy. Whose stark dark hair was drenched in the heady sheen of sweat.

He was as sexy as ten kinds of sin, and twice as handsome, and he was studying her through heavily lidded eyes as if she was the most fascinating creature he'd seen in years.

Um . . . yes . . . that's why her mind had wandered. To keep from dealing with the feelings his hot-to-trot gaze churned inside her.

She let out such a long sigh that everyone in the room swiveled to stare. She kept her face blank and examined her fingernails, pretending she'd discovered a ragged cuticle.

From the moment Axel had strolled into the therapy room with his pro-athlete swagger and princely sense of entitlement, she'd been mesmerized.

Spellbound by the way his fitted T-shirt hugged his intricately muscled body. Then he'd stripped off the shirt, giving her an even more arresting view. A thick head of lush brown hair curled around his ears, and those powerful thighs strained at the seams of his workout pants.

Whew.

It wasn't like her to ogle hunky guys. Okay, yes, she could appreciate the perfect male specimen as much as the next woman. But normally the sight of a well-constructed body didn't carry her away.

For one thing, as a physical therapist, it was unprofessional. For another, just because a guy was hot didn't mean he had a lick of substance.

But sometimes, the visual was too compelling to ignore. Case in point, Axel Richmond.

She was glad she was merely here as a trainee observer, and not his physical therapist.

Big. Darkly tanned. Rugged. Hard-edged. He exuded a savvy, urban, streetwise vibe that blasted a shiver up her spine. He was the kind of man who could seriously derail a woman's life if she gave him half a chance.

Especially a woman who'd grown up in the safe cocoon of a town called Stardust, where houses were charming and colloquial, yards were tree-shaded and expansive, fences were white-picket, and most of the townsfolk had Texas roots that ran five generations deep, but spiked with Louisiana flair. From crawfish boils to boggy swampland to the way people pronounced "praline." (*Pray-leen* for the rest of Texas, *prawl-een* in the eastern border counties.) Stardust was a perfect place to stay in a haunted B&B, catch lightning bugs in a jar on a muggy summer's evening, celebrate the Fourth of July, trade tall tales with the locals, and watch pine trees grow.

In the best Bugs Bunny imitation Kasha had ever heard, Axel said with a sarcastic tone, "Aww, what's up, Doc?"

Kasha hid a grin and Axel caught her hiding it. And his gaze turned knowing.

Snap!

The sizzle between them was as volatile as dynamite and just as dangerous.

Dr. Harrison pushed his glasses up on the bridge of his nose, rubbed the spot between his eyebrows with the pad of his thumb. "Your recovery is not progressing as quickly as we'd hoped."

Axel struggled to contain the ghost of a wince, layering a smile on top of the hurt as if over-icing a lopsided cake, trying to make it look better.

"How's that possible? I've been pushing myself to the limit. Working out eight, nine hours a day. I'm ready to get back out on the mound. More than ready. Hell, I'm *desperate*." Axel said the last word as if a dentist had wrenched it from his mouth.

A painful truth.

Dr. Harrison darted a glance at the Gunslingers' general manager, Truman Beck. The GM shook his head. Both Beck and Harrison exchanged concerned looks with Rowdy, who stood to one side, arms folded over his chest.

Rowdy knew what it was like to be in Axel's position. His career had ended abruptly after a baseball bat–wielding assailant had attacked him outside a Dallas nightclub three years earlier.

"What?" Axel demanded, a dismal note in his voice. The guy might be a typical cocky jock, but he was aching. "What aren't you telling me?"

Dr. Harrison cleared his throat. "Your range of motion has actually worsened since your last exam."

Axel's face crumpled as surely as if he'd taken an uppercut to the jaw from the fist of a heavyweight prizefighter. To his credit, he recovered quickly, shaking it off, hardening his chin, straightening his spine. Tough. He was tough.

His right hand clenched closed in his lap, his left palm lying open on his knee. He licked his lips, an I-freaking-hate-being-vulnerable glaze clouding his eyes. "So where do we go from here?"

Another tense, three-pointed exchange of glances between Dr. Harrison, the general manager, and Rowdy.

Kasha's stomach tightened.

"We're just as anxious to get you back on the field as you are to get there," said Truman Beck. "Dr. Harrison has consulted colleagues across the country about your case and . . ."

"There is a cutting-edge procedure we'd like to try." Dr. Harrison fiddled with his tie.

"Why haven't we tried it already?" Axel shoved a hand through his hair, his frustrated brow cleaved.

"Because," Rowdy said, "although the surgery has rapidly restored functioning in some people, in other cases it's actually made things worse."

"Ah shit." Axel pulled a palm down his face.

Dr. Harrison gave Axel a booklet. "All the statistics are here, and of course we would use the doctor who invented the procedure, which increases the chances for a positive outcome."

Beck stuck his hands in his front pockets and rocked from the balls of his feet to his heels. "It's your best option."

Using the TV monitor in the corner, Dr. Harrison started a Power-Point presentation on the innovative surgical procedure. Axel stared at the screen, but Kasha could tell he wasn't absorbing much of it.

Her sympathy shifted, bloomed to full-on empathy.

Axel's gaze smashed into Kasha's so sharply she softly gasped at the impact. The sultry expression in his eyes said, *You, me, another time, another place, fireworks!*

Thank God it wasn't another time or place. Kasha didn't do fireworks. Ever.

Purposefully, she schooled her face, making it unreadable. She wasn't going to let Mr. Hotshot Pitcher know how much he affected her.

When the presentation was over, Dr. Harrison switched off the television and turned his attention back to Axel. "So when should we schedule the surgery?"

Axel grunted. "Why do I feel like I'm being railroaded?"

Dr. Harrison raised his palms. "Mr. Beck needs to prepare for the future—"

"And you want to know whether to move me to the sixty-day disabled list or not," Axel said flatly.

"Yes," Beck confirmed.

Axel jumped to his feet, his hands clenched by his side. "You don't have to put me on the sixty-day DL. Give me a shot at the mound. I can play through a little pain."

"We tried that two weeks ago against Denver, and not only did we lose the game, but apparently it set back your recovery." Beck slowed his speech as if talking to a wayward child, pausing to let the news sink in. "The key question here is whether you can get better without aggressive intervention."

Axel's face paled and he looked as if he might throw up. "And if I refuse to have the surgery?"

"Then I can't guarantee your future with the Gunslingers."

"You say that like anything is guaranteed in baseball." Axel's laugh was harsh, humorless. "Let's be straight up about it. What you're really suggesting is that if I don't have the surgery, I'm out."

"Not at all." Beck backpedaled. "I'm saying you have some important decisions to make concerning your career."

Axel sank back down on the bench where he'd been sitting, grim determination stretching his lips taut. He shot a glance at Rowdy. "I know *they* want me to have the surgery." He nodded at Beck and Harrison. "But you've been where I'm at. What's your opinion?"

Rowdy rubbed his jaw. "It's not my decision."

"But do you believe the risks of the surgery outweigh the rewards?" Axel pushed, intensity vibrating off his hard-muscled body.

He seemed a lone warrior, carrying a bedraggled shield, raising it to his chest for another round of exhaustive fighting.

His weariness plucked something inside Kasha, and she had the strangest urge to touch him, soothe him, reassure him that he was not alone.

"You have to weigh the odds," Rowdy said. "Does the surgery give you a better chance of getting your pitching arm back over more traditional methods?"

Axel picked up the booklet Dr. Harrison had given him, and glowered at the data as if he were to scowl hard enough it could change the facts. "According to this, the surgery ended the career of thirty percent of the players."

Dr. Harrison cleared his throat. "But forty percent returned to the game with improved pitching stats. As you can see for yourself, the remaining thirty percent returned to their previous level of performance. Odds are in favor of the surgery."

Beads of sweat popped out on Axel's brow. He raised his head, swept his gaze around the room, and landed on Kasha again.

She made the mistake of meeting his deep brown eyes, and stumbled over the sharp desire in those dark depths. She braced herself not to react, even as she felt a hot flush pinch low in her body. She drew herself up tall, stretching out all of her five feet, eleven inches.

"Hey Sphinx," he said. "What do *you* think?"

"Are you speaking to me?" she asked, keeping her voice low, temperate.

"You're the only one here with a stony face." He waved at the collected managers, coaches, administrators, and medical personnel. "I can read what everyone else is thinking. Beck is rolling around dollars and cents. Stilts over there," he said, nodding at the Gunslingers' diminutive media liaison, "is planning a palatable press release. Doc is stumped on how to proceed with my rehab without the chancy surgery, but he doesn't want to admit it. Rowdy feels I shouldn't do it, but he's caught between a rock and a hard place and can't say so. But you, you're new, and you have no dog in this hunt. What do *you* think?"

Oh, but she did have a dog in the hunt. She needed to keep this job, and going against management was not smart.

"Ahem." Dr. Harrison pushed his glasses up onto the bridge of his nose again even when they didn't need pushing. "I know exactly how to proceed. We'll—"

"But you . . ." Axel said to Kasha, ignoring the physician. "You play your cards right up against your vest."

"That's because I don't have an opinion," she said mildly, even though her heart was pounding. Why?

"Everyone has an opinion."

"I don't yet have enough information to form one," Kasha murmured. "And either way, my opinion doesn't matter. I'm simply a physical therapist here to do whatever I'm assigned."

"There is nothing simple about you, Sphinx," he said, his tone oozing testosterone. "You're more complicated than everyone in this room put together."

His comment was a heat-seeking missile that shot straight into her gut. Every gaze in the room zeroed in on her, some people actually looking at her for the first time.

To keep from squirming under the scrutiny, Kasha breathed in gently through one nostril, slowly exhaled through the other. "I just met you. How could I possibly know what's best for you?"

"You've got good instincts."

"You can't know that."

"But I do. I've been watching you working out with the injured players. I see how you are with them. Caring but appropriately detached. Calm. Encouraging. You know when to push, and when to let a player figure things out on his own."

"I'm breathlessly flattered," she said, injecting her voice with sarcasm because she *was* flattered by his attention. Kasha wasn't accustomed to giddy feelings. She didn't like the sensation. It made her feel out of control.

"I didn't mean it as flattery," he said. "I call it like I see it. So tell me the truth, what do you think about my situation?"

"You really want my honest opinion?"

"Raw and undoctored."

"You don't need the surgery."

"No?" He arched his eyebrows as if he'd expected her to tell him to go ahead with the procedure. "Why's that?"

"You're not the only one who's been watching," she said.

His mouth twitched into a smart, edgy smile. "You've been watching me too?"

She flapped a hand at the elaborate facility they were in. "It's a big wide open space with lots of mirrors."

"Voyeur."

The air crackled with sexual electricity. Kasha couldn't believe that the others could stand so close to them and not flinch from the heat. It was all she could do not to fan herself. She battled against the steamy sensations that Axel's smile triggered inside her, a fireworks show of sparks and flames.

He moved then, rotated his injured shoulder, and tried to smooth away the grimace tugging his brows inward with a quick smile. It was unconvincing.

Pain.

He was hurting.

But it was more than mere physical pain. Emotional pain was inset deep, tucked away from the casual observer. His pupils darkened as she stared into him. Sharpening her attraction.

Kasha's throat went dry. She should keep her mouth shut. It was the smart thing to do.

"What did you see when you were watching me?" Axel prodded.

"They push you too hard." She waved a hand at the group. "It's understandable because you're a moneymaker. But more than that *you* push you too hard."

"Too hard?" he scoffed. "There's no such thing."

"That take-no-prisoners attitude has worked to get where you are," Kasha said. "But now it's not working anymore."

His nod was almost imperceptible. He knew it intellectually, but his heart resisted. He possessed such singular focus that backing off and slowing down felt like failure.

"You're not giving yourself the time and space you need to heal," she went on. "You've got this mistaken belief that if pushing hard is good, pushing harder is better. It's not. *That's* why you're not improving."

"Ms. Carlyle," Dr. Harrison barked. "You've overstepped your boundaries."

She knew it, and a sense of dread washed through her. She was a probationary employee. They could fire her without cause.

And then what would she do about Emma? She was struggling to pay off school loans from getting her doctoral degree in physical therapy; without this job, she wouldn't be able to afford both her debt and Emma.

But she kept her voice even, reasonable. "He asked my opinion."

"And you should have kept it to yourself," Dr. Harrison snapped. "Axel, don't let this woman influence your decision. *You* are in control of your care."

She should let it go, humble herself, try to hang on to the job, but Kasha simply had to say one more thing. If she kept quiet, and Axel went through with the surgery and the results turned out badly, she would never forgive herself for not speaking up.

"Try my way first," she said. "Take some time off. Give your arm a rest. Try massage and gentle therapy. Try hatha yoga. You can always have the surgery later—"

Truman Beck interrupted. "This innovative surgery is so groundbreaking, that if he has it now, there's a chance he could even be back on the roster by the All-Star break. Granted, we'd move slowly and he wouldn't see much action until we were certain his arm had fully healed, but it is a reasonable possibility. Data backs it up.

"And if the surgery fails," Kasha said, "not only is his career done for, but it could have long-lasting consequences for his overall health."

"We could have you scheduled for surgery in two days," Dr. Harrison said.

Kasha shifted her gaze to Truman Beck, who was shooting her the evil eye. Axel's current therapist, Paul Hernandez, didn't look happy either. The man had his hands on his hips and a dour expression on his face.

Terrific, she was making enemies left and right.

"Well, Ms. Carlyle?" Axel cocked his head, but did not drop his gaze.

Her heart knocked heavily as if she'd been running full-out. She had the oddest urge to drop panting to the floor, sink her face into her hands, try to block the sensations surging through her body.

She wondered if perhaps she was dreaming this. Axel's stare, the way he made her feel, the intense, undeniable attraction, the muddle of her mind. She should tell him no. Firmly. Clearly. Save herself.

Instead, she murmured, "I can't make any promises except to give you my best."

"That's all I ask. You've got the job. How, where, and when do we start?"

"Axel," Dr. Harrison said. "Ms. Carlyle is a probationary employee and she is still working on her certification in sports medicine. If you're not going to go through with the surgery, at least use Paul."

Axel growled. "She's the one who had the stones to speak up against this rush to surgery. *She's* the one I want."

"This . . . this . . ." Dr. Harrison sputtered, "is highly unorthodox."

"What's it going to hurt to give her a chance?" Axel said. "Unless there's a good reason why not. You did say it was my decision."

Truman Beck glared at Kasha as if he blamed her.

Axel got to his feet, towered over the general manager. "The surgery is no guarantee that will happen. Let's give Kasha a chance."

"Is this what you want?" Beck asked Kasha.

No. This was not what she wanted.

Why had she opened her mouth? What was wrong with her? It was like an unsolvable math problem she'd been given seconds to work out in her head. "I will help Mr. Richmond to the best of my abilities. But we need a quiet place to work. Somewhere out of the city so he won't be distracted from his recovery."

"You could stay at my place," Rowdy offered. He and Breeanne still had a sprawling second home in the country on the banks of Stardust Lake that they rarely used. "I have a home gym, and Kasha lives right there in town. Easy. Convenient."

Everyone looked at Beck for approval.

The skin on Beck's jowls wobbled. "A week, Ms. Carlyle. I'll give you a week. If we don't see some improvement in Axel's arm by then you're out of a job. Understood?"

Punished. She was being punished for speaking her mind.

"Well?" Beck snorted.

Kasha gulped, nodded, and prayed she was right about Axel's condition and that she could indeed help him. "Yes, sir," she said, and reached down deep inside for the bravery that had pulled her through a dicey early childhood. "But I have a contingency."

"*You* have a contingency?" Beck's tone was beef-jerky dry.

Great. She was going to blow this job before she ever got started. She pressed her feet hard into the floor, anchoring herself, but kept her knees loose. "I do."

Respect crossed Beck's face. "Yeah? And what's that?"

"If I *can* improve his arm in a week, then you take me off probation and make me a regular employee without the three-month waiting period."

Simultaneously, Beck flicked both index fingers against his thumbs. Kasha held her breath. Had she gone too far?

"Pretty sure of yourself." Beck growled. "Making demands."

No, she wasn't sure of herself at all, but she'd stepped up to the plate; she had to follow through or he would think her weak, and so would Axel. "If I'm going to risk my job going out on a limb, then I deserve to be rewarded if I'm proven right."

Beck stared at her long and hard and finally laughed. "All right," he said. "You've got a deal."

Kasha starched her spine to keep from sagging in relief. Her gamble had paid off. In a week's time, if she'd made improvements in Axel's arm, her insurance benefits would kick in and so would her pay raise and she could move forward with her plan to get custody of Emma.

Beck swung his gaze to Axel. "And you. If she hasn't helped your shoulder by this time next week, I'll expect you to consent to surgery."

"If it's not better, I will." Axel nodded, but the look he shot Kasha said, *Don't let me down.*

CHAPTER 2

What the hell had he done?

When Truman Beck lobbed a pitch for surgery, Axel choppered it straight into the ground. Why? He shook his head, puzzling out his motives. Why had he picked rest over surgery?

Rest when you die. That was his motto.

And yet, here he was, going against management, throwing his lot in with a novice physical therapist, agreeing to take it easy.

After parting remarks, the rest of the team dispersed, leaving him and Sphinx alone. He caught her staring at his bare chest.

Feeling self-conscious about his tattoo—he didn't want her asking questions—Axel reached for a T-shirt from the gym bag at his feet, but took his time wrestling into it, careful of his right shoulder, which throbbed painfully whenever he moved quickly.

Bull by the horns.

That was the only way to handle the situation. He'd gotten them both into this. Time to huddle and figure out how they could work together to heal his shoulder and get back out on that mound.

Kasha stood like a serene mountain, calm in the face of a stormy sea, and he was reminded of a stylized print of Mount Fuji dwarfed by a tsunami, which hung in the hallway of his parents' house. The

print, *The Great Wave off Kanagawa* by Katsushika Houkusai, had the
same effect on him as she did—powerful, magnetic, controlled.

"Looks like it's just you and me, kid," he joked, but it came out
sounding flat and uninspired.

She said nothing. Did not smile. Did not frown. Did not move
toward him. Did not walk away. Neutral. She was absolutely neutral.
Switzerland had nothing on this chick.

He ran a hand through his hair to tame his nerves, and turned
to face her. Why did she make him so nervous? He didn't do nervous.

She was tall, only a few inches shorter than his six-foot-two. Her
skin was a creamy latte color, rich and toasted. Her thick straight
hair—such a dark color of brown that it was almost black—was
plaited in a single braid that hung to the middle of her back. High
cheekbones, gentle chin, intense chocolate eyes.

His tongue stuck to the roof of his mouth as he fumbled around
for the right words. While he'd never been a glib playboy, he'd never
had problems talking to women.

Until now.

He wished he had time to regroup. Fully think about his decision. He considered telling her he needed a shower before they got
into it, but she looked as if she knew a stall tactic when she heard one.

Her eyes settled on him, at once both infinitely gentle and deter-
minedly tough. The sun came through the window, bathing her in
a halo of yellow light.

Looking at her, he thought about the time he'd been hiking outside Durango with Dylan before he'd gotten sick.

It was November, after baseball season was over, but before the
snows really set in. They had crested the ridge together and saw a startling mix of orange and purple and blue. They were so surprised by
the sight they'd stood with their mouths hanging open, their booted
feet stopping simultaneously in the crisp frost. In that moment—as
in this—the view stirred something in him that he couldn't fully
explain. Stunned by the play of shadow and light, he desperately
wanted to take a picture, capture her on his cell phone. Solidify the

image so he could review it later and see if he could figure out why she was so extraordinary.

If only she wasn't so damn sexy. Even dressed in the unattractive uniform of chinos and polo shirt, she exuded ripe sensuality. Why couldn't she have been middle-aged and plain? Or better yet, a guy.

The sun shifted, a cloud moving over, and the moment broke. A ping of loss stabbed him, and for no good reason, he felt as if he'd missed out on something important.

"Well," he said and then repeated, "Well," because he'd forgotten what he'd planned on saying. "Where do we go from here?"

"You start resting."

"Yeah." He pressed a palm to the back of his neck. "About that—"

"Backtracking already?" She stepped to the side, as if standing directly in front of him was too intense.

"I'm not a big fan of taking it easy." He watched her from the corner of his eye as he picked up his foot and tied his shoelace, pretended he wasn't watching her.

"You're conflicted," she said. "It's understandable. And it's clear you're very physical." She raised one eyebrow, shot a glance at his biceps.

"Straight up."

"Humble too."

"And lovable." He grinned. "Don't forget lovable."

Kasha snorted.

"I've amused you?"

"Greatly. Now back to rest and relaxation."

"Good old R&R." He cocked his head, perplexed by the sensations surging through him—lust for sure—but there was something more. Something rich and mystic he could not remember experiencing before. "What does that look like exactly?"

"You really don't know?" she murmured in an I'm-not-believing-this-guy tone.

"Are we talking about sleep in?" he blabbered to keep from analyzing his feelings.

"That could be an option if you're not getting enough sleep.

But you don't want to oversleep. That's just an excuse to avoid your problems."

"Problems? I've only got one problem. My screwed-up shoulder."

"What about the issues that got you in this shape in the first place?"

"Issues?" Axel scowled, rotated his arm. "I don't have any issues besides the shoulder."

She smirked. "You wouldn't be where you are if you weren't an overachiever tackling the world as a contest to be won."

"Is that right?" He leaned in closer.

"In my observation," she went on a bit primly, "you're eager, responsible, goal-oriented, persistent, organized, and enthusiastic."

"Not seeing the problem."

"You tell yourself that if you don't push, push, push, you're a loser. Did your parents have high expectations of you?"

"Don't all parents?"

"You're an only child?"

"Yeah," he admitted.

"In the gifted and talented program at school?"

"Yes," he mumbled. Was he that easy to read?

"Just because you're not always on top doesn't mean you're a loser."

"Um . . . by definition, yes it does."

"It's not true."

"What's not?" He blinked, having lost the point.

"That if you're not always achieving something you're a loser. It's not fact. It's only something you believe. It has no basis in reality."

He didn't know how she knew so much about him. It was scary and unnerving. "What's wrong with that?"

"Nothing is wrong with that. But every positive trait has a shadow side."

"Meaning . . ."

"The bright and shiny Tin Man from *The Wizard of Oz* got so focused on his job of cutting down trees that he rusted up in the rain."

"And I'm the Tin Man?"

"Chop, chop, chop."

"Are you saying I don't have a heart?"

"I'm saying that too much reliance on any particular trait leads to imbalance. In your pursuit of being the best pitcher ever, your shoulder has rusted up. More wood chopping in the rain will not solve the problem."

"What about chopping wood in the sunshine?"

"The rust has already set in. The only cure is to stop chopping, and oil up."

"Hmm," he said, taking a step toward her. "Oil up. Now that has possibilities."

She didn't miss a beat. "Are you flirting with me?"

"Maybe."

"Well, stop it. We're going to be working together, and I won't tolerate flirting."

"Just trying to lighten the mood."

"The mood doesn't need to be light. We were making a list of your strengths and weaknesses. Let's stick to that."

"What about your strengths and weaknesses." He took another step forward to see if he could unsettle her.

She drew in a slow, calm breath, did not back up, did not show any reaction at all. Her dark eyes remained quiet and shuttered. "We're not talking about me. You're the patient."

"Ah, so you can dish it out, but you can't take it."

"You're flirting with me as a distraction because you don't want to take a hard look at yourself."

Was he?

He raked a gaze over her body, the swell of her breasts, the curve of her hips. C'mon, any straight single guy in his right mind would want her. "I'm flirting with you because you're a hot, sexy woman."

"Do you feel compelled to flirt with every woman you're attracted to?"

"No." He widened his grin. "But you're special."

"Stop it."

"Why? Are you married? You're not wearing a ring."

"I'm not married, but my marital status has nothing to do with it. I'm your therapist."

"Technically Paul is my therapist."

"Not for the next week."

"But after next week can we . . ."

"No."

"Why not?"

"Because if next week is successful, I'll continue to be your therapist."

"What about after that?"

"Mr. Richmond," she said in a schoolteacher voice. "This is an inappropriate conversation."

"I've been a bad boy simply because I find you attractive?"

"I'm not judging you," she said. "I don't label your behavior as good or bad. It's either effective or ineffective. Flirting is ineffective for your treatment, and it makes me uncomfortable. Let's stick to the topic. Your constant drive to succeed is causing problems, and I suspect not only at work, but in your personal life as well."

Damn! Her perception was uncanny. His last relationship—albeit not a serious one—had broken up because of all the time he spent working out.

"Lady," he said. "You don't know me at all."

She looked at him with such pity it made him mad. "Who's Dylan?"

He slapped a hand over his heart, over the tattoo, even though his T-shirt hid it from her prying eyes. "Let's get something straight. You don't get to ask me about that. Ever."

"He was very important to you." Her eyes were sad, but she wasn't taking it personally.

Axel was not going to talk about Dylan. He made a verbal U-turn, switchback. "So the heartless, rusted Tin Man. That's me in your book?"

She paused, nodded, her head gliding loose and smooth. "Balance. You need balance in your life. That's what I'm saying. You've hit the wall."

"And?"

"Now comes rest. Or you could run after Truman Beck and tell him you changed your mind about the surgery. It's your choice. I have no vested interest in the outcome. In fact, if you went through with the surgery, it would get me off the hook."

"You didn't seem to have much trouble putting yourself on the hook in the first place," he pointed out.

"I have to speak up when I see something that needs speaking up about."

"You're the crunchy granola type."

Amusement lit her eyes. "I strive for peace, harmony, and balance in all things."

"So then you go and rock the boat with management? Contradictory."

"Some things are more important than peace, harmony, and balance."

"What things?"

"Principles. I couldn't let them bulldoze you into something that you were obviously on the fence about. Sometimes, you have to put up a fight."

His muscles tensed. "Why am I the battle you've chosen to take on? You don't owe me anything."

She took a deep breath in segmented parts, filling her belly first, then her mid-chest, finally the tops of her lungs. Strong. In charge. Her breasts rose brilliantly, swelling with air, alive with it. He'd never been fascinated with anyone's breathing before, but now he was.

"Because you're on the verge of crashing and burning," she said.

"Really?"

"You know it too. Deep down. That's why you put off the surgery. And it's why I offered my opinion."

"You didn't offer it, Sphinx. I pulled it out of you."

"You took my advice."

They stood there staring at each other and he had the most overwhelming urge to kiss her.

Kiss her hard. Kiss her long. Kiss her deep. Kiss her until both of them were hot and sweaty and panting for air.

She must have seen the desire in his eyes because for the first time, she looked uncertain and stepped back.

That move made him want to close the gap she'd created, span the distance, rub the corner of her wide, peach-hued lips with his thumb, and coax out a smile. But he wouldn't. If she was going to be his therapist, he would keep his hands to himself.

"This place is impressive." She dodged his gaze by glancing up at the domed ceiling that let in a flood of sunshine. "State-of-the-art facility. Cutting-edge equipment. Highly trained therapists. It's adding to your sense of failure."

"Huh?"

"You're thinking, hey, I've got the best of everything to heal and I'm not healing, what's wrong with me?"

"Busted." He laughed even though it wasn't funny. "So what are we going to do about that?"

"Take you away from all this." Finally, she surrendered a hint of a smile. "I'll file a treatment plan with Dr. Harrison, and we'll use Rowdy's house in Stardust for your rehabilitation."

"I'm not much of a country person." Axel shook his head. "I grew up in Houston. I'm a fast-paced urbanite. I'd rather stay in Dallas."

"All the more reason to get out in nature. It'll help. I promise."

"Why can't I rest at my condo where I can call for takeout whenever I want?"

"Precisely because you can call for takeout. A healthy diet is part of the healing process. Rowdy has a couple who look after his ranch. Mr. Creedy keeps the grounds. His wife is the housekeeper and cook. I'll make a meal plan for you that Mrs. Creedy can follow."

"I eat healthy . . ." he said. "Most of the time."

"With me on your case, you'll eat healthily all of the time."

"So you're a nutritionist too?" Yeah, okay, his tone was smart-assed, but she was talking about dragging him to the hinterlands of Bumfuzzle Nowhere.

"Actually, I do have a certificate in nutrition."

"Overachiever."

"No more so than you."

"Let me guess. You're a vegetarian."

"You say that as if it were a dirty word."

"No, just boring."

"Are you planning on fighting me every inch of the way? Because if you are, let's stop this right here, and you can call the GM and tell him you've changed your mind about the surgery."

Axel cocked his head, studied her. Her expression was neutral, her eyes noncommittal. Did anything ever rock her serene cool? He had a mad urge to do something, anything to rustle that glossy surface, to find the jagged edges hiding below the water's surface because he knew those edges had to be there. "It depends."

"On what?"

"Whether you can make this thing happen or not."

"Have a little faith," she said. "I know what I'm doing."

He paused, still stuck on his dilemma. His instinct was to push. Always. Passion and determination had carried him this far, and it was hard to resist. But he'd hit a wall, and she was right.

"Okay." He raised his palms. "Let's do this. Haul my ass out to Mayberry. I'm putting my career in your hands."

But even as he said it, he knew keeping his word was next to impossible, because he had no idea how to slow down. None.

He'd been going full bore since the moment he could walk and nothing stopped him. Even when Dylan got sick, he'd kept going because working through grief was the only way Axel stayed sane.

He studied Kasha, felt a twinge of pity. Whether she knew it or not, the woman had her work cut out for her.

CHAPTER 3

Five hours after she got stuck being Axel Richmond's physical therapist, Kasha sat in her car outside the group home where her half sister Emma lived. This was her fifth visit to the renovated Victorian on the corner of Moonglow and Pearl Street in an older part of Stardust filled with stately houses and long-limbed sheltering trees.

She was still struggling to wrap her head around the miraculous news that she had a biological sibling. The lawyer's out-of-the-blue call six weeks ago had changed everything, including the way Kasha saw herself.

Remembering that world-rattling phone call, she closed her eyes.

"Kasha Carlyle?" asked the polished-as-glass male voice.

She had stopped to answer the phone on the way to put a load of laundry into the washing machine, and she had dropped the basket at her feet. Her first leery thought was *Oh crap, I don't remember giving my number to any guys recently.*

"Yes," she said, injecting her tone with a distant, don't-much-care note.

"My name is Howard Johnson—"

"Howard Johnson? Like the hotel chain?"

He sighed, mumbled almost imperceptibly, "I should have

changed my name years ago," before he said in a louder voice, "Yes, like the hotel chain, and the Mets switch-hitting third baseman."

"That's got to be annoying."

"You don't know the half of it," he muttered, but marshaled his professionalism and went on. "I'm an attorney for the estate of Jane Compton."

"I don't know a Jane Compton," she said, but she tightened her grip on the cell phone.

"You might know her by her stage name, Bunny Bongo."

"No," Kasha said, realizing that she wasn't breathing, but she felt no urgency to take a breath. "Sounds like a stripper name."

"She was."

"Oh well, there you go. What's this Bunny . . . er . . . Jane Compton got to do with me?"

Howard Johnson exhaled sharply. "She asked that I contact you in the event of her death."

Kasha's chest grew tighter and tighter and tighter and still, she couldn't seem to make herself breathe. Her voice came out high, and streaky from lack of oxygen. "Why?"

"Because she was the mother of a twenty-three-year-old mentally challenged daughter, named Emma, who happens to be your half sister. Emma has been living in a group home for the past year while her mother was in hospice, and you're her only living relative."

Kasha had dropped the phone, sat right down in the middle of the laundry basket, and instead of breathing, she'd thrown up.

Even now, nausea swept over her again.

Opening her eyes, Kasha practiced a breathing technique she'd learned in yoga class. Inhale to the count of four. Hold the breath to the count of seven. Exhale to the count of eight.

Calm down.

The past was over. It had been out of her control, none of it was her fault, and it couldn't be changed. Accept. Forget. Forgive.

All that mattered now was Emma.

Clutching the car keys in her palm, Kasha got out and strode up the sidewalk, her stomach shaky the same way it had been the four other times she'd visited. She hadn't yet told her adoptive parents about Emma. Didn't know how to start the conversation. The last thing she wanted was to hurt them.

Be honest. You're not ready to relive the pain. As long as she didn't have to talk about the past, she could handle it. Putting words to it would bring everything back up again.

Besides, she'd convinced herself it was better to wait until she'd made her final decision about Emma before she broke the news to her parents.

Kasha knocked on the door, and a few seconds later the smiling housemother, Molly Banks, opened it.

"I'm sorry I didn't call first," Kasha apologized. "But I was hoping to see Emma."

Molly bit her bottom lip, and her gray eyes clouded. "It's not that I mind you seeing her, but routine is such a comfort to our young women. Unexpected disruptions can cause behavioral issues."

"I don't mean to make trouble, I just . . ." Kasha felt the car keys bite into her palm. "I needed to see her."

Molly said nothing, pressed the tip her tongue to her upper lip as if holding back her opinion.

"But I'm making this about me, aren't I? And not what's best for Emma." Kasha shook her head, the unshed tears tasting brackish in her mouth. She took a step backward. "I'm sorry. I'll go. When can I see her again?"

Molly's face softened. "We were just about to sit down to dinner. Would you like to join us?"

Her stomach churned and she didn't think she could eat, but she needed to see Emma again. Needed a reminder of why she was working for the Gunslingers. "Yes. Please. Thank you."

"Come on in." Molly held the door wide, and moved aside.

Kasha walked over the threshold, and into the tidy house that smelled like fresh-cut lemons and fabric softener. Molly escorted Kasha into the dining room where the members of the household were grouped around the table, standing behind their chairs, waiting for permission to be seated. Like Emma, the other five young women had Down syndrome.

The walls were painted sunny yellow. The chairs were plain and sturdy. The table was set with heavy plastic dishes.

"Ka'cha," Emma exclaimed, her eyes widened behind the thick lenses of her round glasses, and she raced over to envelop Kasha in a tight bear hug.

She hugged her sister back, overwhelmed by the rush of love. How was it possible for her to so completely love a young woman she had no idea existed six weeks ago?

Emma slipped her arm around Kasha's waist, rested her head against her shoulder, announcing to the room at large, "My titter."

The other residents surrounded Kasha, calling her name, begging for her attention.

Emma scowled, squeezed Kasha's arm, and announced in a loud, petulant voice, "My titter."

Molly smiled tolerantly, but her expression was harried as she shooed the other girls back to the table. "I'll find an extra chair."

Kasha felt guilty for disrupting the meal. She should have called. Why hadn't she called? Um . . . because she'd been afraid Molly would tell her not to come. "Anything I can do to help?"

"Ask Dixie." Molly disappeared into another room.

On her previous visits, Kasha had learned that the cook, Dixie, lived in her own apartment at the back of the property. Before Kasha could head to the kitchen to see if Dixie needed help, Molly's husband, Cliff, came home from his job as a postal worker. That set off another round of stampeding girls as they ran to greet him.

Over the heads of the six residents hugging him fiercely, Cliff gave Kasha a good-natured smile. "Molly didn't tell me we were having company for dinner."

"She didn't know," Kasha said. "I apologize for dropping in unannounced."

"We do appreciate advance warning." His voice was kind, but firm.

"I'll make an appointment next time."

"But . . . we're always happy to have visitors." He clapped his hands, sending the giggling young women back to their places.

Molly returned with another chair, and she and Cliff rearranged the table settings so that Kasha could sit next to Emma.

Dixie came around to put meat loaf on the plates.

"No meat loaf for me." Kasha put her hand over her plate when Dixie got to her.

"My titter only eat vegetable," Emma explained.

"Oops," Dixie said. "I forgot."

One of the other girls crinkled her nose. "Eww. I hate veggybles."

"Well," Molly said, picking up a bowl of potatoes that Dixie had deposited on the table at her elbow, and passed it around. "You're going to eat yours, Haley."

Once everyone at the table had food on his or her plate, the makeshift family said grace. Then Molly gave the signal and they started eating. All conversation stopped for a few minutes as everyone dug in with gusto. Dixie retreated to the kitchen. Kasha felt odd and out of place.

Until Emma reached under the table to pat Kasha's knee and whispered, "My big titter."

Kasha had three adopted sisters she loved dearly, but she had never experienced the instant connection she'd felt with Emma from the moment she first saw the girl's dark chocolate eyes, the exact same color as her own.

They both had the same creamy latte skin, and the same thick, black hair inherited from their biological father, who'd been part Native American, part Ethiopian. Immediate recognition—soul recognition—of someone she'd never met before had punched Kasha in the gut, left her wrung out and reeling.

We belong. She's part of me.

By her third visit, Kasha experienced an overwhelming urge to become Emma's legal guardian, and assume custody of her. Provide her with a permanent home. She'd talked to Howard Johnson and he got her to agree to wait six weeks before moving forward with the process.

"Give yourself a chance to get to know her," he said. "To see if this is really the right step for you both."

The six weeks had passed, and the urge hadn't subsided. In fact, it had grown even stronger. She wanted Emma.

Kasha had taken the job with the Gunslingers because of her sister. But joining the sports team had been a big adjustment, going from the head of the physical therapy department at Stardust General, caring mostly for elderly patients, to a probationary position working with cocky, handsome baseball players in the prime of life.

Her friends teased her and made "hot body" jokes, and asked her if she could introduce them to members of the team. But in all honesty, Kasha preferred working with her senior citizens.

Seniors truly needed the skills she taught them in order to stay in their own homes or to be able to walk again or improve their balance to prevent falls. While the ballplayers were chasing the peak of athletic perfection.

It was definitely a paradigm shift. Normally, her job entailed motivating people to work harder, but with hard-charging guys like Axel Richmond, she faced the opposite challenge.

Axel.

She set herself up for trouble when she'd voiced her opinion and agreed to work with him one-on-one. If she blew this, she'd lose her job. The job she needed to provide well for Emma.

Once she was off probation, she'd not only be making double her previous salary, she would have the best insurance available. True, Emma had Medicaid, but Kasha was determined her sister would have access to the finest medical care money could buy.

So why had she spoken her mind today? Was it an unconscious form of self-sabotage?

Subconsciously, could she be having second thoughts about becoming Emma's legal guardian? She could always backtrack. Advise Axel to get the surgery, tell him she was wrong, let herself off that hook. All it would take was a phone call.

Did she want out?

She glanced over at her half sister and instantly felt the hard tug of love. Emma beamed up at her as if Kasha was the most amazing thing she'd ever seen.

And Kasha felt her heart melt into a puddle of goo. If the look on her face matched the sweet goopiness in her chest, no one could ever call her Sphinx.

Looking past those heavy glasses into Emma's dear, trusting eyes, Kasha felt utterly changed. Tears for all she'd lost, tears she never allowed herself to shed, burned at the back of her throat. All these years Emma had been living in the same town, and Kasha had not known of her existence.

Sadness for everything she'd missed swept over her, for the terrible tragedy and dark secret that had kept her and Emma apart for twenty-three years.

Breathe. Just breathe.

The past couldn't be changed. The future was nebulous. Tomorrow would always be tomorrow. They lived today. This minute. Now.

And that was the most amazing thing about Emma. She only knew now. And Kasha, who'd spent her life trying to live down the past and find peace in the moment, needed that.

Needed it far more than she could express.

For all her limitations, Emma was centered, and grounded in a way that not even fifteen years of daily yoga practice had given Kasha.

"You not eatin' you pea," Emma said in a singsong voice.

"Well look there, so I'm not." Kasha smiled at her younger sister and ate a spoonful of peas to please her, and made a funny face that had Emma giggling.

"You're so good with her," Molly murmured. "A natural nurturer."

Kasha almost laughed. In her family, the nurturer title went to her sister Jodi, who loved taking care of the guests who visited her quirky B&B made from boxcars. Jodi was the oldest of the four adopted Carlyle sisters, and only ten months Kasha's senior.

One boyfriend had even told Kasha that she didn't have a nurturing bone in her body. A few had called her a cold fish. The nickname Ice Princess had been thrown around a time or two by guys in high school and college.

But she was glad that people couldn't see the emotions seething inside her. Glad she had learned the skill to hide her vulnerability. Glad she was nothing like her violent, unpredictable biological parents.

They finished the meal, which included a dessert of apple crisp, and Kasha helped clear the table and wash dishes. The young women teased and laughed and had a wonderful time, and when the chores were done, Kasha had an hour to spend with Emma before the household began bedtime rituals.

Emma took Kasha by the hand and led her to the bedroom she shared with Haley. They sat on the floor of the clean, simple room, coloring in a Disney Princesses coloring book. Emma claimed the purple crayon, and announced purple was her favorite color.

"Mine too," Kasha confessed.

"We the 'ame." Emma wriggled like a happy puppy.

"Which princess do you like best?" Kasha asked.

"Ja'mine," Emma said. "'He look like me and you."

"Jasmine does look like us, doesn't she?" True indeed. Except for Emma's features marked by Down syndrome, Kasha and her half sister looked remarkably alike.

Emma reached over and gave Kasha a hard hug. "I love you, titter."

Kasha cupped the back of Emma's head in her palm and whispered the words that were normally so hard for her to say. "I love you too."

"Color!" Emma announced, and swatted Kasha's hand. "You color now."

"Oh sorry, I didn't realize I was holding up the works."

They lay side by side on the floor, busily coloring in the coloring book. The girl stuck her tongue out while she worked. It seemed to help her concentrate. Kasha could smell her strawberry perfume, and Emma's shoulder brushed right up against hers.

Sometimes life was like the surface of a tranquil lake, calm, smooth, serene. But all it took was one stone dropped from the hand of a child, one twig fallen from a tree branch, one fish breaking the surface to cause ripples that fanned out, waved, rocked, disturbing everything.

Ripples.

Finding out about her half sister was the small stone plunked into the quiet lake of Kasha's life, and the ripples were still growing, widening, spreading out.

Change. Like it or not, change was here. And it was time to decide whether to roll with it, fight it, or ignore it.

Emma's beaming face made up Kasha's mind. First thing in the morning, she would call Howard Johnson and tell him she was certain that she wanted to become Emma's legal guardian and to start the paperwork.

This wasn't going to be easy, but she was ready to become her sister's surrogate mom.

WHILE KASHA WAS having dinner with her half sister at the group home, Axel was sitting alone at a tall bistro table in his condo eating a premade salad he'd picked up at Whole Foods, and drinking a pilsner.

The television was on in the living room, a replay of one of his best games, and he could partially see it from where he sat. As he watched himself wind up for a beautiful hundred-mile-an-hour fastball, he winced.

Great arm. Great game. Those were the days. Except he hadn't fully appreciated what he had until it was gone.

Naïve. Arrogant.

He'd foolishly believed he could power through anything to achieve his goals. He'd learned the hard way that some things simply could not be achieved by a bulldozer mindset and can-do attitude.

But the thought of doing nothing went so far against the grain of Axel's belief system that it made him physically sick to his stomach.

He pushed the salad away, got up from the table, and paced the length of the galley kitchen. Everything was new and shiny and modern and cookie-cutter, like every other condo in his neighborhood. Granite countertops. Cocobolo cabinets. Solid hardwood flooring. Stainless steel appliances.

The place was both gorgeous and soulless. It wasn't a home.

How could it be a home? He was rarely here and had no one to share his life with. Not that he'd wanted that. Not since he'd lost Dylan.

Axel put a hand over his heart, breathed out his grief. It served no one.

Action. Baseball. It was the only thing that had kept him sane in those nightmarish, thundercloud days after Dylan's death.

He moved into the living room, his mind replaying the events of the day. Fact: He was attracted to Kasha Carlyle. Had been from the moment he'd watched her glide into the sports medicine facility the previous Monday.

Fact: He wanted her more than he should.

Fact: For some unimaginable reason he'd agreed to hole up in the country with her for an entire week and do nothing, when he could be having surgery to fix his pitching arm.

Fact: He wasn't dreading it.

Fact: He was really disturbed by all of those facts.

Quandary? What was he going to do about these feelings?

Should he: (A) Call Dr. Harrison and tell him he wanted Paul Hernandez as his therapist while he rested instead of Kasha? (B) Call the general manager and tell him he was ready to go ahead with the surgery? (C) Rock on with the current plan, but do his damnedest to keep his desires in check?

Decisions. Decisions.

If he tossed Kasha in favor of Paul, he was afraid it would reflect badly on her and she'd lose her job.

Option B was tempting, but he couldn't seem to quell the nagging voice that told him Kasha was right about resting his shoulder.

That left option C. The most appealing and the most troublesome, because he wanted to hang out with Kasha, and that was the problem.

She reminded him of the willow tree that had grown in his parents' backyard at his childhood home. Tall and slender, able to bend in the wind, but not break. Rooted deep, anchored and stable.

Controlled. So very controlled.

If he could control a baseball the way she controlled her emotions, he'd be headed straight for the Hall of Fame.

It all came down to what was best for his career.

He slumped on the couch in front of the TV, stared at the screen. Instead of seeing his younger self whipping a ball across that plate at a batter who swung hard and missed, he saw his dream play out the way he'd visualized it a million times.

On the mound at Yankee Stadium, leadoff pitcher, last game of the World Series, pitching a no-hitter; the crowd chanting his name, Axel, Axel, Axel; the smell of popcorn and peanuts and hot dogs in the air; the guys in the bullpen happy for the win, but jealous it wasn't them leading the charge; kids in the stands, holding up mitts, praying for a fly ball to land in the pocket of their gloves, everyone watching and waiting with breaths held for him to strike out the last batter.

From the time he was seven years old, he'd fallen asleep with that image in his head. Awakened with it.

And when he was twenty and his casual girlfriend, Pepper Grant, had gotten pregnant, he'd offered to marry her because the thought of being a dad thrilled him to pieces.

Pepper rejected his proposal because she said she couldn't tie him down like that, and they didn't really love each other the way they deserved to be loved. But they both loved that baby something fierce. Pepper had been an awesome mom, and he had the utmost respect for her.

Raising Dylan had only strengthened his resolve to be the very best example he could. He did it through his actions, not just words.

Work hard. Commit. Never give up on your dreams.

He had firmly believed that, and he'd done his best to instill those values into his son.

Without Dylan, what did it all mean? So what if he achieved the pinnacle of success? Without Dylan, the dream was sawdust in his mouth.

But without the dream, what else was there?

He'd worked his entire life for this. Dylan had cheered him on, been his biggest fan, his strongest champion. Letting go of the dream now would be like letting Dylan down in the most fundamental way. Betraying his beliefs.

Axel leaned over and opened the drawer in the coffee table, took out a undersized baseball glove closed around a baseball, a soft cleaning rag, and conditioning oil. The glove was so small that he could only wriggle three fingers inside.

Gently, he rubbed the leather, felt his heart pump hard with every stroke, and knew he had no choice. He had to do everything in his power to reach his goal. If that meant resting, that's what he'd do.

In memory of his son.

Axel blinked, swallowed, and with the tip of the cleaning rag wiped away the single salty tear that had fallen into the pocket of his dead son's glove.

CHAPTER 4

Per arrangements with Rowdy, Axel arrived in Stardust on Wednesday evening, May eighteenth. Gentle therapy sessions with Kasha were to start in the morning, and then the following Thursday he would return to Dallas for Dr. Harrison to reexamine him and determine if Kasha's "take it easy" plan was working.

In the meantime, Axel was stumped.

What the hell was he going to do out here in the sticks? Granted, there were plenty of distractions in Rowdy's house—big-screen TV, recordings of innumerable baseball games, state-of-the-art video technology for video gaming, heated swimming pool, hot tub, a class-A home gym, and even a zipline that ran down to the edge of the lake.

But Axel was an extrovert. He needed people around. Stimulation. He met the live-in caretakers, Boston and Zelma Creedy, but they weren't big talkers, and after they showed him around the place, they took off on a golf cart to their cottage several acres away.

Leaving Axel twiddling his thumbs.

He prowled the grounds. What was he supposed to do? He'd been in the house for only one night, and already he was bored out of his skull. He had nothing to think about but the constant ache in his shoulder, and how far he was falling short.

At eight o'clock on Thursday morning, Kasha showed up with that smooth, butter-don't-melt-in-Iceland look on her face, a tablet computer tucked under her arm, and an efficient snap to her step.

Her glossy dark hair hung down her back in its customary braid, and she wore her uniform—blue chinos and a green polo shirt with the Gunslingers logo. The outfit didn't look good on anyone, but on her, somehow it did. Her exotic sloe eyes locked onto him with a determined sense of purpose.

"Good morning," she said crisply. "Let's get to the gym."

Without waiting on him, she turned and headed for the sliding glass door that led to a garden courtyard, and the detached home gym beyond. For a second, it stumped him how Kasha knew the gym's location, and then he remembered she was Rowdy's sister-in-law.

He ambled after her, rotating his shoulder and wincing against the pain. On the opposite side of the swimming pool stood the glass building that looked like something out of an architectural magazine.

Axel had worked out in plenty of commercial gyms half this size. Through the glass walls, he could see Kasha heading toward the massage table in the far corner. When he pushed through the door, classical music floated out to greet him.

"Ugh." He crinkled his nose. "Could we put on some Kanye instead?"

"No," she said. "Mozart stays."

"Snooty."

"Not snooty," she corrected in an even tone. "Soothing. Soothing music soothes tense muscles."

"You gotta be kidding."

"On the table." She patted the massage table. "And take off your shirt."

"Straight to the point."

"Which is why I'm here." Her face was a blank canvas.

He had no idea what she was thinking. He wished he had paints so he could draw a smile on those full wide lips of hers. "Why are you so uptight?"

"I'm not uptight. I have a job to do, and I'd appreciate it if you'd just let me get to it."

"Message received." He raised both palms. "No idle chitchat."

"I'm glad we understand each other. Now if you please . . ." She gestured toward the table. "Take off your shirt."

He obliged.

Her gaze flicked to his bare chest. Her controlled expression gave away nothing, but in her eyes he saw a quick flash of interest before she managed to snuff it out.

Curiosity about the tattoo? Or was she admiring his muscles? The former made him uncomfortable, the latter made him smile.

She cleared her throat, stared at the table pointedly.

He took his time climbing up on it. She might be in charge, but she wasn't in control. He'd asked for her to be on his case. She was working for him, and it didn't hurt to remind her.

"On your stomach," she said. "We'll start with moist heat to loosen up your shoulder."

He rolled over, got settled, closed his eyes, listened to her moving around, and caught the faintest hint of her scent. She smelled of raindrops and moonlight, of lavender and sage. The fragrance wasn't strong enough for cologne, most likely body lotion or shampoo.

She rested a moist heat pack on his right shoulder, and his body started to relax. He hated to admit it, but she was right about the Mozart. Between the heat and the music and the lulling fragrance, he actually drifted off to sleep for a couple of minutes, jerking awake when her hand touched his bare flesh.

Gently, she massaged his shoulder, her strong fingers pressing into his skin, and instantly Axel got hard. At least he was facedown, but that didn't stop the ache. *Quit thinking about her.*

Pretty damn hard to do when Kasha's outer thigh was touching his hip.

Axel squeezed his eyes closed. Gulped.

"Does that hurt?" She lightly caressed the ball of his right shoulder joint.

"Um, no, why?"

"You tensed up."

Well, yeah lady. You're the sexiest thing since black silk stockings with the seam running up the back.

"It's . . . uh . . ." he stammered. ". . . hot in here."

"I'll turn down the thermostat." She stepped away, momentarily giving him breathing room.

But it didn't last long or help much. The second her hands touched him again, he was as hard as marble.

"Are you always this tense?" She clicked her tongue. "No wonder you're not healing."

No, no, not always this tense, only when he was around gorgeous physical therapists with enigmatic dark eyes and magic fingers.

"We're not going to get anywhere until you relax. What do you normally do to chill out?"

"Exercise."

"I'm not talking about exercise. How do you unplug from work? Read? Watch TV? Play video games? Listen to music?"

"I don't have time to unplug. I'm thirty, and injured. If I'm ever going to make it to the top I have to give one hundred and ten percent."

An amused laugh rolled out of her, soft as fairy dust.

"What's so funny?"

"Excuse me? You are the big time."

"The Gunslingers are an expansion team," he said.

"So what?"

"It's not the same."

"How much more 'top' does it get, Axel?"

"Pitching for the Yankees, the finest team in baseball."

"That's a matter of perception," Kasha said. "I thought the best team in baseball is the one who won the last pennant."

"Best is transitory, you're right," he said. "That's why I said finest team. Historically there's no team with as much history and heart and can-do spirit as the Yankees."

"I'm certain there are millions of baseball fans that will argue the point."

"The Yankees are iconic. They're synonymous with baseball."

"Why is playing for the Yankees so important to you? Let's face it, especially when the odds are slim that things will actually go your way. When it comes to trades, a lot of that stuff is beyond your control."

The old anxiety and uncertainty hit him in the chest, and he hardened his chin against the massage table. No room for doubt. He was going to make it to the Yankees or die trying. Nothing or no one was going to dissuade him. He was determined to make Dylan proud.

A salt lump knotted in his throat and he swallowed hard. He wouldn't talk about Dylan. Couldn't.

"You're tensing up again." Kasha's fingers kneaded his back. "Try to relax."

"I can't stop thinking how far I'm falling behind."

"Do you know how many people would kill to be where you are?"

"Yeah," he said. "I know how lucky I am, but that doesn't stop me from wanting more, and at my age, I don't have much time left to achieve it."

Kasha sighed.

"What?" he asked, turning his head to glance over his shoulder at her. Her face was in profile. Her eyelids lowered halfway, her chin dipped down slightly.

"I can see I've got my work cut out for me."

"Sorry, it's just who I am."

"Is it really?"

He snorted. "Yes."

"Think back to before you were consumed with baseball."

"My mind doesn't stretch back that far."

"You don't have any other hobbies?"

"Who has the time?"

"You do. Now."

"I see your point. Let me give it some thought."

"Since you don't have a hobby, we'll do mine."

"Which is?"

"Yoga."

He groaned.

"Stop complaining. I gave you a chance to come up with something you enjoyed. You didn't, so we do things my way. I'll change into my yoga clothes and meet you outside on the lawn."

"You carry yoga clothes around with you?" he asked, his pulse leaping at the thought of seeing her in yoga pants.

"I keep a change of clothes in my car."

"You had this yoga thing planned all along."

She gave him a "maybe" shrug and a whisper-smile. Oh, she was a sly one.

"Do I need to wear anything special?" he asked, sitting up on the massage table.

"You're good in those sweatpants, but you can put your T-shirt back on. And grab a yoga mat from the closet."

Five minutes later, he had a yoga mat spread out on the back patio a few feet from the swimming pool, the morning sun reflecting off the water, scattering prisms of light over the ground. He smelled chlorine and coconut-scented sunscreen.

Dressed in black skin-tight yoga pants, a black and red tank top layered over a red sports bra, Kasha glided out of the house as if skating on a cloud, and frankly, he couldn't stop staring at her. The woman was a walking wet dream.

She carried a purple tote bag with a yoga mat sticking out of it. She unrolled the mat, bent over to spread it on the ground.

He studied her boldly as she bent over. The yoga pants looked brand-new and clung to her curves, and he thought, *I'm in love with those pants.*

She straightened and came to stand on a spot in front of him at the end of her mat, and indicated he should do the same on his mat, and then she led him through a series of poses in what she called a grounding process.

"Turn off whatever is bothering you," she soothed. "Close your eyes and just be here now."

Yeah, like that was so easy.

But the more she talked, the more the sound of her voice lulled him, and before long, he wasn't thinking about anything except for breathing the way she taught him to breathe and holding the poses.

Even the hot sexual thoughts banked to a low simmer.

Okay, maybe this yoga thing wasn't so nutty after all. In those few minutes he felt more calmed and controlled than he'd felt since . . . well, since he couldn't remember when.

They were doing side arm stretches and he was swinging along at a steady clip, when she cautioned, "Easy does it. Explore the edge, but don't go over it."

"Explore the edge? What does that even mean?"

"Feel the power of the stretch. But if there's the least bit of actual pain, back off."

He grunted, and stopped extending as far as he could.

"Good job," she encouraged him.

"I feel like I'm revving my engine with the transmission in park."

"Then back off more."

"If I do that, I'll barely be moving."

"Then barely move." She slowed her own pace to demonstrate.

"At this rate my shoulder won't heal until I'm eighty."

Her smile was enigmatic, slight and light.

"What?" he asked, mimicking her movements, rotating his body from side to side with painstaking motions that were actually starting to feel really good in his shoulder.

"I was thinking of what you'll be like at eighty."

"How's that?"

"You'll be winning wheelchair races down the hallway of the nursing home and goosing the nurses not smart or fast enough to get out of your way."

"I don't know whether I should feel flattered or insulted."

"Your choice," she said. "Arms straight out at your sides, shoulder height, palms up."

"This isn't hard," he said.

"Not yet." There was that knowing smile again, as if she held the keys to heaven and she wasn't going to let him in until he proved himself worthy. "Make tiny little circles with your fingertips as if they were paintbrushes, and you were painting the walls."

"That I can get into."

"Slow down."

"You're starting to sound like an echo." He snorted.

"I'll stop repeating myself when you hear me."

"I don't see how this is helping much. It's just stretching, and not very strenuous stretching at that," he grumbled.

"Last time I checked, I was the therapist and you were the patient. Why don't you just let me do my job?"

"Great, fine, okay." He chuffed out a breath and slowed his movements. "Ow, this is getting harder."

"Uh-huh."

"Are you always such a tough taskmaster?"

"Close your eyes," she said. "Focus on what you're doing, nothing else in the world matters but painting those walls. Nothing else exists."

"Um . . ." He cleared his throat. "Your voice exists."

"Widen the circles," she instructed, ignoring that.

"Right. Focus. I'm focusing." Except that he wasn't. His shoulders were burning, and her lavender-sage smell was tangling up in his nose, and her voice was heating up his blood. He dropped his arms.

"Arms up," she said, perky but insistent.

"They're tired."

"I know. Mine are too. Arms up."

Grunting, he raised his arms. "Is this painting almost finished?"

"The longer you complain, the longer it takes."

"You're punishing me?"

"Don't have to. You're already punishing yourself by focusing on your discomfort. Just focus on what you're doing, ignore everything else."

"Like when I'm pitching?"

"Exactly like when you're pitching."

They exercised together for a while longer, Axel obeying her commands, keeping his eyes closed, and moving with intent and purpose. And when she told him it was time to get on his back for floor stretches, he was surprised to discover thirty minutes had passed.

"We're winding up already?" he asked, surprised by his disappointment that it was almost over.

"Half an hour is long enough for your first yoga session. Roll over onto your stomach." She demonstrated, rolling over onto her belly, and giving him a great view of her gorgeous rump sheathed in those yoga pants.

He tried his best not to stare, failed utterly.

"Pay attention to your breathing," she chided. "Not my butt."

He closed his eyes, but he could still see the shape of her round fanny burned into his retina. He opened one eye, peeked over at her, found her staring at his ass. "Focus, Sphinx."

"I am," she said, not looking the least bit guilty for having been caught ogling his butt. "I'm the therapist, my job is to study your form."

"If telling yourself that makes you feel better, go right ahead. I know the truth."

"It is the truth." Her voice was maddeningly calm. What would it take to get a rise out of her?

"But if I look at you—"

"You're gawking."

"You make it sound so cheap."

"Not cheap. Predictable. Now ground your pelvis against the floor, and raise both legs in the air."

"Have you ever noticed how provocative some of these yoga poses are?" he asked.

"Predictable."

"I feel so common," he joked.

She ignored that. "Now raise your arms out in front of you like you're Superman flying off to save Lois Lane from some baddies."

He raked his gaze over her as her chest lifted up off the floor, while her hipbones stayed firmly rooted against the yoga mat. "For it's hip-hip and away I go," he teased.

"That's Underdog, not Superman."

"What's the difference?"

"One's a dog, one's a man . . . oh . . . I see your point."

"Aha!" Axel crowed. "You do have a sense of humor."

"And release the pose," she said mildly, not letting him get to her. "Time for Superman to land."

"Aah, and just when I was beginning to enjoy the flight."

"On your back in Savasana."

"What's that?" He sat up.

"Corpse Pose."

"Seriously?"

"It's a pose of total relaxation. Of surrender." She flipped onto her back, legs slightly apart, arms at her sides, palms facing up.

"Vulnerable position," he commented, still sitting.

"I had trouble with it at first too," she said. "Just try it."

"You did?"

"Being vulnerable is not my strong suit," she admitted.

"And yet here you are, all laid out in Sa-whatever-vana."

"You're avoiding the process. You've done great today, it's been a successful morning, don't blow it."

"All right, all right." He swung around, lay down on the mat next to her, unable to tell her the real reason he didn't want to lie down faceup. What if he got aroused again?

But her eyes were closed and she looked so peaceful, a barely-there smile curling up the corners of her lips. She was right. It had been a good morning.

He rested on the mat, his shoulder muscles feeling tired but no longer aching the way they normally did when he pushed himself with free weights or the machines. It was a peaceful tired, a good kind of tired, and for the first time since his injury, he truly felt hopeful that everything was going to work out.

KASHA LAY BESIDE Axel feigning calm. A hundred different thoughts popped in and out of her head. Some yogi she was. Couldn't shut down her mind chatter for a two-minute Savasana.

Snap out of it. Get straight. Breathe.

But whenever she inhaled, she could smell his scent—slightly musky now from the exercise—and she could feel heat radiating off his body, could hear his breathing too, the deep, masculine sound as he filled his lungs, held it for a beat, and then let it go long and smooth.

The sound lulled her, made her feel as if she were being rocked by gentle ocean waves. She realized they were breathing together, and it was not the patient following the therapist, but the other way around. She had fallen into *his* breathing pattern.

Alarmed, she held her breath.

And then he held his too.

Ah good, back in charge. Today had gone well. A little massage. A little yoga. As long as he did what she told him, he was going to have improvement in his range of motion.

That sure of yourself, huh?

Terrific. Doubting herself? No room for that. She had to make this happen. Not only for her sake and for Emma, but for Axel's as well. If he didn't learn how to slow down, he was going to blow his arm out for good, and that would be the end of his dreams.

She opened her eyes and turned her head to study him.

Even at rest, he looked like a man on the verge of springing into action. Maybe it was all those hard-packed muscles glistening in the sun. God, he was gorgeous. If she wasn't his therapist . . .

But she was. No place for unprofessional thoughts in this relationship. He needed her help, and that's what she'd give him. That's *all* she would give.

"What now?" Axel mumbled in a sleepy voice.

"We're going to do a guided meditation called yoga nidra." She sat up. "To put you in a state of deep relaxation."

He opened one eye. "What do I have to do?"

"Shh, just keep your eyes closed and listen." She sat cross-legged on her mat. "The military uses a version of yoga nidra called iRest to help heal servicemen and women with PTSD."

"Okay," he said. "Just remember, you've got my career in your hands."

Yes, that was the nerve-wracking part, but she was confident she could help him. "I'm going to place a special buckwheat pillow over your eyes to block out the light."

She fetched the pillow from her tote bag, reached over to settle it over his eyes. She tried to do it without touching him, but he shifted slightly, and her fingertips brushed against his forehead.

Singed. Dammit!

Axel sucked in his breath at the same time she jerked away and lost her balance, falling backward onto her mat.

Thank God, he couldn't see her. She righted herself and brushed a dusting of perspiration from her upper lip with the back of her hand. She could not keep reacting so viscerally every time she touched the man.

"Kasha?" he murmured.

"Still here." She cleared her throat, and found herself smiling. "Sink down into the mat. Feel the earth supporting your body."

Her own body grew heavy, leaden, as it often did during meditation, but this was different somehow, as if she were tuning in to his rhythms, experiencing the sensations with him.

And in those sensations, she blossomed, and grew.

This was nuts. Absolutely nuts. She was imaging a connection that wasn't there. He was a client. She was his therapist. So what if he was a hunk? It was a line that could not be crossed.

She guided him through the meditation, modulating her voice low and tranquil, hiding her emotional turmoil with soft words, and soon he was breathing slowly and deeply, snoring slightly, completely and utterly relaxed, maybe for the first time since he was a child.

The magic of yoga nidra; it had the power to still the most turbulent mind. Considering the crazy way Axel made her feel, maybe it was time she started practicing the technique on herself.

CHAPTER 5

Kasha had no more than walked into her house after her day with Axel than her cell phone rang. It was the lawyer.

"Hello Mr. Johnson," she said.

"Got your message," Howard Johnson replied. "I know the six weeks are up, and you still want to pursue custody of Emma. But while that's admirable, before you take that final step, I think it wise for you to first spend some time with your sister outside the group home setting."

"Why?"

"To fully understand what you're up against."

"I appreciate your concern." She kicked off her shoes at the back door, savored the feel of the cool tile under her bare feet. "I'm in the medical profession, and I'm well aware of Emma's challenges."

"Being aware of the challenges and living with them on a daily basis are two different things. You are essentially taking on a parental role."

"I know that."

"She's a child in an adult's body."

"I can handle it." Kasha trailed into her bedroom.

"Even so," the lawyer said. "I encourage you to take this extra step. Let me put the wheels in motion, and make arrangements for you to take Emma home with you for an overnight stay and see how you two click outside of a controlled environment."

Kasha blew out her breath, took out her earrings, and set them on the top of her dresser. "I'd really rather just get this process started. I know I want her."

"Do you have a bedroom set up for Emma? Have you hired someone to look after her while you're at work?"

"Not at the moment, but neither one of those should take me long to set up. I can handle those details while you're drawing up the paperwork."

"Your job is in Dallas. You're going to have to move there eventually. Have you thought about how such a move will affect Emma?"

"There will be more opportunities for Emma in the city," Kasha said. She had thought about it a lot. In Dallas there would be services for Emma that didn't exist in Stardust. It was another reason she'd taken the job with the Gunslingers. "It will be an adjustment, but we can weather it."

"Your heart is in the right place, Ms. Carlyle. But have you considered whether or not Emma will be happy living with you? As excited as you both are to have found each other, you are virtually strangers."

Kasha sank down on the end of her bed. More than anything in the world she wanted to share her life with Emma, her only living blood relative. And only part of it was making amends for her biological parents' sins.

But the lawyer had a point. In the end, she wanted what was best for Emma, not herself. She had to make sure she was doing this for the right reasons.

"You make a good case," she admitted. "Please make arrangements for me to take Emma for a few days."

"Smart decision," Howard Johnson said. "I'll move forward with that, and we can get together with Emma's foster parents for a time that's convenient for both of you."

Kasha hung up, and paced her bedroom.

It was time to tell her adoptive parents about Emma. Dread over digging up ancient history had her avoiding this conversation for too long. She needed their guidance as she went forward with gaining custody of her half sister, and the longer she waited to break the news, the more hurt they would be that she hadn't confided in them from the beginning.

Why hadn't she confided in them from the beginning?

In the bathroom, she undressed to her underwear and stood examining herself in the mirror. Studied the thin vertical scars carved into the tops of her thighs. Traced them with her finger. Counted them out.

There were a hundred and three of them, each an ugly badge of shame.

Old now.

Silvered.

They'd been there for so long that most days, she barely noticed them. But she was permanently marked by her past. The scars were a constant reminder of where she'd come from, and where she never wanted to return.

And on some level she was terrified of slipping back there. Even though logically she knew she'd come out on the other side of her trauma, a primal fear lurked deep in the recesses of her brain.

"It's okay. You're all right," she soothed. "You beat it."

Shaking off the fear, she showered, and dressed and headed over to her parents' house, guiding her Prius over the railroad tracks that crossed Main Street. She drove past Timeless Treasures, her parents' antiques store, and took a left to round the block.

The closer she got, the higher the guilt tower grew. In this neighborhood the houses were older, mostly frame—Craftsman and farmstyle, Victorians and Cape Cods. In the yards sat garden gnomes or metal cutouts of pink flamingos or Texas flags.

It was a good place to grow up, a safe place full of love and caring and community. A long way from where Kasha had spent the first seven years of her life.

Outside her parents' home cars filled the driveway, spilled out onto the street. What were all the vehicles doing here? Were her gregarious parents throwing an impromptu party on a Thursday night?

Sucking in her breath, and her courage, Kasha parked at the curb, drummed her fingers on the steering wheel, and studied the yellow Victorian with white gingerbread trim and a wide, welcoming veranda. The coat of paint was new. The house had been gray when she was growing up, with red trim. The metal roof was new too, her parents investing in it after one too many hailstorms. Poplar trees, tall, thin, and stately, flanked both sides of the house just inside the white picket fence. Underneath each front window was a flowerbox flush with pink and purple petunias.

She did not remember the night she took refuge in this house; that dark night was forever buried in her damaged childhood psyche. But she did remember the day she walked up the sidewalk with Dan and Maggie Carlyle after the adoption was final, enveloped in the open arms and welcoming smiles of her new sisters.

Knuckles rapped against the window, startling her. She jerked her head around to see her other brother-in-law, Jake Coronado, who was married to her oldest adoptive sister, Jodi, standing there holding a tote bag.

Jake also played for the Gunslingers, and he currently had the highest batting average on the team. "How come you're sitting out here all by your lonesome?"

"How come you're here at all? No game tonight?"

"Travel day. We're playing in Houston tomorrow, so instead of heading out with the team, I came home to spend time with Jodi. I'll leave tonight after the party, and catch up with the team there."

"What party?" Kasha's chances of getting her parents alone to tell them about Emma dimmed.

"You're not here for Trudy's celebration?" he asked.

"No, I just dropped by to see Mom and Dad. What's Trudy celebrating?"

Trudy was their next-door neighbor, a spunky, tattooed senior citizen who'd once been a Vegas showgirl, but she was now an artist with an appealing folk art style.

"She's having a gallery showing in New York."

"No kidding?"

"Impressive, huh."

"Sure enough." Kasha bobbed her head. "Is Rowdy here too?"

"Naw, too much on his plate. He's already in Houston with the team. But Breeanne's inside."

Kasha opened the door and got out. "What's in the bag?"

"Jodi forgot the apple pie she made, and I had to circle back to the B&B to get it," Jake said.

"Pregnesia strikes again." Kasha chuckled.

"I had no idea pregnancy could make women so forgetful. But on the upside, when she gets mad at me, she forgets it quickly." Jake grinned like a naughty schoolboy.

"This too shall pass, and soon you'll have an adorable baby to love and a wife with her elephant memory back."

"True," Jake said. "I'm ready for both."

"Not the least bit nervous about tackling fatherhood?"

"With Jodi as my partner, I'm not scared of anything." Jake opened the door for Kasha. "She's my heart and soul."

Okay, it did sound a bit sappy, but Jodi and Jake were amazing together, and Kasha might have been jealous if she weren't so happy that her sister had found her great love.

They walked through the front door together and headed for the kitchen. Jake called out, "I'm back, everyone, apple pie in hand, and look who I found lurking outside."

"Hi, honey!" Her mother wiped her hands on her apron and came over to give Kasha a vanilla-scented hug. "I'm glad you made it. I roasted a whole cauliflower for you. I found the recipe on the Internet. It got lots of five-star reviews."

Although her family members were steadfast carnivores, they honored her choice to go meatless. Her mother went out of her way to prepare tasty vegetarian meals for her, and Kasha appreciated the effort. Mom bustled around, pulling things from the oven.

"What can I do to help?" Kasha offered.

"Check to see if everyone has something to drink." Mom turned the burner off under a pot of black-eyed peas.

Jodi was sitting at the kitchen table drinking lemonade. Jake hurried over to drop a kiss on his wife's forehead. Jodi wrapped her arm around his neck and pulled his head down for a proper kiss. Jake put his hand on her extended belly, and then they looked at each other as if they'd invented sex.

Kasha turned away, feeling embarrassed for witnessing their private moment. She stepped out onto the back porch to check on the dozen or so guests gathered around her father, who was manning the barbecue grill. They all had drinks in their hands.

"Anyone need a refresher on their drinks?" she called. Everyone shook their heads, so she stepped back inside as her mother was taking the roasted cauliflower from the oven.

"How did you know I was coming over?" Kasha asked.

"I left you a voice message," Mom said. "Although I didn't hear back from you, I knew you'd want to help Trudy celebrate her big success."

"I had my phone turned off while I was working with Axel Richmond," Kasha explained. "And I forgot to check voice mail when I left his house. I didn't even know about Trudy's big news. I was dropping by for . . ." She didn't want to say why she was really dropping by. Not now. Not in front of other people. ". . . a visit."

"How are things going with Axel?" Jake asked. "Richmond is pretty intense. He's got his demons."

"No worries there," Jodi said, resting her head against Jake's shoulder. "At her old job, Kasha's nickname was the Exorcist."

Kasha sat down across from Jake and Jodi. "Demons? What do you mean?"

Jake shrugged like he wished he hadn't opened his mouth.

"Is there something I should know?" Kasha pushed, even though she normally wouldn't have done so. She was not the type to stick her nose into other people's business, but it was her job to help Axel get back on the mound.

"Axel's working through some personal stuff," Jake mumbled.

"You mean besides his injury?"

Jake shifted uncomfortably in his seat. "I don't like talking about someone behind their backs."

"This isn't gossip," Kasha said. "My only concern is for Axel's welfare. I am his therapist."

Jake shot Jodi a look, and she nodded. The corners of his mouth skewed, and he let out a reluctant noise. He scratched the top of his head. "It's not a secret, anyone who follows baseball knows about it, but no one on the team discusses it. Out of respect."

"Respect for what?"

"Dylan."

Chill bumps crawled up the nape of her neck. "The name Axel has tattooed on his chest."

"Yes. Dylan is . . . was . . . his son."

She'd suspected Axel was sensitive about the tattoo, and the angst in Jake's eyes told her Dylan was no longer alive. "Dylan died?"

"Yeah."

A tug of sympathy, hard and heavy, hit her low in the belly. No wonder Axel pushed himself so hard. It was his way of surviving grief. Her heart sank. "Oh no."

Jake nodded. "Over two years ago now."

"What happened?"

"Some kind of rare cancer. Dylan was just eight years old."

Kasha's knees weakened and she dropped down into a kitchen chair. She felt dizzy, unanchored by the news. "That's awful."

"Axel's never really bounced back from it." Jake tapped his finger restlessly on the table.

"How could you ever come back from something like that?" Jodi asked, and protectively rubbed her belly.

Jake slipped his arm around Jodi's shoulder and pulled her close. She rested her head on his chest, and a grateful smile tipped up her lips.

Kasha pushed aside the twinge of envy that pinched her. "Thank you for telling me, Jake. It does help to know what's going on with Axel."

"Do be careful," Jodi cautioned.

"Careful about what?" Kasha canted her head.

"Axel is easy to fall for."

Kasha blinked at her sister. "Why are you cautioning me about that?"

Jodi shrugged. "He's a good-looking guy. You're single, he's single . . ."

"And I'm a professional who would never blow my career or reputation by crossing a line with a patient."

"I wasn't suggesting that." Jodi spread her palms out on the tablecloth. "We just don't want to see you get hurt."

"I won't," Kasha said, wondering how Jodi had guessed at her attraction to Axel.

No mystery, she told herself. Axel was hot. He'd make most any available—and some who were not—woman's womb wiggle.

The back door opened and Suki came bouncing in.

The youngest Carlyle sister was a live wire who instantly brightened any room she entered. Petite five-two, Korean by birth, thoroughly American in personality, and she loved stylish fashions. Today she had on a short beige macramé skirt and black V-neck tank top, and Roman sandals.

"Dad needs more barbecue sauce," Suki said.

"Fridge," Mom directed.

"Hey, Stretch." Suki wriggled her fingers at Kasha on the way past.

"Hey, Short Stack."

"Kasha, could you take this platter of corn on the cob out to the picnic table?" Mom asked.

"Sure." Kasha carried the corn outside, mentally gauging her chances of getting her parents alone to tell them about Emma. Odds were against her.

Table the discussion for another time. One more day wouldn't make much difference. Enjoy the party. Go home. Get some sleep. Get up tomorrow, and go do her job. She was good at keeping her lips zipped.

Too good, some might say.

Dad came over with a pair of tongs in his hands to give her a peck on the cheek. "I put some portabella mushrooms on the grill for you."

"Thanks, Dad." She hugged him hard.

"You're in a sweet mood. What's up?"

"Just happy to see you." Her mind drifted back to Axel, and the knowledge he'd lost his young son. Life was so short and so precious. "I'm grateful to have you, and so glad you're still here."

Dad gave her a sideways look. "Something troubling you?"

Before she could tell him that she wanted to talk to him and Mom later, sixty-something Trudy, adorned in colorful tattoos and multiple piercings, sashayed up to them. Over the years, Trudy had been something of a surrogate, avant-garde grandmother to the Carlyle sisters, and she was like one of the family.

"Did you hear my big news?" Trudy's eyes sparkled.

"I did. Congratulations, Trudy. You deserve this so much."

"I knew eventually my passion would pay off." Trudy chuckled. "I got a new tattoo to celebrate. Wanna see?"

To be polite, Kasha nodded.

Trudy tugged the corner of her shirt down her right shoulder to reveal fresh ink that said: "Live passionately or not at all."

"It's a statement," Kasha said. One she didn't agree with. She'd spent a lifetime squelching passion, because she knew how much damage it could do.

"You've got to let go of the reins sometime," Trudy said. "And just let yourself feel."

A bubble of resistance pressed up Kasha's throat. She ironed on a smile. "I'll keep that in mind. Congrats again, Trudy."

"Thanks." Trudy beamed.

Kasha caught sight of her sister Breeanne sitting on a lawn chair by herself, underneath the elm tree where a tire swing used to hang when they were kids. Breeanne looked forlorn. Kasha grabbed a lawn chair and went over to sit beside her sister.

Breeanne had been the first child their parents had adopted, even though she was younger than Kasha and Jodi. She had a heart condition that had been a constant part of family life when they were all growing up, but today, at twenty-seven, after multiple surgeries, Breeanne had made a full recovery.

"Why you are sitting over here by your lonesome?" Kasha asked.

Breeanne made a halfhearted attempt at a smile. "Just needed a little time to myself."

"Do you want me to leave?"

"No. You're the one person I do want to see. Just being around you calms me down."

"Is something wrong? Are you and Rowdy—"

"Oh no, no. Rowdy and I are fine. In fact marriage is the most amazing thing." Breeanne perked up. "I love him so much."

"I can see it on your face."

Breeanne reached over to pat Kasha's hand. "I know you're going to find your true love too."

Kasha shrugged. "I'm okay even if I don't."

Breeanne's mouth turned down and her eyes went sad. "Honestly?"

"I don't need a man in my life to be happy."

"Have you found a key to the hope chest yet?" Breeanne asked.

"To tell you the truth, I haven't been looking."

It might seem an odd question to some, but two years earlier, Breeanne had found an antique hope chest at an estate sale. It was an unusual trunk, possessing five individual compartments contained inside one wooden box, each compartment with its own lock. On top of the lid, a cryptic message had been carved.

Kasha had it memorized because for the past year, ever since Jodi married Jake and she passed the hope chest on to her, it had been sitting in her living room functioning as a coffee table.

Treasures are housed within, heart's desires granted, but be careful where wishes are cast, for reckless dreams dared dreamed in the heat of passion will surely come to pass.

Kasha didn't have to worry about passionate wishes backfiring. She never did anything in the heat of passion. She knew firsthand just how destructive passion could be.

The elderly woman who sold Breeanne the hope chest had told her that if she made a wish before she unlocked the compartments, her wish would surely come true. Romantic, Breeanne had fallen in love with the silly legend. The old woman had no keys for the trunk's locks, but on a wish and a prayer that any skeleton key might work on a skeleton lock, Breeanne bought the hope chest.

Breeanne, Jodi, Suki, and Kasha had gone through every skeleton key they could find in Timeless Treasures, and none of them worked. Oddly, neither of the two locksmiths in Stardust could open up the trunk without drilling into the locks. Nor could they adequately explain why they couldn't unlock it.

The hope chest sat unopened for several days after Breeanne bought it, until Suki came up with the idea of making skeleton key necklaces. Suki sold the necklaces in her online Etsy store to great success, and used up all the keys in the store. She'd put a sign in the window offering to buy skeleton keys for a dollar.

The next day, a mysterious customer brought in a key that had fit the lock on the trunk's fifth compartment.

Taking the saying on the chest to heart, Breeanne had made a wish as she'd opened the compartment, asking for a boost in her writing career. Right after that, she'd gotten a call from the agent who'd snubbed her for over a year, telling her local sports hero Rowdy Blanton was looking for a ghostwriter from their area.

Inside the compartment, Breeanne had found a smaller box with another cryptic saying etched into that lid, and when she opened the smaller box, Breeanne discovered a cheetah scarf that felt soft only to her and Rowdy. To everyone else, the scarf felt rough and scratchy.

Breeanne took it as a sign that she and Rowdy were meant to be.

Romantic, yes, but it didn't really mean anything, at least not to Kasha's way of thinking.

But then Breeanne gave the trunk to Jodi after she and Rowdy married. Jodi found a skeleton key in an antique evening bag she'd borrowed from Timeless Treasures on the same night she met Jake while crashing a high-society wedding.

The key had fit the fourth compartment in the trunk, and when Jodi opened it, she'd found an exotic perfume that only she and Jake could smell.

Still, Kasha remained unconvinced that the trunk had special wish-granting powers. In her mind, it was self-fulfilling prophecy, and nothing more. How could it be more than the power of suggestion? Her sisters had wanted to fall in love, so their minds had invented a fantasy to match what they found.

Kasha wasn't interested in searching for a key. The last thing she wanted was a passionate relationship. If she ever did get married—not that she was even thinking along those lines—it would be a sane, sensible agreement. Not some wild, ardent union based on over-wrought emotions.

Breeanne put a hand on Kasha's knee. "You can't give up on love."

"I haven't given up because I was never looking for it in the first place."

Breeanne clucked her tongue. "Love is the most wonderful thing in the world."

Kasha shifted in her seat, and wished she hadn't gotten into this conversation. "Forget me. What's got you down in the mouth?"

"I saw the doctor today—"

"Is it your heart?" Kasha's pulse jumped, and she wrapped a hand around Breeanne's thin forearm.

"No, no. I didn't see my cardiologist." Breeanne nibbled her bottom lip, and pushed a lock of long blond hair behind her ear.

"Who?"

A tear slipped down Breeanne's cheek, then another, and another.

What now? Kasha's chest tightened. Felt helpless in the face of her sister's tears. She dug around in her purse, found a tissue, pressed it into her sister's hand. Awkwardly, she patted Breeanne's shoulder. "There. There."

Breeanne swiped at her cheeks, but it didn't staunch the flow of tears.

Fear twined around Kasha's throat. "What is it? You gotta tell me."

"Rowdy and I went to see a fertility specialist . . ." Breeanne paused. Hiccupped. "And the tests came back." She hitched in a breath, closed her eyes. "Because of my longstanding health issues, and the medications I was on for so many years, I most likely won't ever be able to have children of my own."

"Oh, Bree," Kasha whispered. "I'm so sorry."

Breeanne pressed the tissue against her nose, her shoulders wobbling with the force of her grief.

"Have you told Mom and Dad?"

"Not yet. I was hoping to tell them this evening, but I can't bring myself to put a damper on Trudy's great news."

"It's a blow. I can only imagine how much it hurts. But there's always adoption. Look how well we turned out."

"I know, I know. I'm trying to be practical and mature about it." Breeanne blinked. "And I don't want to suggest that adoption is somehow less than having your own children. I don't believe that, not for a second, but there's some biological need inside me to have someone that's my blood kin. Do you know what I mean?"

Kasha thought of Emma, felt her throat squeeze in empathy. "Yes," she admitted. "I do."

"I know it's selfish." Breeanne tore the sodden tissue in half. "But it's the way I feel."

"It's not selfish," Kasha said. "It's human. You've been delivered a blow and it's okay to grieve. You shouldn't feel ashamed or guilty for it. And I'm sure Mom and Dad will say the same."

"I don't want to hurt them," Breeanne said. "Do you know what I mean?"

Yes, she knew exactly what her sister meant, which was part of the reason why she hadn't already told her parents about Emma. She'd been waiting for the perfect time. Clearly, the perfect time was not now. Breeanne's news came first.

Relief rushed through her, and if she were being honest, she'd admit she was grateful for the reprieve. But postponing the inevitable wrapped a hard skin around the pebble knotted in her stomach, growing dread the way an oyster grew a pearl.

And fleetingly, for one awful minute, she wished she'd never found out about her half sister.

CHAPTER 6

On Friday morning, Kasha grabbed a can of V8 juice from the fridge, and drank it in lieu of breakfast on her way up to Rowdy's sprawling ranch house. During the drive over, all she could think about was what Jake had told her the night before about Axel and the loss of his son, Dylan.

When she arrived, Mrs. Creedy, the petite, gray-haired housekeeper in Harry Potter glasses, answered the door. "Axel's around back."

She followed the housekeeper out the back door through the courtyard, rich with native East Texas plants, to find Axel pitching into a baseball rebounder on the other side of the swimming pool.

What? She rubbed her eyes in disbelief. Was he freaking kidding her? She'd specifically told him to rest his shoulder. Pitching was not resting.

"From the look on your face, I'm guessing he's in a mess of trouble," Mrs. Creedy said.

"Trouble isn't the half of it," Kasha muttered, and sank her hands on her hips.

"Honey, if you think you can make that one toe the line, you're in for a world of hurt. Mr. Creedy and I are off to run errands. You're on your own with him for the next couple of hours."

Mrs. Creedy shook her head and went back inside, closing the sliding glass door behind her.

Kasha wanted to cling to the housekeeper's hand and beg her not to leave her alone with him, because she simply didn't trust herself around him. Instead, she donned a Miss Badass persona, squinting hard and shading her eyes with the flat of her hand.

Axel wore loose-fitting gray gym shorts and a white T-shirt so worn she could make out every honed rib beneath the thin cotton. Athletic shoes clad his feet, and his dark thick hair—damp from either sweat or a recent dip in the pool or both—was slicked back off his forehead.

The sun caught his cheekbones, showcasing his profile. He was lean and hard, and every time he threw a pitch or caught it on the rebound, he winced.

Dammit, was the man intentionally trying to undermine her efforts to heal him? Or was he just that ruthlessly stubborn?

When he turned and saw her standing there, his face dissolved into a hot smile that gave the sun a run for its money. He was utterly irresistible.

Easy, she told herself.

No matter how irresistible he might be, she *had* to resist him. Axel was her patient, and any sexual feelings had no place in a professional relationship. She had a job to do. No ifs, ands, or buts. She wasn't here to be charmed. She wasn't some simpering groupie who lost her mind every time he flexed his muscles. She was here to rehabilitate his arm.

End of story.

The knot in her stomach had everything to do with the fact he was not following the protocol she'd set up for him, and nothing to do with the fact that her heart was pounding so hard she could barely think straight.

He dropped the smile, turned back to the rebounder as if daring her to do something about it, and flung the ball again.

Oh dude, it's on like Donkey Kong.

Squaring her shoulders, Kasha marched closer until she was only a foot away, crossed her arms over her chest, glowered, and said, "Ahem."

He kept pitching.

Big surprise. The man was mulishly stubborn.

She cleared her throat again, louder this time, and dropped her hands to her hips. He had a glove on his left hand but kept fielding the ball with his right. He stared straight ahead, not glancing her way, continuing to rhythmically toss and catch the ball. Testing her?

"How long have you been doing that?" she asked quietly.

His shrug was a casual glide, so polished he didn't miss a beat with the catching and throwing. "An hour or so."

"Is there something about the word 'rest' that you don't understand?"

"Not in my vocabulary."

"Ah," she said. "So all you need is a definition. Try this one on for size. Rest: to cease work or movement in order to relax, refresh oneself, or recover strength."

"You don't say."

"I do say. That's why my lips are moving."

He turned to her, caught the rebounding ball without looking, and met her gaze, a wicked gleam in his eyes; dangerous business, but having fun.

Air stalled in her lungs, and her pulse popped painfully in her throat. Why was she doing this? What did she know about supreme, high performance athletes? What if she was wrong about rest?

Great. Now he had her second-guessing herself.

Don't think of him as a supreme athlete, she reasoned. *Think of him as OCD. He can't stop testing limits. Think of him as an injured guy who'd lost his son and was using work to keep his grief at bay.*

Her pulse skipped and her gaze shifted to his heart, to the dark ink of the tattoo she could make out through the thin white T-shirt. Scolding him wasn't going to work.

Kasha smiled gently and forced herself not to gnaw on her bottom lip. Maybe she could turn this around.

A long moment passed, and a bead of perspiration pearled on his forehead. She deepened her smile to show friendly teeth, vague and nonthreatening.

He smacked the ball into the pocket of the glove, closed his fingers around it, and dropped his left hand to his side. His stance was loose-kneed, but aggressive. "You got a point to make?"

He was such a big guy, tall and solid. Kasha wasn't accustomed to men towering over her. She was five-eleven and a hundred and fifty-five pounds, bigger than a lot of men. But beside him, she felt downright fragile, and that was disconcerting.

"You know if your arm doesn't improve by next week all you have to do is have surgery. But I'll be out of a job."

"They won't fire you," he said as if she was being ridiculous.

"I'm a probationary employee who went out on a limb. Of course they'll fire me."

He ducked his head, ran his hand up the back of his neck, shifted his weight. He used his smile to apologize. "I got up this morning and I intended to take it easy. I was going to go for a walk and then I saw this rebounder in the garage and I got excited and . . ." He shrugged like a kid caught playing hooky. "I was going to toss the ball around for just a few minutes, and time got away from me."

"Be honest. You planned to stop just before I got here."

"Guilty as charged. My bad luck you showed up early."

A clot of anger lodged in the center of her chest. "If you don't give a damn about your long-term health, fine by me. I'll tell Truman Beck I was wrong about my ability to help you, and ask him to assign you another therapist."

"You're not going to do that." He grinned as if he just decided he liked her better when she yelled at him.

Nothing doing. She wasn't giving him the satisfaction of losing her temper. Purposefully, Kasha ironed her expression blank. "As if you know me so well."

"You're an open book."

"That's the last thing I am. You're just trying to rile me."

"Is it working?"

"No it's not. I get what you're doing. You're deflecting attention off yourself and onto me."

"Pitcher's gotta pitch," he said.

"You think that's clever?"

"Yeah." He spread his grin like plaster, thick and rough. "I do."

"If you're determined to pitch," she murmured, lightening her tone. "At least do it safely."

"Meaning?"

"Throw underhanded."

"Like a girl?"

"And pitch to me instead of the rebounder."

The contours of his face tightened. "I can't pitch to you."

"Why not?"

"I throw hundred-mile-an-hour fastballs for a living, Sphinx."

"Not right now you don't."

"Go ahead. Rub it in."

"I'm beginning to think you really do want that surgery," she said.

"I don't."

"Then why are you being so difficult?"

"I can't pitch to you."

"Why not?"

"I might hurt you."

Kasha clenched her jaw. "Do I look soft and delicate to you? I can take anything you can dish out."

He eyed her up and down. "Oh yeah?"

"Absolutely."

"Okay." He chucked the glove to her. "Here you go."

She snagged the mitt in midair. "You need a glove too."

He rolled his eyes. "Fine. Rowdy's got extras in the gym."

"I'll go get it. You take a break." She picked up the rebounder and carried it with her to the gym, and wondered where she could hide it to keep him from doing this again. Maybe she could enlist the Creedys to keep an eye on him whenever she wasn't around.

When she came back with the extra baseball glove, she found Axel sprawled in a chaise longue poolside, a pair of mirrored sunglasses over his eyes, and she knew with absolute certainty he was staring at her legs in the chino Bermuda shorts that were part of her uniform options.

"You don't have to wear your uniform when you're working with me," he said.

"I prefer it," she answered. "Helps to keep things professional."

"Uh-huh," he said in a sultry voice so sexy it curled her toes. Now that was unprofessional. She had to stop letting him affect her like this. Making her stomach melty and her breath quicken.

She tossed the extra mitt to him. He reached up as effortlessly as if he were swatting a fly. But she noticed he reached with his left hand, not his dominant one. Was his right arm hurting from pitching against the rebounder? Or had using his left arm become a defensive strategy?

"Do you still want to do this?" she asked, punching her fist into the pocket of the well-worn leather glove.

"You bet." Languidly, he drooped one leg over the chaise, pushed off with the other leg, and straightened upright.

Once again, she was struck by his height, and his presence. She tossed her head, the end of her braid swishing against her spine, and crouched like a catcher.

"Ready?" he asked.

"Yes."

He lobbed her an underhanded ball so soft she had to stretch out long to reach it before it hit the ground.

"While I appreciate that you're taking it easy on your arm, you don't have to treat me like glass. You're pitching underhanded. It's okay to put a little power into it. I'm tough as an old boot. Toss the ball to me as if I were a guy."

"But you're not a guy."

"Seriously? Are you a chauvinist on top of being a hardhead?"

"Sphinx, in case you haven't noticed, there are physical differences between men and women." He ogled her. "I'm all for equal rights and equal pay and equal whatever, but biology is biology."

"Throw the damn ball with some force," she growled, confused as to why she was goading him to put more power into the pitch. She should be happy he was taking it easy. Why wasn't she happy?

The next pitch came in hot, blasting hard into her glove. Kasha caught it, but the momentum caused her to rock backward, and if she hadn't been a dedicated yoga devotee, she would have lost her balance and ended up on her butt on the cement.

"Better?" He smirked.

"Perfect. How's your shoulder?"

"Fine. Feels loose. Easy."

"Great."

The next pitch that he let fly was harder than the last, but she was braced for it this time, or so she thought. It was higher than his previous pitch too, and she had to spring up to catch it. She stretched her arm high overhead, kept her eyes on the ball, moved—back, back, back.

Her heel came down on something firm but squishy, and her first thought was, *Snake!*

Freaked out, Kasha jumped, stumbled and realized too late it was a garden hose. She felt her feet go out from under her. She wind-milled her arms in a vain attempt to right herself. The baseball glove flew off her hand, and she was airborne.

Falling in midair. A weightless, surreal, holy-crap sensation.

And she tumbled over the edge of the swimming pool into the deep end, her body breaking the surface of the water. At the shock, her heart momentarily stopped.

The impact wrung the air from her lungs. Stunned, she batted at the water, her mind whirling. In that split-second drift of panic, she heard a loud splash, felt waves slap against her as strong arms encir-cled her waist and hard-muscled legs entwined with hers.

"I've got you," Axel said, his voice muffled and watery.

At his touch, a warm peace spread over her and she grinned idi-otically. *Seriously, Kasha?*

He lifted her up, tugged her head out of the water, and whis-pered, "Oh shit, you're bleeding."

She wanted to tell him it was no big deal, but she was feeling a little woozy. Why was she bleeding? Where was she bleeding?

Eyes closed, she did a little mental inventory. Feeling out her body. But honestly, she was so distracted by his arms around her that she couldn't really process anything.

She tried to look around, to see the blood for herself, but he had her in such a tight grip she could hardly breathe, much less swivel her head.

Axel towed her toward the side of the pool. She thought about protesting, breaking free, but it felt kind of nice here in his arms.

Warning! Dangerous thoughts ahead. Pull out. Pull back.

"Stop thrashing," he growled. "Just relax, dammit."

Oh yes, because that was so easy to do when the hunkiest of hunks is hauling you soaking wet from a pool.

Kasha willed herself to go still and let him be in charge, which, granted, was not easy. She was used to being in control. Her hair was in her face, plastered against her eyes, and she couldn't see. Apparently the band holding her braid had broken. She blinked, making a motorboat noise, blowing out her breath through wet lips.

"Here we are," he said when he reached the ladder, treading water to keep them afloat. "Can you grab hold?"

"Yes, sure." She was alarmed to hear her voice come out wobbly and small.

She lifted a hand to push her hair from her eyes, and startled when her fingers grazed her temple and discovered it was tender to the touch. Blood mixed with water trickled down her palm, and the smell of chlorine burned her nose.

The sight of her blood sent her head reeling and her stomach lurching. She lost her grip on the ladder and slipped backward.

But Axel had hold of her. "Steady. Steady." His breath was warm on her skin. "You okay?"

"A little dizzy," she admitted. "What happened?"

He kept his arm latched around her waist. He peered at her temple. "Looks like you scraped the side of your head against the cement on the way down."

"Oh," she murmured, annoyed at the wooziness, and alarmed at how rubbery her limbs felt. "Okay."

In order to keep her steady, Axel pressed his hip against her butt for stability, and boosted her up the slippery ladder. Closing her eyes against the dizziness, she managed to belly flop onto the edge of the pool.

Grunted.

Rolled over onto her back.

Surprised at how heavily she was breathing, Kasha opened her eyes, her long wet hair clinging to her body like seaweed, and looked up into Axel's handsome face.

"Are you all right?"

She nodded. Or thought she did, but he looked so concerned that she wondered if she just imagined that she nodded.

"Kasha?" His tone was sharp, anxious. "Can you hear me?"

Uh-huh. She moistened her lips to tell him she was fine, but she was so mesmerized by those smoldering dark chocolate eyes of his, she couldn't focus.

She shivered, cold despite the heat of the direct sun. "F . . . f . . . fine."

"You don't look fine." He swore under his breath. "I shouldn't have played catch with you."

"It was my fa . . . fa . . . fault." A fresh shiver shook her spine.

"You're still bleeding," he said. "C'mon, we've got to get you cleaned up." He got to his feet, extended a hand to hoist her up.

She teetered as blood rushed to her feet and her head buzzed.

"Whoa there." He put a hand to her back. "Are you—"

"Fine," she said, struggling to get control of herself. "Stop asking."

His lips pressed into a line that said, *Not believing you for a second*, and he took command, encircling her wrist with his thumb and forefinger and hauling her toward the house. Her wet shoes squished and squeaked against the walkway.

"Wait," she said when they reached the back door.

"What?" he snorted.

"I can't go dripping water all over Rowdy and Breeanne's hard-wood floors."

"Don't worry, I'll clean it up later. We need to attend to that wound."

She balked, digging in as she tried to kick off her sneakers on the welcome mat. "Wait, wait. Hang on."

He snorted, but stopped long enough to let her shed her shoes, opening the sliding glass door while he waited.

His feet were bare. He'd been wearing flip-flops, and he'd lost them somewhere along the way. His shorts were plastered against his skin, molding to the hard angles of his body, and through the wet material she could see the outlines of his impressive male package.

Oh holy guacamole.

She gulped. What was wrong with her?

"You've lost color in your face," he said. "Are you okay?"

She nodded, her bare feet sinking into the nubby rubber mat, although she was feeling hot, and there was that darned dizziness.

"Kasha?" Concern tinged his voice.

She swayed. "Uh-huh."

"You're about to pass out."

"No, I . . ." She stumbled.

He caught her, swung her up into his arms.

"No, wait," she said, fighting against the wooziness. "Put me down."

"Stop struggling or I'll drop you."

"Put me down."

"Nope." He hefted her up in his arms, and carried her over the threshold.

No guy had ever picked her up, much less carried her anywhere. "I'm too big for this."

"I'm bigger."

He was quite large, all sinew and muscles. The man made her feel petite, and that was a completely novel sensation. She probably shouldn't be noticing that right now. Not when his arms were cradling her backside, and he smelled so good and she was feeling a little spacey.

"Okay," she said. "Let's get this over with."

He carried her into the bathroom, set her down on the closed toilet lid, reached for a large bath towel from the rack, and bent over her to wrap it around her shivering body.

It was just the two of them in a small, enclosed space. She looked up as he raised his head and they were eye to eye. Nose to nose. Lip to lip. Her mind raced down uncharted terrains of lust and panic.

Axel leaned in, almost as if drawn by a strong magnet, pulling him toward her. Kasha felt her mouth soften and round of its own accord.

Instinct.

Nature.

His chest was heaving just as hard as hers, and he was as wet as she was and his hair was stuck to the side of his head in a totally adorable way.

And Kasha thought crazily, *If he doesn't kiss me first, I'm going to kiss him.*

CHAPTER 7

Kasha's lips were so close, so hot and tempting, that for one insane second Axel forgot that she was shivering and that blood was trickling down her temple and that they were in a bathroom, for chrissakes.

As if hypnotized, he couldn't stop staring at her, nor could he stop thinking, *I want to kiss her. Hard. Long. Hot.*

He could already taste them, those lips. Smell the sweet tanginess of her lemon-drop breath. He ached to press his mouth to hers, explore the contours, shape, and outline. Nibble and taste and tease.

Her dark-eyed gaze was pinned on him, and her breathing was so shallow, he wasn't sure she was breathing at all. Was the wound on her head more than a simple scrape? Had she actually struck the edge of the pool? Could she have a concussion?

Then again, he was the one entranced. Maybe he'd hit his head.

All he would have to do in order to kiss her would be to lean forward by an inch and . . . Compelled, he leaned in, and a stream of water drizzled from his hair onto her nose.

She didn't react.

Axel shook himself, stepped back, and snapped his fingers in front of her face. "You still with me?"

"Here," she croaked in a deep-throated voice that sounded damn sexy.

Feeling like a jackass for his caveman thoughts, Axel tacked on an easy smile. "You all right?"

"Yes, yes." She sounded irritated.

He studied her a minute, not knowing what to tackle first, getting her out of wet clothes or attending to her wound. She shivered again, and her nipples beaded up so hard, he could see them through her bra, shirt, and the towel he'd draped around her shoulders.

The bleeding had stopped, and there wasn't a knot forming. Dry clothes first. First aid second.

"Take off your clothes," he said.

"What?" she asked on a soft gasp.

"Not with me standing here," he amended. "I'm going. Leaving." He gestured toward the door. "To take off my clothes. Alone. In the other room."

She stared at him.

He was overexplaining, but he couldn't seem to stop, not when she was looking at him like that. "And then I'll get dressed and come back with something for you to wear. I saw some chick clothes in the front hall closet."

Just shut the hell up, Richmond.

"Chick clothes?" She sounded amused.

"You know, dresses and lace and stuff. I don't know who they belong to . . ."

"My sister Breeanne."

"Oh yeah, Rowdy's wife."

Kasha's eyes glittered. She seemed to enjoy throwing him off his game. "So I'm supposed to sit here naked and just wait for you to come back?"

Fresh images of Kasha naked popped into his brain. "Um . . . here are more towels." He took a stack from underneath the cabinet, set them on the counter. "I'll be right back."

He rushed out of the bathroom, and he could have sworn he

heard her chuckle. He let out a quick breath, and clambered upstairs. He changed and went to the hall closet where he'd seen women's clothing. He grabbed a blue flowered sundress and hurried to the downstairs bathroom where he'd left Kasha.

Heart thumping erratically, he knocked on the door with two knuckles. "You decent?"

"Depends on what you mean by decent."

He opened the door a crack, shoved the dress through it.

"No underwear?" she asked.

"Sorry. I didn't think about it. I'll let you handle that after I tend to your head wound."

"I can dress my own wound. I'm in the medical professional."

"Not up for discussion. I'm going after the first aid kit, and when I get back I'm coming in."

"Not if I lock the door."

"Then how will you dress the wound? There's no medical supplies in that bathroom."

"Just go get the kit." She huffed.

Grinning, he went after the kit, and when he returned he announced, "Ready or not, I'm coming in."

He opened the door to find her trying to zip up the back of the blue dress. Her hair was wrapped up in a towel to keep her wet hair off her shoulders. She looked gorgeous in blue, and cute as all get-out with her hair in a towel turban.

The dress fit snug across the breasts. Kasha's younger sister was not as well endowed as Kasha, nor was she as tall. The hem hit her high mid-thigh, when on her sister it would have been knee-length.

Her wet clothes, bra and panties included, were draped over the towel rack inside the shower. No underwear. Beneath that thin cotton dress, she was naked.

"Here," he said, moving inside, setting the first aid kit on the vanity and trying his best not to think about her nakedness. "Turn around."

She squirmed as if to get away, but there was nowhere to go. The wall was in front of her, and he was behind her. She chuffed, still struggling with the zipper.

"Turn around," he commanded.

She looked like she wanted to argue, but then she slowly pivoted to face the wall, exposing her back to him.

He put a hand to her waist.

She wriggled away.

"Hold still."

She grunted, shook her head, but finally stopped moving. Good thing he couldn't see her face. He had a feeling she was glaring bullets.

He tugged on the bottom of the zipper with one hand, stretching the material taut, and reached up with the other to grab the zipper's tongue. His fingertips touched her bare skin, and he was happy to discover she was warmer. He finished zipping her up, and patted her shoulder. "All set."

"Thank you," she mumbled.

"Now sit back down."

"If you're going to insist on bandaging me up, I'd rather stand."

"Woman," he said, "you are stubborn as the devil."

Kasha grinned and he realized with a start that it was the first time he had seen an honest-to-goodness heartfelt smile on her face.

It was an electrical smile that transformed her from aloof, exotic goddess to playful girl next door. She hid a lot from the world. Her eyes widened and her cheeks rounded and her chin dissolved into a sexy dimple.

"Now that's a treasure," he said.

"What?"

"That rare grin."

"What do you mean? I smile all the time."

"Not like that. Not from the heart. Not like you really mean it."

"What can I say? I enjoy frustrating you."

He grinned right back. He'd been the one to make her smile like that. "Watch out, or I'll have to change your nickname from Sphinx to Smiley."

"Don't you dare," she said. "I've grown quite fond of Sphinx."

"You like being mysterious."

She lifted a shoulder as the smile slipped away, but that amazing grin lingered in his mind, a forever image he could call up in the future whenever he thought of her. "Not really. I'm just not a big talker or a fan of expressing my every emotion."

"Huh? Most women love dissecting their feelings. Then again . . ." He met her gaze. "There's nothing usual or ordinary about you."

"Are you saying I'm not feminine?"

"Not at all. You're a deep thinker who doesn't waste time on self-pity or self-indulgences."

"Oh, I don't know about that," she mused, her voice taking on a sultry sexiness. "I've been known to take a bubble bath while eating Häagen-Dazs coffee ice cream straight from the carton. That's pretty self-indulgent."

Terrific. Now he had a persistent mental vision of Kasha in a claw-footed bathtub surrounded by bubbles while she licked melting ice cream off her lips, unbraided hair falling around her like a velvet curtain. He imagined crawling into the bath with her, and his body hardened all over again.

Ah hell. This would be so much easier if she wasn't so incredibly hot. He couldn't believe she wasn't married. What was wrong with the guys in this town?

Reining in his urges, he opened up the first aid kit, took out an antiseptic wipe to clean the area at her right temple. With her hair wrapped up in the towel and out of the way, it was easier to see the wound. He moved closer, used the wipe to dab at the wound.

She clenched her teeth, hissed in a breath.

"Sorry," he said. "But it has to be done."

"I'm not a very good patient."

"No?" He gasped, feigning shock. "I would never have guessed."

She stuck out her tongue at him, a sweet, sexy pink tongue that disarmed him completely.

Holy shit, he was in trouble.

Carefully, Axel cleaned the wound. No swelling, or immediate bruising, just a nasty scrape. Dylan had gotten plenty of skinned knees and elbows and he knew what to do.

Kasha lowered her eyelids and murmured, "You're surprisingly gentle."

"Surprisingly? What? I can't be gentle because I'm a big guy?"

"It's not only your size, it's the sheer force of your personality. You're kind of overwhelming."

"And yet you don't seem overwhelmed."

"I didn't say I was overwhelmed. I said you were overwhelming."

"Immune to my charms, huh?"

"Absolutely."

"Why is that?"

Kasha rolled her eyes to the ceiling. "Does every woman in the world have to fall all over you? Is your ego that big?"

"Are you trying to deny this spark we've got going on here?" He quirked up one corner of his mouth in a devilish grin that always worked.

"Are you trying to fan it?"

"C'mon, you know we've got chemistry."

"Explosions have chemistry; that's not a ringing endorsement."

"What's wrong with explosions?"

"They destroy things."

"Ah," he teased, "but what a way to go."

"No!" She barked so harshly, his smile vanished. Her hands were trembling and her eyes went dark. "It's a terrible, terrible way to go."

Whoa. He'd never seen her like this—anxious, angry, aggressive. Guilt flooded him. Had she lost someone close to her in an explosion? Crap, what if someone she loved had died in an explosive way. Damn his big mouth.

"Kasha . . . I . . . I didn't mean . . . I didn't realize . . ." He jammed a hand through his hair. "I'm such a dumb ass."

"Gotcha," she said lightly, as if she'd been joking all along, but her hands were trembling, and she couldn't completely bury the fear in her eyes.

"Whew," he said pretending to be relieved, but still worried by what he'd seen. She had demons he knew nothing about. *So do you, buddy, so do you.* "The truth is, I don't feel sparks like this often. It's hard not to fan it."

"I don't believe for a second that you don't feel like this on a regular basis. You must get tons of women throwing themselves at you. My brothers-in-law are ballplayers. I've seen the groupies that hang around the bullpen. I'm not an idiot."

"Just because there's a buffet doesn't mean I eat junk food."

"Rrright. I'm certain if you put your mind, and that deadly wink of yours, to it, that you could charm the panties off just about any woman you wanted."

He laughed.

"Something I said tickle your funny bone?"

"When I was a teenager I developed this eye tic that went into hyperdrive whenever I got nervous. And when you're a sixteen-year-old boy, asking a girl out is plenty nerve-wracking. My eye would start hopping and twitching and the girls thought I was weird and avoided me. Of course that made me more nervous, which in turn led to more eye twitching."

"Vicious cycle."

"Yeah."

"So what happened?"

"My mother hauled me to a doctor who said all the energy drinks I was downing in order to keep up hours and hours of baseball practice was causing the tic. Mom didn't know I was drinking them, and she gave me an earful. I gave up Red Bull and the twitching stopped."

"And girls have been lining up ever since."

"Pretty much." He chuckled again, brushing back a strand of her hair that had come loose from the towel, tucking it behind her ear. The touch, her skin, the intimacy of the small room, all served as a solid thump to his chest.

"Are you finished cleaning that yet?" she murmured.

"Time for ointment, and adhesive bandage."

"I can take it from here."

"You could," he agreed. "But I'm already doing it, so you might as well let me finish." He reached into the first aid kit for the antibacterial ointment, and when he turned back toward her, tube in hand, he couldn't help noticing the imprint of her nipples straining through the material of her dress.

For chrissakes, Richmond, stop looking down. Keep your eyes on her face.

Kasha seemed keen on not looking at him either. She stared over his shoulder as if fascinated by the seascape painting on the wall behind him.

He put a small dollop of ointment onto a cotton swab, touched it to her temple.

She flinched.

He took hold of her chin with a thumb and forefinger. "Hold still. It will be over in a sec."

"That's what she said," Kasha deadpanned.

Chuckling, Axel shook his head. "You look all serious and quiet and then you drop these little humor bombs so unexpected that they sail over most people's heads."

"But not yours."

He guided her face toward his until she had no choice but to meet his gaze. "Not mine."

She held his stare without the ghost of a grin, joked, "That's what she said."

Damn but he liked her. A lot. More than he'd liked anyone in a long time. Why did she have to be his physical therapist? "You're a sly one, Kasha Carlyle."

She looked amused, and didn't deny it. "My mother calls it clever."

"It's always the quiet ones."

"Hmm," she said. "That's a generalization if I ever heard one."

"Why are you so quiet?" he asked, unwrapping the adhesive bandage.

"I've discovered that you can learn more by keeping your ears open and your mouth shut.

"Was that directed at me?"

"Simple statement of fact. If you own it, that's your problem."

"You're a complicated woman, Sphinx."

"Slap a Band-Aid on the side of my head, Richmond, and let's get back to your therapy." Her tone was no-nonsense, her eyes unreadable.

He had no clue what she was thinking, but he certainly knew where his thoughts had strayed. Back to her lips, those soft, curvy, I-need-to-be-kissed-and-kissed-hard lips. "I thought my therapy was supposed to be resting."

"Some of your therapy, not all. Besides, you are not resting right now. You're patching me up."

"How do you know I don't find this restful?"

"Do you?"

Hell no. Being this close to her made him so tense and worked up that he could hardly stand himself. He stared into her bottomless eyes, framed by thick, dark lashes. He could smell her, feminine and earthy, his favorite scent in the world. God, but she was gorgeous.

"Axel?"

"Uh-huh," he said, surprised to hear his voice come out slow and dreamy.

"If you're not going to put that Band-Aid on my head, please get out of the way so I can do it."

Keeping his eyes locked on to hers, he moved in so close there wasn't an inch of space between their bodies. His chest was almost touching her breasts. Breasts unburdened by a bra. His body got even tighter.

Particularly below the belt. Erection. He was getting a hard-on.

Quick. Stats. Think of baseball stats. Mentally, Axel started reciting the pitching stats of the greats—Nolan Ryan, Cy Young, Sandy Koufax, Tom Seaver . . .

Kasha poked him with her elbow.

Startled, he yelped. "What was that for?"

"Just checking to see if you slipped into a coma." She laughed again.

The sound made him forget all about Nolan Ryan's seven no-hitters, his attention focused one hundred percent on the tall, leggy beauty with her hair wrapped in a fluffy towel, and the erection won.

Surprise claimed her eyes, but only for a moment; she quickly wrangled herself under control and her expression returned to default. Deadpan.

He broke out in a sweat. They were too damn close and that's all there was to it. He shifted his hips away from her, but his butt bumped into the vanity. There was nowhere to go.

"Stuck between a rock and a hard place," she mumbled so softly he wasn't sure he actually heard her.

Axel couldn't get the Band-Aid on her head fast enough, but in his haste, he stuck part of the adhesive strip on the strand of hair that had escaped her turban.

"Ouch."

"Sorry, sorry." He yanked at the adhesive, but it didn't unstick.

"Ow, you're pulling my hair." She moved, brushed against his erection. Her eyes rounded. "Oh crap."

Panic seized him as his body reacted instinctively to the contact, and his hips rolled against her. "Sorry, sorry."

"Stop moving!" she gasped.

"You stop moving."

They both froze, and their eyes met. God, he was nothing but a caricature of a horny jock. Pathetic.

"It doesn't mean anything," he said trying not to sound desperate. "Normal biological reaction. It happens. No big deal."

"So—"

"Ignore it. Ignore me. I'm just going to let you . . ." He gestured at her temple where the Band-Aid only half covered her wound and the other half stuck in her hair. "Take care of that."

Kasha's lips were pressed together in a straight line, but her eyes were twinkling. She looked amused, and that really flabbergasted him. She thought it was funny that he'd gotten a boner while patching her up?

"Ah," she teased, and stared pointedly at his groin. "But who is going to take care of that?"

HAD SHE ACTUALLY said that?

Appalled at herself, Kasha watched Axel hightail it out of the bathroom, his blue jean shorts cupping his splendid butt, the muscles of his legs as hard and strong as that other, wholly masculine muscle that she'd accidentally bumped against.

Why had she said that?

Axel.

He was to blame. He brought out things in her that no one had ever brought out. A wild playfulness she didn't even know she had. It bothered her. A lot. She was a professional. Here to do a job. She was not going to let sexual attraction screw this up. Her reputation was on the line. Her behavior from here on out could either make or break her career.

But she needed underwear, and she wanted out of Breeanne's sundress that was both too small and too skimpy on her. And she had to do something with her hair. Ack! They might as well call it a day and start fresh tomorrow.

Kasha squared her shoulders, wrapped her wet clothes up in another towel, and went in search of Axel. She found him in the living room, pacing like a caged lion. He stopped the second she came in.

"Listen," they both said at once.

"You go first." He waved in her direction.

"No, you."

"I insist."

She paused. Thought about the best way to handle this embarrassing situation so it would not affect their working relationship. "Repeat after me," she said, tucking her wet, towel-wrapped laundry under her left arm.

"Okay."

She tapped her chest three times with her right fist. "Cancel, cancel, cancel."

"Cancel, cancel, cancel," he repeated, and copied her hand gestures.

"Erase, erase, erase." Using the same fist, she lightly tapped her forehead.

A bemused Axel followed suit.

She moved to the crown of her head. "Delete, delete, delete."

By the time he finished saying, "Delete, delete, delete," they were both grinning.

"Incident gone. Never happened," she said.

"Reset switch, huh?"

"Exactly."

"I'm good with that."

"I'm going to go home now," she said. "Your assignment for the rest of the day is to take it easy. No more rebound pitching. I'll see you tomorrow."

He looked utterly relieved. "So what went on in the bathroom—"

"What bathroom?"

"Gotcha." He winked.

But she couldn't help feeling she was in over her head.

CHAPTER 8

On the drive back to her house, her damp clothes in the passenger seat behind her, wet hair pulled up into a soggy ponytail, Kasha tried to convince herself that she and Axel hadn't almost kissed—twice—in the bathroom of her sister and brother-in-law's second home.

That Axel hadn't gotten an erection, and that she hadn't accidentally knocked against that impressive hard-on.

He wanted her.

The scary thing? She wanted him right back.

Drumming her fingers on the wheel, she realized she was fidgeting and tried to calm down with slow, deep breathing.

It didn't work.

Her sexual feelings for her client were totally inappropriate. How did she stop feeling them?

You can't help what you feel, she told herself. *But you can help acting on those feelings.*

Her stomach dipped with the curves in the road. The big question here was could she keep her feelings hidden from him? Yes, he was sexy as all get-out. Yes, he was drop-dead handsome. Yes, all she wanted to do was wrap her legs around his muscular waist and pull him into her.

Desire recognized. Acknowledged. Dismissed.

But what if you can't stay detached, whispered the dark part of her soul.

What if too much bad DNA ran through her blood? She had never been put to the test. Not since she'd started yoga and learned to sublimate her impulses with devotion to her practice. Not since she'd made a conscious effort not to follow in her biological parents' footsteps.

Restlessly, Kasha shifted in the seat, felt her throat burn at the memory of the way Axel had looked at her, his brown eyes as lusty as her dark heart.

She fiddled with the satellite radio, trying to find music that would tamp down her untamed thoughts. She found a station with soothing spa music, but it only irritated her. She switched to easy listening, but that wasn't any better. Country music whined tinny in her ears. She punched the search button, trying to find something that was not on her normal presets.

A hard-driving rock beat poured from the mp3 player, and caught her right in the gut, hard and throbbing and primal. The running drumbeat pulsed hot blood throughout her veins, spreading heat through her body.

She felt wildly, viciously alive.

And from where she'd been, that was a very bad thing.

Terrified, she snapped off the player, and realized she was trembling. What was happening to her? The long-dormant passions she held off for so long roared inside her. Wanting out. Wanting Axel.

No. No. She would not give in. She would not become like her biological mother. She was stronger than her DNA.

What to do? What to do? Quit her job? Considering her growing feelings for Axel, that was the smart thing.

But if she walked away from this assignment, she'd lose her position with the Gunslingers. Truman Beck had been adamant about that, and Rowdy wouldn't be able to do anything to save her.

And if she lost her job, she'd have to wait to get custody of Emma, at least until she paid down her mountain of school loans. Years. It could take years.

Loneliness, the kind of which she hadn't felt in over two decades, walloped her. She thought of how elated she'd been to discover she had a sister. How amazed at the instant love she'd felt for Emma from the first moment she saw her. How her immediate impulse had been to move heaven and earth to take care of this vulnerable, motherless girl. How deep down, she'd found a glimmer of hope that she could finally make amends for what her biological mother had done.

She knew what it was like to be completely alone in the world, and what a desolate feeling! But the love of the Carlyle family had changed the course of her life, and that was what she wanted to do for Emma.

Without even knowing she meant to do it, Kasha didn't go straight home to shower and change, but instead drove to the house at the corner of Moonglow and Pearl. She wouldn't go in. She hadn't called ahead, and besides, she wasn't wearing underwear.

She stopped at the curb.

She'd been doing this a lot lately. Sitting outside a house, working up the courage to go in. What was going on with her? Six weeks ago things had been so easy, so ordinary, so worry-free.

She thought yoga was the answer to all her problems. That she'd conquered her insecurities, gotten a handle on her troubled emotions; that she could survive any challenge with dignity and grace.

And then she found out about Emma, and everything shifted.

Restlessly, her fingers stroked the steering wheel. She forced herself to stop, pressed her palms together in front of her heart, slowed her breathing, and whispered a healing mantra.

Some of the residents of the group home were in the side yard, which was fenced with decorative black wrought iron, playing basketball on an asphalt driveway court. Emma had the ball and she was double dribbling full-out on her way to the basket. Her sweet face was turned up to the sun, a magnificent smile on her face. She was fully in the moment, fully alive.

Looking at her half sister, those sloppy, soppy, messy feelings of love swamped Kasha. "Sister," she whispered. "I love you so much."

Get out of here before Emma sees you.

She was about to slide the Prius into drive when her cell phone rang. Kasha fished it from her purse, already freaking out that it might be Axel. She wasn't ready to talk to him.

But it wasn't.

At the sight of Howard Johnson's name on the caller ID, Kasha exhaled loudly and answered. "Hello?"

"Ms. Carlyle?" His voice was clipped, professional, but underneath she heard something else. Concern? Censure?

"Yes?" Kasha rubbed her chin, and watched Emma block another resident from making a basket. Atta girl.

"I've gotten permission for you to take Emma Cantu home with you for two days."

Kasha caught her breath.

"Ms. Carlyle? You there?"

"Yes, yes. I'm here."

"Have you changed your mind about seeking custody of your half sister?"

She looked across the street at darling Emma. The girl had wandered away from the game to pluck a dandelion from the yard. Emma blew on it, and giggled as the dandelion seeds scattered in the air. How innocent. How pure.

Kasha's chest tightened. "No."

"You're certain you want to move forward?" His tone stiffened, starchy and dry. He disapproved.

"How many times do I have to say it for you to believe me? I want custody of my handicapped sister."

"It's not that I don't believe you."

"What then?"

He hesitated, said, "A close friend of mine has a child with Down syndrome. It's not an easy road you've chosen."

"I didn't choose this path," Kasha said. "The path chose me."

Howard Johnson made a noise she couldn't quite decipher, part respect, part you-have-no-idea-what-you're-in-for.

"It's just not very often I see an attractive single woman willing to stunt her own life in order to take care of a handicapped sibling she didn't even know existed. You're a rare bird, Ms. Carlyle."

He didn't understand how Kasha's parents had already con-
demned her to a stunted life, and Emma was actually her salvation.
Caring for her sister was a way to right her parents' wrongs, to do
something noble, to soothe the wounds tragedy had flayed.

Heal herself. Make amends.

"Well then," he said. "Let's schedule a weekend for you to take
Emma. The best time for the Bankses is either the Sunday and
Monday of Memorial Day weekend or the last weekend in June,"
Howard Johnson said. "Do either of those work for you?"

"Sooner rather than later. I prefer Memorial Day."

"All right. I'll call the Bankses to confirm and I'll get back to you
with the arrangements."

"Thank you." Kasha switched off her phone, and shifted her attention back to Emma, who was spinning around in a circle, her
arms outstretched, laughing for all she was worth.

And Kasha felt a joy unlike anything she'd ever felt before. Her
sister.

Her destiny.

Her salvation.

Her redemption.

AFTER THE POOL incident, Kasha grew more guarded. Axel couldn't
blame her. Things had gotten out of hand. He expected her to back
off. What he hadn't expected was his reaction. He wanted her even
more than he had before.

*You only want her because you can't have her. It's just the thrill of the
chase that's got you amped up.*

Yeah. Maybe. He hoped so. That explanation worked for him.
He was in control here, not his dick. As long as Kasha was his therapist, absolutely nothing was going to happen between them.

End of story.

But all his good intentions flew out the window whenever she
massaged him, and he started thinking those treacherous thoughts
again. The day after they'd almost kissed they kept personal con-

versation to a minimum, focusing on the task at hand, and after that they managed to get things on a professional keel. At least on the surface.

The rest of the week passed in a reassuring sameness. They did gentle yoga in the mornings, and then Kasha put him through his paces with specific free weight exercises targeted for his shoulder, and general cardio, followed by a swim in the pool or the lake, and ending with a guided meditation underneath the pine trees.

With each passing day, Axel felt himself grow stronger, his range of motion increasing, but more than that, he felt calmer, healthier. Kasha's prescription of gentle exercise and lots of R&R seemed to be working. He was ready to get back on the field. In just a week, his mind had shifted from defeated to hopeful.

And it was all because of her.

On Thursday, May twenty-sixth, it was time for him to check back in with the Gunslingers. Axel knew his shoulder was more supple, and there was definitely improvement in his pain level, but Dr. Harrison's examination would prove if the gains were actually measurable.

He and Kasha could have driven to Dallas together, but since Axel didn't know if he'd be returning to Stardust or not, he packed up his belongings just in case, and they took separate vehicles.

Axel didn't realize how tense he was until he met up with Kasha in the employee parking lot of Gunslinger Stadium, and she took one look at him, smiled gently, and whispered, "Breathe."

Uncanny, the way she could read him.

She breathed with him, four slow deep inhales, holding their breath to the count of seven, exhaling for the count of eight. It was surprisingly intimate.

His body loosened as his lungs emptied.

"Feel better?" she asked when they'd done ten rounds.

"Yeah." He pinned her with his gaze, felt his blood churn.

She rubbed her palms together briskly, her smile slipping a little at the corners. "Let's do this."

Once they were inside, Kasha waited in the corner of the examination room with the usual entourage, including Rowdy and Truman Beck. Dr. Harrison moved toward him to begin the exam, but Axel raised a palm and shifted his gaze to the general manager. "There's something I want to say before we get started."

Beck grunted. "What's that?"

"Right here, right now, no matter what the outcome, I want you to promise me you won't fire Kasha. If the therapy didn't work, it was totally my fault. There were many times over this past week that I didn't follow her instructions."

Beck folded his arms over his chest and shot a glance over at Kasha, who was her usual cool, serene self.

God, Axel wished he had her self-control. She was amazing.

Beck said nothing for a long moment.

Ah crap, was the GM going to balk?

Finally, Beck nodded curtly at Kasha. "Agreed."

Kasha's face didn't change, but her shoulders dipped in a move so slight he was sure no one else noticed her relief.

"And, if I have improved," Axel went on, feeling pretty damn confident he *had* improved thanks to Kasha, "you'll live up to your promise, take her off probation, and give her the raise and health insurance she'd got coming as a permanent employee."

"You certainly wound him up," Beck said to Kasha. "I hope this cockiness is a good sign."

Kasha lifted her chin confidently, and her confidence fed his. "Axel's worked very hard to do what was necessary to heal his shoulder."

Damn, he loved the way she said his name.

He winked at her, but she didn't wink back, and he was left feeling as if he'd thrown a pitch to a batter who hadn't bothered swinging.

Dr. Harrison poked and prodded, measured and tested his muscle strength and shoulder rotation with both high-tech and low-tech methods, offered only noncommittal grunts and pensive hmms.

Every time Axel felt himself tensing, he would glance across the room at Kasha and catch her gaze and remember to breathe slowly and deeply, and he would feel his body loosen with each measured breath.

She was the calm at the bottom of the ocean—deep, silent, undisturbed. Whenever he peered hard into her unwavering brown eyes, Axel felt himself pulled below the surface to a place he had not been before, a deep and comforting place full of hope and light.

"Well?" Truman Beck asked, folding his arms over his chest, after the exam was over. "What's the verdict, Doc?"

Dr. Harrison glanced up, looking mildly surprised. "I do see some improvement. Not vast. It has only been a week, but there is definitely a measurable difference."

Beck grunted in happy surprise.

"Congratulations." Dr. Harrison shook first Axel's hand, and then Kasha's. "Whatever you're doing, keep up the good work. Let's schedule a follow-up appointment in two weeks to make sure we're staying on track."

"Um," Kasha said. "I have to say something."

All eyes swung to Kasha. The hairs on the back of Axel's neck bristled. He didn't like the look in her eyes.

"Yeah?" Beck hooked his thumbs in his belt loops. "What is it?"

"It might be a good idea if you replaced me with Paul Hernandez. That way Axel can stay here in Dallas, be close to the facilities—"

"No," Beck said.

A small flicker of alarm lit up Kasha's face but she quickly whisked it away. "Pardon?"

"You heard me." The GM stepped closer, a move designed to intimidate. Axel tensed, felt his hand fist involuntarily. "You agreed to serve as Axel's therapist, and you're going to follow through with your agreement, just as I'll follow through with mine."

Kasha opened her mouth, closed it again without saying a word, and exhaled in two parts. It was a technique she'd taught him designed to release tension. It might not show in her face or body language, but she was stressed.

"Unless," Beck said, "you have a damn good reason why not."

"Um . . . um . . ." Kasha stammered.

"Well?" Beck glowered. "Do you?"

Kasha drew herself up tall, her eyes unreadable. "I don't know if Mr. Richmond and I are well suited."

Beck's gaze switched to Axel. "You got a problem with her?"

"No," Axel said.

"There you go." Beck spread his arms wide. "You're on the case, Ms. Carlyle, until the job is done."

Kasha gave a curt nod, swallowed, accepted her fate. "Yes, sir."

"I'm glad we all understand each other." Beck headed for the door. "See you back here in two weeks for the follow-up exam."

Beck, Harrison, and the rest of the entourage left. Only Rowdy stayed behind.

Rowdy was eyeing them both, and Axel couldn't help wondering if the field manager sensed the attraction pulsing between him and Kasha. If Rowdy knew what Axel was thinking about his sister-in-law, he'd likely punch his lights out.

"What's going on?" Rowdy asked.

"Nothing. I'm going to slide on out of here. See you back in Stardust," Kasha told Axel, and hurried out the door.

Leaving him alone with Rowdy.

His field manager settled his hands on his hips. "Something I should know about?"

"Nope."

"Mr. Creedy told me there was an incident in the pool. Care to explain?"

"Kasha fell in and scraped her temple on the rough cement. I pulled her out and doctored her up. She's fine now."

"She fell in?" Rowdy looked skeptical.

"She did."

"Kasha, the yoga girl? Who is the most balanced person I know both mentally and physically, fell into the pool?"

Axel shrugged, tried his best to stay loose and noncommittal.

"And you went in after her?"

"Hey, she hit her head. I didn't know if she was knocked out or not. I had to go in."

"How did that happen?"

Axel shifted from foot to foot. "We were playing catch."

"Kasha? Playing catch?"

"It was part of my therapy." Axel offered up a sheepish grin. "And she's a lot more fun than you might imagine."

"Oh really?" Rowdy said. "You know more about her in a week than I do, and I've been her brother-in-law for two years?"

"I didn't say that."

"So there you both were, wet, alone . . ." Rowdy trailed off.

The conversation shot Axel back to that moment. How he'd pulled Kasha from the pool and carried her into the house. How they'd been squeezed into that enclosed bathroom together, so close her scent breached all his boundaries. Looking into those endless brown eyes, her head wrapped so fetchingly in that blue towel, breathing in time with her, feeling more alive than he'd felt since . . .

Well, since Dylan had died.

Oh shit. He was in deep, and now he got why Kasha had told Beck she wanted off his case. The sizzle between them was too hot to handle.

But he *would* handle it. Axel rotated his injured shoulder, loosening things up, shaking unwanted thoughts from his mind. She was healing him, and he couldn't jeopardize that. Kasha was his ticket back.

"You're not going to do anything to put her job in jeopardy," Rowdy said, looming over him. It wasn't a question, but an implicit statement.

"Absolutely not."

"Because the Carlyles are family. Breeanne's sisters are *my* sisters."

"Gotcha." Axel bobbed his head, pushed up off the exam table to level the playing field.

"You're not hooking up with Kasha?"

"What?" Axel feigned effrontery. "No. Of course not."

"Because while she looks tough, underneath it all, she's a big softie."

"Kasha is safe with me," Axel promised, holding up both hands and wagging them back and forth.

"Glad we got that straightened out," Rowdy said.

"Um . . . me too." Axel swallowed against the heavy feeling weighing down the center of his chest. Feeling Rowdy's stern glare boring through him, Axel pasted on a smile, acted like he was the most contented guy on the face of the earth.

"You still interested in going to the Yankees?" Rowdy's abrupt change of subject caught Axel off guard.

Was he? "Hell yes. Why? Is something up? Have they expressed interest?"

Rowdy shook his head. "I'm just information gathering. No trades are gonna happen until you're healthy. First get that shoulder healed."

"I'm working on it," Axel promised, wondering exactly what Rowdy wasn't telling him. Was a trade to the Yankees in the offing? Just the thought of it sent a thrill buzzing through his veins. "Doing my best."

"Good," Rowdy said. "That's all that counts."

Axel didn't believe that. Not for a second. What counted was not just healing, but coming back stronger than ever. That is, if he wanted to live his dream of playing for the Yankees.

Right now, that dream seemed awfully fuzzy and very far away, despite the good news he'd just gotten from Dr. Harrison. And now he was going to go back to Rowdy's house in the country and would continue to see Kasha day after day.

On the one hand, it was great.

On the other? It was an unqualified mess. He was her patient, and he wanted her. Desperately. Wanted her, but couldn't have her. Had to keep his hands off her, because she was his best chance of reclaiming his lifelong dream of pitching for the Yankees.

And he simply could not jeopardize that.

CHAPTER 9

Kasha had mixed feelings about Axel's improvement. She was happy for him and the fact that she still had a job. Yay!

But part of her was worried about her ability to control herself around him. Ever since that day she fell in the pool, her grip on her self-control had been tenuous. And now she had two more weeks of putting her hands all over his hot body as she guided him through his therapy.

It was too much.

Until now, until Axel Richmond, she'd had no trouble sublimating her sexual desires. But there was something about him that torched all her best intentions. Which was precisely why she should stay away from him.

But she couldn't. Their futures were intertwined.

He was her job.

It was essential she never forget that.

Grateful that she hadn't had to drive home with him, she returned to Stardust resolved to keep her feelings to herself. Too bad she couldn't do the same with her hands.

Late that afternoon she walked into her house on the edge of Stardust and circled the hope chest coffee table in the middle of her living room.

Seriously, she should give the thing to Suki. No hope chest wishes for her. If she did indeed get custody of Emma, it was most unlikely she'd find a guy who'd want to marry a woman with the lifelong responsibility of caring for a mentally challenged younger sister.

And she had no problem with that. Her sister was the most important thing in the world to her. Much more so than some fictional future husband she wasn't even sure she ever wanted.

At the thought of Emma, her heart hopped, and she couldn't help smiling. She was going to have her sister on Sunday and Monday of the upcoming Memorial Day holiday.

But she still hadn't told her parents about Emma. The family had been in a tizzy over Breeanne's infertility news and she wanted to give them time and space to digest it.

Is that the only reason? Could it also be because you don't want to have to revisit the night Dan Carlyle found you covered in blood in their garden shed?

Yes. True, true, true.

That wasn't the full reason. Total honesty here, she'd been putting off saying the words, because saying them would open that old can of worms she'd buried deep. With the news of her half sister had come understanding. She finally knew the reason her biological parents were dead.

Because Emma existed.

While the good part of Kasha wanted her sister with all her heart, did a small ugly dark part blame the girl? And ultimately, that's what Kasha was avoiding facing.

The cause of the scars.

The black spot on her soul.

She'd fought so hard to come back from that terrible place. Kasha ran trembling hands over her upper thighs.

Unsettling and unresolved feelings swirled around inside of her. Whenever she felt like this she knew the cure. Had discovered the secret to grace under fire when she was a disturbed fifteen-year-old and frantic with ferocious feelings.

Yoga.

That's what she needed right now. It would help her sort this out.

Kasha was in the middle of a headstand when there was a knock on her door. Before she could decide whether she wanted to invite the visitor in or not, Suki bounced into the room wearing an extremely short denim skirt, jade green leggings, and a tight-fitting green silk shell.

"Just how much freaking yoga do you practice?" Suki asked, sinking down into a cross-legged position in front of Kasha.

Sighing, Kasha slowly lowered her legs to the floor, and sat up to face her sister. "As much as it takes."

"Something eating you?"

"What makes you ask?" An errant bra strap had slipped down her arm, and she tucked it back inside her striped tank top.

"You over-yoga whenever you're upset."

"How do you know I'm overdoing it? This might be my first yoga session of the day."

"Is it?"

"No."

"How many?"

"Third one," Kasha admitted.

"Three hours of yoga by five in the afternoon?" Suki clicked her tongue—tsk, tsk. "Spill it. What's bugging you?"

"Nothing," she said.

Suki sent her a chiding stare.

"Nothing I want to talk about," Kasha amended.

"Trouble at work?"

"What was it you wanted?"

"How could you be having problems on the job? You're working with some of the hottest guys in sports. Oh!" Suki snapped her fingers. "Is it a drool issue? Can't stop drooling over the hunks?"

"I'm not letting you get to me," Kasha said mildly.

"Should I redouble my efforts?"

"Just tell me why you're here?"

"That doesn't sound very warm and welcoming. Where's your yogic spirit?"

Kasha cleared her throat.

"Right, you're not rising to the bait." Suki pantomimed curling her index finger into a hook, and latching it around her mouth and into her cheek.

"Correct. I'm not a catfish."

"I brought you something." Suki rotated, sat back on her feet, knees against the floor. She reached for her purse—a green bejeweled drawstring pouch she'd made herself—loosened the pucker, and pulled out a skeleton key.

Kasha rolled her eyes.

"Don't be dismissive. Someone brought it into the antiques store today and I have a good feeling about it because it has the same heart-shaped handle as the two keys Breeanne and Jodi found. Of course, I immediately thought of you."

"Lucky me."

"You're supposed to say, Thank you, Suki." She shoved the key into Kasha's hand.

Kasha palmed the key. It was warm against her fingers. "Thank you, Suki," she parroted.

"Well . . ." Suki cocked her head, rested her hands on her knees.

"Well what?"

"Aren't you going to open the trunk?"

Kasha shook her head.

"Aww, c'mon. Why not?"

"I don't believe in that silly prophecy."

"How can you not believe?" Suki stared at her as if she were a lemon growing on a turnip vine. "After what happened with Breeanne and Jodi?"

"They didn't find their true love because of a magical hope chest, Suki. It makes no logical sense."

Suki whacked Kasha's forehead with the heel of her hand.

"Ow." Kasha pulled back. "What was that for?"

"Being so damn duh."

"Duh about what?"

"You need a guy. You're thirty. Your ovaries are withering on the vine."

"Why do you give two figs about my ovaries?"

"Well, now that Breeanne can't have her own kids, it's time for you to step up to the plate. Jodi's already doing her part."

"Me? Why not you?"

"I'm only twenty-five, far too young to settle down. But you? You're headed for spinsterhood fast."

Kasha rolled her eyes again.

"Let's try the key. What's it gonna hurt?"

Kasha waved a hand at the hope-chest-turned-coffee-table. "Have at it. Be my guest."

"You have to open it."

"Why? Seriously, go ahead."

"Because Jodi gave the hope chest to you."

"Big deal. Now I'm giving it to you."

Suki sank down on the floor, looked at Kasha with disappointed eyes. "You don't believe in the prophecy. You've got a PhD. You are too smart for that. I get it. But Kasha, what if you're wrong? What if there is a little magic in the world? A little woo-woo stuff no one understands, but it works just the same? You of all people, Miss Yoga Girl, ought to be able to get behind that."

"Practicing yoga doesn't make me gullible."

"As I recall you were the one egging Jodi on when she didn't want to open the trunk."

"That was Jodi. She needed love in her life."

Suki leaned over to knock Kasha on the forehead with her fist. "For a smart chick you can sometimes be really thick."

"Oh for crying out loud, give me the damn key." Kasha held out her hand, irritated that she was letting Suki get to her. "Odds are it won't fit any of the remaining locks anyway."

Kasha crawled to the trunk, stuck the key in the top lock, and tried to turn it.

Suki wailed, "Nooooo!" and clutched the sides of her head with both hands.

She startled. "What is it?"

"You didn't make a wish first."

"That's okay, the key didn't turn anyway."

"Oh good." Suki dropped her hands, straightened her shoulders. "Move on to the next lock, but this time *make a freaking wish first!*"

"Stop yelling."

"Stop messing with my head."

Kasha blew out her breath. To keep Suki happy, she would make a wish. What did she want? She paused, read the cryptic message engraved on the lid of the trunk.

Treasures are housed within, heart's desires granted, but be careful where wishes are cast, for reckless dreams dared dreamed in the heat of passion will surely come to pass.

Heat of passion.

That's what scared her. To the core of her being. To the seat of her soul. Her biological parents had been passionate people, who loved and warred violently in equal measures.

And that passion destroyed them. Kasha wasn't passionate about anything, and she was not reckless.

You were reckless. Almost. With Axel.

Kasha shook her head. She had to forget about the kiss that had not happened. She hadn't crossed a line.

"What are you going to wish for?" Suki asked. "You don't have to tell me, but you have to make a wish."

Kasha read the hope chest lid again. What was her heart's desire? Emma.

She wanted Emma, and she had an excellent chance of getting her without the silly prophecy. And wanting her half sister was neither reckless nor passionate. Safe wish. Safe bet.

Smiling at Suki, she slipped the key into the second lock, wished silently, *Emma.*

The key did not turn.

Disappointment hit the bottom of her belly, and for a silly second she thought, *I'm not going to get Emma.*

Darn, she was letting Suki get her worked up. Cool. Calm. Breathe.

"Go on." Suki nudged her with her toe. "Try the third one."

The third one was the last one because Breeanne's key had opened the fifth lock, Jodi's the fourth.

Wishing she hadn't started this mess in the first place, Kasha wrapped her fingers around the old metal key gone warm in her palm, and slipped it into the third lock.

Please, let me gain custody of Emma.

Turned the key. The lock clicked.

Kasha gasped.

"It opened!" Suki squealed. "I knew it would work. Holy cow, Kash, it opened. Lift the lid."

An undercurrent of emotion she couldn't name raised goose bumps on Kasha's arms. Now that the lock was opened, she did not want to look inside. All she wanted was to lock it up again.

But Suki wasn't going to sit still for that. She cleared her throat loudly, drummed her fingers on the hope chest, "Growing old waiting on you."

Forced into a corner, Kasha pushed back the hinges on the third compartment of the hope chest to find a rectangular wooden box inscribed with another saying.

To sip, to savor, one drink of love intoxicates two spirits, fusing one to the other forever in infinite passion beyond time and space.

Kasha felt the breath slip from her lungs in a long, soft pull. She didn't inhale, not even when her chest started to ache and her head buzzed dizzily.

Passion.

That word again. She wanted no part of it. Or what was in that box. Passion destroyed. Wrecked lives. Ruined people. Crushed souls. Killed love.

"Kash?" Suki sounded worried, touched Kasha's shoulder with a gentle hand. "You okay?"

Finally, she inhaled, felt her entire body go cold. "Fine."

"You sure?"

Kasha forced a bright smile, but she could tell Suki wasn't falling for it. "Terrific."

"Want me to open the box for you?"

"Maybe we shouldn't open it at all."

"You afraid there might be something to the prophecy?"

"No." *Yes.*

"Then open that sucker up. I have a feeling there's vino inside," Suki said.

Reluctantly, Kasha opened the box, and just as Suki predicted, there was a bottle of wine inside it. The label was sepia, the lettering faded. She could barely make out that it was a merlot dubbed True Love.

She turned it over. The bottled date was unreadable, and it did not contain the surgeon general's warning. Around the neck of the bottle, tied with a thin white string, was a small piece of yellowed paper, and written in the flourishing script of a quill pen were the words: "TASTE ME."

A similar Alice in Wonderland type message that had been on Breeanne's scarf—"TOUCH ME." And Jodi's perfume bottle— "SMELL ME."

"I'll get a corkscrew and two glasses." Suki hopped to her feet.

"I'm not drinking it."

Suki stopped, whirled around, and sank her hands on her hips. "Excuse me?"

"I have no idea where that bottle came from, or how old it is. There's no winery name on it. The wine could have turned."

"It's sealed. I'm sure it's fine."

"I'm not rolling the dice."

"C'mon, what's the worst that could happen? It tastes like vinegar."

"Or it's loaded with organic arsenic."

"A small amount of arsenic is in many wines. One sip won't kill you." Suki turned and headed for the kitchen.

"Why are you pressuring me?" Kasha called after her.

Suki reappeared with a corkscrew and a single wineglass. "Don't you want to find love?"

"I didn't wish for love, and even if I did I wouldn't be laying it all on the turn of a key."

"What did you wish for?"

"I'm not telling you."

"Scaredy cat."

"Not rising to the bait." Kasha stood up, stretched, and was surprised to see she was holding tight to the wine bottle.

"If you don't believe in the prophecy, then what are you scared of? Drink the wine."

"Be my guest." Kasha shoved the bottle at her.

Suki shrugged. "I'm not turning down wine, but if it's like Breeanne's scarf and Jodi's perfume, I'm betting I won't be able to taste anything."

Kasha wished her sister would go away, but she didn't know how to tell her that without sounding rude.

Suki set down the glass on the hope chest, opened the wine, and poured a couple ounces in the glass. She swished the wine around, sniffed it. "Smells like red wine vinegar." She took a swig and made a face. "Tastes like red wine vinegar. Ugh. You're not missing anything."

"Mystery solved." Kasha recorked the bottle, picked it up along with the corkscrew and the glass, and headed for the kitchen. "Now I can pour it out."

"Wait." Suki put a restraining hand on her arm. "You're really not going to try it?"

"No."

"Well, don't pour it out. Just in case you change your mind."

"Tell you what. You can have it. Do whatever you will with it."

Suki wrinkled her nose, but accepted the bottle Kasha thrust at her. "It tastes like vinegar to me, but I might do a taste test with other people. See if I can find your soul mate for you."

"Seriously, Suki, it will probably taste like vinegar to me too."

"Never know until you try."

"If I try it will you hush?"

"Yes." Suki clapped her hands. "Oh boy."

"I have no idea why you care so much."

"Because if it works for you that will be three times the hope chest worked, and if it worked for you guys, it will work for me too."

"You could take it now for all I care."

"Wine." Suki pointed at the glass. "Drink."

Kasha lifted the glass to her mouth. She could already detect the fresh, fruity aroma, and it smelled good. Very, very good. Not vinegary at all. Uh-oh. She put a blank expression on her face.

Suki snored, pretending she'd fallen asleep while waiting.

All right. Kasha took a sip and her tongue sang. She let the wine sit in her mouth. Sweet, complex, and nuanced, it was more than just the best wine she'd ever tasted, it was the stuff of legends. Heavenly, exalted, incomparable. She wanted to snatch the bottle back from Suki and down the whole thing in one greedy gulp.

Instead, she made a big show of wincing. "Bleech. You're right. Pure vinegar."

"Really?" Suki's face fell. "Bummer. I was so sure it would taste good to you too."

"Sorry. No."

Suki's shoulders slumped. "Can't win 'em all, I guess."

"No, no, you can't." Kasha stiffened her grip on the stem of the wineglass, forced herself not to grin at the deliciously golden taste.

Heaving a sigh, Suki headed for the door. "I guess I better get back to work."

"You can leave the bottle if you want," Kasha said. "I'll pour it out."

"No way." Suki clung to it. "I'm going to let everyone else give it a taste. I bet it tastes sweet to someone. Obviously, you're not the person who was supposed to have the hope chest. That's all."

"Umm, okay. Bye." Kasha tried not to gaze longingly at the bottle as Suki went out the door.

But the minute her sister was gone, she sank down in a comfortable chair and slowly sipped the rest of the wine in the glass—wine that would make angels weep with joy—and licked up the very last drop.

CHAPTER 10

During the therapy session on Friday morning, May twenty-seventh, the day after Axel's appointment with Dr. Harrison, by silent, mutual agreement, both Kasha and Axel maintained a professional attitude—no flirting, no lingering glances, nothing to inflame the burning embers.

It didn't matter.

The air clumped thick with sexual tension. Even when Axel was across the room, working out on a machine, Kasha could feel the strength of their attraction.

Adding to the pressure was the fact that the groundskeeper and his wife were out of town for a long Memorial Day weekend. She and Axel were alone on the sprawling ranch. No one to come in and announce that lunch was ready. No one mowed the yard outside the glass gym. No other eyes on them.

Alone.

The daily morning massage was the hardest part of all. To distract herself from the feel of his hard muscles and pliant bare skin, Kasha broke the silence. "What's it like being on the pitcher's mound?" she asked, desperate for neutral ground.

Axel didn't say anything for a moment, and his breathing was so slow and regular, she thought he'd fallen asleep, but finally he said, "For me? Now?"

"Well, obviously not now, but before you injured your shoulder."

He made a soft groan of pleasure as she kneaded the back of his neck, and the sound tugged her female parts. Control. She had to stop these crazy sensations before they went any further. Forcefully, she focused on what her hands were doing, blanked her mind.

Rub. Stroke. Squeeze.

Axel Richmond's body.

"Stepping onto the mound after a decade in the business is like putting on your favorite pair of worn-out blue jeans."

"Oh?" Too much air came out of her lungs, and her head felt tight and dizzy, the way it had when she'd sipped the hope chest wine.

"It's a perfect fit. Comfortable, secure, and I feel more like myself than at any other time. It's like coming home."

"Does the crowd ever make you anxious?"

"No. When you're in the zone, the crowd doesn't exist."

The zone.

That's where she needed to be. Just the work. Axel didn't exist in any way except as the work. His was just a back, and she was massaging it. Could be anyone's back really.

Except it wasn't just anyone's back.

"It's me and the batter and the ball. That's all I see, but I see it with extraordinary clarity if that makes any sense. Each time I'm on the mound, the game is new and fresh."

"Beginner's mind."

"What?" he sounded surprised. "How did you know?"

"It's a yoga thing."

"You understand."

"When you master something, you're able to see both the small details and the big picture. The forest and the trees."

"That's it. I see the game as if watching every frame of a movie. When I throw a ball, it's as if it's moving in slow motion instead of a hundred miles an hour. When the batter swings, I see not only all the possible outcomes, but the meaning of those details from the lens of the entire game."

"Wow," she said. "You've become the sport."

He paused, considering that for a moment. "Yeah, maybe."

"There's only one problem with that."

"Which is?"

"Who will you be when the baseball ends?"

"I try not to think about that," his voice turned edgy, his muscles tensed.

"You're thirty, and injured. You should be thinking about it."

"I know, but taking my eye off the ball feels like . . ."

"What?"

"Never mind."

"Failure?" she guessed.

"Death," he mumbled so quietly she wasn't sure she heard him.

"Everything comes to an end eventually." She touched him gently with the flat of her hand, soothing his fears. "It's the cycle of life."

"Yeah well, I intend on fighting it with everything I have in me. Baseball is my passion. My life. I know I can't pitch forever, but I could be a staff coach or a field manager like Rowdy. I could become a commentator, or a baseball scout. Maybe work in the front office. Who knows? Maybe I'll become a sports agent."

"Those careers take different kinds of talents. Are you a good teacher? Do you have the right personality for a color commentator? Are you good at contract negotiations? What suits your personality?"

He didn't answer.

"You haven't really thought beyond your pitching career."

"Not much," he said, sounding slightly hostile. "I've been focused one hundred percent on my dream."

"Which is pitching for the Yankees in the World Series."

"Yes. I'll think about what comes after, after."

"What if you never achieve this dream? It is an extreme long shot."

"Playing in the major leagues is a long shot. I made that. I'll make this. Failure is not an option."

"Why not?"

His muscles rippled, and she knew, even though she couldn't see his face, that he was clenching his teeth. "It's just not."

She let that go, slid her hands down his spine, making her touch as soothing as possible. She waited until he'd relaxed a little before she ventured, "What did you enjoy before you ever picked up a baseball?"

"I forget."

"If baseball didn't exist, what would you do for a living?" she encouraged, trying to get him to understand that he was so much more than his career.

"I wouldn't want to live in a world without baseball," he said.

"Why does it mean so much to you? If you could get at the reason, you could find your inner truth and then you would understand that constantly striving for success can never fill what's empty inside of you."

"I'm not empty." His voice was angry again. "My life is full to the brim." But even as he said it, his voice wound up. A sound that said he was trying to convince himself as much as her. "I have my work, my friends, the team. I don't need anything else."

He moved away from her, sat up, glared hotly at her as he grabbed for his T-shirt. "Hey, you don't get to judge me."

"I'm not judging you. I—" She broke off.

His glower deepened. He tugged the T-shirt over his head, covering those sculpted abs.

"Jake told me about Dylan."

He froze. His face was stony, a bit of a sphinx himself.

"I . . . I'm so very sorry for your loss."

Axel splayed his right palm over the left side of his chest, and pain filled his eyes.

"I can't begin to imagine everything you've suffered."

"No, you can't." His voice was sandpaper, his eyes stormy.

"Do you ever think about having more children?"

"You can't replace one child with another," he growled, his right palm welded to his boy's name tattooed forever on his heart.

She was screwing this up royally. Everything she said seemed to make things worse. "Axel . . . I . . . you're closing yourself off to so much more."

"You don't have kids. You don't know what it's like to lose one. You don't get to have an opinion on how I should lead my life."

"You're right," she whispered. "But I do know how important family is. I'm adopted. All of my sisters and I are. And even though I love my adopted parents with every cell in my body, there's a hollowness inside of me that I didn't even realize was there until—"

A long silence stretched between them. They stared at each other. An eon seemed to pass, neither one of them moving or speaking. Gauging each other. Mapping the lay of the land. Their relationship was shifting, but where was it going? More importantly, how did she stop the drift?

"Until what?" he prompted.

Why had she started this? Kasha ducked her head, struggled to keep her emotions from showing up on her face. Breathe. She inhaled deeply, raised her head to meet his intense gaze.

"Until what?" he repeated, his tone telling her that he was not going to drop the topic.

"Emma," she said, because she'd been unable to talk about her half sister to anyone else but Howard Johnson, and the secret was eating her up.

It felt safe to tell him, and that truly surprised her. She trusted him. Why, she didn't know, but the second she mentioned Emma's name, she felt an emotional weight roll from her shoulders, and it was only then that she realized how heavy it was.

His eyes softened, and his shoulders relaxed and he dropped his hand to his knee. "Who's Emma?"

Kasha smiled at the same time tears burned her nose. She gritted her teeth to make sure the tears did not slide into her eyes. Sphinx. Strong as steel; steady as stone. "My biological half sister."

Axel blinked, studied her for a heartbeat before he said, "You just recently found out about her?"

How had he guessed? She nodded, touched the tip of her tongue to the roof of her mouth. Pressed her palms against her upper thighs.

"Seven weeks ago." Slowly, she told him about the out-of-the-blue call from Howard Johnson, and how the news had rattled her to her core.

"So your biological father had a child out of wedlock."

She nodded, held her breath, hoped he would not ask more about her father.

"You've met Emma?"

Kasha's mouth twitched involuntarily. If it was this hard to talk to Axel about Emma's condition, how was she ever going to tell her family? But she had to tell them. Today. She was getting Emma on Sunday and her family expected her for their annual Memorial Day weekend bash.

"Yes," she whispered.

Axel frowned with concern. "Your meeting with Emma didn't go well?"

"It went amazingly well."

"But?"

How did he know there was a "but"? "She's got . . ." Kasha bit her lip. "It's not . . ."

He held up a palm. "Hey, it's none of my business. You don't have to tell me."

"I want to tell you. I need to tell someone."

His eyebrows shot up on his forehead. "You haven't yet told your adoptive family about Emma?"

Slowly, Kasha shook her head.

"Why not?"

Kasha took in another steadying breath. "Emma's different. She's not like everybody else."

Axel studied her, head cocked, looked genuinely interested in her problems. "What do you mean?"

"She has . . ." Kasha gulped, watched Axel's face carefully, looking for judgment. "Down syndrome."

He paused, hooked his belt loops with his thumbs, his eyes full of sympathy, and nothing else. "That's rough."

"Yes." Heat flooded Kasha's body, her limbs going loose, and weak. "When I was a kid, I had fantasies about having a secret brother or sister. Blood kin. And when it happened, my world turned upside down."

"Finding out about Emma's condition dashed your expectations," he said softly.

That was pretty insightful of him. The expression in his eyes said he understood about dashed expectations. But of course, he did. He'd lost his son. Her issues were nothing compared to his.

And his capacity for empathy astounded her.

"Kasha," he murmured, and reached out to touch her arm. Lightly. Comforting. Nothing sexual about that touch, but instantly the temperature in the room shot up twenty degrees.

She swallowed, shifted away from his touch. Too much. It was too much. He was too much. "Emma's handicap doesn't make me love her any less. In fact, I might love her even more because of it. The minute I looked into her face, I felt a connection unlike anything else I've ever experienced. Axel, she's a part of me."

"That's a lot to hold inside for seven weeks."

Kasha rubbed a palm over her mouth. "It's a relief to say it to someone. Thanks for letting me rehearse with you. I think it's going to be easier now to tell my parents."

"Glad I could be of service. If you want to talk more." He shrugged as if it was no big deal, and his eyes cradled her as if she were a rare and delicate glass. "I've got one good shoulder if you need to lean on it."

She smiled helplessly. Oh, he was a charmer. "Thank you for that."

"So . . ." He patted his left shoulder. "Go ahead, let it out."

"I'm petitioning the court for custody of her," she blurted, startling herself. What was it about him that made her want to confess everything?

Axel's eyes widened. "Big step."

"It's why I need this job so badly. I'm still paying off school loans, and the pay is double what I was making in my previous job. Plus the health insurance is the best there is, and while Emma does get Medicaid, she's got a lot of health issues and I want to make sure she'll get the best health care money can buy."

"I get that."

She closed her eyes briefly, tried to imagine what he must have gone through with his sick child. He probably understood what she was facing more than she did.

"You're strong," he said.

"So are you." She heard the admiration in her voice, recognized how much she respected him. He was a good guy.

"Emma's lucky to have you."

"No, I'm lucky to have her. She's incredible, so sweet, and innocent. She makes me feel . . ." Kasha paused, trying to decide how to name her feelings. "Important. Needed. She gives me a sense of purpose."

"I get that." The tilt of his head, the angle of his eyebrows told her that for whatever reason, he did understand.

"Every time Emma sees me she gets a big smile on her face." At the thought of Emma's dear face, Kasha couldn't contain her own huge grin. "She can't make the sound 's,' so she calls me her 'titter.' It's so cute."

"You sound like you're in love."

"I am." Kasha pressed both hands over her heart. "She is an amazing girl, although I should say young woman. She's twenty-three."

"What is her mental age?" Axel asked.

It was a legitimate question, but it made Kasha feel defensive, and she had to wonder about her feelings. Emma had mental challenges, true, but Kasha didn't want her sister pigeonholed by a number. "She reads on a third-grade level."

"So it will be like having an eight-year-old for the rest of your life."

Kasha could feel herself bristle. Nothing about Axel's expression or his body language suggested he meant anything negative by the comment, but she couldn't help feeling resentful. Emma was an incredible human being no matter what her capabilities.

"Yes," Kasha said. "And I'm fully prepared to accept that responsibility."

Axel looked at her with such respect and admiration it immediately dissolved her defensiveness. He was on her side. Her heart fluttered, and she dropped her hands.

"Do you have any idea how amazing you are?"

"I'm not amazing at all," she protested. "I never expected to feel so overwhelmed by love, but I am."

"You're a good person, Kasha Carlyle." His eyes were as tender as a whisper. "I'm honored you shared that with me."

"I don't know why I did." Feeling self-conscious and hating it, she lowered her eyelashes. "Maybe I was using you as practice. I have to tell my parents about her tonight. I've put it off as long as possible. I'm picking Emma up tomorrow. I have her for the weekend and it's my first time having her stay with me overnight."

Suddenly, she was acutely aware of just how alone they were. She noticed that he hadn't shaved in a couple of days, and had a sexy stubble thing going on. Her nostrils flared on the scent of coconut massage oil mixed with his heady masculine fragrance.

Compelled by a force that she could neither explain nor resist, her gaze was drawn to the shape of his mouth—perfect color, shape, and size.

Kiss-worthy lips.

A vivid image of kissing him flashed in her head, and she could almost feel his mouth on hers. Moist. Weighted. Delicious.

Twin spots of heat burned at the backs of her knees, spread quickly up her thighs. Alarmed by her wayward thoughts and feelings, Kasha turned away and started putting away supplies and equipment.

Axel joined in.

"I've got this," she said. "You're the patient. You rest."

"I'm not going to sit here and twiddle my thumbs while you slave away."

"Breaking down a massage table is hardly slave labor."

"Sphinx, I'm used to being part of a team, helping out. For now, we're a team, and I'm not letting you carry the load alone, so get over it."

It wasn't her independence or need to be in control that wanted him to back off. Rather, it was this ridiculous attraction she felt whenever she was near him.

"Please," she said, trying not to sound desperate. "I've got this. Why don't you go take a shower while I finish up?"

"Nope," he said cheerfully, nudging her out of the way so he could break down the massage table. His hip against hers was electric, and it was all she could do not to gasp at the contact.

She started to argue with him, but decided to let it go. He was standing too darn close and she stepped back. "Don't hurt your shoulder."

"I won't."

She pressed her fingertips together, tried not to fret, and mumbled, "Cocky."

"I heard that." He finished folding the table, propped it against the wall, and turned to her with a laser beam grin.

Why did he have to be so pulse-jerkingly handsome?

"You're just one big ear."

"I do have great hearing."

"Must be annoying when you're playing baseball."

"I block all that out when I'm on the mound."

"Oh yeah, so you said," she murmured, and still avoiding his gaze, looked out the glass wall of the gym to the pool.

Looking at the pool made her remember the day she'd fallen in, and that made her remember the close quarters of the bathroom, and how close his hot lips had been to hers. Absentmindedly, she reached up to touch the scrape at her temple that was nearly healed.

"Kasha."

"Uh-huh."

"Look at me."

No. Don't wanna.

But Kasha wasn't a coward. She raised her chin, gave him her

coolest noncommittal stare, and got tangled up inside those spectacular dark eyes.

"Go to lunch with me," he said.

"What?" she mumbled, so mesmerized by him that she was only
vaguely aware that he'd spoken.

"The Creedys are out of town for the holiday weekend, and I'm
a horrible cook. There's a good chance I'll die of food poisoning if
left to my own devices."

Absolutely not. That's what she should have said. She was in
enough hot water being his therapist, much less socializing with him.

Instead, she hesitated.

He took her hesitation as a yes. "Great. I'll shower and change
and grab my car keys and you can take me to the best place in
town."

Say no.

But then she thought, hey, at least in town, at a restaurant, they
wouldn't be alone. And the way lust bombarded her every time she
saw, touched, heard, or smelled him, that was a good thing.

"Okay," she mumbled. "But this isn't a date."

"Of course not." He blinked at her as if that was the silliest thing
he'd ever heard, and then she felt embarrassed for having said it.

"Go shower," she said, pointing at the door. "I'll finish up here
and then be waiting for you at my car. I'm driving. No discussion."

His grin cracked open as if he was a fisherman who'd just reeled
in the catch of a lifetime.

Nervously, she reached for the coconut-scented massage oil,
meaning to cap it, but the outside of the bottle was slippery and it
fell from her hands, spilling oil all over the front of her clothes. It
drenched the entire room in the smell of the tropics, and had her
thinking of palm trees and umbrella drinks and Axel in a Speedo.

Heat that started at the backs of her knees rose all the way to the
nape of her neck.

Frig, she was covered in massage oil and all she could think about
was having sex with him.

"Hang on." He grabbed for paper towels from the sink, and moved toward her as if he was going to start dabbing her.

She snatched the paper towels from him. "I've got this. Go."

"But you're covered in oil."

"I keep a change of clothes in the trunk of my car."

He stared at her for a long moment. His smile was sly. And everything inside her ached and hummed. "You can have the downstairs bathroom. I'll shower upstairs."

"Great." She made shooing motions with one hand as she dabbed at the oil on the front of her chest with the other. And realized belatedly that the oil made her nipple visible through her shirt.

And that he'd already seen it.

"Go."

"Yes, ma'am." His dangerously handsome eyes danced, amused.

Her body responded, going soft and warm and wet and treacherous. As she watched him walk away, she couldn't help wondering how she was going to survive another two weeks without breaking every rule in the book.

CHAPTER 11

When Axel came out of the house to find Kasha standing beside her green Prius, he smiled a proud, hit-the-jackpot smile, slightly self-conscious about how happy he was, like some Hallmark greeting card prince on one knee, clasping a glass slipper in his hand, a sappy sentiment written in scroll script: We fit!

Because that was how he felt.

Joined. Connected. He and Kasha fit like a lock and key.

She was amazing. A grounded, logical woman who took life with a steady, unwavering gait, and stole his breath with those soulful dark eyes.

Important to an intensely ambitious guy who'd spent much of his clueless life blundering around as if he were a china-closet bull.

She wore a billowy white shirt that rippled over her skin like water whenever the wind blew. It was belted at the waist with a wide gold snakeskin-print belt, and the material was so gauzy, he could see the white camisole she had on beneath.

Yellow skinny jeans hugged her long legs, showing off the curve of her calves, the slim taper to her ankles, and her long, lush, almost-black hair was done up in a single braid that hit her mid-back.

Her lips were the color of raspberry stains, sweet and darkly bright. She looked like a regal bird peering down from a lofty perch, contained in her distance, high, serene, supreme.

She was so incredibly beautiful, and he ached for her. Wanted her. Intensely. Desperately. Shockingly.

He wanted to pull her into his arms and plant hot kisses all over her gorgeous face. Wanted to coax a smile from her, trace his tongue along that brilliant mouth.

She was so strong, so resolute, so damn determined not to let anyone see what lurked beneath—fear, longing, vulnerability. She was so hauntingly vulnerable, but it took an observant eye to see it past her tall stature, enigmatic dark eyes, and proud chin.

She'd been brave for so long. She didn't know how to put down her shield and look around to see that she was safe. She needed to accept herself and that hot fire of passion she struggled so hard to deny.

Why? Why did she fight so hard to keep from being who she was?

"We're going to the Honeysuckle Café," she said. "They serve out-of-this-world veggies, and if you're so inclined, the chicken-fried steak is their best seller."

"Okay." He walked around to the passenger side door. "Not a date."

"I do have to warn you about one thing," she said as they climbed into the car.

"What's that?"

"The Honeysuckle Café is inside Timeless Treasures, my parents' antiques store."

"You're taking me to meet the parents? A bit soon, isn't it?" he teased. "This is our first date, after all."

She gave him a don't-go-there-or-I'll-put-you-out-of-the-car stare. "It's not a date and if you're going to insist on calling it a date I'm not leaving the driveway."

"Okay."

"Just FYI, Dad's a huge baseball nut. He was over the moon when my sisters married major league players. And he'll talk your ear off about it. He and his brothers played minor league ball when they were young."

"I love talking about baseball."

"We're here," she announced a couple of minutes later, parking at the curb outside a converted Victorian house on Main Street.

Kasha led him into the antiques shop. Chimes tinkled as the door opened and closed, and they walked into a whoosh of scent—lavender mixed with the yellowed smell of old books, mixed with the tint of oil paintings, mixed with sweet earthiness of caramelized onions—and quaint vintageness—ornate highboys and beaded purses; lace tablecloths and spindly-legged chairs; gaudy glass jewelry and colorful cigar boxes; butter churns and copper kettles; ostrich feathers poking from tall wicker baskets, ruffling in the air of the overhead ceiling fan; a gold-framed movie poster from *Gone with the Wind* (Frankly my dear, I don't give a damn) covering part of a side wall. Frank Sinatra on a record player singing "I've Got You Under My Skin."

A middle-aged man and woman were standing behind the checkout counter in the middle of a smooch. The man's arms were around the woman's waist, and she was looking up at him as if he was the center of the universe, apparently unconcerned whether anyone caught them in a romantic moment or not.

Axel smiled. The couple reminded him of his parents, many wedding anniversaries marked, and still flagrantly in love.

"Mom, Dad," Kasha said. "This is Axel Richmond. Axel, these amorous folks are my parents, Dan and Maggie Carlyle."

Grinning sheepishly, the older couple broke apart and turned to face them.

"Honey, Axel Richmond is the star pitcher for the Gunslingers. I know who he is," Kasha's father said. He wore a white button-down shirt with the sleeves rolled up to the elbows, and a pair of faded jeans.

Maggie Carlyle's cheeks pinked and she pushed back a strand of blond hair lightly tinged with gray from her forehead, offered him a beaming smile.

"Axel." Maggie Carlyle extended a hand. "Welcome to Timeless Treasures."

"Pleasure." He shook first Maggie's hand and then Dan's. "Always nice to meet a fellow ballplayer, sir."

Dan waved a dismissive hand, but he grinned like a boy. "Nah, I only played bush league ball. You're the real deal."

"Baseball is baseball," Axel said. "It's all for the love of the game."

"You got that right!" Dan bobbed his head as if Axel had said something profound.

"It's his deepest passion." Maggie patted her husband's chest and leaned against his side.

"You're my deepest passion," Dan corrected, dropping a kiss on his wife's upturned face. "But baseball is a close second."

"Almost upstaged by a white ball with red stitches." Maggie laughed and hugged her husband hard. "At least you're honest."

Axel glanced up to the open balcony of the second story, where books abounded. Along the balcony railing stretched a lethal-looking calico cat, her eyes narrowed to snooty slits, tail swishing rhythmically. "Um . . . y'all, I think that cat is about—"

Without looking up, everyone simultaneously jumped back. A second later the cat hit the counter, swung her head around, and looked disappointed that she hadn't startled anyone. Twitching her tail, the calico strolled down the length of the counter before dropping to the floor, and eeling around Kasha's legs.

Kasha bent to pick the cat up. "You're an ornery little puss, aren't you, darling?" she cooed, and scratched the calico under the chin. The cat purred loudly. Kasha's face softened as she stroked the kitty.

"This is Callie," she explained. "My sister Suki saved her from Hurricane Sandy when she was going to school at NYU. Now Callie is the store mascot."

"A scary mascot." Axel eyed the railing where the calico had been sitting moments before.

"The vet says she suffers from PTSD, and that's why she drops down off the balcony onto people. It makes her feel secure and in control."

"Uh-huh." Axel didn't know about that diagnosis. To his way

of thinking, the calico was in primal stalk mode, and scaring people was fun for her, but what did he know about cats?

"We were headed to the Honeysuckle for lunch," Kasha told her parents. She put Callie down on the floor and dusted her palms against her hips.

"Enjoy your lunch," Maggie said. "Nice meeting you, Axel. I hope we'll be seeing more of you."

"Count on it," he said, and his heart rejoiced when he saw a tiny smile edge up the corners of Kasha's mouth, and realized that he felt better about the future than he had in a long time.

"His shoulder rotation improved by a full millimeter. That means he'll be staying at Rowdy's ranch for two more weeks." Kasha beamed.

"Congratulations!" Maggie hugged her daughter. "Your new career has sprouted wings. I'm so proud of you."

"And congrats to you too." Dan slapped Axel on the back. "You'll be back on the mound before you know it. Our Kasha is a miracle worker."

Axel met Kasha's eyes. "She's unlike any therapist I've ever encountered."

She didn't blush at the praise, or even offer up a smile. She stood calm, serene, full of positive self-esteem. She accepted her talent without ego. She knew who she was. He loved that about her.

"The Honeysuckle closes for lunch at two-thirty, and it's almost two now." Kasha motioned in the direction of the delicious smells.

He turned to follow her, and as he did, Axel saw the elder Carlyles draw closer and smile into each other's faces as if watching the sun come up on the best day of their lives.

His parents were equally soppy in their mature love, and he wondered if he would ever have that. The only person he'd ever loved completely, and unconditionally, without doubt, hesitation, or reservation, was Dylan.

At the thought of his son, sadness squeezed his chest and he momentarily closed his eyes. He'd been thinking of Dylan a lot lately, and it hurt. More than he wanted to admit. Without the long, punishing workouts to keep his mind occupied, he had too much time for dark thoughts.

"Axel?" Kasha asked, her voice soft and low.

He opened his eyes, stared into her intense gaze.

"Are you all right?"

He smiled, easy but totally manufactured. "Sure."

"Pain?"

"Nothing I can't handle."

"Do you want to go back to the ranch?"

"No way. I've been looking forward to getting out." Screw his demons. He felt like a prisoner out on work release, privileged to just be here.

"Okay." She hesitated.

His gilded, brushed-on smile wasn't fooling her for a second, but she let it go and opened the interior door of Timeless Treasures that led into the Honeysuckle Café. She stood in the orange glow of the sunshine spilling in through the sparkling clean window, the light cutting through the thin material of her white shirt, giving him a peekaboo view of her excellent body.

"Come on," she prodded, having no clue that he was so stunned by her beauty that his legs had turned to cement.

She didn't wait for someone to seat them. Instead, she headed for a wooden bench booth in the corner. "Permanently reserved for members of the Carlyle clan as long as it's not already taken," she told him. "Perks of Mom being best friends with the owner."

Red and white checkered tablecloth on the table, drinks served in Mason jars. Wurlitzer in the corner playing a Hank Williams tune. Red Coca-Cola napkin dispenser. The menu written on a chalkboard, comfort food with a gourmet twist: chicken-fried steak with chipotle cream gravy, mac and cheese with guanciale, buffalo sliders, and slimmed-down soul food.

Creative and yet appealingly ordinary.

A thirty-something waitress hurried over and greeted Kasha with a hug. It surprised Axel to see Kasha hug the waitress back.

Kasha was normally so reserved he didn't think of her as much of a hugger. But here, she was in her milieu. Among family and friends.

He was the outsider.

"I know you want the veggie plate," the waitress said to Kasha, and then turned to Axel and held out her hand. "Hi, I'm Venus."

"Axel Richmond."

"Honey," Venus said. "No need for introductions. Everyone in Stardust knows who you are. We're a Gunslingers town. Sorry to hear about your injury."

Axel rotated his right shoulder. "It's much better now. Thanks to Kasha."

"Isn't she an angel?" Venus gushed. "She got my granddaddy up walking again after he broke his hip. Doctor said he would be bedridden for the rest of his life, but Kasha would have none of it. Let me tell you, you could have knocked old Doc Prescott over with a feather when Granddaddy walked into his office under his own steam."

Axel met Kasha's gaze. "She is something."

Kasha's cheeks flushed and she quickly glanced away.

"What'll you have?" Venus asked Axel.

"I'll have the veggie plate as well."

"Good choice. It's awesome. Course everything at the Honeysuckle is awesome."

"You can eat meat if you want," Kasha said. "I won't judge."

"Veggie plate," Axel said, not taking his eyes off Kasha. He'd eat dirt if he thought it would impress her.

"It comes with lentils for protein," Venus said. "I'll go put your order in and bring you some water. Anything else to drink?"

"Water's fine," Axel confirmed.

When Venus was out of earshot, Axel said, "She thinks you hung the moon and the stars, and you know what?"

"What?"

"I agree."

"Stop it." Kasha rolled her eyes.

"I mean it."

"You're flirting."

"I'm paying you a compliment."

"You're messing with my head."

"Or you could try this on for size. 'Thank you, Axel.'"

"Don't make me regret this lunch," she said.

Even though this wasn't a date, Axel couldn't help feeling that electrical thrill of a first date was going really, really well.

Yo Richmond. See those hot coals in your hand? You're juggling fire. If you don't want her to quit as your therapist, knock it off.

He stared at her.

She stared back, totally badass.

What should he do? (A) Stop coming on to her because things couldn't end well. (B) Say screw it, and just do what he'd wanted to do since the day he met her, and kiss her like tomorrow would never come. (C) Slow down, but hang in there because the best things in life were worth waiting for?

C. Definitely C.

Their food arrived. Venus arranged it on the table in front of them and gaily said, "Bon appétit," and off she went.

Axel looked across the table at Kasha and knew he would always remember this moment. She was surrounded by plump vegetables: roasted red bell peppers and butter-yellow corn on the cob, purple cabbage, and broccoli sautéed with olive oil and garlic; her fork clinking softly against the bone white plate, an expression of foodie-in-heaven bliss on her face.

He was so busy watching her eat that he forgot his own meal.

"Is something wrong with your food?" she asked.

"No. It's terrific." He paused, swallowed. "Just like you."

"Axel," she chided. "You simply can't keep saying things like that."

"Why not? It's true."

"It's flirty. We talked about this."

"No it's not. Flirty is silly, teasing. I am serious. You are terrific."

"I'm your therapist."

"Still terrific."

"We can't . . . this isn't . . ."

"What?"

She dabbed her mouth with a napkin, that plump, raspberry mouth that made his mouth water. "I should never have come out with you. We didn't call this a date, but it's a date and . . ." She put down her fork. "Here we are. Being datey."

"At the Honeysuckle Café."

"Eating a vegetable plate," she said. "You're eating a vegetable plate to please me."

"So what? Nothing wrong with that."

"It's unethical for me to have a relationship with you," she said a bit primly.

"I'm not talking about a relationship. I'm simply saying I admire you. Don't make a bigger thing of this than it is."

She leaned back against her chair, eyed him uneasily, and took a sip of water.

He wished he could say what was really on his mind. *I like you. I think you're special. I want you. Maybe when I'm healed and you're no longer my therapist we could . . .*

But he knew what would happen if he pushed. She wasn't a fan of pushing. And even once he was healed, he might end up traded to another team on the other side of the country. It was his life's ambition to play for the Yankees. What if all his dreams came true, and he got what he wanted? He'd have to leave Texas, and he knew for a fact that long distance relationships just didn't work. He'd tried it and failed more than once.

Getting ahead of yourself, buddy. Way, way ahead.

Nothing might ever happen between him and Kasha. Between him and the Yankees. Hell, even between him and a healthy shoulder. She was right. He had to stop with the compliments and the flirting and the lusting. Although there were no guarantees he could stop that last one. He had no right to push. He had nothing to offer her.

Yet.

Unnerved by his thoughts, Axel clenched his fork, tension tightening his jaw muscles, and he draggled in a covert inhale to steady the clipped rhythm of his exasperated heart.

He didn't move. Didn't speak.

She must have seen it in his eyes. Somehow, she knew what he was thinking, sensed his frustration. Her dark eyes turned darker still until they were almost black underneath the glow of the cutesy red lanterns dangling overhead. She reached out a hand as if she were going to touch him, but stopped midway across the table.

Axel sat frozen, his gaze fixed on hers, unable to exhale.

She dropped her hand to the breadbasket, picked up a piece of cornbread, and examined it as if that was what she'd been angling for all along.

His stomach flopped. Was he imagining her feelings for him? Was he being a fool? Axel didn't fall head over heels very often. But he was seriously afraid that's what was happening. But what if she didn't feel the same way.

Ah shit.

"Sister!" a voice called out.

At the same moment, Kasha and Axel looked over to see a pretty red-haired, pregnant woman about their same age walk over. Kasha stood up and hugged her sister, then waved her into the booth and perched lithely on the outer edge of the seat as if she were an elegant eagle about to take flight.

"Axel," Kasha said. "This is my sister Jodi."

"Jake's wife." Axel reached over the table to shake Jodi's hand. "We met briefly once at the stadium."

"Yes, I remember. Before your shoulder injury."

They made small talk for a while and then Jodi said, "What are your plans for Memorial Day, Axel?"

Axel shrugged, grinned at Kasha. "My therapist tells me I'm supposed to take it easy."

"All by your lonesome?" Jodi pretended to pout.

"Looks like it."

"Well," Jodi said good-naturedly. "Kasha may be able to do all the find-yourself Zen stuff, but for us extroverts it's called boredom."

"Oh, I don't know about that." Axel watched Kasha's face. "I think she's onto something. She certainly got my attention."

Was it his imagination or was a smile twitching at Kasha's lips?

"Be that as it may," Jodi said. "You are officially invited to the annual Carlyle Memorial Day bash at Mom's request. We hope you'll come. Please say yes. Come for Saturday, Sunday, Monday, or all three. We're short of guys since Jake and Rowdy will be at the stadium."

"You party for three days?" he asked.

"It's the Carlyle way," Jodi said.

Kasha's smile winked out. She drilled a hole through him, moved her head imperceptibly. Message received. She didn't want him at the party.

"We're having therapy session six days a week," Axel said. "So Saturday's out. But I'd love to come over on Sunday."

Something bumped against his shin, sharp and insistent. Kasha was kicking him.

"Um," she said. "Don't you have other plans?"

"Nope," Axel said feigning innocence. "None at all."

Another swift kick. Ouch. If stares were daggers, he'd be bleeding from every orifice.

He smiled even wider at Jodi, and sent Kasha a kick-all-you-want-I-gotcha look. "Tell me what time to be there, and what I should bring?"

CHAPTER 12

"Here's what you're going to do," Kasha said to Axel when they were back in her Prius headed for the ranch. "You're going to call my mother, thank her for inviting you to the party, but tell her that you can't make it."

"Nope."

Kasha swung her head around to glare at him. "Excuse me?"

"Not canceling," he said amicably.

"Why not?"

"For one thing it's rude."

"No it's not. Tell her you forgot you had something else to do."

"But I don't."

"Pretend."

"You mean lie?"

Kasha blew out an exasperated breath. He was right about that. "Please," she said, trying a different tack. "Do it for me."

"But I want to go to the party." His voice was light, but it was laced with deeper meaning.

She cast another glance over at him. He had on sunglasses and she couldn't read his eyes. "You can't go."

"Sure I can. I was invited."

"But I will be there. With Emma."

"How can you take Emma with you when you haven't told your parents about her?"

"I will," she said, gripping the steering wheel tighter and wondering why she'd taken him to lunch at the Honeysuckle. She should have expected her family would invite him to the party.

"So why can't I come too?" he asked. "I'm stuck at the ranch all weekend with nothing to do, and you keep pestering me to relax and have fun, but the minute I do, splat, you squash it."

"All right. Fine. Come to the party." Under her breath she muttered, "Maybe I'll skip it."

He didn't say a word, just kept looking at her with kind, understanding eyes, and that freaked her out a little.

"What?" she asked, hunching forward, then catching what she was doing and forcing herself to sit up tall, shoulders back and down.

"What, what?"

"Why do you keep staring at me like that?"

"Like what?"

"Like I'm a delicate flower."

"Is that what I was doing?"

"Yes, and it's annoying." She knew she was overreacting, but she couldn't seem to contain her feelings.

And that bothered the hell out of her.

She did some yoga breathing, and it helped. Marginally. But marginally was better than nothing. When she glanced over, Axel was still studying her.

Then he surprised her completely by reaching over the seat to take her hand, but what surprised her even more was she did not pull away. "I could help you. Be a buffer."

"I don't need a buffer." Her eye twitched. Okay, yeah, maybe she was fooling herself.

"Who better than an objective third party? I'd be like an umpire."

"No need for a referee. Everything is going to be fine," she said firmly. Maybe if she said it enough times it would be true.

"Emma's good with strangers then? And crowds?"

Kasha didn't know. "I'd rather not talk about it right now."

"Just tell me you've got a plan in case things aren't fine. Kids—and I say this knowing Emma is mentally an eight-year-old—are notoriously unpredictable."

He was freaking her out. Could it really be that hard? Bringing Emma to the party?

She would ask Molly Banks for advice. Emma's foster mother would know best how to handle her. She didn't need Axel's two cents' worth, and she moved her hand away.

"You don't have a battle plan." He made a noise of disapproval, halfway between a grunt and a groan, and it alarmed her that his disapproval bothered her "Are you nuts?"

"I'm confident I will be able to handle any bumps in the road." She wasn't, but he didn't need to know that.

"Emma's not just a trophy you can trot out and show off. She's a real person, with feelings, flaws, and faults like anybody else."

"I know that."

"Do you?"

Seriously, was it any of his business? "Why do you care?"

"Because," he said, "I like you, and I want this to go well for you and Emma."

"I'm your therapist, not your friend."

"Um-huh." He looked smug.

"Um-huh what?" She meant to sound churlish, but instead it came out as insecure. Dammit!

"Like it or not," he gloated, "we've got something more than therapist/patient going on here."

"We do not!" she denied, hearing the panic in her voice, feeling a band of heat flare up the back of her neck. She didn't dare look at him.

The air inside the Prius was so thick with sexual tension it was hard to think.

"I'm honestly just thinking about Emma," he said. "When Dylan got to the point where he couldn't walk and had to be in a wheelchair . . . well, let's just say some kids can be cruel."

"Can we drop it, please?"

"What if Emma panics when she's faced with sudden attention from strangers?" Axel asked. "What if she gets scared?"

"I'll take her into another room and talk her down. I don't see why I need a battle plan to take a handicapped young woman to a Memorial Day party. You're overthinking it."

"You haven't been around kids much." He said it as a statement, not a question, and he was right. "I see disaster written all over this."

"Thanks for your vote of confidence."

"It's not against you, I just know how with kids a happy day can quickly go in the opposite direction."

"Good grief, Richmond. I had no idea you were such a worry-wart."

"And I didn't know you didn't have the sense to step out of the way of an oncoming train."

"It's not going to be that bad."

"I hope you're right.

"Emma is sweet and beautiful and amazing and she's my sister."

"And she's used to having your undivided attention and you're taking her to a party where she doesn't know anyone, and—"

"I get the picture." Kasha winced. "Now get out."

"What?" He blinked.

"We're here. Get out." She pointed at the passenger side door.

He glanced at his watch. "It's only three-thirty. We're not going to finish our session?"

She paused, her hand on the shifter, torn between her job and wanting to get away from him and the confounded sexual tension. Knowing that he was right about Emma. "We'll make up the time tomorrow. I'll be back bright and early. Go lie in the hammock and read a book."

"Aren't you afraid I'll get out the rebounder and sling balls around?"

"You won't. You got a good report from Dr. Harrison. You're not dumb enough to mess that up."

"You trust me." He grinned his patented heart-melting grin. "I'm touched."

"You're still not coming to the party."

"You sure? I might get bored enough to hunt down the rebounder from where you hid it. Or worse, drive to the Little League field and see if they'll let me coach."

"You wouldn't."

"Not if I had something better to do." He raked a gaze over her body. He was still sitting in the seat, not getting out.

Kasha groaned, rested her head on the steering wheel. "Okay fine, you can come to the party."

"Woot." He pumped a fist.

"Don't look so smug. You got permission by coercion."

"I never needed your permission. I was invited."

"Too bad that I have to show up."

"You don't want to go?"

"My parents throw a massive party every single holiday, and they expect all of us girls to be there if we can. They love to say that life is too short not to celebrate whenever you can. Honestly, it's a little exhausting."

"I'm an extrovert, sounds like heaven to me."

Kasha raised her chin. "But I'm not complaining. I've got the best parents in the world."

"The second time around."

Kasha flinched, ignored that. "Three days of nonstop festivities. Backyard barbecue, Mom makes these amazing apple fritters, party favors, games, toasts, and on Memorial Day itself, a picnic at the Stardust Veterans Memorial Park."

"How do they afford it?"

"Oh, everyone who comes to the party brings something, and/or contributes money. Sometimes my folks bring in more than they spend, but they just put the money toward the next party."

"And you're going to walk Emma into this hubbub without a plan?"

"Will you let it go? It's my deal."

"You're a planner, Kasha. Why haven't you planned for this?

Why haven't you told your folks about Emma? Why didn't you tell them the minute you found out about her?"

She'd been wrestling with the same questions, unsure of why she was so reluctant.

"I don't know."

"I do."

She stared at him. "Oh yeah?"

"You wanted something that was all yours just for a little while. Your family, while fantastic, are a bit intrusive, and you needed space and distance to sort things out."

She hadn't realized it until he said it, but it was true. "Maybe."

"A secret sister all your own."

Her only living blood kin.

"But then the secret scared you, and you felt bad for keeping quiet, but it was hard for you to share your news because it made you feel too much, and out of control, and there's nothing you hate more than being out of control."

"Wow." Okay. It was as if he'd peeled off the top of her head and crawled right down into her brain.

"We have been seeing a lot of each other," he explained. "What I can't figure out is why you're so scared of losing control."

That was the real secret, wasn't it? The truth about what had happened to her biological parents, the terrible catalyst for every bad thing that had happened in her life.

And she wasn't about to tell him. Not now anyway. Not as long as he was her patient. It was too much sharing. Too intimate. Too personal.

Because right now, with the way he was looking at her full of understanding and insight, all she wanted to do was fling herself into his arms, and confess everything.

God, why had she gone to lunch with him? She'd known it was a mistake and she'd done it anyway. What was wrong with her?

"Get out of the car." Her voice came out like a huff of helium, high and tight.

He clicked his tongue, his eyes full of roguish charm. "Bossy woman. What in the hell am I going to do with you?"

Make love to me.

The unexpected thought jolted her, then filled her with alarm. No! No! She believed she'd gotten that destructive impulse under control, but here it was, stronger than ever.

Why was her treacherous subconscious trying to undo her? Did she want to get fired? Was she losing touch with reality? Why was she fantasizing about a man who was on his way out of her life? Warning. Danger ahead. Stop. Turn back.

"Please," she said, on a desperate whisper. "Get out of the car."

And finally, thankfully, he did.

CHAPTER 13

Plagued by her mounting alarm and Axel's stunning insight, Kasha returned to Timeless Treasures with shaky hands and a leaden heart.

"Where's Mom?" Kasha asked Suki, who was behind the checkout counter. A few customers were browsing the aisles.

"She went home to lie down. She's got a headache and wanted to nip it in the bud before it turned into a migraine," Suki said, without glancing up from the stool where she sat making skeleton key necklaces.

"Oh."

"By the way, I had several people taste your wine and they all say it's nasty. I think I'll pitch it out."

Kasha's pulse quickened at the thought of that sweet wine getting dumped. "No need. You could stick the bottle in the trunk of my car."

A sly light lit Suki's eyes. "No sense in that when I can take care of it for you."

"I'd like to keep the bottle. It's pretty."

"Aha!" Suki gloated, hopping off the stool and pointing an accusing finger at Kasha. "The wine did taste good to you. I knew you were lying."

"Throw the bottle away or not." Kasha shrugged, donned her hippest don't-care stare. "Totally up to you."

"Yogis are supposed to be truthful. Tell me the truth, did the wine taste good to you?"

"No." That was the truth. The wine wasn't merely good. To her, it tasted splendid, grand, magnificent, glorious, excellent, the most perfect wine ever bottled. "Good" didn't begin to cover it.

"Hmph." Suki stared at her hard, sank her hands on her hips.

"I'm going over to the house to check on Mom."

"You're no fun." Suki looked disappointed and went back to bending a ring clasp on a silver chain with a pair of jeweler's pliers.

Kasha went out the back door of Timeless Treasures, down the steps, over the stepping stone pathway, out the white picket fence, and into the yard of the Victorian house on the other side of the alley.

"Mom," she called, as she entered through the back door.

"In here, sweetheart." Her mother's voice drifted from the living room.

Kasha walked in to find her mother sitting in the lounge chair, an ice pack on her forehead, a bottle of ibuprofen and a tube of analgesic ointment on the tray table beside her.

"That bad?"

"Darn headache has been nibbling at me all morning. Trying to get ahead of a migraine. This is a holiday weekend, and I still have lots of work to do." Mom sighed. "But what are you doing here? Where's Axel?"

"He's back at the ranch. Would you like me to massage your temples?"

"Oh, that would be heavenly, sweetheart. Thank you so much."

Kasha went into the kitchen, got a chair, and brought it back. She put Mom's lounger in full recline position. After arranging the kitchen chair at the head of the lounger, she sat down to rub Mom's temples.

"Ahh," her mother said. "You've got the magic touch."

"Why didn't you tell me about the migraine when we came into the store earlier?" Kasha applied gentle pressure.

"You were with Axel," Mom said. "I didn't want to get in the way."

"You're never in the way. Family is family."

Her mother sucked in a deep breath, and Kasha eased off the pressure. Might as well go ahead and tell her about Emma. They were alone, no interruptions.

She cleared her throat. Was now really the right time when Mom was fighting off a migraine?

"How have things been?" Mom asked. "You've been quieter than usual the last few weeks."

Her mother's familiar vanilla-scented cologne filled Kasha's nose. She'd always associated that soft scent with kind, tranquil love. "The new job has its challenges. There's that long drive for one thing."

"When are you going to get an apartment in Dallas?"

This was it. The perfect segue.

Um, Mom, you remember my real—er . . . biological father? Well, it seems that twenty-three years ago he left his sperm with someone besides my biological mother.

"I was waiting until I got off probation."

"But you're off probation now, right? Because of all the success you had with Axel? That's what Breeanne said Rowdy told her. Is that right?"

"Yes, but it just happened on Thursday. I'm not jumping into anything."

"You were always our most cautious daughter," Mom murmured. "But all those road miles are taking a toll on your car. Although I do hate to see you leave Stardust."

Kasha stroked her mother's forehead.

Tell her.

She hesitated. Bit her lip. And thought about what Axel had said. That she enjoyed having a secret because it was something that was all her own.

"Axel seems like a really nice guy," Mom said.

"He is."

"Handsome too."

"Mom," Kasha warned. "Don't play matchmaker. He's my client."

"But if he wasn't your client?" her mother asked, her voice rising as if catching a hopeful updraft.

"Moot point. He is." Her gut tightened.

Silence stretched between them. Kasha tried to think of something casual to say, but all she could think about was Emma.

"May I ask you a question?" Mom reached up to touch her arm.

Kasha wanted to say no because she feared it was going to be about Axel, but she couldn't say that. "Sure."

"Why did you go to work for the Gunslingers?"

"Working for the Gunslingers is an excellent opportunity. Extra money. Wonderful insurance," Kasha said mildly.

"You've never been the kind of person who was motivated by money." Mom's voice grew lower, slower. "You're my most grounded child. Down to earth. No stars in your eyes. You understand what's truly important."

She felt like such a traitor by her instant connection to Emma, her need for blood family. Oh damn, she should have told her parents the minute Howard Johnson called her about Emma.

Her mother pushed the button on the recliner to lower the legs and raise the back of the chair. "But you loved your job at the hospital. You were head of the department and they haven't found a replacement. You love Stardust. There's got to be more behind the job change than money."

Kasha could barely push scratchy words up her throat and over her lips. "There is."

Her mother's eyes were soft, accepting, gentle. "I knew something had been eating on you. Whatever you have to tell me, sweetheart, it's going to be okay. I promise."

The secret she'd been pushing back for seven weeks burst from her in a torrent of words. She told her mother everything. About how shocked she'd been at Howard Johnson's call, her fears, her shame, her joy.

She talked about the moment she'd been introduced to Emma, about the instant connection she'd felt, how incredible it had been when Emma flung herself into Kasha's arms and proudly crowed, "My titter!"

She admitted why she'd taken the job with the Gunslingers, and her heartfelt desire to get custody of Emma, and bring her into her life forever.

Throughout it all, the love in her mother's eyes never wavered. Why had she been so afraid? And it was only when Mom handed her a tissue that Kasha realized soft, slow tears were rolling down her cheeks.

She never cried. Why was she crying?

Her mother pulled her into her arms, held her tightly, whispered against her neck. "Shh, shh, it's all right, sweetheart. It's okay."

"You're not mad at me for keeping Emma a secret from you for so long?"

"Not at all. I just wish you had told me so that you didn't have to go through all that by yourself, but I honor your right to deal with this in the way that's best for you."

"I'm sorry I—"

"You have nothing to apologize for." Her mother leaned over to kiss her forehead.

"My old family crap is bleeding over into your life," Kasha said, resting her head on her mother's shoulder. "That's not fair to you and Dad."

"None of that was your fault, Kasha. You can't take on your biological parents' sins as your own. You're completely innocent." Mom squeezed her tightly. "I can't imagine how shocking that must have been for you to learn your father had a child out of wedlock when married to your mother. That you have a biological half sister."

Kasha bobbed her head. "Even worse, all these years Emma was right here in Stardust and I never knew about her."

"I suppose after all that happened, Emma's mother wanted to lie low and stay out of the limelight," Mom mused. "Although I can't believe the police didn't find out about her during all that—"

"The case was pretty open and shut." Kasha swallowed. "I guess there wasn't much reason to explore my mother's motives beyond the obvious."

"Are you doing okay? This didn't bring up any of your old . . ." Her mother's gaze dropped to Kasha's thighs, to the site of her darkest shame. ". . . issues?"

Kasha ran her palms over her upper thighs. Closed her eyes, swallowed hard. Thank God, she no longer had the impulse to cut herself. "I conquered that a long time ago. With help from you and Dad."

"It was yoga that pulled you out of it."

"But you were the one who enrolled me in my first yoga class."

"Have you told Jodi and Breeanne and Suki about Emma?"

"No."

"You poor dear. You've been holding this inside?"

"I told Axel," she confessed.

For a flicker of a moment, her mother looked hurt, but she quickly recovered and tacked on a smile. "That's understandable. You're around him all day long and it's often easier to tell a stranger something this personal than your own family."

"Thank you for supporting me."

"Always, darling. Forever." Her mother straightened. "Now for the tough part. Are you really sure petitioning the court for custody of Emma is what you truly want?"

"I have no doubt in my mind, but the lawyer insisted that before I make the final decision, I bring Emma home to stay with me for a couple days."

"That's wise. There are a lot of challenges involved in caring for a young adult with disabilities."

"I'm not going to abandon Emma just because she's got challenges." Kasha straightened her shoulders. "Where would the four of us girls be if you and Dad had shied away from our challenges?"

"I'm not suggesting that," Mom said. "But you should know what you're getting into. For Emma's sake as much as your own."

"That's what Howard Johnson said."

"It's only smart. Raising children is not an easy task, and from what you've said, Emma will be perpetually eight years old."

Kasha rubbed two fingers over her mouth. "Did you ever regret adopting the four of us? Especially considering Breeanne's heart condition and me with my . . . ." Kasha waved a hand at her thighs, indicating the deep scars hidden by her pants.

"Never!" Mom said fiercely. "Not for a second. You girls fill our lives with so much love. Hard times only made the good times that much sweeter."

"That's what I want to have with Emma," Kasha said. "That's why I'm already in one hundred percent. Taking her for the holiday is only a formality."

"I think that's so noble of you."

"I'm not doing it to be noble, Mom. I'm doing it because I truly love her. Until I met her, I didn't understand how it was possible to love someone so quickly and absolutely, but I do."

"Now you know how I feel about you girls." Her mother patted her hand. "When will you gain legal custody of her?"

"I'm going to call the lawyer on Monday."

"Assuming everything goes well this weekend?"

"I'm calling either way. I want her. But . . ."

"But what?"

Kasha cleared her throat. "I'm afraid of jeopardizing my job with the Gunslingers and if that happens, I won't be able to afford to pay adult day care for Emma. Even at my old job it would have been tight, which was why I applied with the Gunslingers in the first place."

"Why would your job be in jeopardy?"

"Axel," she whispered.

"What about him?"

"I have . . . inappropriate feelings for him."

"Ahh," her mother said, "and how does he feel about you?"

"Mom, that's not the point. He's my patient. It's unethical of me to have feelings for my clients."

"The feelings aren't unethical, but acting on those feelings are. Kasha, are you afraid you're going to act on those feelings?"

She nodded.

"You're not going to act on those feelings. You're an ethical person."

"I can't be certain of that. These feelings . . ." She couldn't bring herself to finish the sentence.

"You're afraid of being like your biological mother." Mom said it as a statement, not a question.

"Yes."

"I know that thought has tormented you for years, but you are not like her."

"She had a mental illness," Kasha said. "My biological father probably did too. You can't deny DNA."

"Nurture is just as important. You're a strong woman, Kasha. You are in control of your destiny. But no matter what happens, your father and I, and your sisters too, are always in your corner. You don't have to go it alone. We're here for you. If you need someone to look after Emma, we can pitch in."

"The dilemma is eating me up. If I stay on as Axel's therapist, I'm terrified I won't be able to stop myself if I'm tempted. But if I quit the Gunslingers, I won't have enough money to support Emma."

"So it comes down to finances. You're not with the Gunslingers because you love the job."

"While I enjoy the job, I'm there because of the paycheck and the benefits. But there's even more to it than that. I'm afraid if I leave the team, Axel will go ahead with the surgery and not give himself the time and space he needs to heal."

"Isn't that up to Axel?"

"Yes, but without me on his side, he's more likely to give in to pressure from the general manager and have the surgery."

"So you're going to base what's right for your life on Axel's career?" Mom asked.

Kasha entwined her fingers in her lap. "I hadn't thought about it like that."

"It's not as if you're in Jodi's and Breeanne's situation. Their husbands' lives do affect their own. But you're single. Why are you choosing his needs over your own? Has Axel given you any indication that he feels the same way about you?"

"He's made it clear he's attracted to me, but he knows a relationship is impossible as long as I'm his therapist."

"Is this attraction more than just physical?"

For me it is. "I don't know."

"That's something for you to get very clear about before you act on anything."

"I know." Kasha hitched in a deep breath. "Okay, say I did leave the Gunslingers. How do I afford to go for custody of Emma?"

"How does anyone afford children? How did your father and I keep expanding our family when there were times we could barely keep our heads above water? We found a way. Every single time we were up against it and didn't know what we were going to do, somehow we found a way."

"Love will find a way, huh?"

"Not to sound like too much of a cliché, but yes. Love will always find a way. Your father and I, your sisters, our friends, the community. We'll all rally around you. Don't let finances make the decision for you. Listen to what's in your heart." Her mother patted her own heart. "Your heart always knows the right answer."

"Thank you." Salty emotions gathered at the back of her throat. "Truly. I can't tell you how grateful I am that you chose to be my mother."

"Honey, don't you get it? Emma is just one more person to love. Of course we'll help you with her. Forever always." Mom leaned over to hug her tight. "Now, do you want to tell your father and your sisters the news, or should I?"

CHAPTER 14

Kasha spent the night at her parents' house. They had a long discussion about her past and Emma, and they reassured her that they would help any way they could as she assumed custody of her sister.

By the time she arrived at the ranch on Saturday morning for Axel's therapy session, she felt both relieved and recommitted to keeping a tight leash on her emotions. She could resist her attraction to Axel. She would.

When there wasn't an answer, she remembered that the Creedys were out of town for the weekend. But where was Axel?

Concerned that he might have slipped back into old habits and was pushing himself too hard again, she slipped around the back of the house, went through the gate, and walked past the pool. Her gaze penetrated the glass building, searching the workout machinery for Axel's ripped, bare-chested body.

It took her a minute to find him because he was not on a machine. Nor was he, as she feared, outside throwing balls into the rebounder without her supervision.

Finally, she spied him. He was sitting in one corner of the gym, an art easel in front of him with his fully clothed back to her. He was intent in his work as sunlight flooded the canvas.

Painting.

He was painting. He'd taken her at her word, and gotten involved in a hobby. Would you look at that? Progress.

Kasha stepped closer, watching him paint. He was in the beginning of a project, the subject as yet to be revealed. Strong, controlled movements, the paintbrush an extension of him, languid strokes; his whole body fully engaged. He was painting in oil, gliding the hessian surface with a broad flat brush, weaving a banner of soft yellow over the existing dark merlot, the tip dancing, conducting an engaging interplay of light and dark.

Awestruck, Kasha stepped closer to the glass wall.

Clearly, this was not a new skill. He'd been painting for a while, and he did it the same way he pitched, with everything he had in him—passionately, wholeheartedly. Standing outside the building, watching him work, encapsulated, engulfed, Kasha felt strangely isolated, and nostalgic for something she'd never had.

He was in a world of his own. Intense. Focused. Persistent. Impassioned. Even through the distance of the glass, she could feel his energy, and his joy. He pulsed with it.

And Kasha was jealous. She wanted what he had, even as she feared it with every fiber of her being.

"Should I bring you a bib?"

Kasha jumped, spun around, saw Breeanne standing behind her, grinning. Sheepishly, she straightened, and tried to come up with a reason she was spying on Axel.

"I've never seen you drool over a guy," Breeanne mused.

"I wasn't . . . I'm not . . . it's not . . ."

"Or stammer for that matter." Breeanne looked like she'd found a secret door leading to a cave filled with pirate treasure. "It's cute."

"Good grief, Bree, he's my patient!"

"Which is what makes your fan-girl crush so absolutely adorable." Breeanne clapped her hands together in delight.

"I do not have a crush on Axel Richmond."

"Uh-huh."

"What are you doing here?" Kasha asked, shifting the subject, spinning things back under her control.

"Um . . . let's see. This is my house too since I married Rowdy."

"Why aren't you in Dallas with your husband?"

"I've never missed one of Mom and Dad's Memorial Day parties. Plus they were going to help me start the adoption process."

Oh yeah, that. Kasha felt a twinge of guilt for being so wrapped up in her own problems she'd forgotten about Breeanne's fertility issues.

The sound of their conversation must have seeped into the gym, because Axel turned from the easel, his eyes still glassy from the dreamy zone of artistic creation. But as soon as her gaze met his, Axel's pupils widened, and a slow, easy grin—like the sun coming out after a long round of thunderstorms—broke across his face.

Kasha's insides turned to jelly, all sweet and melty, and she thought, *Oh hellz to the no.* But she was already a goner and she knew. Had known it for days now.

It's okay. Just because you feel it doesn't mean you have to act on it.

"Ooh," Breeanne said. "He's looking at you the same way you're looking at him." And then she started humming "Crazy Little Thing Called Love."

"Stop it," Kasha mumbled from the side of her mouth as Axel got up from the easel and waved to them.

Breeanne launched into the lyrics, altering them to suit the situation. "Kasha just can't handle it."

"Sister, I love you to the full extent of your life, but I swear if you don't knock it off . . ." Kasha knotted her fists teasingly.

"I'll leave you to him." Breeanne snickered and made a beeline for the house.

"Don't you dare run out on me! Get back here. Don't leave me alone with him."

"Call me and tell me all about it later," Breeanne called over her shoulder and disappeared inside.

Her heart jackhammered. She wanted to tell him to stop being so charming, but that would call attention to the fact he'd beguiled her. She was beguiled. Dammit.

A smiling Axel opened the door. His body strong and hard. His brown eyes lively under thick black lashes. Every cell in her body vibrated and hummed.

"Hey, you," he said.

"Um . . . hey."

"Where did Breeanne go?"

"She had . . ." Kasha flapped a hand over her shoulder. ". . . a thing."

Axel's eyes grazed her body from the top of her head to the feet shod in sensible work flats, but he was looking at her as if she were dressed like a calendar pinup girl. "How long have you been standing here?"

"Uh . . . just walked up."

He shook his head. He wore a pair of old gray cotton gym shorts and a plain white T-shirt dotted with flecks of paint. For the first time since she met him, he looked utterly and completely relaxed. It was a delicious look for him. "Fibber."

"It's the truth," she said stubbornly."

"I could see your reflection in the chrome of the exercise equipment," he said. "You've been here for several minutes."

"If you knew I'd been standing out here for a while, then why did you ask?"

"I wanted to see if you'd tell me that you were spying on me." His tone teased.

"I wasn't spying. How I could I be spying? You were in a glass room. Anyone walking by could see you."

"Whatever you have to tell yourself." He was smirking now.

"You don't have to be so smug about it."

"You enjoy watching," he accused.

She smiled.

"Voyeur."

"You've been holding out on me. You said you weren't passionate about anything but baseball."

"Baseball is my love." His smile softened. "Painting is my therapy."

"How long have you been painting?" she asked, struggling to keep from ogling him.

"Since I was five years old. My mother is an artist, and she gave me an art set for my birthday, and from the moment I picked up the brush, it felt natural."

"You have so much talent," she marveled. "Why did you choose baseball as a career over art?"

"Baseball was something my dad and I did together," he said, his tone full of nostalgia, "and then later with my friends, and Little League. Art is solitary. I guess I'm just an extrovert at heart."

"It was the sense of community that won you over?"

"That and I really love baseball."

When he grinned, she could see him as a gap-toothed seven-year-old with a recalcitrant cowlick, and her heart gave a crazy little skip that terrified her. "And you don't love painting?"

"I do, but I knew I would never be as good at art as I am at baseball."

"Why didn't you tell me about your painting before?"

He gave a boyish shrug as if to say, *Sharing ruins it*. "I do it just for me."

"It's private."

"Yeah."

"I get that."

"Do you?" He stepped closer, his gaze hooked on her lips.

Her pulse quickened, and her breath shortened. Purposefully, she lengthened her exhales, getting back on keel, asserting control. "Privacy keeps it sacred."

"What about you?" he murmured.

"What about me?"

"What sacred things don't you share?"

"If I shared them, they would no longer be sacred."

"Think of it as a bonding exercise," he said. "I know you're a physical therapist, and you love yoga, and that you have an illegitimate half sister who lives in a group home, and you haven't told your family about her yet . . ."

"Actually, I told my parents about Emma last night." She tried to keep her voice level, which was hard to do when unexpressed emotions torqued her chest up tight.

"How did it go?"

She met his eyes. "Better than I expected. Stirred up some tough memories, but we worked through it."

"Wanna talk about it?"

She toyed with the end of her braid. "No."

"Okay." He took measure of her. "Got anything else you want to share? Those tough memories?"

"Not really."

"It's not fair. You know my secret, and I know nothing about yours. We've got an imbalance of power."

"We already had an imbalance of power." She folded her arms, cupped opposite elbows with her palms. "I'm in charge of your healing."

"So." He lowered his voice, leaned in. "Let's level the playing field."

"You feeling vulnerable with all your secrets exposed?"

"Exactly." His eyes twinkled.

She shook her head, but she couldn't ignore him. The man was so alive, so compelling, so freaking hot.

"Come on," he cajoled, tapping his ear with an index finger. "Whisper to me. Your secrets are safe. I won't tell another soul."

His grin was so beguiling that she was coaxed to tell him something small and inconsequential. Kasha lowered her voice, her eyelashes, and her reserve.

"Tell me."

"Promise not to laugh."

"I promise."

"Shh." Her laugh came out huskier than she intended, and she couldn't quite tear her gaze from his, ensnared in a sweet spell she had no business being caught in. "When I was thirteen, I had a major crush on Nick Carter."

"From the Backstreet Boys?"

"That'd be the one," she admitted.

"Ain't no shame in crushin' on the boyz," Axel joked. "Number one boy band ever."

"How would you know the first thing about boy bands?"

"Because teenage girls compare teenage boys to the musicians in their favorite bands."

"Ahh. Makes sense."

They looked at each other and grinned, intrigued by the new secrets they'd found out. Her heart, so long held caged, safe from romantic emotions, filled with the most delirious kind of hope.

"Whenever you smile, Sphinx, it makes me feel as if heaven opened up and rained down gold."

"Ouch," she said, delighted and slightly embarrassed by the adoring expression on his face. "That sounds painful."

"Not at all." He leaned in, all muscles and male. "It hurts so good."

What did he mean? What was he suggesting?

"Axel," she whispered.

"Kasha," he whispered back, his face on fire with light and energy.

She smelled sunshine and oil paint and Axel. She wanted to feel the scrape of his sexy beard stubble against her cheek, to taste his heated lips. As she stared into his beautiful dark eyes, almost the color of her own, she could have sworn she heard harps playing and angels singing. And felt the warm, strong grip of his imaginary embrace.

Too much.

It was all too much. Here she was again, taking a magic carpet ride to fantasyland.

She stepped back to clear her head, clear the air of the seductive sexual current sweeping them both along.

"Well," she said, shaking herself out. "Put away the paints and canvas. It's time to get down to work."

THEY WORKED OUTSIDE in the shade that morning, playing underhanded catch, doing exercises designed to specifically target his type of shoulder injury, practicing beginning yoga poses, following it up with Kasha guiding him through a meditation while he lay in a hammock underneath the trees.

Axel tried his best to shut down his sexual feelings for Kasha, but he was a lost cause. He wanted the woman. Fiercely.

Breeanne came out with a picnic lunch and blanket, but didn't stay to eat with them. "I'm headed over to Mom and Dad's," she explained.

Axel spread out the blanket near the flower garden, sat down, and started laying out the food—pasta salad, raw veggies and dip, fresh fruit—light, healthy fare.

"Nice of her to make us lunch," he said.

"That's Breeanne," Kasha said, hues of admiration, respect and love for her sister in her eyes. "She always puts the needs of others first, even as a kid when she went through heart surgery after heart surgery."

"You're lucky to have her."

"I know," Kasha said, her voice growing huskier, softer. "Things could have gone so differently for me if I hadn't—"

She broke off, and busied herself with peeling a banana, and Axel couldn't help wondering if she'd been on the verge of telling him about how she'd come to live with the Carlyles. The urge to protect her fisted around his spine, hard and insistent. He hadn't felt protective like this about anyone since . . .

Well, since Dylan.

That drew him up short. What did his feeling mean?

Axel studied her.

She was watching butterflies flit among the blooms, her face soft and peaceful, fully absorbed by the beautiful float and grace of the insects. How did she achieve it, this sublime mindfulness?

The breeze ruffled her hair that had fallen loose from her braid, and rippled the material of her white silk blouse. The scent of her shampoo—floral and sweet—drifted over to him, and he admired the way the sun threw dappled lighting through the tree leaves to pepper her caramel skin with a creamy glow.

In that moment, Axel *knew* he had to have her. Not just in his bed. Not just for one night. But in his life.

Forever.

This was crazy. He'd never even kissed her, hardly knew her. And yet it felt as if he'd known her intimately all his life. They had a special, indefinable connection.

Question was how did he convince her? Not to mention, how

did he fit her into his life? She was a small-town girl who was about to gain custody of her handicapped sister, and he was a hard-driving ballplayer with designs on pitching for the New York Yankees. How could two people with such different goals make it work?

Didn't matter. He might not know how right now, but he *would* find a way.

SOMETHING HAD SHIFTED in their relationship after Kasha discovered Axel was a closet painter. She couldn't quite put her finger on what had changed, or why, but change it had.

The formidable sexual attraction was still there; if anything, it was stronger than ever. But there was something more. Something with more weight and heft. Behind the hot, hard lust in his eyes whenever he looked at her, there was added dimension that went beyond physical desire. She didn't know what it meant, but it thrilled her and at the same time terrified her.

What was going on?

She left the ranch that afternoon feeling disoriented and giddy and worried. To calm down, she dropped in on a yoga class, which was much less attended than usual because of the Memorial Day weekend; only the diehard yogis showed up.

One thing was for sure, she needed to get herself in hand, and concentrate on what was important. Finishing this job satisfactorily so she could get custody of Emma. That was her priority. This thing with Axel could not work even if she wasn't his therapist. She was better off not even thinking about him, but even two hours of vinyasa flow could not unstick him from her mind.

She was falling hard and fast and didn't know how to climb off the merry-go-round. But she had to, because everything good in both their lives depended on it.

On Sunday morning after church services, butterflies batted against Kasha's stomach as she walked up to the group home to take Emma home for an overnight stay. She'd readied the guest room, and after consulting with Molly Banks about how she thought Emma would handle the party, she stocked her fridge and pantry with Emma's favorite foods.

The entire household met her at the door to see Emma off. Cliff handed her Emma's luggage, and Molly gave her a sack of medications.

"In the mornings," Molly said, "she takes the pink liquid for her allergies, the white pill to keep her from having seizures, and the—"

Kasha blinked. "She has seizures?"

"Not if she takes her pills," Molly said. "But I can see I'm over-whelming you. I wrote down the instructions, and put them in the sack with her meds. Feel free to call me if you have any questions. Oh, and her doctor's phone number is on the medication list."

"Uh, yes, thank you." Kasha tucked the sack under her arm, as it hit her how little she knew about her sister's medical condition.

Emma was amped up, jumping and smiling and singing a non-sense song. She wore red Bermuda shorts, a red and white striped T-shirt, and red Keds. Her hair was pulled into pigtails with red and white ribbons. Her glasses had slipped down the end of her nose and she looked utterly adorable.

"Try to calm her down if you can," Molly whispered in Kasha's ear. "It's hard to contain her if she gets spun up. Don't let her get spun up."

Spun up? What exactly did that mean?

But Kasha didn't have a chance to pull Molly aside for clarifi-cation. Emma was clutching her hand and dragging her toward the Prius parked at the curb.

Once they were loaded up and buckled into the car, Kasha turned to Emma and said, "Would you like to play a game?"

"Game!" Emma clapped her hands.

"Okay. Take a long, deep breath like this." Kasha demonstrated.

Emma studied her, then followed suit.

"Now let it out slowly." Kasha exhaled audibly.

Emma did the same.

"Here's the game. I bet you can't do that ten times in a row," Kasha said.

Emma stared at her, arms crossed over her chest, bottom lips pouched out. "Lame game."

Yes, okay, it was. "Take ten slow deep breaths and we'll go to a party."

"Party!"

"Deep breaths."

Emma ignored her.

Don't let her get spun up. Molly's words of warning echoed in Kasha's ears. What should she do?

She wasn't going to insist Emma take deep breaths when she seemed so resistant. Kasha smiled softly, and took some more deep breaths herself. If she was calm, hopefully it would calm Emma.

"Would you like to listen to music?" Kasha asked.

"Mu'ic!"

Kasha turned the satellite radio to soothing spa music.

Emma crinkled her nose, reached over, and punched buttons on the radio until she found a hard-driving hip-hop song with shocking lyrics. Satisfied, Emma settled back in the seat, those red Keds bobbing in time to the beat.

Great. From the frying pan into the fire.

She reached over to turn the music down.

"No!" Emma grunted and turned it back up, louder this time.

Um, okay. Kasha bit her bottom lip. She'd not seen Emma like this before, but everyone had off days. No doubt it was the excitement. Patience. Compassion. Understanding. That's what was needed.

Plus, picking her battles. She wasn't going to escalate things by changing the music or turning it down again. Not worth it.

Besides, Molly's warning might have prejudiced her for trouble. She was going to assume everything would work out just fine.

"We're going to have a fun day," she said to Emma.

"Fun!" Emma cried.

"Fun," Kasha agreed, and felt her tension ebb. No expectations. No pressure. She could handle whatever challenges might come her way. In fact, she would look at any glitches as opportunities to get to know Emma better.

"I love you, titter," Emma announced at the top of her voice and unbuckled her seat belt so she could lean over to hug Kasha as she drove.

"I love you too, sweetheart, but please sit down and put your seat belt back on."

Emma was practically in her lap, throwing one leg over the gear shifter and one arm around Kasha's neck, and planting a wet kiss on her temple.

Oh heavens.

Kasha eased off the accelerator and guided the car to the curb as best she could under the circumstances.

"Why we toppin'?" Emma asked.

"Because the car doesn't move unless everyone inside is sitting down with a seat belt on."

"Okay." Emma nodded agreeably, and returned to her seat.

Kasha blew out a pent-up breath. Rule established and followed. Good. Good. She started the car back up again, and Emma was a paragon of virtue for the rest of the ride to the party. Emma even reached over to turn down the music herself.

Everything was going to be all right.

THIRTY MINUTES LATER, Kasha was rethinking her decision about bringing Emma to the party.

Even though her parents, sisters, and friends tried repeatedly to encourage Emma to take part in the festivities, the girl clung to Kasha's side like a cocklebur. Every time someone spoke to Emma directly, she would wrap her arms tightly around Kasha's waist and bury her face against her side.

Not once had Kasha seen her half sister act shyly, and she wasn't prepared for it.

Belatedly, she thought about how Axel had told her to get a battle plan. She should have listened.

"Don't worry," Mom said to Kasha, as she sat at the kitchen table with a trembling Emma and a roomful of guests. "This boisterous bunch takes some getting used to. She'll come around. I've told everyone to back off and give our girl some space."

"I remember it took Kasha a while to warm up to us too," Trudy said. "Lord, that was over twenty years ago."

Kasha put her arm around Emma, and didn't try to coax her to speak.

It wasn't until Suki's cat, Callie, sauntered into the room that Emma lit up. "Kitty!" she exclaimed, and charged for the calico.

Kasha, Suki, and her mother all sprang to their feet at once. With her PTSD, Callie could be unpredictable if someone grabbed her unexpectedly, and Emma looked bent on grabbing her.

"Emma no," Kasha said, trying not to sound panicky. "Don't lunge at the kitty."

But Emma was already squatting in front of Callie, and the purring calico put her front paws up on her knees. The cat stretched out her neck and licked Emma's cheek.

Emma giggled, plopped down on her butt on the kitchen floor, and pulled the cat into her lap.

"Wow," Suki said. "I've never seen Callie take so readily to a stranger. Emma's got the magic touch."

"Kitty." Emma stroked the cat gently, and Kasha felt her shoulders relax.

Callie was the icebreaker Emma needed, and suddenly she was chattering to everyone, and things were good again.

The next trouble came when Suki went outside and Callie went with her. Emma followed the cat, and Kasha followed Emma.

And there was Axel, coming through the gate into the backyard, a bouquet of flowers in one hand, a platter of chocolate-covered strawberries in the other. He wore beige chinos and a black polo shirt, with the collar spread open, showing a bit of tanned bare chest.

Having forgotten about Axel being invited to the party, Kasha stopped, the smell of barbecue in her nose and the sound of kids splashing in the swimming pool drumming through her ears.

He looked at her.

She looked at him.

They inhaled at the same time. Drawing in the same air. Oh no.

"Why did you bring me flowers and chocolate-covered fruit?" she asked. "We're not dating. This isn't a date."

"Flowers are for your mom," he said mildly, his eyes lively with amusement. "Chocolate for the party."

"Oh," she said, feeling stupid. Things were weirdly different now, and she had no idea where they stood.

"Did you want me to bring you chocolates and flowers?"

"No, no, no, no."

"'Cause you made it clear we couldn't date or—"

"We can't. Shh. Someone will hear you."

"You're not going to get fired for talking to me, Sphinx."

"I know. I'm just . . . thrown seeing you out of place."

"You mean on your home turf."

"I didn't think you'd really come," she said.

"Is that Emma?" he asked, motioning with his chin since his hands were occupied.

Kasha turned to see Emma talking to three neighborhood ten-year-old girls who appeared to have crashed the party without their parents. "Yes."

"Can I meet her?"

"Relieve yourself of produce first."

"Good idea."

She walked with him to the back door and into the house, casting a glance over her shoulder at Emma. Gentle Breeanne took Emma's hand and guided her over to the tire swing. And Kasha realized this party would stand out as one of the most pivotal days of her life.

It was the beginning of the change. Once she had custody of Emma, there would be no going back. Things would never be the same.

But she wasn't in this alone. Her family had her back, and by extension, they also had Emma's.

Breeanne pushed Emma in the tire swing. The girl pumped her legs and grasped the rope with both hands; her teeth sank into her bottom lip as if she were concentrating for all she was worth.

Kasha waited at the screen door, keeping one eye on Axel, one on Emma, while her mother gushed over Axel's flowers, and set the strawberries on the sideboard already laden with a massive amount of food.

"How's she doing?" Axel asked close to her ear, his chin hovering over her shoulder as he leaned in to follow her gaze.

Kasha jumped, not realizing he'd snuck up on her. "Rocky start, but things are looking up."

"That's the thing about rocks, eventually they smooth out."

"That sounds uncharacteristically philosophical."

"Maybe I'm starting to see the light at the end of the tunnel." He rotated his shoulder. "Thanks to you."

"Want some lunch?" she asked.

"Those burgers your dad is flipping are making my stomach rumble. Okay if I eat meat?"

"Free country," she said, and toed the screen door open, feeling swoony and claustrophobic from being so close to him.

He followed her down the steps, right on her heels. She could feel him behind her, big and imposing.

"Emma," she called.

Emma was sitting at the picnic table with the three neighborhood ten-year-olds, who were eating watermelon slices and seeing how far they could spit the seeds.

Kasha got an uneasy feeling about the three girls, who were usually quite cliquish. Why were they being so chummy with Emma? "Come here a minute. There's someone I want you to meet."

"Is she your mom?" one of the girls said to Emma. "If she's not your mom, you don't have to do what she says."

"My titter," Emma explained proudly.

"Ahmm, you said 'tit.'" Another girl slapped her hand over her mouth, a calculating gleam in her eyes.

"What's a titter?" giggled the third girl. "Is it anything like a uni-boob?"

Emma's smile slipped, and she looked confused. "*Tit*-ter. 'He my titter."

"That guy is your titter?" The first girl snorted with laughter.

"Oh," said the second girl. "I get it. You don't know how to say sister. It's *sis*-ter. Repeat after me, *sis, sis, sis.*"

"Tit, tit, tit," Emma said.

The three girls were laughing so hard they clasped their bellies and one even rolled right off the picnic bench.

Tears filled Emma's eyes, as she kept crying out, "Tit, tit, tit."

Overwhelmed by a protective rage balling up in the back of her chest, Kasha forcefully exhaled. She wanted to snatch up those tacky girls and toss them out of the yard by the scruff of their necks.

"Emma," she said. "Please, come here."

"Easy there, Mama Hen." Axel put a restraining hand on Kasha's shoulder. "I've got this."

He sauntered over to the picnic table, moving with the loose hips and low-slung gait of a gunslinger.

The three ten-year-olds suddenly didn't look so smug or cocky. They squirmed and glanced down at their watermelon slices. He sat down across from them, right beside Emma. Kasha stood watching him, anxiety climbing up her throat.

"Hello young ladies," he said, his voice light, upbeat, but his eyes dark as thunder.

The girls mumbled, shifted, did everything but meet his gaze. They got up, were about to sidle off when he pointed at the bench. "Sit."

They exchanged uncertain glances.

"Sit," he invited in an obey-me tone.

Simultaneously, all three of them plunked back down.

"I know you girls were just teasing Emma, but I think you might have hurt her feelings. Apologize."

The boldest girl finally raised her eyes to meet Axel's cool stare. "I'm sorry."

"Not to me." Axel's voice was as flat, hard, and level as an anvil. "To Emma."

Kasha's pulse thumped double time. What should she do?

"Sorry," the girl muttered in Emma's direction.

"Not good enough," Axel said amicably. "Tell her why you're sorry."

"Sorry we made fun of the way you talk." The girl tossed her hair.

"It okay." Emma bobbed her head.

"Now you." Axel nodded at the second girl, pointed at the third. "And then you."

Looking unhappy about it, the other two girls apologized.

"Wow," Suki whispered from behind Kasha. "He's my hero."

Mine too. Kasha's heart swelled against her rib cage.

"You should be jumping his bones," Suki said. "Why aren't you jumping his bones?"

"He's my patient," Kasha murmured.

"So quit that job."

"Can we go now?" The first girl raised an insolent chin.

Axel nodded. "But I'm watching you. Toe the line."

The girls got up to leave.

"Don't go." Emma wailed in distress.

The girls turned. Emma chased after them. The girls linked arms and took off.

"Wait, wait for me," Emma cried.

Kasha's stomach roiled, and she went after her sister. "Emma, let's have some ice cream."

The girls slipped through the back gate and hustled down the alley. The gate swung closed behind them, leaving Emma in the backyard, fat tears rolling down her cheeks.

"Wait," she called after the girls. "Wait for me!"

Kasha snagged Emma's elbows before she could push through the gate in pursuit of the girls. "There's homemade ice cream. Let's go get some."

"No!" Emma shrieked, and shook off Kasha's arm.

Kasha was acutely aware that people were watching them. She lowered her voice, flashed the biggest smile she could muster. "Strawberry," she coaxed. "Molly told me you loved strawberry ice cream."

Emma's bottom lip protruded in a petulant pout, and she crossed her arms over her chest, a deep frown cleaving between her eyebrows. "No!"

"We have cookies too. Chocolate chip."

Emma's eyes widened. She glanced down the alley to the backs of the departing girls, and then swung her gaze back to Kasha. "No!"

"Then let's go put on your swimsuit so we can go swimming." Kasha took Emma's arm again, gently but firmly, and tried to guide her half sister toward the house.

"No!" Emma rooted her feet into the ground, solid as stone. Clenched her jaw. Narrowed her eyes. Defiantly wrenched her arm from Kasha's grasp. Balled up her fists. Things were escalating fast.

What now?

Feeling every eye in the yard watching them, Kasha sucked in a fortifying breath. It was starting to dawn on her what it was going to be like to take care of an eight-year-old in an adult's body.

Gone was the sweet young woman Kasha had encountered on her visits to the group home. Emma changed before her eyes, growing hostile and churlish. The same girl who, less than an hour ago, had pressed herself shyly against Kasha's side and clung to her for comfort was becoming aggressive and angry.

Emma planted two palms against Kasha's chest and shoved.

Hard.

If Kasha hadn't been so adept at maintaining her balance she would have fallen backward at the force. As it was, she teetered, wobbled, but quickly righted herself.

Hurt and disappointment flooded her body. Her mouth tasted metallic. Her blood went icy with alarm.

Don't take it personally, she reminded herself.

This wasn't about her. This was about Emma. She'd taken the girl from the safety and structure of the group home and dropped her into a stimulating environment with strangers. What had she expected was going to happen?

Had she expected rainbows and unicorns and cotton candy skies?

Unwise. It had been unwise of her to bring Emma into a crowd on her very first visit.

She'd told Howard Johnson she was prepared for the challenges that came along with custody of her half sister. It was time to put her money where her mouth was. Prove it.

From the corner of her eyes, she saw Axel moving toward them as if to intervene, but Kasha held up a restraining palm. *I've got this.*

He nodded and stepped back, but never took his eyes off them.

Kasha switched back to hold her sister's belligerent gaze. "Emma," she said quietly, calmly. "We don't shove. It's not nice."

Emma's bottom lip quivered.

"I know you're scared," Kasha murmured. "I know those girls hurt your feelings."

"I . . ." Tears misted Emma's eyes, and all the fight went out of her. Her shoulders slumped and she hung her head. "I not normal."

Kasha's heart broke. Just broke right in two pieces. Emma knew she was different, and Kasha couldn't fix it.

"You are exactly who you are meant to be, sweetheart," Kasha cooed. "You are perfect just as you are."

"I bad. I puhed you."

"We all do things we shouldn't do when we're hurt and scared and upset. It's okay. It's going to be all right."

"I torry." Tears streamed down Emma's face. "I torry Ka'cha. I torry."

"Oh, Emma. I'm sorry too." Kasha opened her arms and enveloped her sister in a hug.

Emma wrapped her arms around Kasha, buried her face against her breasts, and sobbed for all she was worth.

Kasha held her tight. Embraced her. Embraced the bittersweet moment full of dread and shame and disappointment and understanding and healing and forgiveness.

For Emma.

For herself.

For them both.

Kasha held her sister for a long moment, blocked out everyone and everything else around them. Existed for a time in the perfectness of those few minutes.

Not judging. No more expectations. Just accepting what was.

Those serene ticks of the clock were calm, blissful, and huge.

Finally, Emma's sobs subsided.

"Would you like to go swimming now?" Kasha whispered. They could fix this. The day could be salvaged. "Or would you like ice cream and cookies? What would you like to do?"

Emma pulled back, looked up into Kasha's eyes, her face rippling with uncertainty and worry and fear. "Ka'cha," she said. "I wanna go home. Plea take me home."

CHAPTER 15

"Don't stress about it," Molly said when Kasha returned Emma to the group home after the incident at the party. "It's the first time she's been out for a visit with anyone since her mother got sick. I expected this."

The minute Emma was back in her environment, she was her old smiling self. Warm, affectionate, happy.

"It takes time." Molly rested a kind hand on Kasha's shoulder. "Give it time."

"Thank you for that. I realize now the party was way too much."

"Would you like to try again next week? Maybe just the two of you?"

Kasha took a steadying breath. "Can I get back to you on that?"

Molly's eyes clouded, and her lips thinned. "You're not going to let this chase you off?"

"Oh no, no. I just need some time to . . . regroup."

"I understand." Molly's tone changed. Grew tight, clipped.

"It's not Emma," Kasha explained. "It was my unrealistic expectations."

"Please don't walk out of her life, because I know that would be so easy to do."

"I'm not. I won't. Ever!" Kasha was stunned that Molly would believe that of her. "I just need to figure some things out."

Molly gave a muted smile. "We'll be here whenever you're ready."

After she left the group home, Kasha returned to the party, to find Axel had already gone. And she felt strangely adrift, and empty.

She stayed for a while watching her parents welcoming guests, filling plates and drink glasses, telling lively stories: Dan and Maggie, the perfect hosts, working in harmony. Extroverts. Soul mates. A team. Forever on each other's side. Making marriage look amazingly easy despite the challenges of raising four adopted daughters, each with her own special brand of baggage.

Later in the day, Mom took her aside and gave her a pep talk about Emma, but Kasha was still feeling melancholy and went on home.

She did an hour of yoga, but couldn't clear her mind of the way things had gone with Emma at the party. She blamed herself entirely. She should never have put her half sister in that situation.

Naïve. She'd been so naïve.

After a restless night, she woke with the realization she needed time alone in nature. Nature had a way of putting life into perspective. At dawn, she pulled her kayak out of the garage, strapped it to the roof of the Prius, and headed out for Stardust Lake.

During the sticky summer months in East Texas, humidity collected on the outside of drinking glasses, melting ice and turning beverages watery in milliseconds. Wind chimes rattled sluggishly in the thick air, while lazy flies buzzed around the back door, waiting for someone to open the screen so they could slip inside. Heat shimmered off the asphalt, a wavering mirage that smelled of hot tar and motor oil. Mockingbirds nested in mimosa trees, waiting until it grew cooler to start singing. Grasshoppers leaped through the tall Johnson grass, leaving tobacco-colored spittle staining the broad blades. The scent of magnolias hugged the town in sweaty fragrance. Kids played sandlot ball. Teens loitered in parking lots. Most days of the week a procession of boats on trailers clogged the highway from town to lake.

But at that hour of the morning, even on Memorial Day, there were only two other vehicles in the boat ramp parking lot, both of them belonging to local fishermen. And the air was still cool and inviting.

She got the kayak into the water, flipped her sunglasses from the top of her head down over her eyes, fitted her cell phone into a waterproof case, put on some music, stuck earbuds into her ears, and cast off.

Natalie Imbruglia was whispering in her ear, "Torn" and Kasha joined right in, singing at the top of her voice as she glided across the water, letting her voice loose when she was all alone in nature.

She hadn't bothered braiding her hair that morning, letting it float free and easy. The strands swung around her as she rowed, a thick cloud of hair that both vexed and delighted her. She knew she was lucky to have an abundance of hair, but it had a mind of its own.

She was in the middle of the lake when a Jet Ski zipped past her, rocking the kayak in its wake. She raised the oar and waited for the water to settle. Up ahead, the Jet Ski made a U-turn, and came barreling straight toward her.

Great. Who was this jerk?

Kasha scowled and narrowed her eyes, prepared to get his AZ number. Just before the Jet Ski reached her, the driver killed the engine, and the craft glided alongside her and she stared into Axel Richmond's grinning mug.

"What are you doing out on a Jet Ski," she scolded, pushing her sunglasses up on her head. "You're risking your shoulder loading that thing into the water."

"Relax," he said, his voice warm and sexy. "Mr. Creedy put the Jet Ski in the water for me before he left for the weekend. When I'm done, it will stay tied at the dock until he gets back. I promise."

What could she say to that?

"So," he said, his gaze strolling over her, taking in the red bikini top and denim shorts she wore, a smile lifting his lips. "How are you doing?"

"Fine, until you splashed me with your wake," she grumbled, even though she wasn't displeased. He didn't need to know how hard her pulse strummed whenever she was around him.

"You're upset because I got you wet?"

Kasha rolled her eyes, but she did feel a distinct softening in her root chakra. Darn him. "Tuck away the clichéd innuendo, Richmond. I'm immune."

"Wanna stow your kayak and come ride with me?" he invited.

Tempted. Oh, she was tempted! "I'm fine."

His audacious eyes kept exploring her body. "Yes," he murmured. "Yes you are."

"Okay," she said. "I'm off now."

"Wait," he said. "Don't go away mad."

She wasn't mad. Far from it. She was charmed, and that was the problem. She stuck her oar in the water, waved a hand over her head, and rowed . . . smack . . . right into a large rock lurking underneath the water's surface. She plowed into it so hard, her teeth rattled.

"Sphinx?" Axel called out, alarm in his voice. "You okay?"

Um, yeah, sure, except water was pouring into the hull of her kayak. Dammit. She'd knocked a hole in the fiberglass.

Great. Super. Terrific.

Axel drifted over. "I hate to be the one to break it to you, but your boat is listing. You've sprung a leak."

"You don't say." Water was already lapping at her ankles. It was a significant hole.

"Heads up," he said.

She looked over to see him holding a rope. She reached up, and he tossed it to her. Used it to reel her over to him.

"Looks like it's fate," he said. "You and me together again."

"Looks like I wasn't watching where I was going," she corrected, but she couldn't help smiling.

"Because . . ."

"You distracted me," she said as he pulled her up alongside the Jet Ski.

His sly grin was wickedly sexy. "So it's my fault?"

"Yes. You're far too good-looking."

"Was that a compliment?"

"Don't let it go to your head."

He put out his hand to help her aboard the Jet Ski. She swung up behind him, and when her legs made contact with his, ignored the tingle between her thighs. Forcibly slowing her breathing, she reached down to tie the kayak to the Jet Ski.

"Where's your car?" he asked.

She gave him directions to the marina boat ramp where she'd left the Prius, and they took off.

When they reached the boat ramp, he docked the Jet Ski and helped her carry the kayak to her car. In the hour that she'd been on the lake, several more cars and trucks with boat trailers had pulled into the lot. People were milling around, putting their boats into the water, smearing on sunscreen, loading up picnic baskets for a day on the water.

Axel helped her carry the kayak to her car and strap it on the roof. She kept an eye on him the whole time to make sure he wasn't compromising his injured shoulder.

"Thank you." She turned to him after they had the kayak secured.

"You're leaving?" He sounded disappointed.

"The kayak is done for."

"But I've got a perfectly good Jet Ski, and no one to play with." He nailed her with his gaze, anchoring her to the spot. "Come play with me, Kasha."

She pulled her hair back into a ponytail with the ponytail holder she kept around her wrist. The ponytail swung against her back, loose and casual. He watched it swish as if mesmerized.

"Please," he said, and she could tell from the way his voice cracked that it took something from him to plead. "I don't want to be alone today."

A flash of deep emotion passed over his face. An emotion she couldn't fully decipher. It seemed part grief, part nostalgia, part loss. His hand went to his chest, but his quick, bright smile made her wonder if she'd imagined it.

But instead of refusing his invitation as she intended, Kasha found herself saying, "All right."

"You mean it?" He beamed, suddenly a boy again, happy and

carefree. To think that she could please him so easily. He made her feel both girlish and powerful.

Dumb. Really, really dumb, this illicit thrill that clipped through her.

Just for today, she promised herself. It was a holiday. Their day off. They were simply riding on a Jet Ski together. Just for today, she would let herself go, be in the moment, and have fun. She would zip herself back up after that.

They returned to the Jet Ski, and she climbed on behind him.

"Wrap your arms around my waist," he called over his shoulder as he cranked the engine.

"I'm good."

"Okay, but don't say I didn't warn you." He took off across the water at a thrilling pace.

Kasha squealed—and she most definitely was not a squealer—at the speed, and the force jerked her back so swiftly, she had no choice but to clamp her arms around his waist in order to keep from sliding off the back.

His abs were granite beneath her fingers, hard and defined and perfect. She shouldn't have enjoyed it as much as she did.

What a scene. A beautiful Memorial Day. Blue skies with just the right amount of cottage cheese clouds.

Her arms latched around the spectacularly tanned body of major league pitcher Axel Richmond as they flashed over the calm surface of the lake dotted with watercraft—three white kayaks, a long banana-yellow canoe filled with Cub Scouts in orange life vests, two sailboats, four green fishing boats, a big black brassy speedboat showing off, and at least half a dozen other Jet Skis, and Sea-Doos.

Breathless.

She was breathless.

Because she felt fully alive, and realized she couldn't ever remember feeling quite like this before.

They skimmed over the glassy surface, deft as a water glider. In the air she smelled coconut sunscreen, engine oil, fertile soil, and earthy lake. She rested her head against the left side of his back, heard his heart thumping strong and hard.

The reality of being here with him like this was as phenomenal as any girlhood fantasy—more so. Axel was a man in every sense of the word. Big. Virile. Ripe with testosterone. Sexy as a midnight tryst. And kind. He'd been so kind and good with Emma at the party. She owed him for that.

Stardust Lake, hometown waterway, was a cheery local hangout with quaint summer homes and long wooden docks just made for flipping cannonballs off of. Picnic tables squatted on retaining walls above the lake that was dotted with fishermen casting rods and reels hung with shiny lures. Bare-chested men, with cavemen smirks, wore swim trunks, and manned smokers and barbecues laden with thick slabs of meat.

They spent the entire day on the lake, taking turns driving the Jet Ski. At lunch, they beached on a small island, drank bottled water, and shared snacks they'd both brought—trail mix and apples, peanut butter and rice crackers, string cheese and red globe grapes. They took a leisurely swim, and chatted about inconsequential things like movies, books, music, and amusement park rides. They discovered they both enjoyed art house films, clashed on fiction versus nonfiction (Kasha loved biographies, Axel was into sci-fi), agreed that alternative rock was the best it had been in years and that nothing in an amusement park beat roller coasters. Axel had been to numerous theme parks, given that his job had taken him all over the U.S., and he told her in some detail which coasters were the best and why.

"One day, we'll hit a few of the best," he said, as if they were a couple, as if they had a future together.

Her heart lurched with possibilities, and she saw herself clinging to him in a roller coaster car, screaming with delight.

Stop it. He's your patient.

Not today. Today they were just Kasha and Axel, not therapist and baseball player.

Dangerous. This was dangerous thinking.

Kasha shook off the sticky feelings, brought her attention back to the moment—to the lake and the man beside her, to the pulse in her body and the thrill in her soul.

They lay in the sand on the island, looking up at the sky, cloud watching and calling out what they spied. "There's a witch on a broom." Or "I see a sad-faced clown." And "Look, a grizzly bear catching a salmon." When Kasha saw a hot dog cloud, the topic shifted to baseball and Axel's dream of pitching for the Yankees.

Whenever he talked about baseball, his eyes blazed with a light that scared her. So much passion! It was frightening to a woman who preferred keeping her emotions in the chiller.

Not the deep freeze. Not frozen. But cool. Settled. Soothing.

His heat, his brightness was such a contrast to the way she lived her life. It both relieved and terrified her. She tried not to let her feelings show on her face, and steered the conversation back to the clouds, pointing out a cowboy roping a calf.

By late afternoon, they'd laughed and talked so much that Kasha's voice was growing hoarse.

"I've never heard you talk this much," he said. "I really like the chatty Kasha."

Honestly, so did she.

"May I ask you a personal question?" he ventured, sitting up in the sand to stare down at her.

Feeling vulnerable with him above her, she sat up too. "As long as I reserve the right not to answer."

"Why did you keep your shorts on when we went swimming?" Axel asked.

"Because I didn't want you ogling me," she quipped past the sick feeling that sprang to her stomach.

"So it has nothing to do with those scars on your legs?"

Kasha splayed both palms over her upper thighs. "How did you know?"

"When you came out of the water the hem of your shorts had ridden up," he said solemnly, sitting up, his gaze searching her face. "What happened?"

Shame vibrated through her, and she felt her stomach heat up.

"I . . . that's none of your . . ." Unable to bear the kindness in his eyes, she ducked her head and busied herself with braiding her hair to keep from looking at him.

He reached over, touched her hand. "It's okay. You don't have to tell me. It doesn't change anything."

She darted a sideways glance at him. "Doesn't change anything about what?"

His eyes were dark, mysterious orbs. "The way I feel about you."

A flutter of panic batted around inside her chest. She did not like where this conversation was headed. She hopped to her feet, tugged at the cuff of her damp shorts. "We need to go."

"There's nothing to be afraid of," he said, getting up.

"I'm not afraid," she denied, even as her knees quaked.

He touched her shoulder, lightly, tenderly. A sick sensation rolled through her. "Kasha, what happened to your thighs? I won't judge you."

He knew.

She could tell from the look in his eyes. She hung her head, touched her chin right to her chest. How could she confess her deepest shame?

He didn't move. Didn't say anything else. Just kept standing there patiently, his calloused palm warm against her skin, his thumb rhythmically stroking her in a circular motion, sending a message. *It's okay, you're all right, I'm here.*

"I . . . I . . ." Emotion welled up in her throat.

No! She was not going to cry. She did not cry. That was not the way she operated.

She hauled in a deep breath, waited a heartbeat, and then broke down, confessed. "When I was a teenager, I used to . . . cu . . . cu . . ." She stumbled over the word, finally got it out. "I was a cutter."

He hissed in air through clenched teeth, and the pressure of his hand deepened. "Oh, babe, I'm so sorry you were in that much pain."

"It's all right now," she rushed to assure him. "Mom and Dad got me into therapy and yoga. Yoga changed my life. It was my salvation."

"Thank God for yoga," he said, and drew her against him.

It was a hug of comfort, not intended to be the least bit sexual. And for the briefest second, Kasha allowed herself to drop her forehead to his shoulder and take solace in his solid masculine body that smelled of sand and sun and man.

She lingered as long as she dared, and then reluctantly she pulled away. There were so many questions in his eyes, but he did not ask them. Instead, he reached down and took her hand, and led her to the Jet Ski.

And all the way back to the marina, she kept thinking, *I could so love this man.*

CHAPTER 16

By the time they reached the marina, it was almost six-thirty and the boat ramp was packed, people milling everywhere. The smell of cumin and garlic from the Mexican restaurant on the other side of the boat ramp wafted over.

A live band hit up a respectable version of The Fabulous Thunderbirds' "I Believe I'm in Love with You." An enthusiastic harmonica player made the instrument wail.

Axel tied the Jet Ski at the boat dock. Various watercrafts were lined up at the ramp. It would be a while before they could pull out.

Giggling twenty-something young women were eyeing him, but he was used to that kind of attention—he was Axel "The Axe Man" Richmond, after all—and he politely ignored them. He had eyes for only one woman. He got off the Jet Ski and reached a hand to help Kasha ashore.

She took his hand. Once he had her on the dock beside him, she did not let go. She hung on. Not interlacing their fingers. The gesture was more casual than that, just the slip of her palm against his, but her skin was warm, soft.

He liked that she hadn't let go. It made him feel as if she was claiming him, but then he wondered if it was more because the dock was shaking as a pack of kids ran up and down it playing chase, and she didn't want to lose her balance.

Either way, he would take what he could get.

He squeezed Kasha's hand, pulled her closer to his side.

She released his hand and stepped away, and he couldn't help feeling he'd blundered somehow.

Axel dropped his gaze to her thighs. The shorts covered the scars, but he couldn't forget what they'd looked like. Long, thin, silvered lines, like someone keeping score with Roman numerals.

His stomach flipped over. He hated thinking of her as a trouble teen in so much emotional pain that slicing her skin was the only way she'd been able to find relief from what haunted her.

Thank God, she had found yoga. He hated to think what might have happened to her if she hadn't.

The fierce need to protect her charged through him, and it was all he could do to keep from pulling her into his arms.

"I had a great time today," she said, looking surprisingly shy. She had so much self-confidence that it was hard to think of her as shy. "Thank you for coercing me into going out on the Jet Ski with you."

"Thank you for being coercible." He grinned and picked up her hand again.

She made a lackluster stab at pulling away, but didn't follow through with it.

"Do you have to leave?" he asked.

"I should go . . ." She gestured toward the Prius. "We've been together all day . . ."

"So?" He used her hand to troll her closer.

She resisted, putting tension on their joined hands, yet not breaking the connection.

"We could share some veggie fajitas." He nodded toward the Mexican joint. "Listen to the band. Grab some margaritas?"

"La Cantina is BYOB," she said.

"Okay, skip the margaritas. But please stay. I don't want the day to end yet."

Kasha hesitated, and he could see she was wavering in his direction.

"C'mon," he coaxed.

"I'm in shorts and a swimsuit."

"I have it on good authority you always keep a change of clothes in your car."

She laughed. "I do have a sundress in the trunk."

"It's settled." Holding fast to her hand, he guided her past revelers on the way to her car.

She hit the trunk release on the key remote, and it popped open. She leaned inside, took out an overnight bag, found a flirty red dress with yellow flowers on it.

He spied a bottle of red wine in the trunk, reached down, and hooked a finger around the neck of the bottle. "BYOB. Boy, you are prepared."

"Oh no, Suki." Kasha hissed.

"What?"

She grabbed for the bottle. "Not that wine."

He held it over his head, out of her reach. "What's wrong with this wine?"

She wrinkled her adorable nose. "Tastes terrible."

"Let me be the judge of that."

She looked helpless, hopeless. "Maybe I should be going."

"Put on the sundress," he said, brooking no argument. "We're doing this."

"Does that alpha man stuff usually work for you?"

"All the time." He gift-wrapped a smile, lifting the corners of his mouth up as far as they would go, putting sparkle in his eyes. "Now come on, beautiful. Vegetable fajitas and wine await."

She hesitated for a moment, as if she should refuse, and he gave her a look that said, *Give in; I'm gonna win.*

"Fine." She caved, and he felt like he'd gotten traded to the Yankees. "But I'm not drinking any of that wine."

She pulled the red sundress down over her head. When the dress settled into place, draping to her ankles, she wriggled her shorts off underneath the dress. The shorts dropped them to the pavement, and he stared at them, mesmerized by her quick change. She picked up the shorts and tossed them into the trunk.

"Teetotaler?"

"No. I just don't like the taste of vinegar."

"Fair enough. You don't mind if I have some." He said it as a statement, not a question.

She shifted her mouth to one side as if she was going to protest, but finally waved a hand. "Suit yourself. I know you will anyway."

"You know me so well," he teased, shutting the trunk. Holding the wine bottle in one hand, he looped his other arm through hers and escorted her into La Cantina.

But even though she went willingly with him, Axel couldn't help feeling it was all she could do not to turn and run away.

BECAUSE OF WHO Axel was, they didn't have to wait in line, but were instead immediately escorted to primo seating on the outdoor deck, the owner hustling to set up a table just for them.

Axel protested against special treatment, but the owner waved him away, saying Axel's appearance in his establishment was an honor and a privilege and would bring in customers. Axel accepted the praise and perks with humble thanks.

"This is embarrassing," he said to Kasha.

"But it happens wherever you go."

He nodded and looked uncomfortable. "The downside of being in the public eye."

"Most people would consider it a bonus."

"I don't believe I deserve special treatment just because I have a talent for throwing a ball. The people who should be getting special treatment are teachers and nurses and firemen and cops."

"But that's not the way the world works."

"No," he said fiercely and held out the chair for her to sit. "But it should."

They were seated right along the water, a bit away from the other diners, a festive multicolored umbrella shading their eyes from the western sun. He dropped into the chair across from her, bringing his energy and his heat, all male and muscled and magnificent. He said nothing else, leaned his head back against the chair, and closed his eyes.

Kasha smiled. Two weeks ago he wouldn't have been able to do that—unplug so quickly and sink into the moment. He'd come a long way in a short time. Progressed much farther than she'd imagined he could.

He opened one eye, peeked at her. "How am I doing?"

"Fine," she said.

"This relaxing thing is hard."

"I'm proud of you. You're getting the hang of it."

"Only because I have a great teacher."

"Only because you had no other choice but surgery."

"True." He laughed. "But you *are* a great teacher."

"You're turned out to be an easier patient than I expected."

They grinned at each other.

The owner himself took their orders, and brought them two wineglasses for the bottle Axel carried. The bottle of wine Kasha had found in the hope chest. He set it in the center of the table.

They fell silent as an ultralight aircraft floated overhead. "Ever flown in one of those?" he asked.

"No."

"Would you like to? I've got a friend who owns a couple."

"Thanks for the invitation, it sounds like fun, but now that I've got Emma to think about I should forgo the risky activities."

"It's totally safe."

Kasha eyed the ultralight overhead. "Um . . . it looks pretty sketchy to me."

"Not as dangerous as a Jet Ski."

"That's probably true enough. But I felt totally safe with you. You really know your way around a Jet Ski."

"I'm from Houston. Spent a lot of time on the ocean."

"A man of many talents."

"What can I say? Women dig a guy who can handle personal watercraft."

"And paint and pitch baseballs and . . ."

"What can I say? I'm a passionate guy."

"I know," she said. "That's what troubles me."

"Troubles you how?" He brushed a lock of hair from his fore-head and studied her with heavily lidded eyes.

"You've got long fingers," she said, ignoring his question.

"Better to grip the ball with, my dear."

"Well, you know what they say about guys with long fingers."

"Long fingers, hard to find gloves that fit?"

She burst out laughing.

"God," he said. "I love that sound."

"You're quite easily impressed," she replied. "You do know that."

"And you're a hard nut to crack."

"Not really," she said, pausing to watch a turtle dive off a rock and plunk into the water. "I've just learned a few techniques to keep my emotions from running away with me."

"Maybe you learned them too well."

"No." She shook her head mildly. "I'm not being dramatic when I say yoga saved my life. I was pretty messed up when I was a teen-ager. Poor Mom and Dad. If I hadn't found yoga when I did . . ." She allowed her words to trail off.

He shifted in the chair, leaning closer.

Kasha kicked off her sandals and tucked both feet up into her chair, underneath her bottom. "The thing is, I like who I am now, and I don't want to risk losing it."

"And I somehow threaten your identity?"

"More like my sanity," she mumbled.

He looked pleased with himself. "How often do you do yoga?"

"Oh, every day. The more I do it, the better I feel."

"It sounds like an addiction."

"No. It's medicine. For the mind, heart, body, and soul."

"But isn't it just stretching and breathing?"

"And that's what's so simply miraculous about it," she said. "I'm sure you experience something similar whenever you're pitching, and you're in the zone. It's transcendent."

"True. Gotta say . . ." He shifted his gaze from her face to her body. "I admire the way you can twist your body into those pretzel positions. How do you do that?"

"Practice. Lots and lots of practice."

"Of stretching and breathing?"

"Yes. You should take a yoga class sometime. See what you're missing."

"Can you do a headstand?"

"Child's play."

"Can I see sometime?"

Kasha hesitated. She wanted to share her love of yoga, but the wicked gleam in his eyes made her wonder if he was asking because he wanted to see her shirt fall down when she went up in the air.

"It's okay if you can't do it—"

"I can do it," she said, knowing she was letting him get to her, but he wasn't the only one with talents. "I'll show you sometime. Maybe."

Axel leaned over and uncorked the wine, and poured it up in the two glasses.

She held her breath.

Part of her wanted to know if the wine tasted as divine to him as it did to her, and another part of her was terrified to find out. It was silly. It was superstitious. But despite that, she still wanted to know.

He raised his glass, stared straight into her, and said, "A toast to the perfect day."

Seriously, how could she not drink to that?

"To the perfect day," she echoed, clinked her glass to his, and lowered her eyelashes.

Her heart kicked up, sending a dizzying amount of blood to her head.

Slanting a sideways glance at him, her muscles tensed, She watched Axel take a sip.

The second the wine touched his tongue, he broke out in a smile. "Vinegar, my ass. *Day-am*, Sphinx, this is the best wine I've ever tasted."

CHAPTER 17

Really? Axel could taste it too?

Kasha stopped breathing. With a trembling hand, she raised the glass to her lips and swallowed. The wine tasted even better than it had before—brilliant and warm and sweet and rich. Just as she imagined his lips would taste.

God, she wanted him to kiss her so badly she couldn't stand it. Even as she understood that desire had the ability to dismantle her life, she could no more stop her thoughts than she could prevent the sun from setting.

"I know why you told me it tasted bad." He waggled a jesting finger at her. "You wanted to keep it all for yourself."

"Uh-huh," she said, because she could barely breathe. Let him think that she was greedy instead of petrified.

He held up the bottle. Examined the faded label. "True Love, huh? Hmm. Gotta say, it's true love between me and this wine, and I'm not much of a wine drinker."

Kasha could hear her own heartbeat whooshing through her ears, rushing hard and fast. *He's the one. He's the one. He's the one.*

No. Couldn't be. Myth. Folly. Active imagination.

But her inner self whispered, *Truth.*

"You like it?" she said, scandalized at how smoky her voice sounded.

"I love it. Best damn wine I've ever had. Where did you get it?"

A flush of emotion pushed at her as she experienced overwhelming emotions—bliss, fear, disbelief, hope, excitement, dread. She set the wineglass back on the table, folded her hands in her lap. She wasn't about to tell him about the hope chest. "Jodi."

"Ask her where she got it. I want to stock up."

Every cell in Kasha's body was trembling, and her blood sang. *It's him. Axel Richmond is your soul mate.* Nonsense. Craziness.

But oh! How she wanted to believe, and that was scariest of all.

To calm herself, she slowed her breathing and turned her attention to the lake. A trio of sailboats listed into the wind, sails rippling whitely under the dusky sky, and the lulling sounds of gently flapping canvas traveled across the water.

She remembered coming to the lakeside when she was young, picnicking with her family, swimming in the cove, sunbathing on the sand. Breeanne would rest under an umbrella with a book while her father fished and her mother spread out the food, and she and Suki and Jodi chased each other along the shore.

The images came to her, a flipbook of sweet, happy memories crowding out the darker ones buried deep in the basement of her brain, memories of the days before she found her way to the Carlyles.

Kasha closed her eyes and bit her lip, trying to keep those visions at bay, but she couldn't help seeing the small girl hiding at the bottom of her closet, or climbing up on the roof to get away, or covered in blood, shivering in the Carlyles' garden shed. But she was safe now. Had been for a long time. She'd put those memories behind her. Hadn't really thought of them since she was a teenager.

Until Howard Johnson called her about Emma and jettisoned her back to the time and place she thought she'd tucked away forever.

"Kasha?" Axel nudged her gently with his foot, dragging the toe of his sandal along the back of her calf.

"Huh?" She blinked at him, surprised to find the sun had set and only tendrils of dying light remained.

"Where did you go?" he asked huskily.

"Nowhere." She offered up a faint smile. "I'm right here with you."

He looked as if he was about to say something, but thought better of it. "Are you all right?"

"Fine. Yes, of course. Why wouldn't I be?" She picked up her wineglass, drank more of the miraculous deliciousness to prove she was fine and having fun.

He scooted his chair around so that they were sitting side by side staring out at the water together, the rest of the diners behind them. He was using his body to wall them off in their own little world and she was more grateful than he could possibly know.

The band, which had taken a break, was back now. Playing a slow, sweet ballad that took her a moment to identify. "Keeper of the Stars."

Axel reached out and laid his hand over hers.

A lump rose in her throat. She closed her eyes, fought back a wave of nostalgia for something she'd never had. Unable to bear the tenderness of his touch, she moved her hand, going for the wineglass.

Took a gulp.

The wine—which tasted of the sweetest corners of heaven— loosened Kasha's reserve, and she kicked off her flip-flops, tucked her feet up underneath her in the chair, and reached back to undo her braid, letting her hair uncoil across her shoulders.

Be careful that it doesn't loosen your tongue.

She was terrified that if she spoke, she'd say what she'd been thinking ever since they started working together.

Take me to bed.

Thankfully, the waiter appeared with their fajitas, and the band shifted into a far less romantic song. Yay.

They shared the fajitas, sitting so close their shoulders bumped from time to time as they reached over to spear grilled bell peppers and caramelized onion slices and meaty mushrooms and roasted summer squash dusted with chili powder and cumin.

They passed each other tortillas and beans and rice; the easy ca-

maraderie that had been with them throughout the entire day returned. They ate and watched the sunset and drank wine and talked
about nothing and everything.

The air around Stardust thickened, and a moist orange hue spilled
across the purple-blue stretch of cooling twilight sky. Kasha inhaled
deeply, relishing the tangy sting of roasted chipotle peppers rafting
on the evening breeze, and released a long, contented sigh.

A perfect day indeed.

"Do you want another tortilla?" Axel asked, lifting the lid on the
red plastic warmer, steam rolling off the flour tortillas.

"I've already had three. You're a bad influence." Kasha laid a
hand over her stomach. "I'm stuffed."

He took the tortilla; filled it with refried beans, rice, grated
cheddar, guacamole, and sour cream; and folded it up into a neat
little pouch. "Mmm," he said, and wagged the burrito in front of her.
"Sure you don't want a bite?"

"You go ahead." She laughed and leaned back against the patio
chair, dropped her hands into her lap, and gazed down the end of the
dock to the lake glowing in the light from the lanterns.

When he finished off the last of the food, the owner brought
them sopapillas. "On the house," he said, and left a bottle of honey.

"We gotta eat 'em," Axel said. "They're on the house."

"You get free stuff all the time, don't you?"

"Yep." He drizzled honey on one of the fried tortilla pillows and
held it out to her. "Open wide."

He was feeding her. If she wasn't tipsy, she certainly wouldn't
let him feed her, but she was tipsy, and she opened her mouth and
leaned in, and when Axel's fingertips touched her mouth, she came
unraveled.

She closed her eyes, closed teeth over the cinnamon-dusted sopapilla, and an involuntary moan of delight escaped her lips. "Ohh,
ohh, so good."

A drop of honey clung to her lips. She flicked out her tongue to
lick it away, and opened her eyes to find Axel staring intently at her
mouth, as if he wished he were that drop of honey.

"This is the best damn wine ever," he murmured, his gaze fixed on her, and breathing as if overcome by a force beyond his control.

"I know," she whispered. Her heart hopped, hyped up and hopeful. There was no such thing as soul-mate-detecting wine. It was insanity to entertain such a crackpot theory, but here she was.

Entertaining it.

She should get up, make an excuse, and tell him she had to go home, but inertia welded her butt to the chair, and she couldn't make herself move.

Truth.

She was sitting beside a famous, powerful male, a major league baseball player, and he was drop-dead handsome and passionate. So damn passionate that he stirred the wildness in her.

A wildness that she ran from.

And she was hot and wet and more turned on than she'd ever been in her life. She fidgeted from fear and guilt and pleasure, sliding her bare feet back and forth across the deck boards, halfway hoping she'd get a splinter and it would jolt her out of this craziness.

Craziness.

The old Patsy Cline song "Crazy" popped into her head. She was starting to want this, want him, too much.

Where was the cork? The stopper to shove back into this bottle and pray it would seal up the genie of desire that the wine had unleashed.

Don't blame it on the wine. You were horny for him long before this.

Yes, but until that first blissful sip, she'd been able to control her urges, govern herself. Now? Her organs and bones, blood and skin were anarchists, demanding revolt.

She stole a peek at him as he lazily tippled more wine into both their glasses, his wrist lightly gripping the neck of the bottle. A tiny shiver at how strong that wrist looked, and how close he was, and how romantic this was.

"Aww," he said, looking into the end of the bottle. "It's all gone."

She felt both relieved—because she was pretty tipsy—and sad—

because it was gone. No more heavenly wine to share with the man of her dreams.

Rein in those thoughts. Headed down a treacherous road here, Kash.

She turned her head, stared out at the water, felt her heart beating, saw firelights flicker, nature's flying lanterns gently lighting up the bushes against the banks, heard the bluesy music, tasted honey and wine and lust. A breeze blew across the lake, and she shivered.

"Kasha," Axel murmured, his voice thick and rich.

"Yes?"

"Are you cold?"

"No!" she said, too fast and loud, afraid he would throw an arm around her shoulder to warm her up.

"I could go get that blanket in your trunk—"

"I'm fine." God, the last thing she needed was for him to make a romantic gesture.

Put an end to this silly drama, and walk away!

Good plan. She was going for it. She planted her feet firmly on the deck, started to push up.

"Look." Axel pointed up. "A shooting star."

Kasha raised her face to the sky, followed the beautiful trajectory of the burning star.

"Make a wish," he said, his voice a silky husk.

I wish you'd kiss me.

Oh fudge, had she actually wished that?

"What did you wish for?" he asked.

"What? You want me to tell you and blow my chances of it coming true?"

"I didn't take you for the superstitious type."

Shows what you know, she thought, and took another sip of wine. "What did you wish for?"

"My shoulder to heal forthwith."

"Forthwith? Where'd you get that? A WWI solider?" Kasha asked, feeling a giggle bubble up from the bottom of her stomach and effervesce into a burp. "Oops." She grinned and slapped a palm over her mouth. "Excuse me."

"I like you this way."

"What? Burpy?"

"Lighter. Freer. Not taking yourself so seriously."

"Meaning you don't really like me when I'm my normal self?"

"Not at all. I enjoy the many sides of Kasha Carlyle. I just like seeing you relaxed. You deserve to enjoy yourself."

"Everyone deserves to relax."

"I'm glad you stayed for dinner with me," he murmured, reaching over to touch her hand again.

"Me too," she admitted, even though she probably shouldn't have. "But I'm going now."

"You are?" He sounded disappointed.

"Yep."

"We killed a bottle of wine. You should stay awhile."

"It wasn't a full bottle when we started."

"Still, I've had too much to drive the Jet Ski back for at least an hour, and I expect you have too. The band is good; it's a beautiful night."

He was right. She hadn't intended on driving. She'd planned on walking home. Her place was only a couple of miles away. And this was Stardust. The safest place on earth. And someone she knew was bound to stop and give her a ride.

"I'll call one of my sisters to come and get me," she said, dreading that conversation.

"Why don't you want to stay?" He ran his thumb over her knuckles.

"Because I'm too close to crossing a line with you."

He leaned in, his voice low and welcoming, his scent distracting. "What line is that?"

"You know." She waved a hand. "This patient-therapist line."

"Oh that."

"Don't dismiss it. This is my career and integrity we're talking about here."

"We've done nothing but share a day on a Jet Ski, a partial bottle of wine, and fajitas."

"Don't play dumb. It doesn't suit you."

"Kasha," he said, "there's nothing wrong with sitting here talking."

If he knew what was going on inside her head, he would not be saying that. She was not going to tempt fate. She was getting out of here. Kasha set down her glass and got to her feet, but her toe caught on a knothole in the board, and she swayed precariously. Only years of yoga kept her upright, balanced.

"Steady." Axel shot to his feet, put out a supporting hand. Touched her elbow. Lit her on fire.

She yanked her arm away. "I'm okay. I'm fine."

He was right in front of her, not two inches of space between them, his masculine scent filling up her lungs and addling her brain.

"You're sucking all the oxygen from the air," she said.

"You're holding your breath," he pointed out. "Breathe, Yoga Girl."

"I have to go."

"So you said."

"Thank you for the Jet Ski ride and dinner and the wine, and—"

"It was your wine."

"You poured it."

"Um . . . okay."

"And the conversation. Thanks for that too."

"Anytime." He smiled a wistful smile that touched her deep inside.

His dark eyes cradled hers and she felt something slip inside her, melting, breaking loose. It was scary and thrilling and exhilarating. He paused, stared deeply into her.

Then he played his trump card. "If you stay," he said, "I'll tell you why I didn't want to be alone today."

CHAPTER 18

Curiosity won.

"All right," Kasha agreed, getting her bearings back. She could handle herself.

"Would you like to walk?" He gestured toward the boardwalk that stretched around the lake from the restaurant, to the marina and beyond.

"What?"

"Walk off the food, the wine."

The magic.

Although Kasha wasn't sure it was possible to walk that off. Or if she even wanted to.

He took out enough money from his wallet for the meal, plus an extra generous tip, left it on the table, and held out his palm.

She couldn't resist sinking her hand in his and allowing him to lead her from the patio dining to the boardwalk, the wooden stairs creaking beneath their feet.

The summery sound stoked something inside her, and in her mind's eye, she saw herself as a long-legged girl in a red and white striped one-piece swimsuit, running giggling over these same white-washed boards, running ahead of her biological parents as they held hands, and stopped regularly to kiss passionately. Anyone seeing would think them the perfect family.

She breathed in the same briny air, rich with the fragrance of Mexican food, that she'd smelled back then, and her head spun, dizzy from the vivid memories and shifting of the light as the sun completely sank below the horizon.

"Where did you go?" Axel whispered.

"How did you know I was off in the past?" Puzzled, Kasha stopped, studied him.

He reached out to press the flat of his thumb between her eyebrows. "You were thinking so hard that you were frowning."

She shook her head, shook out the memories. She wasn't going to unload her baggage on him. The past was gone, and couldn't be changed and she didn't like talking about it. Besides, it was his confession time. "Let's keep walking."

He didn't pester her for an answer, but he did take her arm again, and even though she should have minded, she didn't. Decorative ambient lanterns guided their way. On the sandy beach below the boardwalk, couples nuzzled on blankets and beach towels.

The muscles in her groin clenched, and Kasha averted her gaze, not wanting to stir up sexy feelings for the man beside her.

"Thank you," he said gruffly. "For coming out and making a lonely day one of the best days ever. You'll never know how much today has meant to me."

"I . . ." She gulped, admitted the truth. "It meant a lot to me too."

The moon peeked out from behind the clouds. Not a full moon, but almost. Along the banks, bullfrogs croaked a chorus, welcoming nightfall. Kasha noticed they were breathing in tandem, inhaling the musky scent of lake and each other.

"Now that I've stolen your day away," he said, as they strolled toward the end of the boardwalk, "what are your plans for the evening?"

"It's already eight-thirty. Not much of an evening left." She shook her head, her hair brushing the backs of her arms. She felt a bit wanton with her hair floating loose and free in the breeze.

"You're an early-to-bed kind of woman?"

"Yes. Normally, I'm driving over two hours to get to work at the Gunslingers' facility. I have to leave at five a.m."

"Wow," he said. "That's commitment. Why don't you just move to Dallas?"

"I'll move once I get custody of Emma, although I can see that transition is going to take much longer than I anticipated."

"Yesterday was a setback."

"Eye-opener. I didn't fully realize how complicated life with Emma would be."

"But you still want custody of her?"

"Yes, of course. I'm not going to abandon her just because she's got challenges. What kind of person do you take me for?"

"I didn't mean it like that."

"I know you didn't. I'm probably too sensitive. Those girls yesterday . . . well, you were right. I needed a battle plan."

"Kids picked on Dylan when he got sick." Axel's lips evened out in a tight line. "Human nature can be ugly."

"You handled those girls skillfully."

"Practice. You'll get there."

"Slowly."

"I admire you," he said.

"What for?"

"Not everyone would be willing to make such personal sacrifices for a sister like Emma. Especially a sister they didn't grow up with."

"I don't consider her a sacrifice. She's an invitation to joy."

"You really do love her."

"More than you can know," Kasha murmured, still surprised by the stark fierceness of the feelings that went through her every time she thought about her half sister. She had no idea how she could love Emma so much in such a short amount of time, but she did.

"You've got a huge heart," he said. "If you ever need any help with Emma, or just want to talk, I'm here."

"Axel, I can't . . . we can't . . . ." She toggled a finger back and forth between them.

"Do what?"

"This."

"You mean be friends?"

"Friendship is enough for you?" She rested her back against the wooden railing, looked up into his dark eyes, and saw the answer. No. It wasn't enough for him. It wouldn't be enough for her either.

"Kasha . . ." His voice cracked, and his hand tightened on her elbow.

"What was it about today that made you not want to be alone?" she asked, shifting the conversation back to him.

His eyes darkened, troubled. He hesitated a beat. Two. Three. Moistened his lips. Cleared his throat.

The air between them thickened, and it had nothing to do with the East Texas humidity.

"Forget I asked." She waved a hand like she was shooing a fly. "It's none of my business."

Suddenly, he blurted, "Today would have been Dylan's tenth birthday."

Her heart torqued, wrung itself out. "Oh, Axel. I'm so sorry. I didn't know."

One side of his mouth tilted up in a sad half smile. "Don't feel sorry for me. For eight years I got to be the dad of the most amazing kid in the world. I understand why you want Emma. I really do. Despite the challenges, she'll bring a million blessings into your life. Go get her. You won't ever regret bringing her into your life. I promise you that."

"The joy of having Dylan was worth the pain of losing him?"

He laughed, the sound surprisingly light and joyful. "Yes, oh yes. Life hurts, Kasha. We can't stop the pain or insulate ourselves from it. But I'm sure you already know that." He glanced down at her thighs. "That's why you're so afraid to take a chance on us. You're scared of losing it all."

"You're not scared?" she whispered.

"Hell yes," he said. "But if we let pain keep us from taking chances, then we're barely alive, and what's the point?"

She stared into him and he stared into her and there was nothing around them but water and sky. They didn't hear the muted conversations of the other beachgoers. They saw nothing but each other, and she knew they weren't talking about Emma and Dylan anymore.

"You're braver than I am," she said.

"No I'm not. I don't know what happened to you, but I know it was bad." He dropped his hand, ran a fingertip over the tops of her thighs right where the scars were. "You're incredibly brave."

She inhaled sharply. "You don't know me."

"I do know you," he insisted. "I know you're strong mentally, emotionally, and physically. I know you're kind and loving and hardworking. You've got a wry sense of humor, and you're patient with guys like me who pull bonehead moves like I did with the rebounder. You've been hurt badly, but you didn't let the past define you. I might not know your history, Kasha Carlyle, but I know you."

Kasha stopped breathing, stared into those serious eyes that were quickly becoming so essential to her.

The moment stretched long, and longer still.

His fingers remained on her thighs. She could feel his body heat through the material of her sundress. Could hear the lapping of the water against the shore, and the sound of a passing party barge heavy with the sounds of laughter, conversations, and the churn of a slow-moving outboard engine.

Finally, Axel moved to cup her cheek in his palm. "You don't have to tell me anything about your past. I'm not going to ask."

She didn't know what possessed her. Why she broke. She never talked about her biological parents to people who didn't already know the story.

And rarely even then.

But his eyes were so full of understanding, and she knew in her core that she could trust him. And she wanted, no, correction . . . needed . . . She needed to tell him why she was the way she was.

It wasn't that she couldn't love. But rather because she knew she had the capacity for passion so deep and strong it terrified her. Passion could destroy her.

Just as it had destroyed her parents.

A hundred questions lurked in his eyes, but he asked none of them. He held her with his gaze, cradled her.

"My mother murdered my father," she said in a voice so calm that Axel did a double take, his eyes widening, body stiffening, nostrils flaring.

"What?" He blinked. "What did you say?"

"When I was seven years old," she went on in a low monotone. No emotion. General. Bland. "My mother shot my father with a nine-millimeter handgun she'd bought at a pawnshop three days earlier, and when she finished she turned the gun on herself. One bullet for Dad. One for her. Bam! Bam!"

The last two words echoed across the lake.

Bam! Bam!

Sorrow twisted his face. "Kasha, no."

She didn't feel the impact of the shock beneath his words or react to the stark distress on his face. She iced herself up inside, numbed her feelings. Untouchable.

"That's horrifying," he said.

She went on calmly, as if giving the weather report for a cloudless August day. "My parents fought all the time, cats and dogs. Hot-blooded, the both of them. My mother was Italian and prided herself on how quickly she could lose her temper. As if quickness to anger was a virtue. They were infamous in Stardust."

"That must have been so scary for you."

"The police came out to our house at least once a month. But then my parents would make up. Be all lovey-dovey. Have loud, headboard-banging sex. I remember sleeping with my head under the pillow many a night trying to drown out the sound."

Axel shifted, leaning in closer, but his gaze never left her face; all his attention was on her.

"Tumultuous, people called them. Passionate. And so it went, around and around. They would kiss madly one minute, then an hour later they could be screaming and throwing things at each other."

"Shit, Kasha." He looked like someone had punched him hard in the gut after he'd just stuffed on Thanksgiving dinner. He jammed fingers through his hair, spun around on his heels a full three-hundred-and-sixty-degree turn, came back to plant both palms on the dock railing, shoulders down. "Shit."

"Don't feel sorry for me." She stiffened her spine. "I didn't tell you this so you'd feel sorry for me."

"I wish I had a time machine so I could go back in the past and rescue you."

She laughed a humorless laugh. "Sir Galahad. If you'd saved me, I wouldn't be who I am today."

"Walled up in your ivory tower?"

That hurt. She flinched, but tried not to let it show on her face.

"Hey," he said. "I didn't mean that as judgment. We all have our demons. Just meant you hold yourself apart."

"Aloof."

"Your word, not mine."

"It's not that I don't care."

"I know," he whispered, coming closer. "It's that you care so much." His arms went around her waist, comforting and comfortable. "You're just protecting yourself as a byproduct of the volatile environment you grew up in."

She shrugged. "Plenty of people have it worse. Jodi's biological mom was a drug addict who would go off and leave her home alone for days when she was only four years old. And Breeanne's teenage mom abandoned her at the hospital when she found out Bree had a serious heart condition. And Suki? Her parents disappeared in North Korea and were never seen or heard from again."

"But their suffering doesn't mitigate yours."

"Suffering doesn't make me special. Sooner or later, life knocks everyone down. It's how you deal with the knocks and dings that matter. My biological parents dealt with it badly. They were Roman candles. Heat. Light. Fireworks. Explosions." She stared over his shoulder because she didn't want to see pity in his eyes, and watched the headlights of cars moving on the road above them.

"How did . . ." He paused.

She could feel his warm breath tickle her ear, and the whispery heat stoke arousal deep inside her core.

"What happened the day your mother . . . um . . ." He paused. ". . . did what she did?"

Before she could form an answer, he held up a palm. "Wait. You don't have to answer that. It's none of my business."

"No," she said. "It's okay. I want you to understand me." Helplessly, she leaned into him, absorbing his body heat, inhaling his reassuring scent. "I don't remember that day at all. The last thing I remember about that spring afternoon was walking home from school past the purple hyacinth in the flowerbed as I climbed the porch steps. I remember they smelled so incredibly sweet I wished I could eat them."

Funny the things she remembered. Kasha hitched in a breath. "When the front door shut behind me, it closed down my memory of what happened. One minute I was imagining eating sweet purple flowers and the next I was lying on a gurney covered in a green sheet that smelled of anesthetic and staring up at a piercing bright light overhead. I was in the ER at Stardust General Hospital, and Maggie Carlyle was sitting to my left holding my hand, Dan had hold of my right."

"Oh shit, Sphinx. You found their bodies?"

"Most likely. But I don't remember it."

"Waking up like that must have been so confusing."

"And terrifying," she said. "I didn't know where I was or why I was there. I recognized Maggie and Dan, of course. Jodi was my best friend in grade school, and we were in the same class. I used to slip over to the Carlyles' when the yelling or the lovemaking got too loud at my house."

"So after you walked into your parents' house . . ." He hauled in a steadying breath. ". . . you went to the place where you felt safest."

Kasha bobbed her head. "This is what I've pieced together from other peoples' accounts of that day. Several hours after the shootings, Dan found me hiding in their garden shed, cowering behind planter boxes and covered in blood."

"That must have scared him." Axel winced.

"Dan thought I was injured. Maggie tried frantically to call my parents, but when she couldn't get an answer, she asked a neighbor to watch the children, while she and Dan loaded me into the back of their car and took off for the hospital."

"And you don't remember any of that?"

Kasha shook her head. "When they arrived in the ER, the place was in chaos. Cops were everywhere, nurses were running to and fro."

"Working on your biological parents?" Axel guessed.

"Dad was DOA," she said, still using the robotic voice that allowed her to tell the tale without breaking down. "But my mother held on for several hours."

"That's . . ." He ran a hand through his hair, looked stunned. "I can't . . . there are no words."

"There's nothing to say. Worst day of my life." She dusted her palms together. "But it happened and it's over, and I made it through."

"Thank God you don't remember it."

"Thank God for the Carlyles." She rested her head on his shoulder, and he held her for the longest time, and after a while, she felt settled enough to speak again. "I was so scared that Maggie and Dan might send me away, but from the very beginning they treated me like family. They fostered me, and then adopted me. I was very lucky."

Another heavy silence rolled between them, thick as the gathering damp. Axel pressed his lips to the top of her head. "Do you know why your mother killed your father?"

"The cops figured it was a jealous rage. My father had a wandering eye. But it wasn't until I found out about Emma that the truth cleaved me upside the head. Mom killed him because she discovered he had an illegitimate love child with a stripper. She couldn't live with him, but she couldn't live without him either. Crazy passion." She spit out the last word as if it was a rancid peanut, and she could taste the oily yuck.

"And all those years you had no inkling of Emma?"

"No." Kasha swiveled her head from shoulder to shoulder. "In the wake of the murder/suicide, Emma's mother laid low, impressive because that's pretty hard to do in a town as small as Stardust. I can't imagine how ashamed she must have felt. How guilty. I wish I could have met her. Told her I didn't blame her. I can't begin to fathom what she must have gone through believing she was responsible for what my mother did. I just wish . . ."

"What?" he asked, his voice soft as velvet.

She shook herself, stepped back, offered up a ghost of a smile. "It doesn't matter. The past is past. I can't change it. I'm not responsible for what my parents did. I'm only responsible for me. And hopefully soon, Emma."

"And this?" He trailed his fingertips over her thighs. "What started this?"

Kasha nudged his hand away, splayed her palms over her thighs, closed her eyes, and experienced the sharp edge of her fear.

"It's okay," he whispered. "That part of your life is over. You're safe."

She was, but that didn't mean she couldn't fall prey to her emotions. She hoisted up her chin, her shoulders, and her spirits. "It seems stupid now."

"What does?" His voice was a gentle caress.

"When I was in high school some girls started a rumor that I was the one who murdered my parents, and pinned the blame on my mother. It was high school bullshit, but because I couldn't remember what happened that day, I let the taunts inside my head, and I started to wonder if they were right. Maybe I had killed my parents."

"Sweetheart, you poor kid." He drew her back into his arms again. Part of her wanted to fight his embrace. They were getting too close, but another part of her simply surrendered. It felt so good here in his arms.

"That's why it touched me when you went to bat for Emma with those girls," she said. "Flashbacks."

"Dammit, Sphinx. You didn't deserve any of that, and neither does Emma." His voice rumbled from his chest, big and strong. "I'm so proud of how very far you've come. And Emma is lucky to have you."

"No. I'm the one who is lucky. Emma has opened me up to life."

He looked at her as if she were an angel tumbled from his dreams. "Kasha Carlyle, you are the most beautiful woman I have ever known, both inside and out." He squeezed her against him as if he would never let her go.

Instantly, her body responded, heating up, getting moist, throbbing with a wretchedly beautiful ache.

She wanted him! Past every level of desire imaginable, past rhyme and reason and rational thought!

This, whispered a terrified voice at the back of her head. *This kind of desire is what destroyed your parents.*

He shifted her into the crook of his arm, eyes drilling into her, not taking his gaze off her for a second.

Her pulse leaped, and her knees quaked, and a spasm tore through her throat, and she could not utter a word.

"Sphinx," he whispered. "My beautiful, beautiful Sphinx."

And before she could protest, he kissed her.

CHAPTER 19

A sexual jolt, as sharp and shockingly charged as static electricity, crackled against Axel's mouth the second he touched down on those pretty pink lips.

God, what lips! Pillowy. Luxurious. Honey sweet. Soft.

And yet, at the same time, also firm and strong. A paradox. His Sphinx.

Anxious to taste more of her, he tipped her chin up to deepen the kiss, deliberately taking his time, savoring her heated sugar as he slid one hand up her spine, drawing her closer to him.

And that persistent thought again: *We fit.*

A sliver of a sigh slipped past her lips, and her arms slid around his shoulders, moved up.

Nice. Real nice.

Her fingers pushed up through his hair, her short thumbnails resting against the nape of his neck.

He had a sense of the conflict within her, wanting to pull him closer, while at the same time wanting to shove him away.

As it was, she did neither. Just waited.

All right.

He wasn't holding back. His tongue found hers, and a thrilling flush burned inside him.

She pressed her body flat against his, and he was one hundred percent certain she could feel his erection. She was kissing him now, and he let her take the lead, interested to see what she would do, where she would take this.

When her hands moved to cup his face, a rough groan rolled from his throat, in a sound so foreign he did not recognize it.

Things got a little wild from there. The kisses grew quicker, harder, more frantic—bold, hot, hungry—until they were both perspiring and panting.

Kasha broke it off, leaned back against the railing, her eyes glazed with desire. "I can't do this," she murmured, more to herself than to him. "I won't do this."

"It's okay," he said, his voice coming out harder and rougher than he intended. "It's okay." Reassuring her? Or himself?

"It's not okay. I'm your physical therapist." She fingered her lips, stared at him with abject despair.

"It was just a kiss, Kasha." But he knew in his heart it was not just a kiss. He was in love with her and the kiss was a topper. He loved both this competent, confident woman that he'd come to know, and the lost child she'd once been.

"Inappropriate," she fussed. "I knew I should never have gone out on the Jet Ski with you. That was stupid enough, but then I compounded things by agreeing to dinner with you and drinking that wine—" She gulped, whimpered. "Totally irresponsible."

"It was your day off. Time out."

"Doesn't matter. That was utterly . . ." Her breath came out hot and shallow. "It was—"

"Terrific," he said. "Hot. Sexy. Spectacular. Awesome."

"Well, yes." She waved a hand. "But that's beside the point."

"You're making too much of this," he said, attempting to soothe her, even as his own alarm bells were ringing.

"A patient gives me the best kiss of my life, and I'm making too much of it?" She glowered, but she still looked dazed. Hell, he was surely dazed.

"It was the best kiss of your life?" he couldn't resist asking. Okay, so he had an ego, but the thought that she was impressed with his kiss left him feeling like the king of the universe.

"Don't let it go to your head." She snorted.

He smiled, hoping to get her to lighten up about the kiss.

"Can't let you get cocky, thinking your lips are something special."

"But they are special." He wriggled his eyebrows. *Stop it, Richmond, you're making things worse trying to be charming.* Epic fail. He was headed for an epic fail, but he couldn't seem to shut up. "Right? At least to you, or you wouldn't be making such a big deal of this."

"It is a big deal. I kissed a patient." She wrung her hands.

"Technically," he said, feeling a bit panicky, "I kissed you."

"But I allowed it to happen." She ran distressed fingers through her hair.

He loved the way it moved like a shimmery curtain of dark water, nearly black and oh so thick. God, she was the most beautiful thing on the face of the earth.

"I should have stopped you," she said. "Bitten your lip or kneed you in the groin, or—"

"Except you didn't. Because you liked it."

She smacked her forehead with a palm, as if something monumental had just occurred to her. "It was the damn hope chest wine. That's what caused me to let down my guard."

"Hope chest wine? What are you talking about?"

"It wasn't me. It was the wine. Now that I've got the kiss out of my system, and the wine is all gone, I'll be fine. Absolutely fine," she muttered to herself.

He'd never seen her like this, vulnerable, uncertain, lost. Not even when she fell into the pool and he dived in to save her. All he wanted was to make her feel better.

"Yes," he said, reading her, figuring out what she needed and hopefully supplying it. "I'm sure it was the hope chest wine."

"Good. Great. I'm glad we solved that mystery." She straightened. "I'm going home now."

She turned her back on him and walked away as fast as she could without breaking into a run.

ANGUISHED.

Kasha was anguished over what she'd done. It was the only word she had for the bullet of guilt, remorse, shame, and lust ricocheting around inside her body.

After arriving home from her amazing day and evening with Axel, she put on yoga pants and T-shirt, and at ten o'clock at night went immediately to her mat, and started sun salutations.

And yes, she knew sun salutations were a set to welcome the morning, but the poses helped to strengthen her resolve.

She pushed her body at a punishing pace, trying to outrun her emotions, but it wasn't working. She couldn't empty her mind of him. Yoga, the very thing she'd come to depend on to fix any and everything, failed her.

Sleep failed her too.

Hours later she lay in bed staring up at the ceiling, lips still tingly from his kiss.

She was at a crossroads. If she stayed on as Axel's therapist she risked betraying both herself and her profession in the most fundamental way. And yet, if she quit now, in the middle of things, she put her chances of getting custody of Emma in jeopardy, not to mention leaving Axel when he needed her the most.

It was only a couple more weeks. Soon he would be healed and no longer her responsibility. Surely she could resist the attraction for that long.

But she hadn't been able to resist kissing him. What was that all about?

The wine, she told herself.

It was the fault of the wine. If she hadn't been drunk on True Love wine . . .

Shifting the blame. No. She was responsible for her actions. She drank the wine of her own accord. Her choice. Badly made.

Time for another choice. A better one. A healthier one.

Quit.

Walk away.

Some might say it was the cowardly way. After all, wouldn't a brave woman stay and face her fears, her mistakes, and the repercussions? Face it head-on without hesitation.

No choice. She had no choice. There was only one honorable solution, and Kasha had to take it.

ON TUESDAY MORNING after his thrilling Memorial Day with Kasha, Axel woke feeling out of sorts.

He'd slept like crap.

Unable to get comfortable, his shoulder throbbing after the long day on the Jet Ski, and beleaguered by fevered fantasies of his sexy physical therapist, he'd spent a restless night alone in his big empty bed.

In the drifting remnants of dreams, he savored Kasha's lips again, sweet as the True Love wine they'd shared. She tasted of mysteries and moonbeams, magic and midnight murmurs.

Dumb move.

That kiss.

She was his therapist and he needed her. Hadn't really realized exactly how much he did need her until she'd shown up in his life with her willowy smiles and calm, quiet ways.

He was hard-charging. Or at least he had been for most of his life. He understood what it took to make it to the top of the heap. Focus. Dedication. The refusal to quit no matter how hard things got or how bleak they looked. Pipe dreams were nothing but lofty goals acted upon, and if he knew nothing else, Axel knew how to take action.

That same pragmatism told him he wasn't a kid anymore, and that no matter how hard he battled to achieve the pinnacle of success, at his age, he might never make it to where he wanted to go.

The Yankees.

But that didn't mean he was going to quit trying. This was his last shot. He knew that. He was thirty years old, with his best years on the diamond behind him. If he made a misstep now, it was all over.

The thought of life after baseball sickened him. He felt as if a

small, panicked animal was trapped in the basement of his soul, claw-
ing and scratching mindlessly, desperate to escape.

What would he do without baseball? Who would he be? It was
all he'd ever known. It was the only thing that had brought him back
after losing Dylan. How could he willingly leave it behind?

He needed baseball. He wanted Kasha. Two different things.

But she had his back. One hundred percent. She was a woman
of integrity, and he understood she would always tell him the truth,
painful or not.

Which was why he'd listened to Kasha when everything inside
him had been crying out for him to roll the dice, take the gamble,
accept the odds, and go for the surgery.

Yet, ever since her calm voice had cut through the bullshit bouncing around the physical therapy room that first day, his dream of playing for the Yankees had started to seem emptier and lonelier. And
sometimes he couldn't even remember what he was pursuing it for.

Then he would think of Dylan, and his son's cute boyish face and
earnest eyes, and everything inside him rallied to one, singular goal,
the goal that would make his son proud.

Playing for the Yankees might be a long shot, but every fiber in
Axel's being pushed him forward, as if success was guaranteed. All
he had to do was commit himself to the goal one hundred percent.

He could do this. He would do this. He *had* to do this. Failure
was not an option.

But Kasha held the key. His future hinged on the fulcrum of the
dark-haired, exotic-looking beauty.

She intrigued him.

From the moment he laid eyes on Kasha, her almond eyes calm
and unreadable as she stared at him, he'd been captive. He'd been
bare-chested and cocky and she'd been the only woman in a roomful of managers and coaches and doctors in an MLB therapy room.
He'd immediately wanted to know who this goddess was and why
she was there. And the more interaction he had with her, the more
she fascinated him.

How was she this morning? he fretted.

Axel knew she was beating herself up about the kiss. And he feared she was on the verge of dumping him as a client. He didn't blame her. He'd been out of line, and the last thing he wanted was to cause her any pain.

He pulled out his phone to text her. To say something light and breezy, just to let her know he was thinking of her, and that all was well between them. But he couldn't think of the right words to type. How could he express on a phone screen what he was feeling when he was unsure of where her head was at?

Or his, for that matter.

No. He would wait until she got here. See her face-to-face.

Resolved, he got up before dawn, went into the gym, and got down to work.

BUNDLE OF NERVES.

Kasha finally understood what that phrase meant. Muscles tight, heart beating erratically, she drove to the ranch at her usual time on Tuesday morning. Stomach heavy with the news she needed to deliver.

Axel answered the front door in paint-stained gray gym shorts, a white T-shirt, and a weekend's growth of beard. He looked utterly delicious.

"Mornin'." He gave an irresistible smile.

She pressed her lips together. *Resist! Resist!*

"Okay." He gulped, his Adam's apple bobbing, and stepped aside to let her enter.

The air between them throbbed with tension as she moved past him. Once in the living room, she stopped and turned to face him, her heart thundering so loudly she could barely think. "We need to talk."

"Here?" An uneasy darkness settled into the hollows of his cheeks.

"The Creedys are back?"

"Yes."

"Let's go into the gym," she said, wanting a place where they wouldn't be overheard.

"Sure, sure." He bobbed his head, and led the way.

Kasha couldn't help watching the way his hard-muscled rump moved beneath those shirts. *For crying out loud, stop it!*

Inside the gym, she saw the easel was set up underneath the skylight, facing away from the entryway so that all she could see was the back of the canvas. A plethora of paints were arranged on a small table next to the easel.

Eager for a peek at how much progress he'd made, Kasha rounded the easel.

She took one look at the canvas, startled, and caught her breath. "It's me. You're painting me."

He smiled a sunbeam smile. Nodded.

She exhaled sharply, stunned by the grab bag of emotions surging through her. "I can't believe you're painting me."

There was her face floating on the canvas. She was standing on a boat dock, gazing out across Stardust Lake, a light shawl fluttering around her shoulders, a dozen Mason jar lanterns strewn across the boards behind her. She looked calm, serene, queenly . . .

And untouchable.

Her muscles jerked.

Was this how Axel really saw her? Impervious. Aloof. Self-contained. A sense of isolation pulsed through her, strange and yet all too familiar.

"Why can't you believe it?" he said huskily. "You're beautiful."

"I'm not the kind of woman men paint portraits of."

"Pardon my French, Sphinx, but I call bullshit. You're flipping gorgeous."

"It was not always easy growing up a mixed-race girl in a white-bread world." She waved a hand, signifying Stardust at large. "But luckily times are changing. There were many times I was made to feel ugly."

"People often feel threatened by things that are different. It reflects their ignorance, not your reality."

If she were the kind of woman who blushed, Kasha's cheeks would be heating, but she wasn't, so her cheeks did not burn, but she felt light, airy, and happier than she'd felt since . . . well . . . she couldn't remember ever feeling quite this happy, and it was all because of Axel.

He gave her laughter and levity and playfulness. He'd awakened her from a sleep she hadn't even known she'd been in. He surprised her and delighted her, and every time he smiled at her, she was enchanted. He accepted Emma without reservations, treated her kindly, patiently. He'd gotten under Kasha's skin and in her blood, and she needed him far more than she wanted to admit.

She wanted to let down her guard, let him in, give him the passion she'd been saving up for years, but she didn't dare. Couldn't. Not with so much at stake.

"I . . . I . . . It's not. I'm not . . ." She struggled to find the words to express all the emotions pushing at the seams of her heart.

"What?" he prompted.

"I didn't expect this." Weakly, she flapped her wrist at the painting.

"Here's the question. Do you . . ." He paused, swallowing so forcefully his Adam's apple pumped. ". . . like it?"

"I do," she murmured. "I like it very much, but in it I seem so . . ." She put an index finger to her chin, tilted her head. ". . . faraway."

"You often have that exact look on your face," he said. "As if you're keeping an unknowable secret."

The way he'd captured her was unsettling, and far too eerily accurate. It was as if he could see straight into her, and recognized the dark corners of her soul, and liked her all the more because of them.

Forget about the painting. You can't get sucked in. Say what you came here to say.

Kasha inhaled audibly, steadying herself. "I'm going to call Dr. Harrison and tender my resignation. Effective immediately."

"What?" His jaw dropped and his eyes rounded, and he looked . . . *betrayed.*

"I'm quitting." She said it as gently and kindly as she could.

"No." His chin hardened.

"Yes."

"You're jumping ship midway through my recovery?" Axel stepped closer. The harsh undercurrent in his tone matched the furrow between his eyebrows.

"It's for the best." She fiddled with her college ring on the third finger of her right hand, rotating it around and around.

"Why?"

Kasha tucked her chin in, pulled her shoulders downward, but kept them razor-straight like she did in yoga class, anchoring herself inside her body, pulling everything in to keep her mind from flying away at the sight of his hot, fiery eyes. "You know why."

He glared, hard-edged, accusatory, but she refused to flinch against the blade of his gaze.

"Because of last night." His voice deepened. "Because of the kiss."

"Yes."

"It was just a kiss."

"You know it wasn't."

"We've got chemistry yes," he admitted. "But we don't have to act on it."

"You . . . we . . . already did."

"How about this? Let's forget the kiss even happened. Put it behind us."

"We can't, and you know it. We'll kiss again and kissing will lead to . . ." She glanced away, unable to bear the brunt of his scrutiny. "Other things. I can't betray myself like that. I can't and I won't."

"What about Emma?" he asked. "Won't being unemployed make it harder for you to get custody?"

"I'll get another job. They haven't replaced me at my old position. My parents have already offered to help out anyway they can with Emma. I'll be fine. You're the one I'm worried about."

"Me?" He looked first startled and then his lips plucked upward. "Why are you worried about me?"

"I'm afraid you'll slip back into your old ways. Stop relaxing. Forget about your art." She nodded at the painting. "Push yourself past the point of no return, or give in and agree to the surgery in a desperate bid to get back on the mound."

"If you're so concerned, then stay." His eyes were magnets, pulling her in. "We can work this out."

"We can't. I can't."

They stared at each other for a long time, neither moving nor speaking.

Finally, she moved to the back door, rested her hand on the knob. "I have to go."

Curtly, he nodded.

And didn't try to stop her as she fled.

CHAPTER 20

Axel didn't stop Kasha because his mental wheels were churning. If she left the Gunslingers there was nothing standing in the way of them hooking up. While he hated losing her as his therapist, there was nothing stopping him from hitting a home run.

The red-hot dreams he'd been struggling to suppress came roaring to life, and his body got hard just thinking about her.

She had baggage, sure as shit, but he was the guy to help her unpack. He had a few stuffed bags of his own, and she didn't seem put off.

What about the Yankees? What about your big plans?

If he got what he wanted, he'd be living in New York. And Kasha was anchored to her family, and this town. He couldn't very well expect her to rearrange her entire life for him.

C'mon, Richmond. Honestly? What were the odds that he'd make it to the Yankees? Probably a little better than a million-to-one, but not much. Was he going to let that remote possibility stop him from pursuing the woman he wanted?

He thought of Kasha—the taste of those honeyed lips, the smell of her earthy scent, the feel of her smooth latte skin.

No. No, he was not.

He wanted her. Needed her. Had to have her.

Problem was, how to convince Kasha to give their relationship a chance?

AFTER KASHA LEFT the ranch, she called Dr. Harrison, and he accepted Kasha's resignation without trying to talk her out of it. Which was both a relief and a kick to the ego.

Dr. Harrison told her he would call Axel and arrange for him to return to Dallas. Paul Hernandez would assume his former role as Axel's therapist. And the front office would mail Kasha her final check.

All was well in Gunslingers world.

After that, she went to see her old boss, Linda Smothers, at Stardust General Hospital, and asked for her job back as head of physical therapy.

"Oh thank heavens," Linda said. "I've been beating the bushes for someone to replace you, and we couldn't find a single applicant with your skill set. Yes, yes, please come back. I convinced management they'd have to bump the salary in order to get someone with your qualifications, so you're in for a 5K a year raise."

It wasn't even in the ballpark of her salary with the Gunslingers, but it was something, and Kasha readily accepted without negotiating. She needed a job if she was going to petition the court for custody of Emma.

Speaking of Emma, she also called Molly Banks and arranged for Emma to spend the night with her on Friday. Hopefully this stab at a sleepover would take.

Then she had time to kill.

On Wednesday, she hung out at Timeless Treasures chatting with her parents about Emma and making plans, and then dropped by Jodi's B&B to see how things were going with her pregnancy.

By four o'clock that afternoon she'd run out of ways to occupy herself, and she started thinking about Axel again, and that stirred up a firestorm of emotions.

Stop it. Clear your mind.

Yoga.

But not home alone. She needed to be around other people. She'd go to the yoga studio. Stretch him out of her mind.

But when Kasha walked into the studio she found Axel already there, signing up for the five p.m. class.

She rolled her eyes to the ceiling. Seriously?

"Shouldn't you be in Dallas?"

"I told them I needed a couple of days to pack."

"So what are you doing here? Why aren't you packing?"

"Somebody once told me to try a yoga class," he said. "So I thought I might."

"Okay," she said, ignoring the thump of her pulse. She turned for the door. "Have a good workout."

"You're not staying?"

"I forgot I have some things to do." She jerked a thumb over her shoulder.

"You're letting me run you off."

"I'm not."

"Then do your errands later." His gaze both cajoled and challenged, daring her to stay.

"Kasha," called the instructor from the doorway of the classroom. "We haven't seen you in a while. Come on in."

Because of the long hours created by her drive to Dallas, she hadn't been to the studio much since she'd started working for the Gunslingers.

"Yes." Axel grinned. "Come on in."

Fine. She wasn't going to let him get under her skin. Ignoring him as best she could, Kasha went into the classroom, staked out her usual spot, and unfurled her mat.

A few minutes later, she hung in a Forward Fold, her hands cradling her elbows, her head and shoulder loose in Ragdoll Pose, trying to tame her stampeding pulse and stop thinking about Axel, who was on the yoga mat in front of her.

She wasn't going to look at his butt, no, not she. Her eyes were staying tightly closed.

Not a peek. Not a glimmer.

Kasha turned her head, and from her upside-down position, cracked open one eye.

Hot damn, but the man had an amazing ass!

Both eyes popped open wide.

Fudge. This so was not her. She was proud of her self-control. But dammit, once opened, her eyes refused to close.

"Sweep upward," said the instructor.

Through the material of his cotton T-shirt, Kasha could see Axel's taut ass muscles flex and move. She was so glad that he was in front of her and not vice versa. Although it would be even better if he weren't here at all, invading *her* sanctuary.

Better still if she could stop scoping out his hard body, and noticing how he was built, and thinking about that night at the lake. And remembering just how good he tasted.

"And swan dive down," guided the instructor.

"How am I doing?" Axel whispered to Kasha from between his legs.

"Shh."

"I caught you checking me out. My form okay?"

"Your form is fine. Your mouth, however, moves way too much," she whispered back.

"Wanna go for coffee after this?"

"No."

"My treat."

"You really don't know the meaning of 'no,' do you?"

"Do you have a question, Kasha?" asked the instructor.

"I'm good," she told the instructor. To Axel, she whispered, "Shut up."

Thankfully, he did shut up, and she spent the next hour keeping her eyes focused on the teacher.

"On your backs," the instructor called at the end of the workout.

During the Savasana, the final pose of the session, Kasha lay quiet, unmoving, and when the rest of the class gathered up their yoga mats and drifted out of the studio, she kept her eyes squeezed tightly closed, listening to Axel roll up his mat and walk away. When she was certain the room was empty, she let out a long breath, opened her eyes, and got up.

But when she stepped out into the lobby, there he was, leaning one insouciant shoulder against the wall, throwing her a sunbeam smile. She shouldn't encourage him, but the dangerous part of her she couldn't seem to control smiled back.

Dammit, she was done for.

He held the door open, held her gaze. "Coffee?"

She nodded helplessly, hefted her yoga mat sling over her shoulder, and followed him like it was a foregone conclusion. They walked across the street to the coffee shop, and Kasha couldn't help admiring his height. He made her feel, if not exactly petite, definitely more feminine.

He held the door open for her again when they entered the coffee shop. They placed their order and he guided her to a table. A few minutes later he hopped up to pick up his espresso and her iced coffee.

"Thanks," she mumbled, feeling her body heat the way it did every time she was near him.

Axel pulled his wooden chair closer to hers.

An uncomfortable silence settled over them as they simultaneously sipped their drinks.

"Used up all your witty conversation in class, did you?" she finally asked.

"You told me to shut up." A sly, wry smile plucked the corners of his mouth up in an I'm-not-playing-by-any-particular-rules grin.

"So . . ." Kasha scooted her chair back. "Catch you later. Thanks again for the coffee."

His big palm settled on hers, stilling her. "Stay."

"I'm not a Labrador retriever you can boss around."

"You've never owned a Labrador retriever," he stated with absolute certainty.

"How do you know? I might have."

"You didn't. Otherwise you would know they have minds of their own."

"Since you're comparing me to a Labrador, then you won't be

surprised when I disobey your commands." Kasha slipped her hand out from under his, her pulse bounding wildly, and stood up.

"Actually, I expected you to bolt and run."

Well, fudge. She couldn't very well do what he expected. She plunked back down. This time, his grin was a tad less self-assured, and that pleased her.

"You're staying?"

"Don't push it, dude." She stared at his lips, feeling exasperated and bewildered and horny as all get-out.

"Dude?" His smile widened.

"It's something people say." She shrugged, but the casual gesture didn't do anything to ward off the brushfire building in her solar plexus every time he peered deeply into her eyes.

"Other people say it." He leaned in closer, so close she could smell his thyme-scented cologne. "Not you."

"Hey, apparently I do, since I just said it."

"You called me dude to keep me at a distance."

"Right, because a word is as good as metal armor."

"It can be. The way you wield it. Dude makes me sound silly and shallow."

"If the dude fits . . ." She shrugged again, letting her shoulders linger up around her jawline for a second.

He pretended to pluck his tongue from his mouth and file it against an imaginary whetstone before popping it back into his mouth. "Sharpened and ready to duel. Let me have it, Sphinx."

Kasha rolled her eyes and pressed her lips together tight to keep from smiling. She was *not* going to encourage him.

"I'm being funny," he said, "but I want to have a serious conversation."

"What about?"

"Us."

"THERE IS NO *us*," she said calmly, levelly, and anyone who didn't know her would say she meant it.

But Axel knew better. He knew she kept her feelings wrapped up tight, too afraid of losing control to let them off the leash.

"Why are you so scared of having a relationship with me? I'm not your patient anymore."

"I didn't quit so we could hook up. The reason I can't be with you hasn't changed. I'm still a therapist even if I'm not *your* therapist."

"So?"

"A therapist/patient sexual relationship is wrong because of the inequality of power. When you're a patient, you're vulnerable. For me to engage in a sexual relationship with you puts me in control, and gives me an advantage."

"Sounds like a cop-out to me."

"You're weak, vulnerable. I can't . . . won't take advantage of that fact."

Quickly, Axel stuck both his feet around the rungs of her chair legs, and before she could even react, he yanked her, chair and all, right across the cement toward him.

Her eyes widened as he grasped the back of her chair with both hands and leaned his body over her, his face firmly planted in front of her.

"Anything about me look weak and vulnerable to you, Sphinx?"

Ulp. No.

"You know what I think?" he asked, his voice low, his lips devastatingly close, his knees bumped against hers, his hands gripping both of her shoulders.

She bobbed her head, unable to find her voice.

"I think you're so scared of your own sexuality. That you're terrified of feeling your true power."

How did he know? Could he read it in her face? No way. She'd spent years learning how to keep her feelings from showing on her face, hours in front of a mirror honing her skills. How had her practice failed her?

"No? Fine, go ahead and keep your secrets Sphinx," he said, and shook his head as if she'd greatly disappointed him. "I'm just damn worried about you."

"Don't fret about me." She notched up her chin so he wouldn't see the uncertainty in her eyes. "I can take care of myself."

"You really don't want people scaling your ivy-covered walls, do you?"

"And yet you keep trying to climb them. Maybe I should cut down the ivy and grow something with thorns?"

"Where's a machete when I need one?" He cast a glance around as if searching for a honed blade to slice her defenses to ribbons.

"Wal-Mart. Aisle ten."

"I'm getting the feeling that by the time I got back from Wal-Mart the vines will be so thick I'd need to go back for a chain saw."

"Could be," she said mildly, vaulting over the fact her pulse was pounding hard and fast.

"Okay then, if you're not interested in pursuing something with me, then come back to work for the Gunslingers," he said.

"I can't."

"Because of me?"

"No. Because of me. I broke my code of ethics when I kissed you, and I don't like me very much right now."

"Don't worry." He winked, and the gesture sent a fizz of something hot and strange bursting through her veins. "I like you plenty for the both of us."

"Stop it."

"Stop what?"

"Being charming. It's irritating."

He pulled a face. "First time I've ever heard that one."

"Some people find charm exhausting." She wished she could scoot back, but he held fast to her chair with his feet. She couldn't even get up without tripping over him.

"And you're one of those people?"

"Yes."

"You are such a liar. You are just afraid you'll like me too much, and then, gasp, where will you be? All these messy feelings to deal with. News flash, darling. Life is messy when you're living it full-out."

"No, I'm not afraid of my feelings for you," she said, and crossed her fingers before she sat on her hands.

"Yes, yes you are. And if you like me too much, that means you're having feelings for me, and you hate having feelings."

"You're right about the last part," she conceded, grabbing for her drink and taking a long pull on her straw.

"I'm right about the first part too."

"Or you're just supremely full of yourself. Believe it or not, some people are not impressed with star baseball pitchers."

"These are the same people who find charming exhausting?" He leaned back in his chair, but kept his knees locked around hers. He lowered his lashes and studied her without speaking for so long that Kasha started to squirm.

"No, different crowd." She picked up a sugar shaker, took the top off her drink, poured the sugar in, and stirred it up with her straw, more for something to do than because her drink wasn't sweet enough. "Although there might be a few in both camps."

"Which camp are you in?"

"The I-don't-much-give-a-damn camp."

"Ah," he said. "The Rhett Butler defense. Someone gets under your skin, and rather than deal with it, you pretend you don't care."

"Is it working?" She slid a glance at him.

"Not so much."

She took a drink. Made a face. "Ugh."

"You just put salt in your drink."

"So I see."

"Me too."

"You put salt in your coffee?"

"No, I see that you're trying to hide just how much you're attracted to me. That kiss at the lake meant something to me, and I think it meant something to you too. Otherwise why let it chase you off?"

"I'm not doing this." She folded her arms over her chest.

"Then why did you come for coffee?"

"I needed a jolt of caffeine."

"You keep lying like that and that gorgeous nose of yours is going to grow into an elephant trunk. You want another iced coffee?" He nodded at her salty drink.

"I'm good," she said.

"Yes you are," he agreed and then kissed her right there in the coffee shop.

She didn't resist even though she was fully aware of the eyes trained on them, knowing this was going to be all over town by nightfall.

Kasha didn't care anymore. She was a grown woman, not that far off from thirty-one. She no longer worked for the Gunslingers. He was no longer her client. There was nothing standing in the way of her taking him as a lover if that's what she wanted.

Kasha kissed him back, spearing her fingers through his hair, cupped her palms around his ears, realizing he was doing the exact same thing to her. Pinning her to the chair, holding her in place as he leaned across the table to drink her in. He tasted of coffee, rich and potent, and she couldn't get enough.

He kissed her shoulder and then her neck. What a miracle it was to be here with him. To be with this man, feel the brand of his mouth upon her skin. He pulled back to study her and she looked up into his face, and she was suddenly struck by who he was. One of the top baseball pitchers in the country, and he was kissing *her*.

"Oh my," she whispered.

"What is it?" His warm breath feathered the hairs along her temple.

"Nothing." She ducked her head.

Everything.

He titled her face up to him, kissed her again. "Tell me."

"You're *the* Axel Richmond."

"So?"

"It's a lot of pressure being with someone like you. Expectations. I don't want to disappoint."

"You won't."

He dragged her upward until she was on her feet and bent across the table the same way he was, the two of them meeting in the middle, the infernal table between them preventing full body con-tact and she thought, *Where can we go from here?* But his mouth was so blistering hot she stopped thinking at all.

The coffee shop burst into applause and Axel said, "You wanna get out of here?" and Kasha murmured, "Yes," and the next thing she knew they were in his sporty BMW speeding toward Rowdy's ranch.

CHAPTER 21

It took a full ten minutes to get up that hill. There was time to come to her senses. Time to back out. Plenty of time to change her mind.

But Kasha did not change her mind.

Axel stopped the car in the middle of the driveway, killed the engine, and hopped out to come around to her side to open the door, but she was already out, flinging herself into his arms.

He spun her around and crushed her mouth with his and she was dizzy and breathless and crazy.

Breathe.

She tried, but her lungs refused to cooperate. They pumped wildly, her chest moving up and down, but no air exchanged. Somehow, her top was unbuttoned and so was his shirt and they were both rumpled, lips glistening from the wet heat of their kisses, and he looked as bushwhacked as she felt.

"Bed," he gasped.

"Bed?" She blinked as if it was a foreign word, her mind so soaked with sensation she couldn't think.

"Do you want bed . . ." He grunted like a caveman and glanced down at the terrazzo entryway. She followed where his gaze went, and shivered a little. "Or floor?"

"The Creedys?" While the groundskeeper and his wife had their own cottage several acres away, they could show up at the ranch house anytime.

"Right." He nodded vigorously. "Bed."

"Bed," she echoed.

He grabbed her hand and dragged her up the stairs behind him, her heart a jackhammer in her chest, slamming against her rib cage.

"Wait," she said outside the door of the guest bedroom where he was staying.

"What?" His voice came out rough and strangled.

"Condoms."

He patted his back pocket. "Been carrying them around with me since the day we met."

"Cocky bastard." She grinned.

"Aren't you glad?" he growled.

"Yes," she admitted as he sank his mouth on hers again and waltzed her into the bedroom.

"Wait." She splayed a palm over his chest.

"What?" He groaned, shallow and reedy, as if there were no oxygen left in the room.

"We need to talk."

He groaned again, deeper and full of frustration. "What about?"

"You. Me. Us."

"What about us?"

"What this means."

He chuffed, exasperated, and jammed fingers through his mussed hair. "What do you want it to mean?"

"What do you want it to mean?"

Stalling out, his hand dropped to his side. "No matter what I say, I'm going to get my butt in a crack."

"I'm not in a place for a relationship. Not while I'm in the process of getting custody of Emma, and introducing her into my life."

"Okay, I can live with that." He nodded, but his lips tightened and thinned as if he disagreed.

"Really?"

"I'll take what I can get."

"That's it?"

He paused again, looked confused, asked in a hopeful voice, "You want more? 'Cause—"

"No," she lied, because she wanted so very much more that it terrified her.

"So casual. Just this one time?" he asked, and she felt slightly sick to her stomach. He paused, looked her squarely in the eyes. "You sure that's what you want?"

"You're talking too mu—" She didn't get to finish the last word because he lowered his head, lowered his eyes, grabbed hold of her, and pulled her up flush against his chest.

He eased his knee between hers, parting her legs, cupped her face with both hands, and kissed her—hotly, wetly, thoroughly.

Their body heat mingled and she melted into him. His hands slipped from her face to her shoulders and then ambled on down to cradle her breasts, and she thought, *The sexiest pitcher in major league ball is groping me*, and she chuckled against his lips.

"What's so funny?" he asked.

She slipped her arms around her waist, and opened her eyes, peeked up at him. It was great to be with a guy who was taller than she was. He made her feel petite and über-feminine. "You. Me. This."

"That's funny?"

"Far-fetched."

"Why?"

"Why what?"

"Why do you find the idea of us being together far-fetched?"

She opened her mouth, realized she didn't have a good answer, and shut it again. "Are you going to stand here talking all night or take me to bed?"

He thought about that for all of two seconds. "Bed."

"Good man."

"Good ain't the half of it, sweetheart. Just you wait and see." His grin went wicked, and before she knew what was happening, he bent and scooped her into his arms.

"Put me down!" she exclaimed. "I'm too big for you to be carrying. You'll hurt your shoulder!"

"It's already hurt."

"Axel!" She didn't try to fight because she might throw him off balance and cause more problems. "Put me down!"

"I hate having limitations," he growled.

"Tough. You're not Superman. Deal with it."

Grudgingly, he lowered her to the floor.

"Thank you." She straightened.

He took her hand and led her into the bedroom, Kasha's heart skipped. She could still leave. There was time. No line had been crossed.

But then he turned back and looked at her so sweetly that every last bit of fear drained away, and she knew she would follow this man anywhere.

HE'D AGREED TO a one-night stand simply to get her into bed, but Axel wanted so much more. This wasn't just about sex. Not by a long shot.

But he'd have to think about that later. Right now he had a lush, sexy woman in his arms, and he wasn't about to blow it.

"I can't wait to peel those yoga pants off you," he whispered.

"What are you waiting for?" She fluttered her eyelashes in a coy gesture that was very un-Kasha-like.

"I just want to look at you for a moment." He stepped back, raised his hands like he was framing a camera shot. "Store it in my memory."

She was so beautiful. Her sloe-eyes dark and mysterious, her hair caught up in a high ponytail showing off her exquisite bone structure, her impossibly perfect ears, her straight regal nose, her full lips moist and inviting, her white bra visible beneath her unbuttoned shirt.

"Want me to get my cell phone?" she teased.

"Nope. This moment is private, and all mine."

The Sphinx cracked a big grin, and *boom,* she was no longer the Sphinx. Her smile caught him low in the belly, spread pressure and heat straight to his groin.

Axel felt dizzy and weak-kneed and over-the-moon in love with her. He shook his head to clear it, but nothing doing. He was in so deep he knew there was no getting out of this unscathed.

Moreover, he didn't care.

She shrugged the shirt down one shoulder, slanted him a sultry gaze that tightened every masculine muscle in his body. Slowly, she slid it off the other shoulder, let the shirt drift to the floor.

Taking in her lithe, muscular body with ample curves in all the right places, his eyes almost bugged out of his head.

And when she turned her back to him, and unlatched her bra, he was salivating.

The bra joined the shirt on the floor, and when she turned back to face him, and unveiled those perfect breasts, he almost cried out in painful joy. He felt as if he'd waited his whole lifetime for this moment.

This woman.

"Kasha." He breathed her name and let the sound fill his lungs, his heart, his blood, until every cell throbbed with vibration. *Kasha. Kasha. Kasha.*

"Well?" One elegant eyebrow went up on her forehead.

Speechless. He was speechless. Struck dumb by her beauty.

"Are you going to stand there staring all night, or make your pitch, player?" Heat and affection for him danced in her eyes, and he laughed because being with her felt so damn good.

"I'm so glad you quit," he said. "I thought this was never going to happen."

"It still shouldn't be happening," she said. "But you're hot, and I'm weak."

"Thank God for that." His palms itched to cup the weight of her breasts.

"You better make a move before I back out," she threatened, sinking her hands on her hips.

He sobered. "I don't want you to do anything you'll regret, Kasha."

"I'm regretting that it's taking you so long to get to it." She eased the waistband of her yoga pants down over her hips, giving him a glimpse of a pair of white thong panties, leaning over in a sexy little backbend that showed off her tiny waist and curvy rump.

"Actually . . ." He ogled her, admiring how the Lycra fit her like a second skin. "I was thinking I should hop in right about now and finish shucking off those pants for you. Although it does look like they've been spray-painted on."

Kasha folded the waistband down another turn, wriggling her hips. "Easy as peel-and-eat shrimp."

"Mmm," he said. "You're making me hungry, and not for seafood."

"Me too," she murmured, soft as silk.

"I like the taste of salty, earthy things. Oysters . . ." He let his gaze drift to the sweet V between her legs, and was rewarded when she shivered.

"Oh yeah." Her voice was husky, wet.

He closed the space between them until they were almost touching, breasts to chest. And her heart was pounding so hard he could see her pulse beating at the hollow of her throat. "I've been fantasizing about this from the moment we first met. I can't think of anything but you."

"That sounds limiting."

"Not at all. In my daydreams we're always doing the most adventuresome things." He lowered his head until he could feel her breath on his cheek, and he stopped just millimeters short of her lips.

"I hope I don't disappoint, since you've built this up so much in your head."

"You could never disappoint me."

"You say that now . . ."

"It's gonna be great." He wrapped his arms around her back and pulled her up flush against him. She let out a soft little sound of surrender that unraveled him on several different levels.

Her body was so hot beneath his palms and he thought, *I'm not going to last five minutes.*

She kissed him. Tentative. Quick.

Axel groaned and captured her lips, not going to let her get away with drive-by kissing. No sir. "All or nothing, babe," he said, and speared her with his tongue.

She inhaled sharply, those grapefruit breasts rising fast and hard against him. He closed his eyes, struggled for control, instinct urging him to toss her on the bed and slide right into her warm wetness.

Easy does it. Slow and steady wins the race.

She kissed him back, hot and sweet, and he opened his eyes to find her staring at him.

"Christ, I want you," he whispered against her mouth, a teasing tickle of sensation moving across his upper lip. "I wanted you the minute you strolled into the Gunslingers locker room looking all mysterious and mystical. I wanted you when I dragged you soaking wet from the swimming pool. I wanted you when you latched onto my waist on the Jet Ski. I wanted you—"

"I want you too," she cooed, her eyes ablaze with lust and need.

"It's more than that, Kasha. More than want. More than need. I . . ." *I love you.* How did he say it without scaring her?

"Don't," she cautioned, placing an index finger over his lips. "Don't ruin the moment. Just be here with me now. Don't say anything else. Just take me. Do me. Make me feel good."

Axel didn't need to be asked twice. He sank to his knees, and on his way down grabbed hold of the waistband of her yoga pants that hovered at her hips, and tugged, stripping them to her knees.

But a clear view of her scars stopped him. He'd caught glimpses of the scars when her shorts rode up when they were out on the lake, but seeing them now, seeing how she'd sliced herself when she was a teen because she was in so much emotional pain, cut him right in two.

She was trembling under his scrutiny, exposed, bare. Her hands threaded through his hair, her head dipped, her eyes closed, her breathing ragged and insubstantial. He cupped her buttocks in his palms, held her steady. Letting her know he was not repulsed.

One by one, he traced over each thin scar as if he could salve her pain with his tongue, heal her past. A hundred and three of them in total, each one about half an inch long, and the width of a pocket-knife blade, lined up in rows like soldiers. Fifty-two on one thigh, fifty-one on the other.

When he finished counting her sorrow of scars, he planted his face against her panties and breathed deeply.

Mine, he thought greedily. *Mine.*

But was she really? He wanted her. Was determined to woo her. Loved her. But how did she feel about him? She made it clear this was just fun. Could he really convince her to take a chance on him, or was he going to end up with a broken heart?

He didn't care. Loving her was worth the risk. Dylan had taught him that lesson. As painful as losing those you love might be, loving was always worth the shattered heart.

Axel squirmed, overwhelmed by need and desire and love and fear.

As if reading his mind, Kasha dropped to her knees and planted her lips on his chest, right on the tattoo of Dylan's name, and kissed away his scars the same way he kissed away hers.

And he knew that no matter what happened, one way or another everything was going to be okay.

CHAPTER 22

Fifteen minutes later, they were sitting naked in the middle of the bed, staring at each other, both of them trying not to show their disappointment to the other.

How could the sex have fizzled when the chemistry between them was so sizzling? When the kiss at the lake had been off-the-charts fantastic? When their foreplay stirred goose bumps.

"You were wrong," she said.

"About what?"

"I did disappoint. Epic fail," she muttered.

"Not epic," he comforted. "And certainly not a fail. More like a mulligan. Think of it as a mulligan. We need a do-over."

"It's not your fault," she mumbled. "Sometimes I can't get there. We put too much pressure on ourselves. Unrealistic expectations."

"You're giving up so soon, Sphinx."

"It's okay. No big deal—"

"It is not okay."

She couldn't meet his gaze. She was in the medical field. Normally sex talk didn't embarrass her, but she was feeling inadequate and just wanted out of here. "Maybe the kiss was so great because it was taboo. I was your therapist then, but now that I'm not, and the thrill of rule breaking is gone—"

"That's not it."

She lifted her eyes and briefly looked at him. "Maybe it is. Maybe that's the only reason we were so hot before. The forbidden fruit."

"That's not it," he repeated with such certainty that she had no choice but to take him seriously.

"Honestly, Axel, it's not you, it's me."

"Stop," he commanded. "It's no one's fault. We just quit too soon."

"Well, you came—"

"And you didn't. That means the party is not over."

"You have no obligation to satisfy me."

"The hell I don't."

"Check your ego, champ. I'm in charge of my own sexuality."

"All right, so let's go again and this time you fully let go. You're relaxed everywhere but in bed. Your self-control is amazing, but in the sack, that's not such a good thing."

"Look, I've got things to do." She pushed her bracelet down on her wrist, eager to just end it.

"You're not leaving until we make this happen."

"You don't owe me an orgasm. You don't owe me anything. Let's just chalk this one up to things that should never have happened and—"

He kissed her. "Shh."

"Your ego is getting in the way," she mumbled around his lips. "You don't have to prove yourself to me. All those groupies can't be wrong. I'm sure you're normally fantastic in bed and it's simply because we just don't mesh . . ."

When she paused to take a breath, he slipped his tongue between her teeth and made a thrilling little maneuver over the roof of her mouth. The trick—whatever it was—lit up nerve endings from her mouth straight to her womb. Wow, okay, she liked that.

He leaned forward, pushing her back against the pillow, her body burrowing deeper into the memory foam mattress. She readjusted her legs, spreading them apart so he could sink between them. They were face-to-face, his eyes peering into hers as if she was the most interesting thing he'd ever come across.

"You're sweating," he said.

"I know." She ran a palm across her brow, shivered.

"It was an observation, not a criticism." He kissed her skin where she'd just rubbed away the perspiration. "Just wanted you to know there's no reason to break out in a cold sweat. I wasn't serious about holding you hostage until you came. You can leave anytime you want."

"I know."

"Are you staying?"

"Depends on what you intend on doing with that tongue."

"Ah," he said. "At last we're getting somewhere."

"You know this might not end up the way you want it to, no matter how hard you try."

"Seems to be the theme of my life lately."

"You'll get your pitching arm back."

"You sound so certain."

"I am."

"How can you be so sure?"

"Because you're not the kind of guy who gives up."

"I'm glad you're starting to realize that." He kissed the indentation between her nose and her lip, his body heavy against her.

Kasha sucked in a ragged breath. She could feel his erection growing bigger, stronger.

He moved to nibble her earlobe and she shuddered. "You like that." It was a statement, not a question.

Helplessly, she nodded.

"Mmm," he murmured against her ear. "Salty. I like salty."

"Too much salt isn't good for you."

"Are you trying to kill the mood? Roll with it, babe."

"Okay." She gasped because he was doing amazing things with his tongue.

"Now here's the way I see it. For some reason, you're afraid to let yourself go with me."

"Maybe," she admitted.

"The challenge"—he tucked a strand of hair behind her ear, his fingers gentle against her skin—"is to figure out how to loosen you up."

"I don't see how I could get any looser," she said. "My body is so loose it feels like liquid nitrogen."

"I'm not talking about your body." His voice dropped lower, deeper. "I'm talking about that razor-sharp mind of yours. You think too much, Sphinx. That's what's tripping you up."

"Is that right?"

"Yep. And it's my job to find a way to turn off your inner critic long enough to get there."

"Good luck with that," she mumbled.

"You're waving a red flag at a horny bull, you realize that, right?" He kissed the tip of her nose. "I can't resist a thrown gauntlet."

"I wasn't making a dare."

"No?"

"No."

"So you don't want me to do this?" He slipped his hands between her thighs, touched her lightly in just the right place with just the right amount of pressure.

"I do not."

"You sure?" He tickled lightly, making her squirm and swallow back a moan of pleasure.

"Stop it," she whimpered weakly.

"This?" he asked, doing something that lit up every nerve ending in her pelvis. "Or this?"

She tingled and burned. "I think . . . I think . . ."

"Yes?"

"I can't think while you're doing that."

"Good. Thinking gets you in trouble."

"I think . . ." She sucked in a gallon of oxygen, did her best to ignore the zings and zaps his fingers stirred up. "I think we should just call it a day. We gave it a shot. The chemistry is a bust. Now we can move on."

"Nope," he said. "You don't get to do that."

"Do what?"

He manacled her wrists to the mattress with his hands. "Withdraw."

"That's not what I'm doing."

"No?" One skeptical eyebrow shot up on his forehead. "Smells like running away to me."

"It's not running away," she said. "I have things to do—"

"Oh yeah? Like what?"

"Grocery shopping."

"That can wait."

"Not really. The grocery store closes at ten and I don't have a crumb of food in the house."

"You're intentionally being difficult."

"And you're doing what you always do. Push."

"You keep saying that like pushing is a bad thing."

"Sometimes it is."

"When?"

Kasha blinked, unable to think of anything, and finally blurted, "When the door says pull."

He laughed. "Are you telling me you honestly don't want to have headboard-bangingly great sex?"

"You're making promises you can't back up."

"Not as long as you keep fighting me. But . . ." He raked his gaze over her naked body, so bold and appreciative that Kasha shuddered. "If you just let go and let loose, nothing could contain you."

"I know."

He canted his head, looked confused for a moment. "That's what you're afraid of? Being off the chain?"

"I like being contained."

"Ah," he said as if someone had turned a lightbulb on and he could see he was in a great vast library instead of a cubbyhole. "What do you think will happen if you let yourself go?"

She shook her head, tried to get out of the grip he held on her wrists, but he was too strong for her.

"You want up?"

"Yes," she said, feeling petulant, but not wanting him to know he'd gotten to her. "Please."

"Points for good manners," he said. "But there's only one way you're getting up from here."

"What's that?"

"Talk."

She rolled her eyes. "C'mon."

"Talk to me. Tell me why you're so closed off."

"You are seriously annoying, you know that? Most guys would be happy if women didn't want to talk about their feelings. But you're at me with a pickaxe and shovel."

"I'm not most guys," he said.

No. No, he certainly was not. He ran his tongue along her collarbone, and instinctively she arched her hips, seeking to press against him. Damn him.

"Score." He laughed raggedly against her neck.

"Look," she said. "You don't have to keep trying. It's not your fault. It's not my fault. It's not anyone's fault. We just didn't click."

"Bullshit," he said softly, trailing his fingers over her breasts damp with perspiration. "We click like a Bic."

"Could we just cuddle?"

"No," he said. "It's time to get down to brass tacks. What gets you hot and bothered?"

"Nothing much," she answered, which was perfectly true. She worked hard to make sure of it.

He pressed his hips against hers. "Role playing? Sex in public places? Feathers? Fur? Handcuffs?"

"It's not going to work. Accept it."

"What turns you on, Kasha?" His husky voice brushed her ears.

You. You turn me on. That's the problem. She closed her eyes. Fought for control.

"Blindfolds?" he whispered. "Tickling?"

"Tickle me and I might pee on you."

"So is that a thing?"

"No! No tickling, no peeing."

"Good, because I wasn't on board with that either."

"We're compatible there anyway," she mumbled.

"Spanking?" he said. "Do you like to be spanked?"

"Only if you let me spank you first."

"That's definitely not happening."

"You might just have to accept that we're not that great in the sack."

"It's a romantic myth that sex is fantabulous the first time out of the gate. Anything worth doing well takes practice. Lots and lots of practice."

"Hmm," she said noncommittally.

"Kidnap fantasies?" he asked. "Bringing food to bed?"

"If you wash the sheets afterward."

"That could be arranged. What else? Ménage à trois?"

"In your dreams, bucko. I'm the jealous type. I don't share my lover with anyone." Kasha didn't even know that until she said it, but damn if it wasn't true. If he was her man, she wasn't about to share him.

And that scared her because it made her think of her mother who killed her father for being unfaithful. She pushed against his hands, wanting up. Wanting out of there. He was pushing her out of her comfort zone, and she didn't like that.

"Hold on," he said. "We're starting to get somewhere. Do you like sex toys? What about having your toes sucked?"

She shivered.

"Oh ho. So that's it? The toe thing?"

Her toes were very sensitive, but she didn't want him going down there, doing that. It would unhinge her completely.

He chuckled like some black-hatted villain in a cowboy movie, let go of her wrists, and slid down the length of her body, his naked skin against hers. She could get away now, but she didn't.

"No," she protested weakly. "Don't."

His mouth was planting a hot kiss at her navel, but he didn't linger there, just kept going down and down and down, dropping a kiss at key points along the way.

"You can stop there," she said when he reached the center of her womanhood. She ran her fingers through his hair, and twisting the strands to hold him in place.

"Not yet, babe. Not yet." He pushed downward.

She clung to him.

"Ouch. You're pulling my hair."

"I know. Leave my toes alone."

"No way. I've got to see what happens when I give those little piggies some attention."

"Please," she whimpered, as he pulled free from her grip, his mouth kissing her upper thigh. "Don't."

"Please?" he said. "Or don't? Those are two different things."

"Don't . . ."

But he wasn't listening. His tongue skimmed over her knee. She fell back against the pillow, weightless, helpless. Waiting. Tingling. Buzzing. The farther south he went, the more her body tightened.

"Wait," she said knowing if she didn't stop him now she never would. "At least let me go wash my feet."

"The rest of you tastes delicious, I'm sure your feet do too."

"Let me go. I'll come back. I promise."

"I don't trust you," he murmured, his mouth pressed against her shin, his hand stroking her ankle.

"I need a pedicure."

"Your feet are beautiful just the way they are."

"I would have gotten a pedicure if I'd have known you were going to be mucking around down there."

"I'll give you one," he vowed. "After."

"I—"

His mouth touched the top of her foot, and his fingers slipped around to knead the arch. Her foot burst into flames, sent a rolling flash fire straight up her leg to lodge in her groin.

Every cell in her body throbbed with each beat of her pulse. Thump. Thump. Thump. A slow heat spread through her abdomen, oozed through her blood.

"This little piggy went to market," he said, and his mouth closed over her big toe.

"Oh!" She inhaled a massive sigh. Of their own volition, Kasha's hips arched right up off the mattress and her head pressed down deeper into the pillow.

He sucked gently and she completely came undone, panting and writhing as his teeth lightly nibbled her toe.

"This little piggy stayed home . . ." He moved to the second toe, leaving her first damp and twitching.

His hand massaged the balls of her feet, rubbing pressure points, creating a sexy rhythm that destroyed her ability to think anything but more, more, more.

"This little piggy had roast beef."

Kasha moaned, wriggled.

His mouth was a vortex, sucking her in, eating her up, driving her through the roof and out of her mind.

"And this little piggy . . . now this delicious little thing . . . had none."

"No . . . more . . ." There was barely enough air in her lungs to carry the words out.

"Oh, lots more," he said. "We've got six more piggies to get through."

"Come here," she said, reaching down to pull him up. "I have to have you right now!"

"I'm not sure you're ready—"

She grabbed him by the neck and tugged him on top of her.

"Mmm, okay, I see there's been a change in plans."

"Shh," she said. "Just shh and do me."

"Yes, ma'am." He grunted, breathing heavy and pressing his chest against her breasts, which were busy drawing in ragged, quick breaths. "Just don't lose it while I get this damn condom on."

"Hurry," she insisted, full of urgency and need. "Hurry!"

"I loved sucking your toes," he said while he fumbled for the condom. "It makes me so horny. Your toes are so hot, muscular but delicate. Strong and salty and . . ."

Kasha groaned and bit down on her pillow.

"There," he said. "All done."

And then he was sliding into her, slick and hot and big and masculine.

Hot fudge sundae, he was glorious. Halle-freaking-lujah. Was she up? Was she down? Was she in? Was she out?

He was in to the hilt, filling every inch of her with his size and heat. The pressure was unbelievable, heavy and hard. He moved painstakingly slow, prodding and pushing, testing to see how much she could take.

She exhaled deep and long. Gripped his shoulder, sank her fingers into his skin. What sweet, sweet torture. She spread her legs, letting him sink deeper into her.

He gripped her hips, yanked her pelvis upward to meet his as he set a punishing pace—thrusting and thrusting and thrusting. His thumb found her hot button and gently he stroked it, pushing her to the outer limits of sanity.

Part of her wanted to hold on to her reserve, to keep leashed the part she feared most—the power of her femininity. But the primal, primitive part kidnapped her rationality and held on for dear life.

"Let go, Kasha. Let it fly," he crooned, moving to readjust the angle of his hips, and the action was enough to send her completely into orbit. "C'mon, babe, come for me."

He pounded into her, the headboard thumping wildly against the wall in time to his energetic thrusts. She opened her eyes and looked up at him, his face full of sweet agony that matched her own. What a beautiful man.

How had she gotten here? What were the consequences going to be? Was she ready for the fallout?

Hush. Enjoy the moment.

"Stay with me," he coached, rocking higher.

She tried to hold back the moan, couldn't. Failed.

"Music to my ears," he said.

She bit her lip, but there was no shutting the gate now. A long, low keening sound shot from her lips, spun around the room, a declaration of her total surrender.

They were galloping together, thundering toward a cliff, heat and moisture, pressure and friction.

Oh gosh, oh wow, oh heaven, oh my.

He rocked inside her, dropped his head, pressed his mouth against her ear and began to whisper the erotic things he wanted to do to her toes. "I want to lather them in whipped cream and slowly lick it off. I want to watch you squish those toes around in a vat of peanut butter."

Kasha wriggled and writhed, shoved past the limits of her boundaries, ensnared in the fervor and the glide and the dread and the beat that he was hammering into her.

And she came so hard she momentarily went blind.

CHAPTER 23

"I have a confession to make," Axel said once Kasha had drifted down from the rafters.

"What's that?" she murmured dozily into the darkness.

"You make me feel more alive than I've ever felt in my life."

"In bed or out?"

"Both."

"That's sweet." She cupped his face with her palm, thought how it was the most handsome face in the whole wide world. "I don't believe you for a second, but great confession."

"That wasn't the confession," he said. "It was a sidebar."

"Oh? What's the real confession?"

"I have two actually. Is that going to be a problem?"

"Depends on what you confess."

He kissed her deep and firm and long, and she kissed him back as if it was the last kiss of her lifetime and she knew it.

"Wow," he said. "Wow."

"I will hear your confessions now," she said in a queenly tone.

"I lied," he said. "No way is this casual."

"I know," she said. "I lied too."

"I wasn't fooled for a second."

"What else you got for me?"

He kissed her again, then pulled her into the crook of his arm and snuggled against her, making sure she felt his erection.

"I meant confession-wise," she clarified.

"Before I tell you, you have to promise not to get mad."

"How can I promise that until I know what you did? What did you do?"

"Not me. You can't get mad at Jodi."

"Did she tell you about the toe thing?" Kasha swatted Axel's upper arm. "Because if she told you about the toe thing . . ."

"No, I figured that one out on my own."

An uneasy feeling rippled over Kasha. "What did you do?"

"I went to see Jodi, and asked her about what you were like as a kid. She gave me the newspaper clippings about your parents' deaths. I wasn't going to tell you I went poking around, but I can't keep anything from you. I don't want there to be any secrets between us."

Kasha wasn't mad. In fact, she was pleased he cared enough to find out more about her. "Why didn't you ask me for the clippings?"

"There's a reason I call you Sphinx. You don't like to talk about your past."

"Still, to sneak around behind my back . . ."

"It was underhanded," he admitted. "I needed to know all the details about what happened to you, and I didn't want to stir up any more bad memories."

"Why did you need to know the details?"

"Why you can't let go and be yourself. Why you're so afraid of your own passion."

She could hear the digital clock on the desk turn over along with her stomach.

"I get it now. Why you're afraid that if you show any emotions at all you'll totally lose control."

Kasha tried to suck in a deep breath, but it was like trying to suck a thick milkshake through a crushed straw. "I'm doing the best that I can."

"I understand, but I needed to know what I'm up against. If you'll ever be able to—" He broke off. Shook his head.

"What?"

"Never mind."

"What?" she insisted, a band of anxiety rising up and squeezing her throat closed.

He met her gaze, and his eyes looked so sad it robbed every bit of air from her lungs.

"Axel?"

"Love," he said. "I wonder if you'll ever be able to love me the way I love you."

Love.

The word quivered in the air between them, a gelatinous thing, half formed but growing stronger by the minute.

"You . . . you . . ." She moistened her lips.

He reached out, took her suddenly cold hand in his warm one. His eyes drilled into hers. "I love you, Kasha. Can you deal with that?"

"But you . . . but I . . . we barely know each other." Oh God, she loved him too. Why was she resisting? Why couldn't she just open her mouth and say the words?

I love you.

"When it's right it's right, and nothing in my life has ever felt so right, except for Dylan. I realized I loved you when we were sitting on that dock drinking wine and you looked at me with those soulful eyes and I just knew you were the one I'd been waiting all my life to find."

The wine. It was back to the prophetic wine. Destiny. Kismet. True love. Soul mates. Her heart was an eagle soaring in the heavens, proud and bold and hopeful. So very hopeful.

But her head, her stubborn head was too terrified to let her heart have what it wanted.

"That's quite a speech, Richmond," she said, trying to make light of his declaration, trying desperately to calm her galloping pulse.

"Are you going to lie there and tell me that you don't feel it too?"

No, no, she wasn't going to deny it. She wasn't a good enough liar to pull that off.

"Are you sure it's me you love and not simply the challenge of me?" Her heart was beating so loudly she feared he could hear it pound.

"That's a legitimate question," he said honestly. "I do love a good challenge and you've put up one helluva fight. But you're the one I love."

"Are you sure it's not just pity," she asked. "Because I was the poor kid whose parents died in a murder-suicide you feel sorry for me."

"Not pity," he said. "Compassion. But I know the difference between compassion and love. I don't feel sorry for you."

"No? Here's the deal, Richmond. I don't want anyone's pity, especially yours." She ground out the words as if she were chewing gravel.

"Do you still have so little faith in me, Kasha?"

"It's precisely because I do have faith in you that I'm scared. I see how passionate you are about baseball, and I know you stir passion in me."

"Passion you'd rather not have stirred."

"Yes."

"That's why you couldn't come," he said. "Until I coaxed you into letting go. You think if you stay above the fray of life, keep your emotions contained, you won't feel any pain. I got news for you, Sphinx. You might not feel any pain, but you won't feel any joy or ecstasy either."

She knew that. Knew it far better than he did.

"Until you let go of the past," Axel said, "you can't move forward into the future."

"Are you hearing yourself right now?" she asked. "What is this? A case of do as I say, not as I do?"

"How do you think I know you're stuck?" he said. "Been there, done that."

"You're still there." She reached out and tapped the tattoo on his chest. "You're still trying to impress a little boy who is no longer here."

He tensed beneath her touch, threw back the covers. "I'm hungry, you hungry?"

"Running away?"

"Want an omelet? I can make us an omelet."

"All right," she said. "Make me an omelet. But we're not through hashing this out. Not by a long shot."

THEY SAT AT the kitchen table, Axel in pajama bottoms, Kasha wearing his paint-stained artist T-shirt that was way too big on her, omelets and two glasses of milk in front of them.

Axel looked at the food. Thought of Dylan. His appetite vanished. Kasha was right. He'd pushed her to release the past when he couldn't do the same.

Hypocrite.

He studied Kasha, wished he'd handled this better. It wasn't how he'd planned to tell her that he loved her, but he'd been so full of the feeling he couldn't hold back.

Absentmindedly, his palm went to his heart, and he felt the strong pump of it.

"What is it?" she asked.

"After Dylan died," he said, "I couldn't understand how my heart could still be beating when his had stopped. It didn't seem fair for me to be alive when that quick, bright boy was gone. It's not supposed to be like this. A parent shouldn't have to bury their child."

Kasha let out a tiny squeak of empathy, pure and swift. "I can't imagine."

Axel gave a curt nod, acknowledging her sympathy. It was all he could manage at the moment.

She reached across the table, placed her hand on top of his. "You don't have to go on. I'm sorry I goaded you into reliving this."

"No. I want to talk about him. I want to let you in. Share all my secrets. Air my dirty laundry."

"Do you have a picture of Dylan?"

He smiled involuntarily, went to get his phone. He showed her the camera roll of snapshots he couldn't bring himself to delete from the device even though he'd already backed them up.

"Oh my gosh, Axel, he's such a handsome child."

The bittersweet tone of her voice tore a hole right through him. Part of Axel wanted to put the phone away to lessen the pain of seeing his son's smiling face, but another part of him, the proud father part of him, wanted to show off his son.

"This one is my favorite." He flipped through the camera roll until he found the shot of him pitching to Dylan, who was wearing a miniature Gunslingers uniform, bat cocked over his little shoulder, feet rooted, expression serious as he concentrated for all he was worth.

"How old was he in this picture?" Kasha asked.

"Six. It was . . ." He gulped. "Just days before we got Dylan's diagnosis."

He closed his eyes, touched the part of his soul that was forever damaged, drew courage from that pain. Dragging in a fortifying breath, he raised his head and met the concern in Kasha's gaze.

"Rhabdomyosarcoma is a cancer of the connective cells of the skeletal muscles," he recited the information by rote. He could never forget the day the doctor said the same words to him and Pepper in that cramped exam room that smelled of antiseptic and citrus air freshener.

Kasha put a palm over her mouth and a world of tenderness in her eyes. Tenderness that clipped him low in the belly.

"The cancer occurs more often in boys than girls," he continued. "If caught early, it has a seventy percent cure rate. If not . . . well . . ." He shrugged, the gesture anything but casual. "The majority of cases are diagnosed before the age of five. Those tend to have a better survival rate. Dylan was six and his cancer was well advanced."

"Did he have chemotherapy, radiation?" Kasha was fully focused on him. Her exotic, dark-eyed gaze never left his face.

"Yep. Full arsenal. Big guns. He was so sick, poor little guy. Whenever I was out there on the field I pitched my heart out. Pitched for an audience of one. My boy."

"How long did he live after the diagnosis?"

Axel couldn't answer at first. His throat was knotted up too tight. Kasha waited, didn't push.

"A little less than two years. My career was soaring, but I wanted to be with Dylan. The little guy insisted I keep playing. He told me he expected me to make it to the Yankees."

He paused, swallowed, remembering the worst days of his life. "That last summer I was on the road ripped me apart. Sometimes, he watched the game from his chair in the chemotherapy center. Every time I pitched I'd tap my thumb against my ring finger. A signal just for Dylan, to let him know I was thinking of him and pitching the game in his honor."

"Oh Axel." Kasha clasped both hands to her heart. "Oh, you poor man. I can't imagine how hard that must have been. Being away from him as he fought cancer."

"Dylan's mother was a great mom. I worked so she could stay by his side 24/7. I worked for Dylan, to make him proud of his old man. But I also worked for me. Playing ball was the only way I stayed sane."

She reached over and squeezed his arm.

"Fame and fortune means nothing when your kid is sick," he said. "You'd give it all up in a heartbeat. Give up your own life to save theirs."

"Emma is beginning to show me that. She's my sister, but I'm assuming a parental role. It's epic."

"Epic is an understatement. Dylan was such a passionate kid. Before he got sick, you should have seen him. He was a much better ballplayer than I was at his age. He could have been one of the greats."

"You're still trying to be great for him."

"Yeah." Tears burned Axel's eyes as he thought of his son. He pinched the bridge of his nose with the thumb and ring finger he'd once used to signal Dylan.

"Then when he got sick, I told him I'd do it for him. Make it to the Yankees. Play in the World Series."

"That's why this dream is so important to you," Kasha murmured. "It's not for the glory or the money. It's Dylan's legacy."

"Dumb, huh." He tried to crack a smile, but didn't quite pull it off, felt his mouth slip back down at the corners.

"No. It's the opposite of dumb. It's brave and plucky and sad and glorious. You *have* to try. You don't have any other choice."

She got it, and her understanding was a sublime gift. "Now you see why I was pushing myself so hard."

Her eyes darkened. "If I'd known about Dylan, I might have recommended you get the surgery."

"Really?" Axel pulled his chin back, studied her.

She shrugged. "Maybe. I don't know."

"I'm glad I didn't have the surgery. Your way is working and I'm grateful to you."

"What about Dylan's mother?" Kasha asked. "Were you guys ever married?"

"No." He shook his head. "Pepper was a baseball groupie. A casual fling. She was a cool girl, but we were too young and we weren't in love with each other, but we both loved Dylan. We had an unusual custody arrangement. Dylan lived with Pepper during baseball season, I had him the rest of the year. And we had unrestricted visitation. Might not work for most people, but it suited us."

"Where is she now?"

"I don't know. We lost track of each other after Dylan died. No reason to stay in contact."

"Have you ever been in love before?" she asked.

He met her eyes, locked on to her gaze. "No. Have you?"

Her bottom lip was trembling. "No."

His heart thumped, gut twisted. She had never been in love.

"Not," she whispered, "until you."

Axel sat up straight, leaned toward her. "What did you say?"

"You heard me."

"Tell me again, oh woman of few words. A man needs to hear these things."

She met his stare head-on. "I love you, Axel."

Pure joy spurted through his bloodstream. He jumped up from the table, pulled her into his arms. "Aw, Sphinx. I know how hard it was for you to say it."

"Come," she said, taking his bed. "I'm better at showing than telling. Let's go back to bed."

"What about the food?" He looked down at their uneaten plates.

"Right now, I don't think either one of us cares about cold omelets."

He laughed then because his heart was full—full of joy, full of happiness, full of love for this wonderful woman.

She led him upstairs, and this time the mood was soft and quiet and somber, and their joining was all the sweeter for it. The playfulness of their first joining was washed away by the sorrow of midnight confessions.

But once they were back inside the bedroom, he pulled her to him, cupping each breast in his palms over the layer of his cotton T-shirt that she wore. She pressed against his touch, made a soft, whimpering sound.

He touched her everywhere—belly, hips, back, butt—lingering in each spot for a moment, not taking his eyes off her dear face.

He smoothed his hands down her sides, his palms curving in at her waist, flaring out at her hips. She swayed against him, and his nose filled with the smell of soap and womanhood. When he dropped to his knees and planted a kiss at the smooth skin between her thighs, she moaned and tangled her fingers in his hair.

She was so beautiful. He loved everything about her. Touching her became as important as breathing. He kissed her between her legs. Short, hot kisses. "I love the taste of you," he whispered.

His fingers slipped around to buttocks taut and lean from regular yoga. "I love the feel of your strong muscles."

The need for her was primal. Something wild inside them both that called to each other, and each other alone. Whenever heaven had made her, they threw away the mold. She was unlike any woman he'd ever met.

"I love your wounds." He kissed the line of silvered scars. "I love everything about you, Kasha. Good and bad and in between. I love every nook and cranny, every curve and angle."

He was half drunk with desire for her, anxious to slip his tongue inside her warmness. He picked her up and laid her on the bed so she would be more comfortable, and climbed up onto the mattress beside her to finish what he started, using his mouth to pleasure her in the best way he knew how.

"Yes," she whispered. "Yes, just like that."

He thrust his tongue inside her and she tightened around him, her soft purr of satisfaction driving him on. All he wanted to do was make her happy.

She wriggled and squirmed and he loved that he was the one doing this to her, enjoying her body as it heated up.

"That's right," he coaxed. "Relax. Let yourself go."

He stayed with her, kissing and stroking, licking and touching, until he felt her body stiffen and she gasped "oh" high and sweet.

And a tremor that started in her core spread out, shaking up her spine in both directions at once.

As she lay quaking, helpless, he kissed his way back up to her breasts, kissed tenderly while he reached over with one hand to find a condom on the bedside table. He was accomplished at such maneuvers, and quickly had it opened and on.

And then they were joined in mindless pleasure as he slid inside her, pushing her to trembling heights. Pleasure built. Friction. Heat. Pressure. He groaned, called her name, spread his fingers through that mass of long, dark hair.

She wrapped her legs around his waist, pulling him deeper inside her.

Heaven on earth. She was heaven right here in his bed. He claimed her lips as he moved inside her, slowing the pace to stretch things out. He didn't want it to ever end.

She surrounded him. Her heat. Her skin. Her scent. Her muscles.

When they came it was together, big and loud and sweaty. He loved it. He *loved* her.

He flopped over onto his stomach on his side of the bed, breathing hard, exhausted. She sat up, gave him a smug smile, her perky breasts standing at attention. He reached up a hand, touched her mouth. "I love it when you smile."

She plumped up the pillows and lay back against them, looking down at him stretched out on his belly. "Worn out already?"

"Why is it that women are jazzed after sex and all men want to do is sleep?" he mumbled.

"Because a man's essence is drained while a woman is filled up."

"Hmm," he said. "I never thought of it that way."

"That was fun," she said. "Can we do it again?"

"While I appreciate your enthusiasm, I'm not as young as I used to be. Can you give me a few minutes to recover?"

"Oh, sure," she said. "Take your time."

"You're just going to lie there and watch me rest?"

"If I had known sex would get you to relax I would have suggested it a long time ago." She grinned.

His face was pressed against the mattress so he was seeing her with only one eye. He studied the scars cut like fringe across the tops of her upper thighs. Reaching out, he ran a finger over the deepest one. "That must have hurt."

"Hurting was the point," she said. "I felt so numb inside, and cutting made me feel alive."

He leaned over to kiss her scars. "I'm so sorry I wasn't there to save you."

"It's okay. The Carlyles saved me, and then I saved myself with yoga."

"You are so strong." He looked at her with so much admiration he couldn't begin to express how he felt.

"Maybe," she said, "in some ways, but weak in others. Keeping my heart closed off was a failing. I realize that now. Emma was the crack that opened the door, but you . . ."

"What about me?" he asked, caressing her nipple with a fingertip.

"You were the dynamite that blew my heart wide open."

CHAPTER 24

It was near dawn when Kasha woke. She lay in bed, listening to the deep sounds of Axel's masculine breathing. He rolled over, mumbled, reached for her. Was he awake?

"Axel?" She breathed.

His arm went around her waist, and he dragged her over, spooned his body against hers.

"Axel?" she whispered again, her heart floating like a butterfly. Love. She was in love with this man and thrillingly scared that she'd admitted it. "Are you sleeping?"

He didn't answer.

She smiled into the darkness. Her nose was permeated with his incredible scent, and she realized how extraordinary this was. Wriggling her toes, she breathed in the moment, pulled it down to the bottom of her lungs, savoring every sweet second.

"Surreal," he murmured.

"So you are awake."

"Uh-huh."

"What's surreal?" She wriggled against him, feeling girlish and carefree.

"You. In my bed. Naked."

"Wasn't that the goal?"

"True." He laughed. "But I thought it was a pipe dream."

"I should be the one who's stunned and amazed. To think I'm in bed with the major league pitcher Axel Richmond. Now that's many a woman's pipe dream."

"But not yours."

"Well," she admitted, "it wasn't, until I got to know you, and then it wasn't so much a dream as a nightmare."

"Nightmare?" He chuckled.

"Not being in bed with you," she amended. "That's not the scary part."

"What is the scary part?" He walked his fingers up her bare arm.

"The fact that when I'm with you I can't control myself."

"No?" He tugged her closer, dragged her across the sheet and into his embrace. Pulled the covers over their heads. "What can I say? I'm irresistible."

"That's what scares me. Your irresistibility."

"Why does that scare you?"

"I can't . . . won't . . . compete with groupies."

"Sweetheart, there is no competition. You're the clear winner. No one else can compare."

"Seriously? You expect me to believe that? I have morning breath and bed head and—"

"You've never looked sexier."

She couldn't see him very well, but she could certainly feel him, smell him. She kissed him.

"Oh," he said.

She thought he was going to scoop her into his arms, and make love to her again, but instead he hopped out of bed and pulled on his pajama bottoms. "Stay right there. I'll be back."

It felt a bit drafty, so she searched around for his paint-stained T-shirt and put it back on.

In the past, her reserve had kept men at arm's length, but that didn't seem to bother Axel. He accepted her for who she was, and for that she was grateful. He was different from any man she'd ever met. She felt comfortable whenever she was around him. Able to let down her guard with him in a way she normally couldn't with people.

Be more her true self.

That puzzled her. Until now, until Axel, she believed it was only possible to be her authentic self when she was alone.

The door opened and in came Axel with two cups of coffee, looking utterly sexy with his scruffy jaw and bed head. He handed her a cup, kept one for himself, and crawled back in the bed beside her.

"Let's spend the day together," he said.

"Aren't you supposed to be headed back to Dallas? Paul Hernandez is waiting for you."

"Oh yeah, that." He sighed. "I don't want to leave."

"I thought you'd be ready to get out of our one-horse town."

"Actually, I've grown fond of country living," he said. "It's nice. Quiet. Relaxing. Who knew I'd want those things?"

"Me."

"You're so smart," he said, his voice shiny with admiration. "One of the many things I love about you."

Love.

That word again. The word that started a tingle in her toes, and quickly spread up her legs to her pelvis and on to her heart, the word that ended up lodged in her head, leaving her dizzy and breathless with possibility.

Love. Yes, she loved this man with all her heart and soul, but there was so much standing in their way. Emma. Dylan. Her past. His future. His dreams. Her dreams. Tugging them in opposite directions.

"We'll work it out," he said, reading her mind. "I don't know how yet, but it's all going to be okay. You'll see."

She looked at him, at her beloved.

How she wanted to believe! So she pretended that she did. Just for a little while, because in this one splendid moment, everything was perfect.

He took her coffee cup from her, set it on the bedside table beside his, hauled her into his arms, and made love to her all over again.

TWO HOURS LATER, they stood on the dock overlooking the lake, the morning sun halfway up the sky, heating things up. Axel's bags were packed—Kasha had helped him—and loaded in his car. He'd drive her back to the yoga studio to pick up her car, but this was their official good-bye.

He'd suggested the walk to the dock, and she happily agreed, sinking her palm into his when he held out his hand. Interlacing their fingers. A solid hand-holding.

Aboard.

She was aboard.

Axel's heart swelled until it seemed to fill his whole chest, crowding out his lungs, making it hard to breathe.

Kasha inhaled deeply, gazed out across the water, a small I-can't-believe-this-is-happening smile hovering at her lips. He couldn't quite believe it either. Love. He was head over heels in love with the most magnificent woman in the world.

Axel reached for her other hand, turned her toward him. Face-to-face.

Her eyes met his. Eyes misted with tears.

It startled him. He'd never seen her tear up. Not even when she told him the truth about her parents. Immediately, he drew her into his arms, his instincts telling him to comfort and protect at all cost.

He loved her with every cell in his body.

She was his woman, and he was her man.

"Are you all right?" he whispered.

"Never better." A single tear rolled down the outside of her cheek.

He kissed it away.

She laughed, a beautiful sound that lifted his soul. She cupped the side of his face with her palm. "You have to go. The Gunslingers are expecting you."

"A few more minutes won't kill them."

"They're going to be so surprised at how much you've healed." She touched his shoulder. "The progress you've made is astounding."

"All because of you," he said, laying credit where it belonged.

He'd tried for weeks to rehab on his own, pushing, striving, grasping, when the key was to step back, relax, and let go.

The key Kasha had given him.

"I'm so proud of you," she said. "You've come so far in such a short time. You faced your fears and the beliefs that had been holding you back. That takes guts, Axel."

The way she said his name, full of pride and delight, lifted him up to rarefied heights.

"All because of you, babe." He tightened his grip on her. "All because of you."

"No, you were willing to make changes. I can't give you that. Only you could make the choice to change."

"I'm not the only one who's been on a journey." He cupped the back of her head in his palm, smelled sunshine on her skin, and stared intently into her inquisitive brown eyes. "You've changed too. You're more open, trusting . . ."

"What can I say?" Her smile widened. "Hurricane Axel blew into my life and turned everything upside down."

He couldn't hold her smile. It was too bright, and he had to leave. "I wish I could stay. Wish you could continue to be my therapist."

"I can't. We crossed a line."

"It was worth it," he said. "Much as I'm going to miss seeing you every day, this was worth it. *You* were worth it."

She nodded.

"I can come back this weekend," he said.

"No. I'll have Emma. We need time alone together, just the two of us, to really get to know each other."

"I get that, but damn, I'll miss you."

"We can text."

"It's not the same."

"And talk."

"Phone sex?" he asked hopefully.

"Who knows?" Her smile turned saucy.

"Tease." He kissed her.

She hugged him tightly, as if their parting were forever and she would never see him again.

"Hey, hey. I *will* be back."

"I'm just appreciating the moment," she said. "I'm so grateful to have this time with you. To stand here on the dock in the sun, even if I am sweating like a stevedore."

"Mmm," he said, kissing the perspiration from her upper lip. "Sexy."

She laughed, and they kissed in the sultry humidity. Christ, he hated having to leave her behind just when their romance was heating up.

"You're not going off to war, buddy." She pulled back. "It's only Dallas. Little more than two hours away."

But they both knew it was more than that. Back in Dallas Axel would get caught up in the momentum of his career, and Kasha would be busy with Emma. Did absence really make the heart grow fonder, or would the adage "out of sight, out of mind" prove true?

"It's time to go." The misty tears were back in her eyes, but she quickly blinked them away.

"Aw, Sphinx." He pressed her against him, hugging her as hard as he dared. "I'll be back next weekend."

"Can't come back until you leave. Go now. I'm already anticipating the reunion sex."

"Me too." He growled and nibbled on her earlobe.

"Stop," she warned. "Or I can't be held accountable for my actions."

He gave her one last long, sweet kiss, and then reluctantly loosened his arms and let her go, his lips tingling from her heat and energy. "I'll call you when I get to Dallas."

"A text will do," she said. "You're going to be busy, I'm going to be busy."

"I'll never be too busy to call you."

"Go." She laughed and pointed in the direction of his car.

The yearning in him whispered, *Screw your career, stay here, your future is here*. And for one overpowering moment, Axel wanted to give in to that overwhelming urge. But he had commitments, and he'd made a promise to a little boy on his deathbed that he'd play for the Yankees, play in the World Series.

It might be an impossible dream, but as long as he was chasing it, he was keeping Dylan alive.

Keeping himself alive.

That hope had driven him for the last two years. Kept him sane when his world fell apart.

"Be careful on the road," Kasha said.

"Good-bye, Sphinx," he said trying his best to sound light and casual.

Swiftly, Axel turned and strode up the dock toward the ranch house, the wooden slates vibrating beneath his weight, his heart beating crazily, his gut begging him to stay. Create a new world. Make a new life.

But he wasn't ready to accept the death of his old dream. For letting go of it meant letting go of Dylan.

At the thought of his son, Axel's heart broke anew.

"I love you!" Kasha called in a loud, clear voice.

Axel stopped and turned back, saw her standing on the dock looking both vulnerable and brave. Chin locked. Shoulders back. Heart forward.

My love.

He was torn between the future and the past. Dylan tugging him back, Kasha luring him forward. He wanted to go to her, drop down on one knee, beg her to marry him.

But he couldn't. Not yet. It was too soon. He needed to give himself to her one hundred percent. She deserved his complete devotion.

And in order to give her that, he had to put his past to rest before he could step forward into a glorious future with the woman he loved.

Question was, how long would she wait for him to get his act together?

CHAPTER 25

Things were going to go more smoothly this time, Kasha promised herself when she picked Emma up from the group home on Friday, June third. It was just the two of them this weekend, getting to know each other.

She'd decorated the guest room to suit Emma's tastes, planned menus that included all of Emma's favorite foods, and had scores of activities slated. This time, she was fully prepared.

Perfect day, she vowed. It was going to be a perfect day.

Except, she realized as they pulled away from the curb, she'd forgotten to pick up cheese for the grilled cheese sandwiches they were having for lunch. No worries, she'd swing by the grocery store. It wouldn't take five minutes.

But she hadn't counted on Emma being completely enthralled with the claw machine that waited inside the doorway of the grocery store, coaxing the girl over with the promises of colorful stuffed animals. Emma raced over, pressed her face and hands to the glass.

"Come along, Emma," Kasha said gently but firmly.

"Wanna play."

"Not today."

"Tuffed animal," Emma insisted, digging in her heels and crossing her arms over her chest.

"We have stuffed animals at home." Kasha held out her hand to her sister and caught her breath. *Please, please don't throw a tantrum.*

Emma's face clouded and her jaw clenched. She was getting spun up.

Kasha felt her own body tensed. Breathe. Project calm energy. The way she handled this blip would set the course of their relationship. "Let's go."

Emma hesitated.

"Now," Kasha said gently, keeping her hand extended. "We're on a schedule."

Emma glanced over her shoulder, looked longingly at the stuffed animals inside the claw machine.

"Come along, sweetheart." Kasha smiled her brightest smile.

The smile won out over stuffed animals, and Emma took her hand. Kasha swept her into the store, felt her pulse rate slow.

The dairy case was all the way in the back, and they had to pass all manner of temptation along the path. Emma stopped at the candy aisle, and again at the chips and snack crackers aisle, but Kasha never let go of her hand, and each time Emma stopped, Kasha would say, "This way," and walk on.

They snagged the cheese and made it back through the gauntlet, and just when Kasha thought they were home free at the checkout counter, the bag boy turned out to be a young man with Down syndrome about Emma's age. He wore glasses as thick as Emma's and his name tag said "David."

Emma took one look at David and David took one look at Emma and Kasha thought, *Uh-oh.*

"Hi!" David smiled at Emma.

"Hi!" Emma smiled right back.

"My name David," he said.

"I Emma."

"Emma." David rolled her name around on his tongue like it was the most beautiful sound he'd ever heard.

They peered into each other's eyes.

The cashier glanced at David and Emma, and shifted her gaze to Kasha. "Looks like love is in the air."

Goosebumps spread over Kasha's entire body. She thought of Emma as an eight-year-old. She'd not once given thought to her sexuality. Now, seeing Emma eyeing David and David eyeing Emma, the reality of it fully smacked her.

Emma's mind might be childlike, but her body was that of a young woman in her early twenties, and as such, she had the natural urges of anyone her chronological age.

Kasha had let go of Emma's hand while she'd gotten out her wallet, and Emma took full advantage of her freedom, scuttling over to stand next to David and stare raptly at him.

Quickly, Kasha snatched up the cheese, and took Emma's hand and hauled her away from David, her heart thumping wildly. "We've got to go."

"Bye!" David called, pushing his glasses up on his nose with one hand and waving with the other.

"Bye!" Emma hollered back.

We're not coming back to this grocery store, Kasha thought. But that didn't solve the problem. While she could avoid the store, she could not avoid Emma's sexuality, and that gave her a whole world of new problems to think about.

Emma chattered about David like a boy-crazy teen all the way home, and Kasha's trepidation grew with each sentence her sister uttered.

Unable to wait until they got into the house to check, Kasha grabbed the sack of medicines Molly Banks had given her. Because the visitation had been cut short last weekend, Kasha hadn't had the chance to go through the list of medications that Emma was on.

She pawed through the bottles looking for a certain one, and when she found it, let out a sigh of relief. Emma was on birth control pills. Thank God for that. She slumped back against the seat, her mind reeling.

"Titter?" Emma asked. "You okay?"

"Fine." Kasha pressed on a shaky smile. "Are you ready to see your room?"

"Can David come vi'it?"

Oh hell no. "David has to work, sweetheart."

Emma's face fell. "Can we go tee him again?"

"Maybe," Kasha fibbed. "Right now, let's go inside and get you settled."

Once Emma saw her bedroom—painted purple, her favorite color—and decorated in a Jasmine motif, she seemed to forget all about David. And she was the excited eight-year-old again, oohing and aahing and examining each item and hugging Kasha and starting it all over again.

Her joy was contagious, and Kasha felt her spirits lift with Emma's exuberant giggle, and then the fun began.

They played with dolls and stuffed animals that Kasha had bought for her. They colored in the coloring books, and took a walk around the grounds of the acre property that Kasha rented.

A laughing Emma chased the swans into the pond. And when she fell in and got soaked, Emma laughed even harder. Then came a shower and dry clothes.

After she blew Emma's hair dry for her, it was noon, and Emma who was accustomed to a strict schedule, announced gleefully, "Lunch!"

Kasha made grilled cheese sandwiches and tomato soup. When they finished, Kasha started putting the dishes in the dishwasher, but Emma insisted they wash the dishes by hand the way they did at the group home. Kasha went along with it.

Whatever it took to make Emma feel happy, loved, and safe. Maybe once her sister was living with her for a while she could convince Emma to switch over to the dishwasher. There was going to be a period of adjustment. She accepted that.

For dessert, they ate ice cream cones on the porch, and Emma took a deep interest in the hummingbirds buzzing around the feeder. And they stood up to watch the tiny flying creatures bicker and fight in the honeysuckle hedges.

With sticky hands, and chocolate ice cream–smeared face, Emma leaned over to hug her tightly and say, "Thank you, titter."

The surge of love washing over her for her sister was so strong it almost knocked Kasha to her knees. She hugged Emma close, rested her cheek against the top of the girl's head.

This was her biological sister. She was connected to Emma in a way she was not connected to any other person on earth.

It felt monumental, this knowledge, the weight of it.

The girl's fate was intricately entwined with hers, and she cherished Emma beyond all reason.

But sometimes, in quick hard flashes, dread and indecision and guilt smacked into her. She had no idea if she was up for the task of becoming her sister's guardian, but she was damn well going to try her best.

Life had given Emma a raw deal. And Kasha's biological mother had made it worse when she killed their father. Kasha was determined to play cleanup, and make amends the best way she knew how.

The rest of the day passed pleasantly. They watched a Disney movie and Kasha taught Emma some yoga. She let Emma play dress-up in her clothes, jewelry, and makeup, but then Emma looked so grown up, Kasha started to worry about the David thing all over again.

Dinner, by Emma's decree was at five. They washed dishes together again, then watched another movie. Emma's bedtime rituals took almost an hour, but at nine o'clock on the dot, she was ready to be tucked in.

Kasha read her a bedtime story, a passage from a Laura Ingalls Wilder book, and Emma was sound asleep before she reached the end of the chapter. She smiled, leaned down and kissed her sister's forehead.

Emma smiled in her sleep, turned over on her side, and snuggled against the purple hippopotamus Kasha had bought.

And Kasha realized it had indeed been a perfect day, perfectly imperfect, and that was okay.

SEVERAL TIMES DURING the night, Kasha got up to check on Emma, and the rest of the time she lay half asleep, listening for any noises from her sister's room. It was their first night together under the same roof. Would Emma have nightmares? Would she wake up confused and disoriented?

But Emma did neither. She slept blissfully through the night.

Kasha, however, was wrung out. She got up at dawn, did a few morning stretches and sun salutations to wake up, and made a cup of coffee.

It'll get better, she told herself, as she took her coffee to stand in Emma's doorway to watch her sister sleep.

She wouldn't always have to be hypervigilant. Once Emma got used to the place and they established their own routine, Kasha could relax into their relationship. The best things in life took time, after all.

Except for falling in love with Axel. That hadn't taken any time at all.

Things felt so easy with him. So right.

Suki would say it was the True Love wine, but Kasha knew it had nothing to do with the wine they'd found in the hope chest and everything to do with the fact that Axel was kind, and funny, and smart, and accomplished.

He was a guy she could trust. A guy she desperately wanted to trust.

But then there was that pesky passion.

On the surface so thrilling and breathtaking, but that was the problem, wasn't it? She didn't want her breath taken. Breath was life.

Without it . . .

She had to stop thinking about Axel. He was in Dallas doing his thing and she was here with her sister. Emma was her main focus. She had to be.

Emma woke up fussy. She didn't want any of the breakfast offerings Kasha had and kept insisting on doughnuts. Kasha tried to get Emma to take her morning medicines, but Emma refused. "Ta'te bad."

"Take your medicine and we'll go get doughnuts," Kasha bargained, wondering if it was a smart tactic or not. This parenting thing was hard.

"Okay," Emma agreed, and gulped down the medication, leaving Kasha feeling like she'd been played.

When they returned from getting doughnuts, Emma prowled restlessly, at loose ends. Kasha suggested several activities, but with each
one Emma would shake her head vigorously and say firmly, "No!"

"It's going to be one of those kinds of days, is it?" Kasha took a
deep breath.

Even though she'd planned to spend the weekend with just the
two of them, it occurred to her that maybe she should take her sister
over to Timeless Treasures. Emma had loved Callie, after all, and the
cat had calmed her down. But the thought of how busy the store was
on Saturdays held her back.

Emma opened the pantry, stared in at the food.

"Are you still hungry?" Kasha asked, worrying that the doughnuts had spiked Emma's blood sugar.

"All wrong," Emma said, and started pulling items off the shelf
and stacking them on the floor.

"Whoa, hold on, what are you doing?"

"All wrong," Emma insisted.

"What do you mean?"

Emma's jaw hardened, set in stone. "Can go on bottom."

"You want to rearrange the shelves?"

Emma nodded, beamed, her thundercloud mood evaporating.

"Okay, have at it. Rearrange the shelves. Do you want me to
help?"

"I do it," Emma said with a proud shake of her head.

"It's all yours."

After Emma finished rearranging the pantry, she started in on
the refrigerator, and then moved to the closets. When she couldn't
coax Emma away from her task at lunch, Kasha called Molly Banks.

"Oh, sorry." Molly laughed. "I forgot to tell you that Emma is a
bit compulsive when it comes to the contents of closets and cabinets
and drawers. She loves arranging things just so."

"Well, that's handy, but she seems obsessive. I can't get her to
stop."

"Hand her the phone, please," Molly said.

Feeling a bit undermined, Kasha handed the phone to Emma,

who was sitting in front of the open hall closet door surrounded by umbrellas, coats, and shoes. "Molly wants to talk to you."

Emma took the phone, listened to Molly, and then handed the phone back to Kasha. She stood up. "Lunchtime."

"What did you say to her?" Kasha asked Molly.

"I just told her to mind you."

"How do I acquire your authority?"

"Give yourself time," Molly said kindly. "It takes patience."

"I can do that," Kasha said.

"I know you can. How are things otherwise?"

"Good. We had a great time yesterday." Kasha considered telling Molly about David, but thought better of it. If she was going to have custody of Emma she needed to get used to handling things on her own. "Sorry I bothered you."

"No problem. Why don't you bring Emma home tonight? The girls all sing in the church choir, and it would be easier on me to have Emma here."

"You're just saying that to give me a break," Kasha said.

"If you want to keep Emma and take her to church tomorrow, that's fine, but if you don't there's no shame, no judgment in bringing her back tonight," Molly said. "You two are still getting to know each other. Small doses might be best."

"I'll take her to church," Kasha said staunchly. "But thank you for the offer."

"I'm here," Molly said. "Just a phone call away."

"I appreciate that." Kasha hung up, feeling as if she'd just barely passed a surprise test.

BY THE END of the weekend Kasha's house had been completely re-arranged to suit Emma, and the girl was happy and laughing again. It fully set in how important organization and routine were to Emma.

Duly noted.

They met Molly, Cliff, and the other girls at church on Sunday morning, and Emma sang joyfully in the choir, her clear, pretty voice a standout. Listening to her, Kasha was so proud she thought her heart might burst from her chest.

Emma hugged her good-bye on the church steps and skipped off to the group home van with her foster sisters without looking back.

"You did great." Molly laid a hand on Kasha's shoulder. "Next time, would you like to take her for a week?"

"Yes," Kasha said. "I would."

"I'll call you when I get a chance to check our schedule."

"Thank you."

Kasha went back home, and feeling completely wiped out, changed out of her church clothes and fell asleep on the couch. She jerked awake three hours later to the sound of the doorbell. Fumbling groggily, she got to her feet and went to the door.

And there stood Axel grinning at her like he'd won a contest, and she was the prize.

Joy bubbled up inside of her, frothy and light, and she was so damn happy to see him that she feared he wasn't real. That she was still asleep and had conjured him up in her dreams.

"Hey, Sphinx," he said. "Are you going to stand there staring at me all evening, or are you going to invite me in?"

CHAPTER 26

Axel had accused her of staring, but he was the one who couldn't look away. They'd been separated for only four days, but it felt like four hundred years to a man in love.

Kasha wore a long blue T-shirt and black leggings. Her feet were bare, her hair floating free like a silky dark curtain, her beautiful face free of makeup. And she was the sexiest damn thing he'd ever seen.

"You're here," she said in a breathless voice that thrilled him. "You're really here."

Without waiting to be invited in, he crossed the threshold, swept her into his arms, and kissed her hard and fierce.

She giggled, and the sound undid him. His Kasha was giggling like a carefree girl? The changes in her from the first day they'd met were miraculous. And it made him proud to think he'd had a hand in her transformation.

"What are you doing here?" she asked, pulling back so she could gaze into his eyes.

"Complaining?" he asked.

"Absolutely not." But the levity vanished from her face, and her tone turned serious as she pressed her palm against his chest. "Everything's okay, right? You didn't . . ." She gulped. ". . . get cut from the team?"

"I didn't get cut," he assured her.

"Then what are you doing here?"

"You're not happy to see me?"

"I'm ecstatic. Just wondering to what I owe the pleasure."

"Good news," he said.

"How good?"

He couldn't read her. "My shoulder is so improved," he said, feeling the same mix of joy, relief, and, oddly, sadness that he'd felt when Dr. Harrison had broken the news, "that I'll back on the roster."

"Axel!" she crowed. "That's amazing!"

"You're what's amazing. It wouldn't have happened without you. Without you, I would have gone for the surgery and still been recovering. Thank you."

"You're welcome." She twined her hands in his hair and pulled his head down for a heartfelt kiss that set his pulse thumped hard against his ribs.

Absorbing the minty taste of her mouth, he inhaled her lavender-sage scent, felt the curvy shape of her firm body in his arms. In the future, as he went back to the mound, moments like this would be few and far between from now until the end of baseball season.

And he was determined not to miss a second of the time they did have together.

"What's wrong," she said, pulling back to look at him, her lips glistening moist from their kiss. "Something's wrong."

God, she was intuitive. He couldn't hide anything from her. "I've got some more news for you, but let's sit down."

"Is it bad? If it's bad, just tell me."

"It's not bad," he said. "But it does present some challenges. Let's get comfortable for this discussion."

She frowned and he could tell she wanted to push him for answers, but she had so much self-control. "Are you hungry? I could make us something to eat."

"Don't cook. I want your undivided attention."

"You're making me nervous."

"C'mere." He took both of her hands in his and led her to the couch, a sturdy, blue, sensible couch with comfortable cushions. Once they were seated, he stared deeply into her eyes, into her.

Kasha was watching him, a cautious smile twitching at her lips, and she steepled her fingers. "So, the news?"

"Yeah, the news." He squeezed her hands, tried to figure out how best to break it. *Just say it.* "I've got . . ." He cleared his throat. "There's been an unexpected development."

She canted her head. "Yes?"

He hauled in a deep breath, let it out long and slow the way she'd taught him. "There's been interest from the Yankees. They were eyeing me for a trade if I came off the DL before the All-Star break."

"Oh." Her mouth turned downward. Was she disappointed that he might be headed for New York City? "But how would that work?"

"Trade details can be complicated," he said with a wave of his hand. "I could go into it, but the rules are crazy."

"I see." Her face was blank, unreadable. She was back to being the Sphinx. "Do you have to—" She broke off.

"I don't have a no-trade clause," he said. "The only way I could refuse the trade is to retire. I know it might sound strange, but I still think I have a few years left—and it's been my dream to play in New York. This could be my only shot at it."

"I wasn't suggesting you don't take the trade." She shook her head vigorously. "This is your big dream and I would never get in the way of that. It complicates things for us, but I was just being selfish."

"Not selfish, not at all. I . . . we're just getting started but I want you to know I consider you part of my life. I want you to weigh in on the decision."

"I'll miss you fiercely, but this is the top of the heap. It's what you've worked your entire career. This is for Dylan. You have to go to the Yankees. End of conversation. It's fated!"

"We should talk through all the pros and cons of me going."

"There's nothing to discuss. Your dream is within your grasp and if you don't go, you'll have to retire. You're not ready for that. And you could resent me forever if I demand that you don't go. This is everything you've worked your whole life for. Close your fingers around the dream, squeeze tight, and hold on with all your might."

Axel nodded, unable to speak past the knot in his throat. She was the most incredible woman on the face of the earth, willing to put his dreams ahead of her own wants and needs. "But what about us?"

"You'd never forgive yourself if you let this opportunity pass you by," she said. "At your age, with your shoulder being iffy, it won't come around again."

True enough. "But there are other opportunities I want to explore." His gaze locked with hers. "Opportunities that will sustain me a lot longer than baseball."

"You know this is realistically your last chance to play for the Yankees," Kasha said. Her practicality was one of the things he loved so much about her. "I won't let you throw it away."

"But what about us?" Suddenly, Axel felt—confused. She was right. He'd been working his entire life for this moment. But there was something holding him back, something he'd never felt before. "We've got something going on here. I've never felt this way about anyone."

"Axel . . ."

"No woman has ever meant so much to me. No one. I love you, Kasha. Nothing is going to change that. We can make this work."

"Yes, we can talk on the phone, text, and Skype . . . and see each other whenever we can," she said lightly, as if that was enough. "And there's always the off season. It's only four months away."

Four months away from her felt like four hundred years.

"This sucks," he said.

Her shrug was casual, accepting. "This is your job. It's not only what you do, but it's also who you are. I knew that when I made the choice to get involved with you."

"You could always come with me." He hoped he didn't sound as desperate as he felt. "We could move in together."

"Emma in New York City?" Kasha shook her head. "I couldn't do that to her. Plus I just got my old job back. I can't bail on them now."

But she could bail on him? Axel hardened his chin. Dammit.

Maybe it was a little unreasonable, but he wanted her to fight. To demand that he retire. To yell and cry "Foul" and get furious. But that wasn't Kasha's way. She didn't do passionate emotions. He understood why, but he couldn't help feeling she didn't believe that they were worth fighting for.

Axel's head spun, desperate to find a doable solution to their situation. But he couldn't see one. He couldn't make her pick between him and her family, job, sister, and Stardust.

She was who she was and he loved her for it. He couldn't ask her to change for him. That was like asking her to cut off pieces of herself to fit into his life.

"It's going to be okay," she said firmly. "Baseball is in your blood. Axel. It's your identity. You told me that you had no idea who you were if you weren't playing baseball."

"That was before," he said, squeezing her hand.

"Before what?"

"Before you."

"Axel," she said. "I can't be a replacement for baseball. You need a purpose. I can't be everything to you. I have my job, my family . . . Emma."

"I know," he said. "After Dylan died, everything I did was about baseball and when I lost that with my shoulder injury . . . well, you pulled me out of a tailspin and I can never repay you for that."

"Yes you can," she said, clearing her throat and putting sternness in her voice. "By going back to what you love."

"Are you saying you're tired of me hanging around?" He tried for a grin but couldn't quite pull it off.

"I'm saying you have to give your career one last shot, to grab your dream, or you'll always wonder what might have been. Yes, one day you'll have to give up your glove, and you'll find a way to deal with it. But that day is not today. There are a lot of games still left in that arm. You have to pitch again. If not for me . . ." She chuffed in a lungful of air, her gaze slamming hard into his. ". . . for Dylan."

"And that means I have to leave the Gunslingers, leave Texas . . ." He stared deeply into her. "Leave you."

"We'll work through it, Axel. If this relationship is meant to be, we'll find a way to make it work. If it's not . . ." She lifted a shoulder, kept her Sphinx mask firmly in place. "So be it."

"Kasha—"

"You have to do this, Axel. I won't be the reason you gave up on your dream. Like I said, if you leave the game for me, you'll resent me for it, maybe not now, maybe not for a long time, but one day you will. I'm sorry, but I simply can't let that happen."

"We're getting ahead of ourselves," he said. "It's not a done deal yet. Anything could happen. Let's just spend the evening together, and cross that bridge if and when we come to it. Can we have sex now?"

"I thought you'd never ask." She laughed and kissed him.

They undressed each other slowly right there on the couch in the living room, taking their time, savoring the moment. That was another thing she'd taught him—how to fully appreciate the moment. They had each other right now. That was really all that mattered.

Right now, he told himself. It was enough.

Once they were naked, they studied each other, taking note. They made love soft and easy and for a long time, Axel holding himself back to make it last. They explored and experimented, trying new things, stretching their knowledge of each other's bodies.

With skill and care, he moved over her, a gentle rhythm, in and out like an ocean wave, bathing them both in wonder and sensation.

When Axel could hold out no longer, he let himself go inside her, aware of every exquisite detail.

Several hours later, after they were wrung out and exhausted, they lay in each other's arms, sedated and sated, drunk on the heady magic of their lovemaking.

"What's this," Axel asked lazily, tracing his knuckles over her bare breasts as they lay in a heap on the living room floor, loving the silky feel of her skin beneath his fingers.

"What's what?" she mumbled, raising her head to see what he was talking about.

"The trunk you're using for a coffee table. It's got a weird saying engraved in the top of it."

"Oh that." She flapped her hand. "It's a hope chest."

"A hope chest?"

"You know. Back in the old days girls would start collecting items for when they got married—linens, dishes, dowry-type stuff. Things they needed to set up housekeeping."

"Pining for a wedding?" He chuckled. "That sounds far too romantic for you."

"I'm not pining. Jodi gave it to me after she got married. My sisters think the trunk is magical."

"Magical?" He snorted a laugh, but when he spied the somber expression on his face, he said, "Oh, you're serious."

"I don't believe it. My sisters do."

"What does this saying mean?" he asked, reading what was written on the trunk. "'Treasures are housed within, heart's desires granted, but be careful where wishes are cast, for reckless dreams dared dreamed in the heat of passion will surely come to pass.'"

"Nothing," she said. "It doesn't mean a darn thing."

"Five locks, huh?" He ran his hand over the five compartments. "That's different. What's inside?"

"Nothing." She blushed.

Damn. She wasn't the blushing type, and yet here she was looking embarrassed and chagrinned and secretly delighted. Hmm. Something was up with the trunk.

"Tell me about it," he said, leaning over to nibble her earlobe. "Do you have hopes in this chest?"

"I didn't," she murmured. "Until I found the wine. Until I met you."

"The wine? What wine? Our wine?"

"True Love," she said, meaning the name of the wine, but the words made him think something else.

True love.

That's what he felt for her. Whenever he looked at her, thought about her, tasted her, touched her, smelled her, his heart swelled in his chest big with hope and desire, with possibilities and tenderness, with joy and excitement, with trust and a steady, quiet certainty that she was the one he'd been waiting for all his life.

"Tell me about it," he coaxed. He wanted to hear her voice, hear her stories, get inside her world and live there forever.

And so she told him, spinning a strange tale of a magic hope chest that supposedly granted the most heartfelt wishes. "I don't believe it, of course," she said, but then she told him how Breeanne had bought the trunk at an estate sale, finally got it opened, made a wish for her writing career that had led her to Rowdy and true love.

She described how Breeanne had passed the hope chest to Jodi, who'd wished for a wild sexual adventure and had gotten that and much more when she hooked up with Jake while crashing a celebrity wedding.

Finally, she told him about how she'd found the bottle of wine in one of the compartments of the hope chest. How it had tasted like vinegar to everyone but him and her.

"That's a little far-fetched," he said when she'd finished.

"I know."

"But that was the best damn wine I ever tasted."

"Ditto." Her voice was throaty, sexy as hell.

"Ballplayers are notoriously superstitious," he said.

"So you believe me?"

"I believe in you and what I feel for you. That's good enough for me."

"Oh, Axel," she said, and kissed him so hard his toes literally curled.

He dipped his head, and lightly bit her neck. "Tell me, what did you wish for? Your career? Hot sex?"

"Emma," she confessed. "The most important thing in the world to me."

"How does that tie into us?"

"I guess it doesn't," she said. "Except I went to work for the Gunslingers because of Emma, and you were my job."

"Hmm," he said thinking that over. He got that Emma was an essential part of Kasha's life, but felt jealous nonetheless. He wanted to be her number one.

Get over yourself, Richmond. Emma is defenseless, vulnerable. She needs Kasha.

Yeah, well, it might be selfish of him, but damn if he didn't need her too.

"You're about to get your heart's desire," he said. "Emma will be yours before you know it."

"Yes," she murmured, her voice quiet and small.

"Doubts?"

"No, not about Emma."

"About us?" he asked, fear clutching his gut.

She wrapped her arms around his neck, peered into his eyes. "About the fact you're wasting time talking when you could be making love to me again."

"On it," he said, reaching for his pants pocket in search of another condom.

And within a matter of seconds, he was inside her, and taking them both to heaven.

THE NEXT MORNING, they shared a breakfast of oatmeal and fruit before Axel went out on the road. The Gunslingers had sent him down to the Minor leagues for a few weeks. He'd play a rehab game or two, then hopefully be back in Dallas for the July 4th game. Kasha returned to her old job at Stardust General, and his days were jam-packed.

Howard Johnson had filed the paperwork for Kasha to get custody of Emma, and they were just waiting for it to make its way through the legal system. In the meantime, Emma was coming to stay with her during Fourth of July week. Mom and Dad and Suki agreed to watch Emma while Kasha worked. She was prepared. Everything was working out on that score.

She and Axel called or texted each other several times a day, sharing the events of their daily lives as best they could via long distance.

Axel called her from the road, telling her about his travels, spinning colorful stories of his teammates' antics. He described every pitch he threw, how he felt afterward in mind, body, and spirit. His voice filled with pride and excitement, but underneath was more—a wistfulness, a tender longing, a quiet sigh—especially when he whispered, "I miss you so much."

She talked about Emma, and how she was slowly integrating her sister into her life. There were ups and downs as she navigated the learning curve of caring for an adult sibling with mental and emotional challenges. How she'd taken Emma swimming at the community pool, and while her back was turned buying Emma a snow cone, her sister spied David, the bag boy from the supermarket, and before Kasha could get to them, they were kissing on the side of the pool. As calmly as she could, she had intervened. Careful not to make a big thing of it, but quickly getting Emma out of the pool and back home. Luckily, Emma hadn't balked too much. It had been a good mood kind of day.

"It's important to appreciate the small victories," Kasha had said to him. "That's what life with Emma is teaching me."

On the Fourth of July, the entire Carlyle clan, Emma included, packed into Jodi's van and made the trip to Dallas to watch the Gunslingers play and Axel make his comeback appearance. While Kasha enjoyed sitting in the stands with her family during the game, and got a kick out of watching Emma's face during the fireworks show, she couldn't help wishing she could be alone with Axel.

As it was, they barely got to see each other. The game had gone into extra innings and it was almost midnight by the time the guys— Rowdy, Jake, and Axel—met up with them. They all grabbed dinner at a twenty-four-hour diner near the stadium, but she and Axel never had a chance to be alone.

The team was playing in Seattle the next day, and they had an early morning flight out. Kasha had Emma, so there was no sneaking off, even for a quickie. Her sister, not accustomed to staying up so late, was fading fast, yawning and dozing with her head on Kasha's shoulder as they sat in the large, round, family-style booth at the diner.

All they were able to manage was a quick kiss in the parking lot where everyone could see. Zero privacy. No chance for hankypanky. But at least they got to see each other in person, and that was better than nothing.

Or at least that was what Kasha told herself.

Until she got home that night, hot and bothered and desperate for him, but she couldn't even call him for the relief of phone sex. She had Emma and her sister was so hyped up from the day's activities, she couldn't sleep. Kasha spent hours trying to settle her down, and it was after three in the morning when Emma finally nodded off.

Kasha poured herself a glass of wine and went to sit on the back porch. She thought of the hope chest wine she'd shared with Axel, stared up at the stars, and whispered his name to the ebony sky.

She loved him in a way that she'd never loved another, and it was as if they were on separate planets. And what she'd wanted to believe was that one of the greatest romances of all time slowly seemed to be slipping from her grasp.

And as each day passed, she felt him drifting away into his life of baseball, while she stayed rooted here in Stardust, going nowhere.

Oh God, she felt so much; how could she be feeling so much—desire, need, desolation, love, hope, joy, sadness, grief?

She was at their mercy.

Once upon a time, dark emotions had driven her to do the unthinkable. She pressed her hands into wounds of her thighs, closed her eyes, felt a fresh flood of hot feelings—good and bad and in between—rushing over her.

Emotions.

So many emotions.

Emotions she'd spent a lifetime trying to avoid, but she wasn't avoiding them anymore. Kasha embraced the chaos. She laughed and cried and punched the lawn chair pillow and surrendered to the very thing she'd spent a lifetime avoiding.

Messy, crazy passion.

Her greatest fear had come upon her.

And it was terrifying and glorious.

CHAPTER 27

Two weeks after the All-Star break, Axel was traded to the New York Yankees.

It was the team he'd dreamed of joining since he was six years old with his bedroom decorated in Yankees memorabilia. He'd gotten everything he'd ever wanted, and he should be supremely happy. Over the moon.

But he wasn't.

All he could think about was Kasha, and how miserable he was without her. He'd been seeing her whenever he could, but it was tough enough during baseball season when he was in Dallas. New York might as well be on another planet.

He couldn't break the news over the phone. He had to see her in person. Hold her. Kiss her. Make love to her.

Axel drove to Stardust, having no idea when he'd be back again, or how this would go. He hadn't called to tell her he was coming for fear his voice would give him away, and she would guess why he was in town.

Kasha lived on the outskirts of town on a small plot of land, the neighbors few and far between. Her cottage looked like something from a fairy tale, small, gray stone, with ivy growing up the walls. Around the sides, like stalwart sentinels, stood protective pine trees. A cobblestone walkway led to the front door from the gravel drive.

Behind the house, he could see a pond with a duo of swans sliding over the glassy green surface. Axel held his breath, enchanted. A
tiny jolt of recognition grazed him, but the impression was ephem-
eral, too hazy to be deciphered. Familiarity tugged at him, a sensation that whispered, *You've come home.*

Before he could get out of the car, the door opened, and Kasha
came out on the front porch, her gaze locked on the darkening clouds
bunching up against sunrise. Her dark hair was loose, sailing about her
shoulders in the wind, her peaceful face tipped up to the troubled sky.

The gauzy light blue maxi she wore whipped about her body,
molding the soft material against the curve of her thighs, and flowing
out behind her. She looked like a goddess—tall and lithe and beautiful and fierce.

She hadn't noticed him yet, and he felt nonexistent without her
attention and at the same time strangely liberated by his invisibility.

The snapshot moment was priceless and he knew as he looked
upon her that this moment would stay with him forever—pure and
crisp and mystical. Kasha, majestic in her stature, her full lips parted
slightly, and in those compassionate knowing eyes that slanted down
slightly at the corners, a gleam of joy and peace, an expression that
both lifted his heart and distressed him at the same time.

Axel stood in awe, watching her, and realization hit like a lightning bolt shooting from heaven—sharp and bright and hot. This
woman was the love of his life and he would never ever feel like this
about anyone else.

He got out, slammed the car door.

She turned, her eyes widening.

He rushed up the walkway to greet her. She stayed rooted on the
steps, and when he reached her, he spied a single tear tracking down
her cheek.

Axel's gut flipped backward and doubled over. Kasha was crying.

"Hey," he said, his throat tightening.

"Hello." She blinked hard, pressed a knuckle to her cheek, blot-
ting away the tear.

He stepped closer. The whisper of her scent, that exotic combination of—frankincense and lavender and sage now mixed with the smell of rain—vibrated the air molecules around them.

"What's wrong?" he asked.

"You're here and . . ." She rubbed the back of her left calf with the toe of her right shoe. "And I'm getting Emma for two weeks this time. Molly and Cliff are bringing her over right now."

There went his hope for a sleepover before he left for New York tomorrow. He eyed her up and down. There were dark circles under her eyes, and a tiredness that weighted her shoulders. He wanted to pull her into his arms and kiss her for all he was worth, but there was a stiffness between them, an unexpected awkwardness.

"How have you been?" he asked. "Feels like forever since we've seen each other in person. Those Skype sessions aren't the same thing."

"Great." She bobbed her head. "I'm doing great. What are you doing here?"

"I came to bring you something. A gift . . ." *Before I move fifteen hundred miles away.*

"You didn't need to do that. Seeing you is gift enough." Her smile was anemic. Something was wrong. *Yeah, you're leaving her.*

He walked back to the car, went around to the trunk, and took out the picture frame wrapped with a big red bow. Carried it back to her.

"I finished the painting," he said, feeling like a little boy offering a wildflower bouquet to his first girlfriend.

"When did you have time?"

"All those nights I couldn't sleep while thinking about you."

"Oh, Axel," she said, as if her heart were breaking. She took the portrait from him, studied it for a long time, a mist of tears clouding her beautiful eyes. "You've made me look like a movie star."

"To me more beautiful than any movie star."

"Thank you," she murmured. "I love it. You're an amazing artist."

He grinned sheepishly, embarrassed. He tried to shift his expression, searching for just the right balance of strong macho self-esteem, and humble lovable guy.

"How come you don't keep it?" she asked. "Start a collection. One day you'll have a gallery showing. I just know it."

"I wouldn't want to damage it when I . . ." He pressed his lips together. He was doing a piss-poor job of breaking the news.

"When you what?" she asked, her body stiffening as if she knew something was up.

He took the portrait from her, leaned it against the porch railing, took her hands in his, met her gaze head-on. He could avoid it no longer. "When I move to New York City."

She gasped, and her eyes widened, and he watched the interplay of emotions war across the face—surprise, delight, disappointment, sadness. "Axel, that . . . that's wonderful news. Your dream has come true."

"Yeah," he said, his voice coming out rough and husky.

"You don't look happy. You should be over the moon."

"I would be," he admitted, "if it didn't mean leaving you."

"This is a joyous moment for you," she said. "You must revel in it."

"I can only do that if you agree we can make this long distance thing work." He squeezed her hands as anxiety gripped his gut.

She shook her head like she'd lost something irreplaceable, pulled her hands away from his grasp.

His heart took an express elevator to his feet. "Kasha?"

"How is that even possible, Axel?" Her voice was quiet, calm.

He couldn't decide if it was because she'd already gotten over him, or because she'd completely anesthetized her feelings. She had a talent for it.

"You'll be in New York," she continued. "My life is here. My family is here. I'm working on getting custody of Emma. "But it's okay. You're where you need to be, and so am I."

"But I don't . . ." He paused, swallowed past the enormous lump in his throat. ". . . want to leave you."

"Nonsense," she said. "This move is all you've ever wanted. You told me so yourself. It's the dream you dreamed with your son. You must go. You've got an unstoppable passion for baseball."

"I've got an unstoppable passion for you." He held his arms at his side. It was all he could do not to touch her again, pull her against him, kiss her until they were both crazed with lust, but he couldn't do that. She had to come to him.

His gazed locked with hers.

A sad expression tilted the corners of her mouth downward. "Axel," she said, in a tone that ice-picked him straight through the heart. "I've never felt about anyone the way I feel about you, but . . ."

"No." He shook his head. "Don't say it."

"Can't we just keep this breakup clean and easy? No mess. No fuss. No drama."

"Quiet." He fisted his hands, felt his heart shrivel in his chest. "That's the way you want it."

"Yes."

"Calm."

"That's right." She nodded and smiled a tense smile no one would buy into.

"Passionless." He put extra emphasis on the word, knowing it made her twitchy. Good. Let her be uncomfortable. As long as she felt something, she wasn't shutting down completely.

"Passion isn't the issue here," she said.

Frustration roared through him. He stabbed fingers through his hair, let out an exasperated breath. "The hell it's not."

He didn't need to see the stark panic in her eyes to know she was scared. He could feel it coming off her in icy waves. Axel clamped his hands on her shoulders, but she dropped her gaze, refusing to glance up at him. "Look at me, Kasha."

"It's not going to change things."

"Look at me," he said, using a soft voice on her just like she'd used on him, wielding calmness as a weapon.

Finally, she lifted her chin and crashed headlong into his gaze. "Can't we just let the relationship be what it was? A great fantasy, one for the storybooks, but it was a fantasy nonetheless."

"No." He gritted his teeth. "Because for me, it is so much more."

"Don't," she whimpered, stepped back, and folded her arms over her chest. "Please . . ."

"I love you, Kasha Carlyle, and no matter what happens between us, I always will."

"Axel," she said, "I love you too, but this simply isn't going to work."

"Why not?" he asked, standing there feeling like she'd run him through with a sword. "Because you won't let it?"

"The truth is . . ." Her eyes turned heart-smashingly sad. "It's not the distance. It's not your move to New York. It's not the fact we would be apart six months out of the year."

"What is it then?"

"I feel so much for you that it's tearing me to shreds. My feelings are too dangerous, too combustible. You leave me shaken, and wrecked, and crazy. And that terrifies me. I can't be like my biological mother. I won't."

"Oh, Sphinx," he whispered. "You can't be. You would never be like her. What will it take to make you understand that?"

"You can't know that. What if I inherited her Mad Hatter genes?"

It hurt him to see how tormented she was, hurt even worse that he couldn't fix it. Fact. Her mother had murdered her father in a crime of passion. That couldn't be changed or solved.

Not ever.

If she couldn't see her way clear, disassociate herself from her mother's actions, there was nothing he could say or do to change her mind.

"I see," he said, his shoulders slumped, his mouth tasting of ashes.

"It's not you," she said. "It's never been you. You are splendid. Exceptional. And you'll make someone a fine husband. Just not me."

"Kasha." He reached out a hand, desperate to comfort her, but she spun away, the heartbeat in her throat pounding wildly out of control.

"See what you do to me?" she said, placing her hand over her racing pulse as if trying to hold it inside. "When I'm around you, even my blood can't go through my veins at a normal pace."

"This is insurmountable?"

"Yes," she said. "I can't bear to feel this way. Please, just go. Let's forget what we had together. It was just lightning in a jar. Nothing we can build on. Let it go, Axel. Let me go."

"Yeah." He bobbed his head, licked dry, cracked lips. "You're right. Sensible. Calm. That's what we need. Love and passion, well, it's for crazy people, right?"

She whimpered, soft and low and agonized. "Please, please leave. Before Emma gets here."

He raised both palms, stepped back. "That's the way you want it, I'm gone. The last thing I want to do on the face of this earth is to make you feel scared or unsafe, and it looks like that's exactly what I've done. So don't worry. I'm out of your life. As you wish. It's over."

IT KILLED KASHA to break things off with Axel, but it was for his own good. As long as his thoughts were with her in Texas, he wouldn't be able to focus on his career.

And it wasn't as if she didn't have her hands full. Taking responsibility for Emma changed everything. Her half sister's needs *had* to come first.

Her heart was breaking as she watched him drive away, and when she picked up the painting he'd given her and took it into the house, her heart broke again.

The portrait was haunting. In it, she looked ethereal, untouchable, caught between water and sky, seemingly part of the clouds, floating in an ethereal white gown. Her face had no expression, her hair windblown. The way he used shadow and pigment evoked a single mood.

Deep melancholia.

Was that how he saw her? Alone. Isolated. Untouchable. The painting itself was lovely, but it made her feel so sad.

She stowed the portrait in her bedroom, unsure where to put it, just as Molly and Cliff showed up with Emma.

Now, as she saw Emma come running up the sidewalk toward her, the biggest smile in the world on her face, Kasha knew she'd absolutely made the right decision.

One good thing had come out of her dark past. Her sister.

Kasha caught Emma in her arms and gave her the biggest hug and told herself everything was going to be all right.

That day, they did everything Emma wanted to do—fishing, going to the park to swing on swings, getting ice cream, going to Timeless Treasures to see Callie. By the time she got Emma fed, bathed, and into bed, Kasha was exhausted. She'd not had a spare moment to think about Axel.

She fell diagonally across the foot of her mattress and dropped instantly asleep without even taking off her clothes.

Sometime later, she woke disoriented. For a moment she didn't know where she was. She blinked, realized she was upside down in bed, searched for the digital clock on the bedside table.

Two a.m.

Yawning, she shook herself awake enough to change into pajamas and go check on Emma. She pushed open her sister's bedroom slowly to keep the hinge from creaking and peeked inside.

The bed was empty, covers thrown every which way.

An icy sheet of terror iced up her back. Where was Emma?

Don't panic. Check the other side of the bed. Check under the bed. Check the closet. Check behind the curtain.

She upended the room. No Emma.

"Emma!" She scurried into the third bedroom that served as her home office. Empty. She raced into the living room and saw that the front door was standing wide open.

"Emma!" she screamed, and ran out onto the cool cobblestones.

The night was dark and silent. No moon, and only a scattering of stars. An owl hooted. She could see nothing but trees and shadows and the pond.

"Oh my God, the pond!" Kasha sprinted over the rough pavers, stumbled when she hit the grass, and stubbed her toe, but she didn't let that stop her. "Emma!"

She reached the pond glimmering blackly and gulped in great gobs of air, saw the pristine white swans sitting in the middle of the pond.

But there was no sign of Emma.

She pulled her hair back with her hands so it wouldn't fall down in her face when she studied the ground looking for fresh footprints. No bare feet other than her own.

Thank God, thank God, not in the pond.

Where?

No idea. Had Emma just left? Maybe she was sleepwalking. Or could she have been abducted?

She grabbed her keys and her cell phone and headed for the Prius to go search for her sister.

Her cell phone rang.

It was Molly Banks. "Kasha," Molly said gently. "She's here, she's safe."

"You've got Emma? Oh thank God. I'll be right over to get her."

"Honey, it's almost three in the morning, and we're all exhausted. Emma is already sound asleep in her old bed. Why don't we just wait until daylight?"

"Yes. That's a better idea."

"In fact, since tomorrow is Sunday, we'll just go ahead and take Emma to Sunday school and church with us and then you can come over for Sunday brunch and pick her up then. How does that sound?"

"Yes, yes," she babbled. "Thank you, Molly. You are amazing."

"I've been doing this awhile, honey. These sorts of things happen. It won't take you long to get your sea legs."

"How did she get all the way across town? How did she know where to go?"

"Actually, I got the call from David's mom."

"David? The bag boy from the grocery store?"

"Emma tried to climb in through David's bedroom window. Apparently, she and David had a rendezvous planned."

"But how?"

"Emma's a lot craftier than you might imagine," Molly said. "She's got a cell phone and knows how to use the GPS app. You have to remember she's *not* eight years old."

"Oh my gosh. What if . . ." Kasha closed her eyes. "Did she and David . . ."

"No. His parents heard the commotion, and intervened. When his mother asked Emma where she lived, naturally, she gave them our address."

"I can't believe I let her out of my sight for a second." Guilt chewed through her like a buzz saw. She'd been so complacent.

"You have to sleep sometime. You're not a prison warden. Please, don't worry. Everything turned out all right. She's safe and that's the important thing," Molly said. "Go on back to bed. Try to get some sleep. Things will look much better in the morning. I promise."

CHAPTER 28

But Kasha couldn't go back to sleep, and as soon as it dawn broke, she went to see her mother.

She found Mom filling the hummingbird feeders on the front porch. The second her mother looked up and saw her, she set down the pitcher of sugar water and hurried toward her, eyes wide with concern.

"Where's Emma?" her mother asked.

"At the Bankses."

"What happened?"

"It's a long story."

"Do you have a fever?" She placed a hand on Kasha's forehead.

Did she look that bad? "I'm fine, Mom."

"You're not fine. When did you eat last?"

Kasha shrugged, unable to think about food. "Really, I'm fine."

"You always were so hard to mother, so independent. I admire that about you, but sometimes, Kasha, you have to let people help you."

"Really, I'm good."

"Something's wrong or you wouldn't be over here at seven o'clock on a Sunday morning."

"Mom—" Kasha started to protest, but clamped her mouth closed.

Her mother was right. She'd been independent to the point of aloofness. It had never been her intention to shut her family out; rather, she'd wanted to keep from caring too much, keep her heart safe, in case they decided at some point they didn't really want her after all.

But keeping her heart detached hadn't worked. Not with her family. Or with Axel either. It was time she accepted the fact that she needed other people.

"You look exhausted, sweetie. Go pop into your old bed while I make you some oatmeal with bananas and walnuts just the way you like it."

Unable to resist, Kasha went upstairs to the room that used to be the one she and Jodi had shared. She curled up in the middle of the four-poster bed, wrapped herself in the handmade quilt, and sobbed and sobbed and sobbed.

She hadn't cried like this since . . . well, she could not remember ever crying like this. It was desperate grief, lonely and hollow and forlorn.

A few minutes later, the bedroom door opened.

She closed her eyes, willed herself to stop bawling, but the tears just came harder and faster. She felt her mother settle onto the bed with her, draw her into her arms, and mold her body around Kasha.

Mom held her, simply held her, and Kasha let her. The way she'd been unable to let her as that tough, troubled seven-year-old tomboy Maggie and Dan had brought into their home twenty-three years ago.

"You want to tell me what's so terrible?" Mom crooned.

Haltingly, she told her about Emma, and then started crying all over again. "I've failed her."

"Shh." Mom rocked her gently. "Shh, it's all right. Emma is safe. She's fit as a fiddle. Nothing happened with that boy."

"It's not just that. Remember what happened at the Memorial Day party. That thing with those mean girls, how Emma shoved me? I don't know how to handle her."

"You just got off to a rocky start. Happens in every new relationship. Do you remember your first day here?"

"No."

"I don't blame you. It wasn't a day to remember. When we put you to bed, in this very room, you snuck off in the middle of the night and hid in the garden shed again."

"I did?"

"Yes. And the next night, and the night after that, but on the fourth night, you stayed in your bed."

"I get what you're saying, but I eventually grew up. It's always going to be like this with Emma. Mentally, she's always going to be eight years old, but physically, she's a grown woman."

"Agreed. It is a different kind of challenge."

Kasha pulled a palm down her face. "I thought that I could do this. Provide a good home for her. Be there for her. Love her the way my father never got to." Fresh tears spilled into her throat, cut off her words.

Mom reached for a handful of tissues from the box on the bedside table and tugged them into her hand. "You can do this, Kasha. If you let us help you. Let our friends and community help you. You don't have to go it alone, sweetheart. You never have."

Kasha sat up. Swiped away the tears. Blew her nose. "I hate asking people for favors."

"I know." Her mother reached over to brush a lock of hair off Kasha's forehead. "But helping makes people feel needed. We want to help you. Just like you want to help Emma."

"I can't figure out how to integrate her into my life so that she'll be safe and happy. I don't know how to be a mother."

"You know," Mom said softly. "Here's something to consider. You don't have to move Emma out of the group home. You can still have legal guardianship for her care, but you can allow her to continue to live with the Bankses."

"But—"

"But what? Think about her. Her friends are there. She feels secure in the group home. You can still visit her, and take her to your house for weekends and holidays. You don't have to go at this thing full bore."

"Emma didn't grow up in a group home. If it was all she'd ever known, that would be one thing, but until her mother got sick a year ago, Emma was cherished and loved, had a family of her own, a room of her own."

"She's adjusted to life with the Bankses."

"How can I leave her in the group home just because it would make things easier for me? For my relationship with Axel?"

"You're feeling guilty over something that was never your fault or your responsibility," Mom said. "No one would think less of you if you don't take Emma to live with you."

Kasha tossed the wad of tissues in the wastebasket beside the bed, drew in a heavy sigh, traced a finger over the pattern of the quilt. She recognized this patch. It came from the pink and white pinafore she'd worn to court the day her adoption was finalized. When she'd arrived at her forever home.

"Maybe," her mother said, "you're just using Emma as an excuse to avoid your feelings for Axel?"

"But how can I have both? He's in New York living his dream. I can't go there to be with him, even if I did leave Emma in the group home. I love her, and she needs me in a way that Axel doesn't."

"Are you sure you're not the one who needs her?"

"What do you mean?"

"You need Emma to make amends for what your mother did. She took away your father. Took away your family. Deep inside, you feel like if you can make things right with Emma, you can compensate for what your mother did."

Kasha stared at her mother, stunned by her insight.

"You can't change the past. You can't undo what your mother did. But you can put love out into the world. You can fully heal and you can make this work. With Axel and with Emma."

"I don't see how I can fit both Emma and Axel into my world." Kasha shook her head, gulped back the salty lump of tears sitting high and hard in her throat.

"Your father and I managed with four girls, and running our own business. We got by with help from family and friends. If the love is there, you'll find a way."

"Yes, but none of us were handicapped, and Dad wasn't a professional baseball player on the road more than he was home."

"No, but Breeanne's health issues left us juggling medical issues even more complex than what you'll have with Emma. We had trouble making time for our relationship."

"And I saw the toll Breeanne's illness took on our family."

"That's why it might be better for you to leave Emma where she is. You can make a place for her in your home and your heart, but it doesn't have to be 24/7. You don't have to jump into the custodial role with both feet."

Kasha looked her mother in the eyes. She couldn't hurt her by saying what was on her mind. That Emma was the only real blood relative she had in the world. She felt connected to her younger half sister in a way she could not explain.

"I can't fully understand what you're going through," Mom admitted, lowering her voice. "This is your decision. Just know that whatever you decide, the family supports you one hundred percent."

"Thank you," Kasha whispered. "That means more to me than you can ever know."

Her mother reached over to squeeze her arm. Her touch was warm and soft, nonjudgmental, and accepting. "You've been through a lot of changes lately. You don't have to make any decisions right now. Get some rest. Sleep on it. Things will look clearer after you've had some rest. To go with the oatmeal, I'm going to make you some hot cocoa just like when you first came to us and couldn't sleep. Do you remember that much?"

"I could never forget it," Kasha said, tears misting her eyes again. "The kindness you always showed me when I came over to play with Jodi was the reason I hid in your shed on that awful night. I knew you would never let anything bad happen to me. I chose you and Dad."

"Oh, Kasha." Tears were running down her mother's face now, flowing in a steady stream. "I'm so sorry such a terrible thing happened to you, but so happy you wanted us as your forever family."

"That's what I want for Emma," Kasha said. "The same kind of unconditional love that I found here."

Mom wrapped her arms around Kasha and hugged her tightly. "You'll give it to her, darling. I have absolutely no doubt about it. But maybe that means the greatest gift of love you can give her is letting her stay right where she is."

KASHA'S LIFE WAS an upended jigsaw puzzle and she had no idea how to go about piecing it back together.

A few days had passed since she had broken up with Axel, but it felt like weeks. She didn't answer the phone, didn't even check her messages. It was like time didn't exist. She'd called in sick, too, and though she knew she'd have to get back in action in a day or so, she decided it was worth it to take this break. She wasn't any good to anyone anyway.

Emma's legal papers had come in the mail that morning, and they lay on the table ready for her to sign, alongside a grilled portabella mushroom sandwich fresh off the panini press, but she couldn't concentrate on either one.

Axel was to blame for her confusion. No matter how hard she tried, she could not stop thinking about him. But she had to do what was right for Emma. Her own needs and wants didn't matter.

Long ago, she'd resigned herself to a life without romantic love. She cultivated calm and her sphinx face to keep passion—and men— at a distance. She'd managed to arrive at thirty years of age without any entanglements or messy emotional attachments.

And while she might not have been truly happy, she'd been content enough with her life.

But then Emma had come along, and that led her to go to work for the Gunslingers, and that led her to Axel, and that move had changed *everything*.

Axel had shaken her complacency, dismantled her reserve, and penetrated her stony ramparts. He'd stripped her of her defenses, left her raw and aching and exposed.

Worst of all, he'd unleashed her passion.

He'd shown her what she'd been missing, and at the same time

opened the door to a world of hurt. He'd given her hope and unimaginable joy, and then *his* passion had taken all that away.

She understood his compulsion. Playing for the Yankees wasn't
so much about baseball as it was about hanging on to the son he'd
lost. Passion equaled life to Axel, and as long as he held on to the
dream, he kept Dylan alive in his heart.

The doorbell rang.

Kasha froze, and it was only then she realized she'd been pacing
endlessly back and forth across the kitchen floor, staring at the custody papers, thinking of Axel, and pondering her options.

The bell rang again.

She didn't go to the door. Didn't want company. Willed the visitor to leave.

Another chime of the bell.

Probably it was one of her sisters coming to check up on her.
She'd turned off her phone because she'd just needed some time to
think. And she'd managed to duck them every time one of them
turned up at her house. But this couldn't go on forever. It was time
to face things. Anyway, if she didn't go out into the world soon, she
knew they'd break down the front door.

Ding-dong.

Groaning, Kasha buried her face in her palms. She didn't want to
hear their advice and their murmurs of concern. Didn't want Jodi's
philosophy, or Breeanne's gentle hugs, or Suki waltzing in with a
gallon of mint chocolate chip ice cream and two spoons.

She didn't want to talk. Didn't want to listen. Didn't want to be
sociable. She feared she would break down. Cry. Splinter into a million little pieces, and she feared if that happened, she'd never be able
to put herself back together again.

And then where would Emma be?

Her sister or sisters—it could be all three of them—weren't giving
up. The doorbell rang a fifth time.

Then an insistent fist pounded, a hard, solid rap-a-tap-tap. Asser-
tive. Demanding. That kind of knocking had to be Jodi.

Kasha groaned again. If it had to be anyone, why couldn't it have been gentle Breeanne?

"Kasha, I know you're there. Your car is in the driveway. Open the door."

The hairs on the back of her neck rose. No, not Jodi. Not any of her sisters. Not a feminine voice at all.

Axel.

He was at her front door when he was supposed to be in New York.

Kasha pressed a hand to her mouth. She couldn't talk to him. If she opened the door, let him in, all her good intentions would flee and she'd fall into his arms. Much better to keep quiet, stay still until he went away.

"I'm not going away until you answer this door," he called.

She closed her eyes. *Please, please go.*

"Kasha Carlyle, do not make me knock down this door. I don't know if my shoulder could take it."

She knew he didn't mean the threat, but she sucked in her breath at the thought of it. Had a flashback to her parents' fights when her father would kick down a door or put a fist through the wall because her mother angered him. Passion.

This was why she avoided it.

Passion had a way of turning dark and deadly.

"Kasha, I'm sorry. I shouldn't have said that. I'm just so frustrated right now. Please, open the door so we can talk."

She couldn't make herself open it. She stood in the kitchen trembling, that seven-year-old kid again, terrified by her feelings. *Keep quiet. Lie low. He'll go away.*

But he didn't.

The back door swung inward, bumped against the wall with enough force to make her jump.

She spun around to see Axel standing there, dressed in blue jeans and a plain black T-shirt, his hair mussed, his eyes dark and smoldering. He was breathing as hard as she was, his chest jerking up and down, heavy and fast, as if he'd sprinted a mile in four minutes.

"You're trespassing," she said, her voice high and reedy. "Don't make me call the cops."

"I've been trying to contact you for hours. How come you haven't returned my calls or texts? I was out of my mind with worry." He stalked into the room and kicked the door closed behind her.

It slammed.

She flinched.

"You scared the hell out of me," he said. "I thought you were hurt, or worse . . ."

She straightened, searched around inside for equanimity, found none. Where had her calm gone? How had he disarmed her of her weapon so completely? All she wanted to do was fling herself into his arms and kiss him madly.

"Kasha?" His scowl disappeared and his voice softened. "Are you all right?"

"I . . . I didn't feel like talking."

"Like it or not," he insisted, coming closer, his eyes blazing, his jaw muscles clenched tight, "you're going to talk to me."

"You should be in New York. You're going to get in trouble. We covered all this last week. There's nothing left to say," she murmured, feeling her knees loosen.

"The hell there's not." The force of his personality filled the room, large and energetic, but nonthreatening. "I love you, dammit, and I know you love me too. We can't walk away from a love like this."

She took one look into those smoldering brown eyes and she could not resist him. She did love him with every inch of her heart, mind, body, and soul!

"Axel," she said. "What *are* you doing here?"

He stepped forward, a somber expression carved on his face. Her pulse sped up. Seeing that dark expression made her realize how often he smiled, how startled she was not to see his affable grin.

"I refused the trade," he said. "I'm retiring. How could you not know? It's been all over the news."

Her jaw worked, but no words came out. He'd come home to be with her?

"Are you all right?" he asked, coming to stand beside her.

"I'm fine—" She stopped herself, and dropped her defenses because she knew she could trust him. Knew that he only had her best interest at heart. "That's not true. I'm not fine. I haven't even turned on the TV or gone outside. I've avoided my entire family—and I'm sure they wanted to tell me what you'd decided . . . I've been a wreck."

"I know," he said, moving closer. "Jake and Rowdy both told me how you've been ducking everyone It's okay. You've held your feelings in for so long that now you're finally letting go, it's natural to feel like things are falling apart. They're not. You're okay. You're safe."

"You make me feel safe," she murmured.

"It's not me," he said. "It's us. Together. The hope chest was right. The wine predicted it. True love. No more denying it, Kasha. We're in this."

AXEL COULDN'T WAIT one second longer. He had to touch her, hold her. He pulled her into his arms, crushed his mouth to hers, tasted what he'd been longing to taste.

"Axel," she whispered. "Oh, Axel, how I've missed you."

He bent to scoop her into his arms.

"No," she said as he slipped his hands around her and lifted her off her feet. "I'm too big. You'll hurt your shoulder—"

"Shh, no arguments." He carried her into the bedroom and kicked the door closed.

She wrapped her arms around his neck, held him tightly.

Pride swelled his chest. Pride and joy and love for her. So damn much love he could scarcely breathe.

"I was worried I would forget what you looked like," she said, and laughed nervously.

"It's okay. I'm anxious too. But you're imprinted on the backs of my eyelids, babe. Every time I close my eyes, there you are."

"I couldn't *see* you clearly," she said, "because I *felt* you so hard.

Whenever I tried to imagine your face, I felt it instead. The firm jut of your jaw, the bristle of your beard stubble, the hard calluses on your palms."

She pressed her palm against his cheek, and the backs of her bare knees were warm against his arms.

He closed his eyes, felt queasy joy, her heady lavender scent spinning his mind like a top, his body bathed in her brilliant heat.

The lazily rotating ceiling fan in her bedroom cooled things off minutely.

"But a year without playing baseball," she said. "What are you going to do?"

"Paint," he answered. "Rest. Heal. Spend my days making love to you."

TWENTY MINUTES LATER they lay on their sides in her bed, facing each other, hands stacked beneath their heads.

Kasha gazed into the eyes of her beloved, and experienced an earthquake of desire so strong it rocked her world and in a good way, in the very best possible way. She loved this man with everything she had inside her. Loved him fiercely, deeply, forever, and she was no longer afraid of her feelings.

She had fought so hard against these feelings. Terrified they would turn lethal. Yes, he had changed her, but for the better, so much the better. Whenever she was with him she was more. More herself. More involved. More open to the world.

Because of him, she'd faced her fears and self-doubts and overcome them. She was her own person, free of her tragic family legacy, unhampered by her DNA. She was in charge of her own life. She could make happy, healthy choices without hesitation.

They smiled at each other, big and hard and wonderful. They lay in bed and looked at each other and listened to the sound of the rain drumming on the tin roof, and Kasha felt so much happiness she couldn't stop a single perfect tear from rolling down the side of her nose.

"You're crying," Axel murmured, reaching to blot her tear with his index finger. "Why are you crying?"

"You opened the floodgates," Kasha said. "Look out. I'm likely to cry at a moment's notice these days."

"I can handle it." His smile was smug. He'd ruined her for anybody else and he knew it.

Dusky sunlight seeped in through the half-shuttered plantation blinds. It was raining outside. The wind whipped soggy tree branches against the window, a whispery back and forth like God's paintbrush. It felt so cozy and safe here in Axel's arms.

She looked into his dear eyes and her heart raced, stumbled. She was so happy to be here, and yet she felt unexpectedly, untypically shy. He sat up in a square of dim light falling across his honed chest muscles.

"How are things with Emma?" he asked. "I saw the custody papers on your table."

"As much as I want her to live with me, I've realized that was pure selfishness on my part. Emma needs structure. She needs peers her own age. And she needs more supervision than I can give her. At the group home, she's already got those things. She's settled in. If I uproot her, bring her here, she has to start all over."

"It's a big decision either way."

"And it's not as if I'm abandoning her. I'll see her as often as I can. Bring her home a couple of weekends a month. Be her family. But she is an adult and has a life of her own. I need to respect that. I was seeing her as a child, and that was my mistake."

"This isn't easy for you."

She shook her head, pressed her lips together. "No, but I have to do what's right for Emma, not what's right for me. I was trying to rescue her and she doesn't need rescuing. It wasn't about Emma . . ." Her voice broke.

Axel rubbed the flat of his palm up and down her back. "It's okay, you don't have to talk about it."

"No, I want to talk about it. I need to talk about it. I kept so many dark things buried deep inside of me for so long. I don't want to do that anymore. I love the way you brought light and energy into my life. I'm not going to hide from the truth anymore."

"What is the truth, Kasha?"

Her smile was wistful. "I wasn't trying to save Emma. I was trying to rescue that seven-year-old girl hiding in the Carlyles' garden shed. She was the one who needed saving. Not Emma. Emma had a wonderful mother who took great care of her and kept her safe. And she's got a place now where she fits, where she's happy."

"Oh, Sphinx," he said. "I wish I could have rescued you."

"It's okay." Her smile was shaky. "Maggie and Dan saved me. If it weren't for them, I wouldn't be the woman I am today. But even though they loved me with all their heart, I've always kept a part of myself shut down, terrified of getting hurt. I kept that lonely little girl shut off, cut off, and I thought I'd conquered my emotions. It wasn't until you . . ." She took a deep breath. "Well, you were the one who finally got through to me, Axel, and I'll always be grateful to you for that."

"Kasha," he murmured, his heart swelling with love for her. "You are so brave and strong and I love you with every inch of my heart. Marry me, and make me the happiest man in the world and I'll spend every waking hour showing you just how much I love you."

"You're proposing."

"It's not how I planned it. I was going to get a ring, get down on one knee, the whole nine yards, but I can't wait. I want you Kasha, now and forever. Will you be my wife?"

All the air left her body and she had to remind herself to breathe. "Oh, Axel."

Worry creased his face. "How long are you going to keep me in suspense? I'm dying here."

And then the Sphinx forgot she was mysterious. Forgot she didn't do passion. "Yes!" She flung her arms around his neck. "Yes, I'll marry you."

They laughed and talked and hugged and kissed and made hot, passionate love all night long.

EPILOGUE

The church was packed. All seats taken.

Everyone Kasha and Axel cared about was there to honor their big day—friends, family, members of the Dallas Gunslingers, everyone from Emma's group home, people from the hospital and Kasha's yoga studio.

Jodi, looking fabulous with her figure back three months after giving birth to her baby son, Boone, served as a bridesmaid. As did Breeanne, effervescent with the news she and Rowdy would soon be welcoming twin girls from Guatemala. And so did Suki, who was thrilled when Kasha passed the hope chest on to her after the rehearsal dinner.

Maid of honor Emma waited in the wings with the rest of the party, clutching her bouquet, excitement fueling her eyes. They'd practiced her walk down the aisle two dozen times, making sure she had it down. She could handle it.

And just in case something happened, and Emma couldn't carry out her duties, Kasha had a contingency plan where Suki would shift to maid of honor, and Molly Banks would usher Emma outside. But Kasha didn't anticipate problems, and if there was a hiccup or two? Well, wouldn't that make the story of their wedding day all the juicier?

But Emma was a trouper. She not only came through with flying colors, but captured the admiration of the audience as she swept down the aisle, her head held high. The entire chapel filled with happy oohs and aahs, and applause and encouraging words of approval.

By the time Kasha started down the aisle on her father's arm, her heart was overflowing with blessings. She'd come so far! From the young girl who'd gone through so much as a child, to the rebellious teen who'd acted out to ease her pain, she managed to put the past behind her and passionately embrace the gift of true and lasting love.

On this her wedding day.

Her father gave her to Axel, and stepped back to take his place beside her mother. Kasha raised her head, met her beloved's eyes, and she forgot to breathe.

Axel stood before her, his hair shimmering darkly in the light of the candles flickering at the altar. He was gorgeous in a tuxedo, a specially made baseball-themed boutonniere in his lapel—white rosebud, stitched in red.

He stared at her as if she were the most incredible thing on the face of the earth. He made her feel priceless, treasured.

She fell into his eyes, got lost there.

It ends like this: an unexpected spark, instant attraction, the jolting jab of oh-so-you-feel-this-too? Flash fire in the belly, a corkscrew twist in the center of the chest, a physical ache that punches low and heavy and spreads out hard and fast through muscles and tendons, blood and bone.

Heady.

Erotic.

Exhilarating.

She known it that first day in sports facility; she knew it now.

This here? This was something more.

Stronger.

Bolder.

Scarier.

Coal black eyes melted her resistance, seared it to ash, and in that stopwatch moment her gaze struck, and stuck to that of her husband-to-be. One look, and everything and everyone blended and blurred as white-hot need transported them into their own little world.

Things had changed from that momentous beginning. One part of their life was coming to a close, but there was a whole new beginning opening up to them.

Married. Together. Husband and wife.

And as Axel took her hand, his gentle touch sending electrical pulses throughout her body, Kasha knew one thing for certain.

He stirred passion in her, but it wasn't the dangerous kind. Behind the desire was respect, tenderness, caring . . . love.

Real love. True love. Sure and certain love.

There was nothing tumultuous or crazy about his feelings for her. He was solid, dependable, steadfast. He was a man worth waiting for.

When the minister asked her if she took this man to be her lawfully wedded husband, there wasn't a scrap of doubt.

"I do," she said, gazing into the eyes that meant the world to her. "I do, I do, I do."

And then her beloved kissed her with all the passion he had inside him, and she wasn't scared. Not for a second.

"I love you," he whispered. "Now and forever. No matter what may come. We're in this together, and we're going to have an amazing life beyond our wildest dreams."

With this man, Kasha knew it was absolutely true.

Don't miss the next sweet and sexy novel from
New York Times bestselling author

LORI WILDE

A WEDDING
FOR CHRISTMAS
A TWILIGHT, TEXAS NOVEL

Coming October 2016 from Avon Books!
Read on for a sneak peek . . .

CHAPTER 1

Los Angeles, California
December 23, 7:00 P.M.

Katie Cheek caught a glimpse of herself in the plate glass window as she strode toward the front entrance of the old warehouse-turned-trendy-art-museum in downtown LA, and teetered in her six-inch platform heels.

Whoa!

She stopped. Stared openmouthed. Holy cow, who was that?

Vamp.

Smoking hot in a skintight, scarlet, designer sheath dress she'd borrowed from the closet of Gabi Preston, the woman she'd swapped houses with for the Christmas holidays. Trading in her tiny yurt in the sleepy tourist town of Twilight, Texas, for a Malibu beach condo, knowing full well she'd gotten the better end of that bargain.

Across the street, a man whistled long and loud. "Yo, mommy, I'd love to find you in my Christmas stocking."

Katie blushed, and ducked her head to hide an involuntary smile, liking this new her, and freedom from the fishbowl of her hometown.

That's why she was here, to explore her options. And that included her sexuality.

She had changed a lot since high school. LASIK surgery dispensed with thick-lensed glasses. Braces corrected a severe overbite.

Brazilian blowouts tamed her frizzy curls. Even so, she had never grown comfortable with catcalls and whistles.

"Brillo hair," kids had called her, or other old standbys like four eyes, pencil-neck geek, and train tracks.

In public, Katie would laugh and pretend the name-calling didn't bother her, but when she got home, she'd cry to her mother.

Mom would give her a cookie, kiss her forehead, and say, "You won't always be an ugly duckling, sweetheart. One day you're going to turn into a beautiful swan. Just you wait and see."

The woman in the glass lifted her chin and triumphantly met her eyes. Today, decked out in Gabi's expensive clothing, no one could call her an ugly duckling.

People streamed into the entrance of the star-studded, red-carpet charity event—twinkle lights glittered, two huge Christmas trees laden with numerous ornaments flanked the doorway. The sounds of a band playing, "All I Want for Christmas is You" spilled into the street along with the air-conditioning. It felt strange, celebrating Christmas in warm weather among strangers.

But that was why she'd come here. To escape the claustrophobia of her hometown and the over-the-top, nonstop holiday festivities. Gabi had urged her to use her invitation to the charity ball, relax, have a good time and enjoy herself. So here she was.

It was hard to relax among gold jewelry, Rolexes, Manolo Blahniks, and Rodeo Drive finery. Surrounded by the wealth, opulence and celebrity of Hollywood, Katie's confidence wobbled a bit, and the urge to run flooded her.

Outsider.

She didn't belong. *C'mon, Swan, you got this.* She squared her shoulders, and strutted into the event like she was the star attraction.

And people noticed.

Heads turned. Eyes popped. Several men murmured, "Who's that woman in red?"

Me, she thought proudly. *It's me.* Small town, unemployed girl that everyone back home felt sorry for because her fiancé had died tragically.

But here in LA, over the course of the last three weeks, she'd transformed. No more almost-bride turned widow-to-be. She was free.

Guilt carved a slick hole in her belly. Why did letting go of the dream feel so disloyal? Was it because she'd started to come alive again? Was that so wrong?

Matt had been gone a little over a year, killed in a boating accident, and although there were times when her emotions were still shaky, there were other times when she couldn't even remember what he'd looked like, or who she'd been when she was with him.

That was another reason she'd fled Twilight for the holidays. The house swap gave her a chance to discover who she was without a man or a job or a community.

She was three months from turning twenty-seven, high time to find her real place in the world. Sweep the stars from her eyes. If she'd learned anything this past year, it was this. Romantic fantasies were bullshit and she wasn't going to waste another second on wishes and regrets. She was going to live every day to the fullest.

Girl-Next-Door-Gone-Wild.

Well sorta. Wildish.

Inside the museum, she spied an actor she'd been infatuated with as a kid. An actor who reminded her a bit of the first real life guy she'd ever had a crush on.

Ryder Southerland.

Ugh. Another memory she didn't want tromping in her head.

The actor looked worse for the wear. She wondered about Ryder. She hadn't seen the man in twelve years. How would he look today?

Forget Ryder.

Ancient history so old it had arthritis. Focus. Tonight have fun. Mingle. Dance. She studied the roomful of strangers, and anxiety sent her heart swooping to her feet.

Um, maybe she'd have a drink first. Beeline it to the bar. Yes, indeedy.

But before she could put that plan in motion, her cell phone buzzed inside her purse. She almost ignored it, but what if it was Gabi feeling lonely in a strange town this close to Christmas, and needing a shot of confidence? Twilight, and the town's perpetual

Christmas cheer, could be a bit hard to digest if you weren't in a happy, happy, joy, joy state of mind.

Stepping from the main flow of foot traffic, Katie pulled the phone from her purse and checked the caller ID. No, not Gabi, but rather it was Emma, her sister-in-law, who was married to Katie's brother Sam.

"Hello, Em," she answered, scooting to a nearby alcove, and putting a hand to her other ear to block out the hubbub.

"Auntie Katie?"

It wasn't Emma, but her four-year-old daughter, Lauren, Katie's niece.

"Hi, honey." Katie smiled. Lauren was fascinated with phones, and loved calling people. "Does your mommy know you've got her cell phone?"

"She's inna baffroom. I was gonna play Fruit Ninja, but I saw your pitcher on the phone and calleded you instead." Lauren sounded pleased with herself.

"That's so sweet of you to call me."

"Where are you, auntie?"

"I'm in California."

"Where da?"

"Near the ocean."

"Oh." Lauren paused. "Dat's a long way off."

"It is."

"So you not gonna be home for Pop-pop and Nanny's Christmas party?"

"I'm afraid not," Katie said. "But I'll see you later when I get home on Christmas night."

"But . . . but . . . it won't be the same," Lauren said, sounding years beyond her age.

"I know, but I'll bring you a present."

"From California?"

"From California."

"I miss you." Lauren's voice saddened. "You been gone a long, long time and no one plays tea party with me as good as you."

Katie's heart tugged. When she'd taken off to California for three weeks during the holidays, she never considered how it might affect her niece. "We'll play tea party as soon as I get home. I promise."

"Okay. Bye." Lauren hung up, leaving Katie a bit disoriented. Her body was in LA, but her mind and her spirit had traveled to Twilight.

She tucked her phone in her purse. Glanced around. Now what was she doing again?

Oh, yes, getting a drink to steady her nerves. She snaked her way past people and art exhibits, looking for a cash bar with a short line, and finally found one. She queued up, took a deep calming breath, guilt prickling her for standing up Lauren on Christmas Eve.

"Buy you a drink?"

She glanced over to see a blond man in sunshades, fashionably ripped jeans, and crisp beige shirt with four buttons undone showing off a shag rug chest. He sported impossibly straight, white teeth and a smile that rubbed her the wrong way.

"I'm good, thanks," she said, hoping to discourage him.

The guy couldn't take a hint. He stepped closer, crowding her space. "I won't slip you a roofie, I swear."

She hadn't considered that possibility. As a rule of thumb, people in Twilight didn't get roofied. But the look in his eye and his aggressive body language told her he wasn't above such a stunt.

The band shifted into a bouncy version of "Rocking Around the Christmas Tree" and people started dancing around the exhibits.

Katie glued on a stiff smile, kept her voice light, but firm. "I do appreciate the offer, but I prefer to buy my own drinks."

"Cock tease."

"Excuse me?" Startled, she thought she must have misunderstood what he said.

"You heard me. You stroll in here, wearing a slut dress and fuck-me-shoes and you turn down my offer of a drink? What a stuck-up bitch." He snarled.

Stunned by the creep's verbal attack, Katie stood there with her mouth hanging open, her brain trying to process what was happening.

What shocked her was the fact that no one intervened. If this had happened in Twilight, half-a-dozen gallant cowboys would have jumped to her aid and challenged the guy.

Where was a knight-in-shining-armor when you needed one?

Katie pivoted on her heels, rushed through the crowd. Maybe no one had spoken up because of the way she was dressed. Did people believe she was asking for that treatment?

No.

That was her old childhood insecurity talking. Plenty of other women were wearing formfitting clothes, and sexpot stilettos. Still, it disturbed her to think that the way she was dressed—the clothes she'd worn precisely because they made her feel empowered—had spurred the jerk's ugly behavior.

Shame. She was ashamed.

In her mind she heard the voice of the grief counselor she'd visited after Matt's death. Dr. Finley had been kind, but with a no bullshit approach to life. *The guy is a narcissist, antisocial jerk. Don't let him define you.*

She wasn't, but she was done for the day. She'd had enough of glittery charity galas. Problem was, in the labyrinth of the exhibits, she'd lost her bearings.

Where was the front entrance?

Rounding a corner, she glanced over her shoulder to make sure the creep wasn't coming after her, and smacked hard into a young woman holding a small plate of food.

"Oof!" exclaimed the woman. She had Angelina Jolie lips that appeared to be courtesy of an excessive amount of filler, and an overly thin neck that made her head look like a lollipop on a stick. The woman fumbled her plate, and spilled food down the front of Katie's dress.

The plate clattered to the floor, but thankfully didn't shatter. A big blob of something mushy and green, which Katie initially thought was guacamole, flipped into her cleavage, slid down into her bra.

Ugh. What a mess. She prayed Gabi's dress wasn't ruined.

The Angelina lookalike glowered. "Excuse you."

Katie raised her hands in apologetic surrender. "I'm sorry, I'm sorry. I should have been watching where I was going."

"Yes, you should have," the woman chided, but her tone softened.

The cold green mush that had settled between her breasts started burning her skin. A lot. Katie stared down, and saw a bright red rash spreading over her chest.

"Wh . . . what . . . is that stuff?" She gasped.

"Oh, dude," said Lollipop Angelina. "That's sick. Are you allergic to wasabi?"

Katie didn't know, but her breasts were ablaze. She had to wash it off. ASAP! "Bathroom?"

"Up those stairs." The young woman pointed at a metal staircase leading to a second level.

"Thanks." With energy born of pain, Katie flew toward the stairs in search of salvation, fanning her chest with a hand. But when she got to the bottom of the steps, a red velvet rope was stretched across the bottom, and a posted sign announced CLOSED FOR PRIVATE PARTY.

"BOLO. BOLO. BE on the lookout for a hot blonde in a red dress."

Personal bodyguard Ryder Southerland resisted an eye roll, and muttered into the tiny microphone clipped to his lapel. "I know what a BOLO is, Messer, and I don't need an update every time you spy a good-looking woman."

"*Not* a hot chick alert. Repeat this is not merely a hot chick alert, although she does sizzle. It's Ketchum's stalker."

Les Ketchum, the rodeo star turned country and western chart-topping singer, that Ryder had been hired to protect. Two weeks ago Les had broken things off with a buckle bunny in possession of a mean streak who couldn't seem to take *hasta la vista, baby*, for the brush-off it was.

Ryder's entire body tensed, and he pressed a hand to the Bluetooth device that fed Messer's voice into his ear. "You sure?"

"Pretty sure."

"Where?" Ryder leaned over the balcony railing, scanning the well-heeled crowd milling in the art gallery below.

You'd think a hot blonde in a red dress wouldn't be that hard to spot, but since it was a celebrity-studded holiday bash, a surprising number of women were wearing red. And sun-drenched LA had a knack for manufacturing blondes.

"You got Ketchum in sight?" Messer asked.

"Yes." Ryder swung his gaze to his client who was kissing a busty redhead known for her appearances in makeup commercials, underneath a bouquet of mistletoe. "Does your red-dress blonde look armed?"

"It'd have to be in her purse. That dress is spray-painted on. Couldn't hide anything underneath that."

"Can you still see her?"

"Negatory. She disappeared in the crowd."

"Stop talking, and freaking follow her."

"I'm trying, but some drunk sitcom-actress just took off her top, and there's a hundred guys in my way."

This time, Ryder did roll his eyes.

Trite. His job was trite. Protecting spoiled celebrities from overly zealous fans who thought getting near them meant something special. But after four years in the Middle East, and an unpleasant bout of PTSD, Ryder was good with trite.

And working for his former platoon leader's personal security business in LA was a long sight better than crawling home to Twilight where small town minds had branded him disreputable years ago.

Pathetic.

He was twenty-nine years old, had been a decorated MP in the U.S. Army, and yet he couldn't shake the old childhood wounds, and the names he'd been called—bad boy, punk, troublemaker, delinquent, thug.

Ah, his youth. Those were the days.

There was only one family in the whole town he gave a fig about, and that was the Cheeks. The family who'd taken him in when his father kicked him out and no one else would touch him.

His favorites of all the Cheeks was his best friend Joe, and the other was Joe's kid sister, Katie. He hadn't talked to Joe since his friend had moved back to Twilight to take over his ailing grandfather's Christmas tree farm that summer. And it had been two years since they'd seen each other in person, back when Ryder had crashed at Joe's place for a couple of months after he'd been discharged from the Army, and was struggling to get his act together.

And as for Katie?

In his mind she was still the gawky fifteen-year-old who'd flung herself into his arms and kissed him. And that had been the last time he'd seen her, but he couldn't help wondering what she looked like today.

Head in the game, Southerland. Katie ain't nothing but a fond memory.

He leaned farther over the balcony railing for a better look, watching the circular metal staircase that led to the second story exhibits. The party was in full swing. The band blasted Christmas songs. People packed in close dancing, drinking, eating canapés served by tuxedoed waiters passing through the throng.

The crowd was eclectic. Young and old, trendy and traditional, dressed down and dressed up, an equal mix of male and female. The majority of them were wealthy, or plus ones of the wealthy. Ironic, how much money was being spent raising funds to benefit the poor. Why not just give the money to the homeless?

He scanned the three exits he could see, each one manned by museum security, and finally caught sight of Messer trapped in a bottleneck near the entrance.

He counted off the attractive blondes in red dresses, one, two, seven, a dozen. Was one of them Ketchum's stalker?

Concerned, he glanced back at Ketchum. The celebrity and his woman of choice, who had shifted to the bench exhibit seating near the restrooms, were still in a lip-lock, hands all over each other. The second floor was reserved for special VIP sponsors, and Ryder was the threshold guardian to their domain.

From his peripheral vision, he caught movement at the top of the staircase. A blonde. In red. Hurrying.

Hurrying, hell, the woman was full-on running.

Immediately, Ryder tensed, and his hand touched the Taser at his hip. He didn't want to use it, or the concealed Sig Sauer in his shoulder holster. Discretion was a big part of his job. Diplomacy another.

Besides, she was a woman. He was big, and she was small. Body block, and choke hold ought to do it, and that was only if she was unreasonable.

He didn't want things getting messy.

In two long strides, he reached her, and for a split second, he was struck by the notion that anyone watching them might assume they were lovers rushing into each other's arms.

Except she showed no signs of slowing down, her gaze fixed to the spot where Ketchum sat kissing the redhead. This had to be the stalker, hyped up with rage, jealousy, adrenaline, and god knew what else.

Instinct, honed from numerous tours in the sandbox, took over and he reacted without hesitation. It happened during the space of a single breath. Grabbing her by the arm, flipping her onto her back, falling atop of her, pinning her to the floor in a four-point restraint.

"Stand back, people!" Messer shouted. Ryder felt rather than saw his colleague herding people down the steps. "Nothing to see here. Go downstairs and enjoy the party."

Ryder's hands manacled her wrists. His cowboy boots locked spread-eagle around her ankles. The woman was panting.

And so was he, because he realized not only was she not Ketchum's stalker, but he *knew* her.

Ryder peered down into her face. A familiar face despite the fact it had changed a lot over the past twelve years.

Katie Cheek.

What in the blazes?

All the air exited his body in one hard puff.

Her features were softer, thinner, and prettier than ever. The glasses were gone, and so were the braces, and instead of frizzy untamable, dishwater blond curls, her hair was straight and lush and golden.

Yes, she'd changed a lot, but he would recognize her anywhere.

Yep. Katie Cheek, all right.

It was his high school buddy's kid sister, all grown up, and curvy in the most dangerous places.